"Does he make you sizzle?"

"I don't..."

"You see, it's such a waste," he said, and suddenly he was even closer. His hand came up and cupped her chin, forcing her to look up at him.

"I wouldn't mind if it wasn't Philip. I've known since Ben died that nothing could bring back what was between you and me."

She should break away. She could break away, she thought wildly. He was only holding her chin—nothing more. She could step back, get into the car and drive home. To Philip.

She could.

"So tell me he makes you sizzle."

"I..."

There was a moment's loaded silence when the whole world stilled.

She tilted her face just a little.

The moment stretched on. The darkness stretched on.

And then he kissed her.

An Unexpected Rescue

Marion Lennox & Tracy Madison

Previously published as *Abby and the Bachelor Cop*
and *A Bride for the Mountain Man*

⟨H⟩HARLEQUIN® MUST LOVE DOGS

ISBN-13: 978-1-335-69092-0

An Unexpected Rescue

Copyright © 2019 by Harlequin Books S.A.

First published as Abby and the Bachelor Cop
by Harlequin Books in 2011 and
A Bride for the Mountain Man by Harlequin Books in 2017.

The publisher acknowledges the copyright holders
of the individual works as follows:

Abby and the Bachelor Cop
Copyright © 2011 by Marion Lennox

A Bride for the Mountain Man
Copyright © 2017 by Tracy Leigh Ritts

Recycling programs for this product may not exist in your area.

Printed in U.S.A.

www.Harlequin.com

CONTENTS

Marion Lennox has written more than a hundred romances and is published in over a hundred countries and thirty languages. Her multiple awards include the prestigious RITA® Award (twice), and the *RT Book Reviews* Career Achievement Award for "a body of work which makes us laugh and teaches us about love." Marion adores her family, her kayak, her dog and lying on the beach with a book someone else has written. Heaven!

Books by Marion Lennox

Harlequin Romance

The Logan Twins

Nine Months to Change His Life

Sparks Fly with the Billionaire
Christmas at the Castle
Christmas Where They Belong
The Earl's Convenient Wife
His Cinderella Heiress
Stepping into the Prince's World
Stranded with the Secret Billionaire
The Billionaire's Christmas Baby

Harlequin Medical Romance

Bondi Bay Heroes

Finding His Wife, Finding a Son

Falling for Her Wounded Hero
Reunited with Her Surgeon Prince

Visit the Author Profile page
at Harlequin.com for more titles.

ABBY AND THE BACHELOR COP

Marion Lennox

With huge thanks to the wonderful Kelly Hunter,
who gave me Kleppy, to the fabulous Anne Gracie,
and to all the Maytoners, whose friendships
bring my stories to life.

To Radar, who was Trouble. I look back on
every moment with laughter and with love.

Chapter 1

If you couldn't be useful at the scene of an accident, you should leave. Onlookers only caused trouble.

Banksia Bay's Animal Welfare van had been hit from behind. Dogs were everywhere. People were yelling at each other. Esther Ford was having hysterics.

Abigail Callahan, however, had been travelling at a safe enough distance to avoid the crash. She'd managed to stop before her little red sports car hit anything, and she'd done all she could.

She'd checked no one was hurt. She'd hugged Esther, she'd tried to calm her down and she'd phoned Esther's son who, she hoped, might be better at coping with hysterics than she was. She'd carried someone's crumpled fender to the side of the road. She'd even tried to catch a dog. Luckily, she'd failed. She wasn't good with dogs.

Now, blessedly, Emergency Services had arrived.

Banksia Bay Emergency Services took the shape of
Rafferty Finn, local cop, so it was definitely time for
Abby to leave.

Stay away from Raff Finn.

It wasn't past history making her go. She was doing
the right thing.

She tried to back her car so she could turn, but the
crowd of onlookers was blocking her way. She touched
her horn and Raff glared at her.

How else could she make people move? She did not
need to be here. She looked down at her briefcase and
thought about the notes inside that she knew had to be
in court—now. Then she glanced back at Raff and she
thought… She thought…

She thought Rafferty Finn looked toe-curlingly sexy.

Which was ridiculous.

Abby had fallen for Raff when she was eight. It was
more than time she was over it. She *was* over it. She
was so over it she was engaged to be married. To Philip.

When Raff had been ten years old, which was when
Abby had developed her first crush on him, he'd been
skinny, freckled and his red hair had spiked straight up.
Twenty years on, skinny had given way to tall, tanned
and ripped. His thick curls had darkened to burned copper, and his freckles had merged to an all-over tan. His
gorgeous green eyes, with dangerous mischief lurking
within, had the capacity to make her catch her breath.

But right now it was his uniform that was causing
problems. His uniform was enough to make a girl go
right back to feeling as she had at eight years old.

Raff was directing drivers. He was calm, authorita-
tive and far more sexy than any man had a right to be.

"Henrietta, hold that Dalmatian before it knocks Mrs

Ford over. Roger, quit yelling at Mrs Ford. You drove into the dog van, not Mrs Ford, and it doesn't make a bit of difference that she was going too slow. Back your Volvo up and get it off the road."

Do not look at Raff Finn, she told herself. Do not.

The man is trouble.

She turned and tried again to reverse her car. Why wouldn't people move?

Someone was thumping on her window. The door of her car swung open. She swivelled and her heart did a back flip. Raff was standing over her—six foot two of lethal cop. With dog.

"I need your help, Abby," he growled and, before she could react, there was a dog in her car. On her knees.

"I need you to take him to the vet," Raff said. "Now."

The vet?

The local veterinary clinic was half a mile away, on the outskirts of town.

But she wasn't given a chance to argue. Raff slammed her car door closed and started helping Mrs Ford steer to the kerb.

There was a dog on her knee.

Abby's grandmother had once owned a shortbread tin adorned with a picture of a dog called Greyfriars Bobby. According to legend—or Gran—Bobby was famous for guarding his master's grave for almost fourteen years through the bleakest of Edinburgh's winters. This dog looked his twin. He was smallish but not a toy. His coat was wiry and a bit scruffy, sort of sand-coloured. One of his ears was a bit floppy.

His eyebrows were too long.

Did dogs have eyebrows?

He looked up at her as if he was just as stunned as she was.

What was wrong with him? Why did he need to go to the vet?

He wasn't bleeding.

She was due in court in ten minutes. Help.

What to do with a dog?

She put a hand on his head and gave him a tentative pat. Very tentative. If she moved him, maybe she'd hurt him. Maybe he'd hurt her.

He wiggled his head to the side and she tried scratching behind his ear. That seemed to be appreciated. His eyes were huge, brown and limpid. He had a raggedy tail and he gave it a tentative wag.

His eyes didn't leave hers. His eyes were…were…

Let's cut out the emotion here, she told herself hastily. This dog is nothing to do with you.

She fumbled under the dog for the door catch and climbed out of the car. The dog's backside sort of slumped as she lifted him. Actually, both ends slumped.

She carried him back to Raff. The little dog looked up at her and his tail still wagged. It seemed a half-hearted wag, as if he wasn't at all sure where he was but he sort of hoped things might be okay.

She felt exactly the same.

Raff was back in the middle of the crashed cars. "Raff, I can't…" she called.

Raff had given up trying to get Mrs Ford to steer. He had hold of her steering wheel and was steering himself, pushing at the same time, moving the car to the kerb all by himself. "Can't what?" he demanded.

"I can't take this dog anywhere."

"Henrietta says it's okay," Raff snapped. "It's the only one she's caught. She's trying to round up the others.

Come on, Abby, the road's clear—how hard is this? Just take him to the vet."

"I'm due in court in ten minutes."

"So am I." Raff shoved Mrs Ford's car another few feet and then paused for breath. "If you think I've spent years getting Wallace Baxter behind bars, just to see you and your prissy boyfriend get him off because I can't make it…"

"Cut it out, Raff."

"Cut what out?"

"He's not prissy," she snapped. "And he's not my boyfriend. You know he's my fiancé."

"Your fiancé. I stand corrected. But he's definitely prissy. I'll bet he's sitting in court right now, in his smart suit and silk tie—not like me, out here getting my hands dirty. Case for the prosecution—me and the time I can spare after work. Case for the defence—you and Philip and weeks of paid preparation. Two lawyers against one cop."

"There's the Crown Prosecutor…"

"Who's eighty. Who sleeps instead of listening. This'll be a no-brainer, even if you don't show." He shoved the car a bit further. "But I'll be there, whether you like it or not. Meanwhile, take the dog to the vet's."

"You're saying you want me to take the dog to the vet's—to keep me out of court?"

"I'm saying take the dog to the vet's because there's no one else," he snapped. "Your car's the only one still roadworthy. I'll radio Justice Weatherby to ask for a half hour delay. That'll get us both there on time. Get to the vet's and get back."

"But I don't do dogs," she wailed. "Raff…"

"You don't want to get your suit dirty?"

"That's not fair. This isn't about my suit." Or not very.

"It's just… What's wrong with him? I mean… I can't look after him. What if he bites?"

Raff sighed. "He won't bite," he said, speaking to her as if she were eight years old again. "He's a pussycat. His name's Kleppy. He's Isaac Abrahams' Cairn Terrier and he's on his way to be put down. Put him on your passenger seat and Fred'll take him out at the other end. All I'm asking you to do is deliver him."

It was twelve minutes to ten on a beautiful morning in Banksia Bay. The sun was warm on her face. The sea was glittering beyond the harbour and the mountain behind the town was blue with the haze of a still autumn morning. The sounds of the traffic chaos were lessening as Raff's attempts at restoring order took effect.

Abby stood motionless, her arms full of dog, and Raff's words replayed in her head.

He's Isaac Abrahams' Cairn Terrier and he's on his way to be put down.

She knew Isaac or, rather, she'd known him. The old man had lived a mile or so out of town, up on Black Mountain where…well, where she didn't go any more. Isaac had died six weeks ago and she was handling probate. Isaac's daughter in Sydney had been into the office a couple of times, busy and efficient in her disposing of Isaac's belongings.

There'd been no talk of a dog.

"Can you get your car off the road?" Raff said. "You're blocking traffic."

She was blocking traffic? But she gazed around and realised she was.

Somehow, magically, Raff had every other car to the side of the road. Raff was like that. He ordered and people obeyed. There were a couple of tow trucks arriving but already cars could get through.

There was no problem. All she had to do was get in the car—with dog—and drive to the vet's.

But…to take a dog to be put down?

"Henrietta should do this," she said, looking round for the lady she knew ran the Animal Shelter. But Raff put his hands on his cop hips and she thought any minute now he'd get ugly.

"Henrietta has a van full of dogs to find," he snapped.

"But she runs the Animal Shelter."

"So?"

"So that's where he needs to go. Surely not to be put down."

Raff's face hardened. She knew that look. Life hadn't been easy for Raff—she knew that, too. When he was up against it…well, he did what he had to do.

"Abby, I know this dog—I've known him for years," he told her, and his voice was suddenly bleak. "I took him to the Animal Shelter the night Isaac died. His daughter doesn't want him and neither does anyone else. The only guy who loves him is Isaac's gardener, and Lionel lives in a rooming house. There's no way he can keep him. The Shelter's full to bursting. Kleppy's had six weeks and the Shelter can't keep him any longer. Fred's waiting. The injection will be quick. Don't drag it out, Abby. Deliver the dog, and I'll see you in court."

"But…"

"Just do it." And he turned his back on her and started directing tow trucks.

He'd just given Abigail Callahan a dog and she looked totally flummoxed.

She looked adorable.

Yeah, well, it was high time he stopped thinking Abby was adorable. As a teenager, Abby had seemed a piece of him—a part of his whole—but she'd watched him with condemnation for ten years now. She'd changed from the laughing kid she used to be—from his adoring shadow—to someone he no longer liked very much.

He'd killed her brother.

Raff had finally come to terms with that long-ago tragedy—or he'd accepted it as much as he ever could—but he'd killed a part of her. How did a man get past that?

It was time he accepted that he never could.

What sort of name was Kleppy for a dog?

He shouldn't have told her its name.

Only she would have figured it. The dog had a blue plastic collar, obviously standard Animal Welfare issue, but whoever had attached it had reattached his tag, as if they were leaving him a bit of personality to the end.

Kleppy.

The name had been scratched by hand on the back of what looked like a medal. Abby set the dog on her passenger seat—he wagged his tail again and turned round twice and settled—and she couldn't help turning over his tag.

It was a medal. She recognised it and stared.

Old Man Abrahams had done something pretty impressive in the war. She'd heard rumours but she'd never had confirmation.

This was more than confirmation. A medal of honour, an amazing medal of honour—hanging on the collar of a scruffy, homeless mutt called Kleppy.

Uh-oh. He was looking up at her again now. His brown eyes were huge.

Six weeks in the Animal Shelter. She'd gone there once on some sort of school excursion. Concrete cells with a tiny exercise yard. Too many dogs, gazing up at her with hope she couldn't possibly match.

"The people who run this do a wonderful job," she remembered her teacher saying. "But they can't save every dog. If you ask your parents for a pet for Christmas you need to understand a dog can live for twenty years. Every dog deserves a loving home, boys and girls."

She'd been what? Thirteen? She remembered looking at the dogs and starting to cry.

And she also remembered Raff—of course it was Raff—patting her awkwardly on the shoulder. "Hey, it's okay, Abby. There'll be a fairy godmother somewhere. I reckon all these dogs'll be claimed by tea time."

"Yeah, probably by your grandmother," someone had said, not unkindly. "How many dogs do you have, Finn?"

"Seven," he'd said and the Welfare lady had pursed her lips.

"See, that's the problem," she said. "No family should have more than two."

"So you ought to bring five in," someone else told Raff and Raff had gone quiet.

You ought to bring five in. To be put down? Maybe that was what Philip would think, Abby decided, though she couldn't remember Philip being there. But even then Philip had been a stickler for rules.

As were her parents.

"We don't want an abandoned dog," they'd said in horror that night all those years ago. "Why would you want someone else's cast-off?"

She needed to remember her parents' advice right

now, for Isaac Abrahams' cast-off was in her car. Wearing a medal of valour.

"Move the car, Abby." Raff's voice was inexorable. She glanced up and he was filling her windscreen.

"I don't want…"

"You don't always get what you want," he growled. "I thought you were old enough to figure that out. While you're figuring, shift the car."

"But…"

"Or I'll get you towed for obstructing traffic," he snapped. "No choice, lady. Move."

So all she had to do was take one dog to the vet's and get herself to court. How hard was that?

She drove and Kleppy stayed motionless on the passenger seat and looked at her. Looking as if he trusted her with his life.

She felt sick.

This wasn't her responsibility. Kleppy belonged to an old guy who'd died six weeks ago. His daughter didn't want him. No one else had claimed him, so the sensible, humane thing to do was have him put down.

But what if…? What if…?

Oh, help, what she thinking?

She was getting married on Saturday week. To Philip. Nine days.

Her tiny house was full of wedding presents. Her wedding gown was hanging in the hall, a vision of beaded ivory satin. She'd made it herself, every stitch. She loved that dress.

This dog would walk past it and she'd have dog hair on ivory silk…

Well, that was a dumb thing to think. For this dog to

walk past it, he'd have to be in her house, and this dog was headed to the vet's. To be put down.

He looked up at her and whimpered. His paw came out and touched her knee.

Her heart turned over. Nooooo.

It took five minutes to drive to the vet's. Kleppy's paw rested against her knee the whole time.

She pulled up. Kleppy wasn't shaking. She was.

Fred came out to meet her. The elderly vet looked grim. He went straight to the passenger door. Tugged it open.

"Raff rang to say you were coming," he said, lifting Kleppy out. "Thanks for bringing him. Do you know when the rest are coming?"

"I… Henrietta was trying to catch them. How many?"

"More than I want to think about," Fred said grimly. "Three months from Christmas, puppies stop being cute. Not your call, though. I'll deal with him from here."

Kleppy lay limp in Fred's arms. He looked back at her.

The paw on her knee…

Help. Help, help, help.

"It'll be quick?"

Fred glanced at her, brows snapping. Abby had gone to school with Fred's daughter. He knew her well. "Don't," he said.

"Don't what?"

"Think about it. Get on with your life. Nine days till the wedding?"

"I…yes."

"Then you've enough on your plate without worrying about stray dogs. Not that you and Philip would ever want a dog. You're not dog people."

"What…what do you mean?"

"Dogs are mess," he said. "Not your style. You guys might qualify for a goldfish. See you later, love. Happy wedding if I don't see you before."

He turned away. She could no longer see Kleppy.

She could feel him.

His eyes…

Help. Help, help, help.

She was a goldfish person? She'd never even had a goldfish.

A paw on her knee…

He reached the door before she broke.

"Fred?"

The vet turned. Kleppy was still slumped.

"Yes?"

"I can't bear this," she said. "Can you…can you take him in, check him out for damage and then give him back to me?"

"Give him back?"

"Yes."

"You want him?"

"He's my wedding present to me." She knew she sounded defiant but she didn't care. "I've decided. How hard can one dog be? I can do this. Kleppy is mine."

Fred did his best to dissuade her. "A dog is for life, Abigail. Small dogs like Kleppy live for sixteen years or longer. That's ten years at least of keeping this dog."

"Yes." But ten years? That was a fact to give her pause.

But the paw…

"He's a mutt," Fred said. "Mostly Cairn but a bit of something else."

"That's okay." Her voice was better, she decided.

Firmer. If she was adopting a stray, what use was a pedigree?

"What will Philip say?"

"Philip will say I'm crazy, but it'll be fine," she said stoutly, though in truth she did have qualms. "Is he okay?"

Fred was checking him, even as he tried to dissuade her. "He seems shocked, and he's much thinner than when Isaac brought him in for his last vaccinations. My guess is that he's barely eaten since the old man died. Isaac found him six years back, as a pup, dumped out in the bush. There were a few problems, but in the end they were pretty much inseparable."

Inseparable? The word suddenly pushed her back to the scene she'd just left. To Raff.

Once upon a time, she and Raff had been inseparable, she thought, and inexplicably there was a crazy twist of her heart.

Inseparable. This dog. The paw…

"He looks okay," Fred said, feeding him a liver treat. Kleppy took it with dignified politeness. "Just deflated from what life's done to him. So now what?"

"I take him home."

"You'll need food. Bedding. A decent chain."

"I'll stop at the pet store. Tell me what to get."

But Fred was glancing at his watch, looking anxious. "I'm urgently needed at a calving. Tell you what, you'll be seeing Raff again in court. Raff'll tell you what you need."

"How did you know…?"

"Everyone knows everything in Banksia Bay," Fred said. "I know where you're supposed to be right now. I know Raff's had the case set back half an hour and I hear Judge Weatherby's not happy. He's fed up with Raff though, not you, so chances are you'll get Baxter off. Which no one in Banksia Bay will be happy about. But hey, if your fees go toward buying dog food, then who am I to argue? Get Baxter off, then talk to Raff about dog food. He gets a discount at the Stock and Station store."

"Why?"

"Because Raff has one pony, two dogs, three cats, two rabbits and, at last count, eighteen guinea pigs," Fred said, handing her Kleppy and starting to clear up. "His place is a menagerie. It's a wonder he didn't take this one but I guess even Raff has limits. He has a lot on his plate. See you later, love. Happy wedding and happy new dog."

Chapter 2

She couldn't go to the Stock and Station store now. That'd have to wait until she'd talked to Raff. Still, Kleppy obviously needed something. What? Best guess.

She stopped at the supermarket and bought a water bowl, a nice red lead with pictures of balls on it and a marrowbone.

She drove to the courthouse and Kleppy lay on the passenger seat and looked anxious. His tail had stopped wagging.

"Hey, I saved you," she told him. "Look happy."

He obviously didn't get the word *saved*. He sort of… hunched.

What was she going to do with him while she was in court?

She drove her car into her personal parking space. How neat was this? She remembered the day her name had gone up. Her parents had cracked champagne.

It was a fine car park. But…it was in full sun.

She might not be a dog person but she wasn't dumb. She couldn't leave Kleppy here. Nor could she take him home—or not yet—not until she'd done something about dog-proofing. Her parents? Ha! They'd take him right back to Fred.

So she drove two blocks to the local park. There were shade trees here and she could tie him by her car. Anyone passing would know he hadn't been abandoned.

She hoped Kleppy would know it, too.

She gave him water and his bone and he slumped on the ground and looked miserable.

Maybe he didn't know it.

She looked at him and sighed. She took off her jacket—her lovely tailored jacket that matched her skirt exactly—and she laid it beside Kleppy.

He sniffed it. The paw came out again—and he inched forward on his belly until it was under him.

Her very expensive jacket was on dirt and grass, and under dog. Her professional jacket.

She didn't actually like that jacket anyway; she preferred less serious clothes. She was five foot four and a bit…mousy. But maybe lawyers should be mousy. Her shiny brown hair curled happily when she let it hang to her shoulders but Philip liked it in a chignon. She had freckles but Philip liked her to wear foundation that disguised them. She had a neat figure that looked good in a suit. Professional. Lawyers should be professional.

She'd given up on *professional* this morning. She was so late.

Oh, but Kleppy looked sad.

"I'll be back at midday," she told him. "Two hours, tops. Promise. Then we'll work out where we go from here."

Where? She'd think of something. She must.

Maybe Raff…

There was a thought.

Fred had said Raff had a menagerie. What difference would one dog make? Once upon a time, he'd had seven.

Instead of advice, maybe she could persuade him to take him.

"You'd like Rafferty Finn," she told Kleppy. "He's basically a good man." Good but flawed—*trouble*—but she didn't need to go into that with Kleppy.

But how to talk him into it? Or Philip into the alternative?

It was too hard to think of that right now. She grabbed her briefcase and headed to the courthouse without looking back. Or without looking back more than half a dozen times.

Kleppy watched her until she was out of sight.

Heart twist. She didn't want to leave him.

It couldn't matter. Her work was in front of her and what was more important than work?

What was facing her was the case of The Crown versus Wallace Baxter.

Wallace was one of three Banksia Bay accountants. The other two made modest incomes. Wallace, however, had the biggest house in Banksia Bay. The Baxter kids went to the best private school in Sydney. Sylvia Baxter drove a Mercedes Coupé, and they skied in Aspen twice a year. They owned a lodge there.

"Lucky investments," Wallace always said but, after years of juggling, his web of dealings had turned into one appalling tangle. Wallace himself wasn't suffering—his house, cars, even the ski lodge in Aspen, were all in his wife's name—but there were scores of Banksia Bay's retirees who were suffering a lot.

"It's just the financial crisis," Wallace had said as Philip and Abby had gone over his case notes. "I can't be responsible for the failure of overseas banks. Just because I'm global…"

Because he was global, his financial dealings were hard to track.

This was a small case by national standards. The Crown Prosecutor who covered Banksia Bay should have retired years ago. The case against Wallace had been left pretty much to Raff, who had few resources and less time. So Raff was right—Philip and Abby had every chance of getting their client off.

Philip rose to meet her, looking relieved. The documents they needed were in her briefcase. He kept the bulk of the confidential files, but it was her job to bring day to day stuff to court.

"What the…?"

"Did Raff tell you what happened?"

Philip cast Raff a look of irritation across the court. There was no love lost between these two men—there never had been. "He said you had to take a dog to the vet, to get it put down. Isn't that his job?"

"He had cars to move."

"He got here before you. What kept you? And where's your jacket?"

"It got dog hair on it." That, at least, was true. "Can we get on?"

"It'd be appreciated," the judge said dryly from the bench.

So she sat and watched as Philip decimated the Crown's case. Maybe his irritation gave him an edge this morning, she thought. He was smooth, intelligent, insightful—the best lawyer she knew. He'd do magnificently in the city. That he'd returned home to Banksia Bay—to her—seemed incredible.

Her parents thought so. They loved him to bits. What was more, Philip's father had been her brother Ben's godfather. They were almost family already.

"He almost makes up for our Ben," her mother said over and over, and their engagement had been a foregone conclusion that made everyone happy.

Except... Except...

Don't go there.

She generally didn't. It was only in the small hours when she woke and thought of Philip's dry kisses, and thought why don't I feel...why don't I feel...?

Like she did when she looked at Rafferty Finn?

No. This was pre-wedding nerves. She had no business thinking like that. If she so much as looked at Raff in that way it'd break her parents' hearts.

So no and no and no.

Raff was on the stand now, steady and sure, giving his evidence with solid backup. His investigation stretched over years, with so many pointers...

But all of those pointers were circumstantial.

She suspected there were things in Philip's briefcase that might not be circumstantial.

Um...don't go there. There was such a thing as lawyer-client confidentiality. Even if Baxter admitted dishonesty to them outright—which he hadn't—they couldn't use it against him.

So Raff didn't have the answers to Philip's questions. The Crown Prosecutor didn't ask the right questions of

Baxter. It'd take a few days, maybe more, but even by lunch time no one doubted the outcome.

At twelve the court rose. The courtroom emptied.

"You might like to go home and get another jacket," Philip said. "I'm taking Wallace to lunch."

She wasn't up to explaining about Kleppy right now. Where to start? But she surely didn't want to have lunch with Wallace. Acting for the guy made her feel dirty.

"Go ahead," she said.

Philip left, escorting a smug Wallace. She felt an almost irresistible urge to talk to the Crown Prosecutor, tell him to push harder.

It was only suspicion. She had no proof.

"Thanks for taking Kleppy." Raff was right behind her, and made her jump. Her heart did the same stupid skittering thing it had done for years whenever she heard his voice. She turned to face him and he was smiling at her, looking rueful. "Sorry, Abby. That was a hard thing to ask you to do this morning, but I had no choice."

Putting Kleppy down. A hard thing…

"It was too hard," she whispered. The Crown Prosecutor was leaving for lunch. If she wanted to talk to him…

She was lawyer for the defence. What was she thinking?

"Hey, but you're tough." Raff motioned to the back of the courtroom, where Bert and Gwen Mackervale were shuffling out to find somewhere to eat their packed sandwiches. "Not like the Mackervales. They're as soft a touch as any I've seen. They lost their house, yet you'll get Wallace off."

"Raff, this is inappropriate. I'm a defence lawyer. You know it's what I do."

"You don't have to. You're better than this, Abby."

"No, I'm not."

"Yeah, well…" He shrugged. "I'm going to find me a hamburger. See you later."

Uh-oh. Maybe she shouldn't have snapped. Definitely she shouldn't have snapped. Not when there was such a big favour to ask.

How to ask?

Just ask.

"You couldn't cope with another dog, could you?" she managed and he stilled.

"Another…"

"I couldn't," she whispered. "I can't. He's still alive. Raff, he…he looked at me."

"He looked at you." Raff was looking at her as if she'd just landed from Mars.

"I couldn't get him put down."

Raff was carrying papers. He placed them on the nearest bench without breaking his gaze. He stared at her for a full minute.

She didn't stare back. She stared at her shoes instead. They were nice black shoes. Maybe a bit high. Pert, she thought. Pert was good.

There was a smudge on one toe. She considered bending to wipe it and decided against it.

Still silence.

"You're keeping Kleppy?" he said at last.

She shook her head. "I'm… I don't think it's possible. I'm asking if you could take him. Fred says you have a menagerie. One more wouldn't…wouldn't be much more trouble. I could pay you for his keep."

"Fred suggested…" He sounded flabbergasted.

"He didn't," she admitted. "I thought of it myself."

"That I'd take Kleppy?"

"Yes," she whispered and she thought that she sounded about eight years old again. She sounded pathetic.

"No," he said.

She looked up at him then. Raff Finn was a good six inches taller than she was. More. He was a bit too big. He was a bit too male. He was a bit too… Raff?

He was also a bit too angry.

"N… No?"

"No!" His expression was a mixture of incredulity and fury. "I don't believe this. You strung out a dog's life in the hope I'd take him?"

"No, I…"

"Do you know how miserable he is?"

"That's why I…"

"Decided to give him to me. Thanks, Abby, but no."

"But…"

"I'm not a soft option."

"You have all those animals."

"Because Sarah loves them. Do you know how much they cost to feed? I can't go away. I can't do anything because Sarah breaks her heart over each and every one of them. Don't you dare do this to me, Abby. I'm not your soft option. If you saved Kleppy, then he's yours."

"I can't…"

"And neither can I. You brought this on yourself. You deal with it yourself." His voice was rough as gravel, his anger palpable. "I need to go. I didn't get breakfast and I don't intend to miss lunch. I'll see you back in court at one."

He turned away. He strode to the court door and she

chewed her lip and thought. But then she decided there wasn't time for thinking. She panicked instead.

"Raff?"

He stopped, not looking back. "What?"

Sometimes only an apology would do. She was smart enough to know that this was one of those times. Maybe a little backtracking wouldn't hurt either.

"Raff, I'm very sorry," she said. "It was just a thought—or maybe it was just a wild hope—but the decision to save Kleppy was mine. Asking you was an easy option and I won't ask again. But, moving on, if I'm to keep him... I know nothing about dogs. Fred didn't suggest you take him, but he did suggest I ask you for help. He said you'll tell me all the things I need to care for him. So please..."

"Please what?"

"Just tell me what I need to buy at the Stock and Station store. I have a meeting with the wedding caterers after work, so I need to do my shopping now."

"You're seriously thinking you'll keep him?"

"I don't have a choice."

He was facing her now, his face a mixture of incredulity and...laughter? Where had laughter come from? "You're keeping *Kleppy*?" He said it as if she'd chosen Kleppy above all others.

"There's no other dogs out there?" she said, alarmed, and he grinned. His grin lit his face—lit the whole court. Oh, she knew that grin...

Trouble. Tragedy.

"There's thousands of dogs," he said. "So many needing homes. But you have to fall for Kleppy."

"What's wrong with Kleppy?"

"Nothing." He was still grinning. "I take it you haven't told Philip."

"I… No."

"So where's Kleppy now?" His grin faded. "You haven't left him in the car? The sun…"

"I know that much," she said, indignant. "I took the car to the park and I tied him to a nice shady tree. He has water and feed. He even has my jacket."

"He has your jacket." He sounded bemused, as if there was some private joke she wasn't privy to.

"Yes."

"And you've tied him up…how?"

"I bought a lead."

"Please tell me it's a chain."

"The chains looked cruel. It's webbing. Pretty. Red with pictures of balls on it."

"I don't believe this."

"What's wrong?"

But she didn't have a chance to answer. Instead, he grabbed her hand, towed her out of the courthouse—practically at a run—and he headed for the park.

Dragging her behind him.

Kleppy was gone.

Her pretty red lead was chewed into two pieces—or at least she assumed it was chewed into two pieces. One piece was still tied to the tree.

Her jacket lay on the ground, rumpled. The water bowl was half empty. Apparently chewing leads was thirsty work. The marrowbone wasn't touched.

No dog.

"He doesn't like being confined, our Kleppy," Raff said, taking in the scene with professional care.

"You know this how?" *He'd chewed through a lead?*

"It's always been a problem. I'm guessing he'll make tracks up to the Abrahams place, but who knows where he'll end up in the meantime."

"He'll be up at Isaac's?"

Isaac lived halfway up the mountain at the back of the town. Raff was looking concerned. "It is a bit far," he admitted. "And from here… It'll be off his chosen beat." He raked his hair. "Of all the stupid… I don't have time to go look for a dog."

"I'll look for him."

"You know where to look?"

"Do you?"

"Backyards," he said. "Never takes the fastest route, our Kleppy." He raked his hair again. Looking tired. "I need lunch. If I'm not back in court at one then Baxter'll definitely get off. You need to do this, Abby. I can't."

Look for a dog all afternoon… "Philip'll kill me."

"Then I guess the wedding'll be off. Is that a good thing?"

Raff spoke absently, as if it didn't bother him if her wedding was at risk. As indeed it didn't. What business was it of his to care about the wedding? What business was it of his to even comment on it? She opened her mouth to say so, but suddenly his gaze focused, sharpened. "Is that…?"

She turned to see.

It was—and the change was extraordinary.

When she'd left him two hours ago, Kleppy had looked defeated and depressed. When he'd crawled onto her jacket he hadn't had the energy to even rise off his stomach.

Now he was prancing across the park towards them,

looking practically jaunty. His rough coat was never going to be pretty. One of his ears flopped down, almost covering his eye. His tail was a bit ragged.

But they could see his tail wagging when he was still a hundred yards away. And, as he got closer…

He had something in his mouth. Something pink and lacy.

What the…?

"It's a bra," Abby breathed as the little dog reached them. She bent down and the dog circled her twice, then came to her outstretched hand. He rubbed himself against her leg and his whole body shivered. With delight?

He was carrying the bra like a trophy. She touched it and he dropped it into her hand, then stood back as if he'd just presented her with a cheque for a million dollars. His body language was unmistakable.

Look what I've found for you! Aren't I the cleverest dog in the world?

She dropped the bra and picked him up, hugging him close. He wriggled frantically and she put him back down. He picked up the bra again, placed it back in her hand and then allowed her to pick him up—as long as she kept the bra.

His meaning couldn't be plainer. "I've brought you a gift. You appreciate it."

"You've brought me a bra," she managed and she felt like crying. "Oh, Kleppy…"

"It could just as easily have been men's jocks," Raff said. He lifted the end of the bra that was hanging loose. There was a price tag attached. "I thought so. He's a bit small to rob clothes lines, our Kleppy. This has come

from Main Street. Morrisy Drapers are having a sale.
This will have come from the discount bin at the front
of the store."

Had it? She checked it out. Cop and lawyer for the
defence, standing in the sun, examining evidence.

Pink bra. Nylon. White and silver frills. About an E
Plus Cup. Room for about three of Abby.

"Very…very useful," Abby managed.

"You'll need to pay for it."

"Sorry?"

"It's theft," Raff said, touching the bra's middle with
a certain degree of caution. It was looking a bit soggy.
"He never hurts anything. He hunts treasures; he never
destroys them. But they do get a bit…wet. Taking it back
and apologising's not going to cut it."

"Will they know he's stolen it?"

"He's not a cat burglar," Raff said gravely, though the
sides of his mouth were twitching. "Dog burglars don't
have the same finesse. He's a snatch and grab man, our
Kleppy. There'll be a dozen people on Main Street who'll
be able to identify him in a line up."

"Oh, my…" And then she paused. Kleppy.

Kleppy was a strange name but she'd hardly had time
to think about it. Now… "Kleppy. Oh…"

Raff looked like a man starting to enjoy himself. "Got
it," he said, grinning. "And there's another reason you're
not offloading this mutt onto me. This is a dog who lives
to present his master with surprises. No dead rats or old
bones for his guy. It has to be interesting. Expensive
is good. One of a set's his favourite. Isaac gave up on
him long since—he just paid for the damage and got on
with it. So now here's Kleppy, deciding you're his new

owner. Welcome to dog ownership, Abigail Callahan. You're the proud owner of Banksia Bay's biggest kleptomaniac—and also the littlest."

A kleptomaniac... Kleppy.

She stared at Raff as if he was out of his mind. He gazed back, lips twitching, that dangerous smile lurking deep within.

She was about to present her fiancé with a kleptomaniac dog?

"I don't believe it," she managed at last. "There's no such thing."

"You want to know how I know this dog?" He wasn't even trying to disguise his grin. "I'd like to say I'm personally acquainted with every dog in Banksia Bay but, even with Sarah's help, I can't manage that. Nope, I'm acquainted with Kleppy because I've arrested him."

"Arrested..."

"I've caught him red-handed—or red-pawed—on any number of occasions. The problem is that he doesn't know how to hide it. Like now. He steals and then he shows off."

"I don't believe it."

"You've already said that."

"But..."

"That's why no one wants him," he said, humour fading. "He's always been a problem. Henrietta's had to be honest with everyone who came to the Shelter looking for the ideal pet. He isn't ideal. Isaac paid out on Kleppy's behalf more times than I can say. He's hidden stuff and he's been accused of stealing himself. Isaac never cared what people thought of him, which was just as well, as there's been more women's underwear end up at his house than you can imagine. He burned most of it—what choice did he have? Can you imagine wandering the town saying who owns this G-string? But he loved Kleppy, you see." The smile returned. "Like you will."

"I… This is appalling."

"I told you to get him put down."

"You know I'm a soft option." Anger hit then, fury, pure and simple. "You know me, Raff Finn. You put this dog in my car because you knew I wouldn't be able to have him put down. You know I'm a soft touch."

"Now how would I know that?" he said softly. "I haven't known you for a very long time, Abby. You've grown up. You've got yourself engaged to Philip. The Abby I knew could no sooner have married Philip than fly. You're a lawyer engaged in getting Wallace Baxter off. A lawyer doing cases like that—of course you can get a dog put down."

His gaze met hers, direct, challenging, knowing he was calling a bluff she couldn't possibly meet.

"You still can," he told her. "Put Kleppy in the car and take him back to Fred. You've made his last hours happy by giving him the freedom for one last hoist. He'll die a happy dog."

You still can.

Say something.

She couldn't think of a thing to say.

She was hugging Kleppy, who had a pink bra somehow looped around his ears.

She still hugged Kleppy.

What Raff was saying was sensible. Very sensible. There were too many dogs in the world. She'd done her best by this one. She'd let him have a happy morning—if indeed Raff was right and Kleppy did enjoy stealing.

But he was certainly a happier dog now than he'd been when she'd first met him. He was warm and nuzzly. He was poking his damp nose against her neck, giving her a tentative lick.

His backside was wriggling.

Take him back to Fred? No way.

She'd always wanted a dog.

Philip would hate a dog.

Her marriage suddenly loomed before her. Loomed? Wrong word, but she couldn't think of another one.

Philip was wonderful. He was her rock. He'd looked after her and her family for ever. When Ben had died he'd held her up when her world seemed to be disintegrating.

Philip was right for her. Her parents loved him. Everyone thought Philip was wonderful. If she hadn't married him…

She *hadn't* married him, she reminded herself. Not yet. That was the point.

In nine days she'd be married. She'd move into the fabulous house Philip had bought for them, and she'd be Philip's wife.

Philip's wife would never bring home a kleptomaniac dog. She'd never bring home any sort of dog. So, if she wanted one…

She took a deep breath and she knew exactly what she'd do. Her last stand… Like it or leave it, she thought, and she sounded desperate, even to herself. But she had made up her mind.

"I'm keeping him."

"Good for you," Raff said and the twinkle was back with a vengeance. "Can I be there when you tell Philip?"

"Get lost."

"That's not kind. Not when you need help to buy what Kleppy needs."

"I'm starting to get a very good idea of what Kleppy needs," she said darkly. "An eight-foot fence and a six-foot chain."

"He'll mope."

"Then he'll have to learn not to mope. It's that or dead."

"You'll explain that to him how?"

"You're not being helpful."

"No," he said and glanced at his watch. "I'm not. I need a hamburger and time's running out before court resumes. You want a list?"

"No. I mean…" The afternoon suddenly stretched before her, long and lonely. Or not long and lonely for her. Long and lonely for the little dog squirming in her arms. Her thief. "I do need a list. I also need a chain." She hesitated. "But I can't leave him here. This morning was only two hours. This afternoon's four at least before I can collect him."

"So take him home."

"I can't." It was practically a wail. She caught herself. Fought for a little dignity. "I mean…it's not dog-proof. I need an hour or so there to get things organised."

"That's fair enough." He paused, surveyed her face and then decided to be helpful. "You want me to ask Sarah to help?"

Sarah. Her eyes widened. Of course. Sarah loved dogs. And… Maybe her first suggestion was still possible. Maybe…

"No," Raff said before she opened her mouth. "Sarah's not taking ownership of another dog and if you ask her I'll personally run you out of town. I mean that, Abby."

"I wouldn't ask her."

"No?"

She managed a twisted smile, abandoning her last forlorn hope.

"No."

"Good, then," he said briskly, moving on. "But she'll enjoy taking care of him this afternoon. Kleppy'll be tired after his excursion. We have a safe yard. The other dogs are quiet—they won't overwhelm him—and you can come by this evening and pick him up."

Go back to Raff's? She couldn't imagine doing that. But Raff was moving on.

"It's a good offer," Raff said. "Take it or leave it, but do it now. If you accept, then I'll lock this convicted thief in my patrol car and take him out to Sarah. I may even do it with lights and sirens if it means getting back to court on time. You can take my list and go buy what you need and get back to court on time as well. Or I leave you to it. What's it to be, Abby?"

"I…" She was starting to panic. Go out to Raff's tonight? To Raff's? She hadn't been there since…

"Unless you have another friend you can call on?" he suggested, and maybe her emotions were on her face. Definitely her emotions were on her face.

"All my friends work," she wailed.

"Then it's Sarah. Tonight, and you *will* collect him." That irrepressible grin emerged again. "Hey, you have a dog. What a wedding gift. To you and to Philip, one kleptomaniac dog. Happy wedding."

He drove out to Sarah with Kleppy beside him and he found the smile inside him growing. Somewhere inside, the Abby he'd once known and loved was still there.

Once upon a time she'd loved him.

That had been years ago. A teenage romance. Yes, they'd felt as if they were truly, madly, deeply, but they were only kids.

At nineteen he'd headed off to Sydney to Police Training College. Abby had been stuck in Banksia Bay until she finished school, and she'd needed a partner for her debutante ball.

He still remembered the arguments. "You're my boyfriend. How can I have anyone else as my partner? Why can't you come home more often so we can practice?"

And more… "You and Ben are totally obsessed with that car. Every time you come home, that's all you ever think about."

They were kids. He hadn't seen her need, and she hadn't seen his. Philip had been home from university; he'd agreed to partner her for her ball and Raff was given the cold shoulder.

They'd been kids moving on. Changing.

They had changed, he conceded, only just now he'd seen a glimpse that the old Abby was still in there. Feisty and funny and gorgeous.

But still…unforgiving, and who could blame her?

He'd forgiven himself. He didn't need Abigail Callahan's forgiveness. He couldn't need it.

If only she wasn't adorable.

Chapter 3

The afternoon was interminable. The case was boring—financial evidence that was as dry as dust.

The courtroom was as dry as dust.

She couldn't think of a way to tell Philip.

All afternoon she was aware of Raff on the opposite side of the courtroom. He was here this afternoon to present the police case. Thankfully, he wouldn't be here for the rest of the week. He was called away twice, for which she was also thankful, but he wasn't called away for long enough.

He was watching her.

He was waiting for her to tell Philip?

He was laughing at her. She knew he was. The man spelled trouble and he'd just got her into more.

Trouble? One small dog, easily contained in a secure backyard. How hard could this be?

So tell Philip.

There was lots of time. The police case went on for most of the afternoon—tedious financial details. She and Philip both knew it back to front. There were gaps while documents were given to the jury. She had time to tell him.

Philip would be civilised about it. He'd never raise his voice to her, especially not in a courtroom. But still...

She couldn't.

Across the court, Raff still watched her.

Finally the court rose. Raff crossed the courtroom and Abby panicked. *Don't say anything.*

"You guys okay?" he asked, and anyone who didn't know him would think it was simply a courtesy question. They wouldn't see that lurking laughter. *Trouble.*

"Why wouldn't we be?" Philip demanded, irritated. He disliked Raff—of course he did. He showed no outright aggression—simply cool, professional interaction and nothing more.

"It's getting close to your wedding," Raff said. "No last minute nerves? No last minute hitches?"

"We need to go," Abby said, feeling close to hysterics. "I have a meeting with the caterers in half an hour."

"I bet there's lots of stuff you need to do." Raff's voice was sympathy itself. "Messy things, weddings."

"Not ours," Philip snapped. "Everything's under control. Isn't that right, sweetheart?"

"I...yes." Just go away, Raff. Get out of our lives. "Are you coming to the caterers with me, Philip?"

"I can't." Philip turned a shoulder on Raff, excluding him completely. "My dad and my uncles are taking me out to dinner and bowling. A boys only night. I thought I told you."

He had.

"That sounds exciting," Raff said, mildly interested. "Bowling, huh. I guess I won't be untying you naked from in front of the Country Women's Association clubrooms at dawn, then."

"My friends…"

"Don't do wild buck's nights," Raff said approvingly. "I guessed that. You'll probably be home in bed by eight. So you're alone tonight, Abby? Organising caterers on your lonesome. And anything else you need to do."

"Could you please…" she started and then stopped, the impossibility of asking another favour—asking him to bring Kleppy home—overwhelming her.

"Nope," Raff said. "Not if you're about to ask me anything that involves the wedding. Me and weddings keep far away from each other."

"We're not asking you to be involved," Philip snapped. "Abby can cope with the caterers herself. Ready to go, sweetheart?"

"Yes," she managed and allowed Philip to usher her out of the court.

She should have told Philip then. She had ten minutes while Philip went over the results of the day, what they needed to do to strengthen their case the next morning, a few wedding details he'd forgotten to cover.

Philip was a man at ease with himself. It was only when Raff was around that he got prickly and maybe… well, that did have to do with their past. Raff had messed with Philip's life as well as hers.

Philip was a good man. He was looking forward to his wedding. His father and his uncles were taking him out for a pre-wedding night with the boys and he'd enjoy it.

She didn't want to mess with that until she must, even if it did mean delaying telling him about Kleppy; even if it meant going to Raff's alone. Maybe it'd be better going alone. Going with Philip… It could make things worse.

"Come round tonight after bowling," she told him, kissing him lightly on the lips. Her fiancé. Her husband in nine days. She loved him.

And if he was a bit dull… He'd had his days of being wild, they all had, before life had taught them that caution was good.

"We should get a good night's sleep," he said.

"Yes, but there are things we need to discuss." He'd like Kleppy when he saw him, she decided. Kleppy of the limpid eyes, wide and brown and innocent.

She should change his name. To Rover? Rover was a Philipish name for a dog.

But Kleppy suited him.

"What do we need to discuss?" he was asking.

Say it.

No. Introduce him to Kleppy as a done deal.

"Just…caterers and things. I don't want to make too many decisions on my own."

He smiled and kissed her and she had to stop herself from thinking dry and dusty. "You need to have more self-confidence. Make your own decisions. You're a big girl now."

"I…yes."

"Anything you decide is fine by me."

"But you will drop by?"

"I'll drop by. Night, sweetheart." And off he went for his night with the boys. His dad and his uncles. Bowling. Yeeha!

And that was the type of thinking that was getting her into trouble, she decided. So cut it out.

Philip was a lovely man. He was handsome. He was

beautifully groomed. They'd had a very nice holiday last year—they'd gone to Italy and Philip had had four suits made there. They were lovely suits. He'd also had two briefcases made—matching ones, magnificent leather, discreetly initialled and fitted out to Philip's specifications. She'd only been mildly irritated when he'd decreed—for the sake of the briefcases—her surname would be his.

What was the issue, after all? She was to be his wife.

But buying suits and briefcases had taken almost half of their holiday.

Cut it out!

It was just… Raff had unsettled her. This whole day had unsettled her.

"So go home and organise your house for one small dog, then go organise caterers," she told herself. "Oh, and pay for Kleppy's stolen goods. Just do what has to be done, one step at a time."

And then go out to Raff's?

Aargh.

She could do this.

She could visit Rafferty Finn.

She could do it. One step at a time.

The rest of the afternoon was full, but Abby and her dog were front and centre of his thoughts. He shouldn't have offered to bring Kleppy home. Not this afternoon. Not ever.

He didn't want her coming here.

After dinner, Raff washed and Sarah wiped, while Sarah told him about her day, the highlight of which had been minding Kleppy.

"He's a sweetheart," his sister told him, her face softening at the thought of the little dog. "He's so cuddly. Why does he love his bra?"

"He's a thief. He likes stealing things. He's a bad dog." He found himself smiling at the thought of strait-laced Abigail Callahan having to front up and pay for stolen goods.

Maybe it wasn't a good idea to keep thinking of Abby. Not like this.

She was Philip's fiancée. Anything between them was a distant memory. It had to be.

But Sarah was looking doubtful. She looked down at Kleppy, snoozing by the fire, his bra tucked underneath him. "He doesn't look bad. He's really cute and Abby's very busy. Are you sure Abby wants him?"

Raff hardened his heart. "I'm sure."

"And Abby's coming tonight?"

"Yes."

"Abby's my friend."

She was. The tension of the day lessened a little at that. No matter what lay between Raff and Abby, no matter how much she hated seeing him, Abby had always been Sarah's friend.

They'd all been best friends at the time of the accident. Ben and Raff. Abby and Sarah. Two big brothers, two little sisters. Philip had been in there, too. A gang of five.

But one car crash and friendship had been blown to bits.

In the months that followed, no matter that Abby had loathed Raff so much that seeing him made her cry, she'd stuck by Sarah. She'd visited her in Sydney, despite her parents' disapproval, taking the train week after week

to Sydney Central Hospital and then later to the reha-
bilitation unit on North Shore.

Back home, Sarah's friends had fallen away. Acquired
brain injury was a hard thing for friends to handle. Sarah
was still Sarah, and yet not. She'd struggled with everything—relearning speaking, walking, the simplest
of survival skills.

They'd come so far. She could now almost live inde-
pendently—almost, but not quite. She had her animals
and their little farm Raff kept for her. She worked in the
local sheltered workshop three days a week, and twice
a week Abby met her after work for drinks.

Drinks being milkshakes. Two friends, catching up
on their news.

Raff would pick Sarah up and she'd be happy, bub-
bly about going out with her friend—but Abby would
always have slipped away from the café just before Raff
was due. Since the accident, Abby had never come back
to their farm. She'd never talked to Raff unless she absolutely must, but she'd never taken that anger out on
Sarah.

"I'm glad Abby's coming tonight," Sarah said simply. "And I'm glad she's getting a dog. Abby's lonely."

Lonely? Sarah rarely had insights. This one was startling. "No, she's not. She's getting married to Philip."

"I don't like Philip," Sarah said.

That was unusual, too. Sarah liked everyone. When
Philip met her—as of course he did because this wasn't
a big town—he was unfailingly friendly. But still… In
the times when Raff had been with her and they'd met
Philip, Sarah's hand had crept to his and she'd clung.

Was that from memories of the accident?

The accident. Don't go there.

"There's nothing wrong with Philip," he told Sarah.

"I want Abby to come," Sarah said, wiping her last pot with a fierceness unusual for her. "But I don't want Philip. He makes me scared."

Scared?

"The man's boring," Raff said. "There's nothing to be scared about."

"I just don't like him," Sarah said and, logical or not, Raff felt exactly the same.

She didn't want to go.

She must.

She gazed round her little house with a carefully appraising eye. She'd hung her wedding dress in the spare room and she'd packed away everything else she thought a dog might hurt.

She'd bought a dog kennel for outside and a basket for inside.

She'd bought a chain for emergencies but she didn't intend using it. Her back garden was enclosed with a four-foot brick fence, and she'd checked and rechecked for gaps.

She had dog food, dog shampoo, flea powder, worm pills, a dog brush, padding for his kennel and a book on training your dog. She'd had a quick browse through the book. There was nothing about kleptomania, but confinement would fix that.

She'd take him for a long walk every day. Kleppy might sometimes be lonely, she conceded, but surely loneliness was better than the fate that had been waiting for him.

And if he was lonely… She might sneak him into the office occasionally.

That, though, was for the future. For now, she was ready to fetch him. From Raff.

So fetch him. There's not a lot of use staring at preparations, she told herself. It's time to go claim your dog.

It was eight o'clock. Philip's night out would be over by ten and she had to be back here by then.

Of course she'd be back. Ten minutes drive out. Two minutes to collect Kleppy and say hi to Sarah. Ten minutes back.

Just go.

She hadn't been out there since…

Just go.

"When will she be here?"

"Any time soon."

He shouldn't care. He shouldn't even be here. There was bound to be something cop-like that needed his attention at the station—only that might look like he was running, and Rafferty Finn wasn't a man who ran.

"She never comes here."

"She likes going to cafés with you too much."

Sarah giggled, hugging Kleppy close. This place was pretty relaxed for a dog. The screen door stayed permanently open and the dogs wandered in and out at will. The gate to the back garden was closed, but Kleppy seemed content to be hugged by Sarah, to watch television and to occasionally eat popcorn.

Raff watched television, too. Or sort of. It was hard to watch when every sense was tuned to a car arriving.

The Finn place hadn't changed.

The moon was full but she hardly needed to see. She'd come here so often, to the base of Black Mountain, that she knew every bend. As kids, she and Ben had ridden their bikes here almost every day.

This had been their magic place.

Her parents had disapproved. "The Finns," her mother had told them over and over, "are not our sort of people." By that she meant they didn't fit into her social mould.

Abby and Ben didn't care.

Old Mrs Finn—everybody called her Gran—had been the family's stability. Gran's husband had died long before Abby had known her, and it was rumoured that his death had been a relief, for the town as well as for Gran. After his death, Gran had quietly got on with life. She ran a few sheep, a few pigs, a lot of poultry. Her garden was amazing. She seemed to spend her life in the kitchen and her baking was wonderful.

Abby barely remembered Raff and Sarah's mother, but there had been disapproving whispers about her as well. She'd run away from home at fifteen, then come home unwed with two small children.

She'd worked in the local supermarket for a time. Abby had vague memories of a silent woman with haunted eyes, with none of the life and laughter of her mother or her children.

She'd died when Abby was about seven. Abby remembered little fuss, just a family who'd got on with it. Gran had taken over her grandchildren's care. Life had gone on and the Finns were still disapproved of.

Abby and Ben had loved it here. They had always been welcome.

And now? She turned into the drive but her foot eased from the accelerator.

"You're always welcome." She could remember Gran saying it to her, over and over. She remembered Gran

saying it to her after Ben's death. As if she could come
back here...

She had come back. Tonight.

This is only about a dog, she told herself, breathing
deeply. *Nothing else. The past is gone. There's no use
regretting—no use even thinking about it. Go get your
dog from Raff Finn and then get off his land.*

Raff never meant...

I know he didn't, she told herself. Of course he didn't.
Accidents happened and it was only stupidity.

Could she forgive stupidity?

Ben was dead. Why would she want to?

He saw her stop at the gate. It was after eight—would
Philip have finished his wild night out? Would she have
him with her?

Maybe that was why they'd stopped. Philip would be
doing his utmost to stop her keeping Kleppy.

Would she defy him? She'd need strength if she was
going to stay married to Philip. She'd need strength not
to be Philip's doormat.

But the thought of Abby as a doormat made him
smile. She'd never been a doormat. Abby Callahan was
smart, sexy, sassy—and so much more. Or...she had
been.

She'd followed him round like a shadow for years.
He and Ben had scoffed at Abby and Sarah, the little
sisters. They'd teased them, and had given them such a
hard time. They'd loved them both. Until...

Until one stupid night. One stupid moment.

He closed his eyes as he'd done so many times.
Searching for a memory.

Summer. Nineteen years old. Home from Police

Training College. Ben home from university. They'd spent weekend after weekend tinkering with a car they were trying to restore. Finally they'd got it started, towards dusk on the day they were both due to go back to the city. They were pumped with excitement. Aching to see it go.

They couldn't take it on the road—it wasn't registered—but up on Black Mountain, just behind Isaac Abrahams place, there was a cleared firebreak, smoothed for access for fire trucks.

If they could get it out there, they could put it through its paces.

He remembered loading the car on the trailer behind Gran's ancient truck, Ben's dad watching them in disapproval. "You should be home tonight, Ben. Your mother's expecting you."

"We need to see this working," Ben had told him and Mr Callahan had left in a huff.

Sarah was watching them, wistful. "Can I come?"

"There's not enough room in the truck."

"What if Philip brings me?"

"Sure. Bring Abby."

"You know Abby's mad at you—and she's not talking to Philip, either."

But neither Ben nor Raff were interested. They were only interested in getting their car going.

And it worked. Up on the mountain, he remembered Ben driving, yahooing, both of them high as kites. Months of work paying off.

He remembered getting out. Swapping drivers. Thinking it was too dark to be on this track, and it was starting to rain. Plus Ben had to get back to have dinner with his parents.

But Ben saying, "We have lights. If I can cope with Mum being fed up, you can cope with a bit of rain. Just do one turn to see for yourself how well she handles."

Then…nothing. He'd woken in hospital. Concussion. Multiple lacerations. Broken wrist and broken ankle.

All he knew of the accident was what was written in the official reports.

Philip had driven Sarah onto the track to find them. He'd turned off the main road onto the firebreak, and ventured just far enough down the break to reach the crest…

Philip had been the only one uninjured. His recall was perfect, stark and bleak.

Raff had burst over the crest on the wrong side of the road, driving so fast he was almost airborne. Philip had nowhere to go. Both drivers swerved, but not fast enough.

Both cars had ended up in the trees. The rain and the mess from the emergency vehicles had washed the tracks away before the authorities could corroborate Philip's story. Raff couldn't be prosecuted—but he had punishment enough. He'd killed his best mate and he'd destroyed his sister. He missed Ben like he'd miss a twin—an aching, gut-destroying loss. He'd lost a part of Sarah that could never be restored.

His grandmother had died six months later.

And Abby?

Facing Abby had been the hardest thing he'd had to do in his life. The first time he'd seen her…she'd looked at him and it was as if he was some sort of black hole where her heart used to be.

"I'm sorry," he'd said and she'd simply turned away. She'd stayed away for ten years.

Her brother was dead and sometimes Raff wished it could have been him.

Which was dumb. Who'd take care of Sarah, then?

Let it go.

Go greet Abby. And Philip?

Abby and Philip. Banksia Bay's perfect couple.

Chapter 4

Raff was waiting on the veranda and Abby felt her breath catch in her throat. She came close to heading straight back down the mountain.

What was it with this man? She was well over her childhood crush. She'd decided today that it was the uniform making him sexy, but he wasn't wearing a uniform now.

He was in faded jeans and an old T-shirt, stretched a bit tight.

He looked good enough to...

To get away from fast.

He was leaning idly against the veranda post, big, loose-limbed, absurdly good-looking. He was standing with crossed arms, watching her walk towards him. Simply watching.

His eyes said caution.

She didn't need the message. Caution? She had it in spades.

"Where's Kleppy?" she asked, and she knew she sounded snappy but there wasn't a thing she could do about it.

"Phil's still on his wild night out?"

"Cut it out, Raff."

"Sorry," he said. Then he hesitated and his eyes narrowed. "Nope. Come to think of it, I'm not sorry. Why are you marrying that stuffed shirt?"

"Don't be insulting."

"He's wealthy," Raff conceded. "Parents own half Banksia Bay. He's making a nice little income himself. Or a big income. He's already bought the dream home. He's starting to look almost as wealthy as Baxter. You guys will be set for life."

"Stop it," she snapped. "Just because he's a responsible citizen…"

"I'm responsible now. Maybe even more responsible than you. What have you got on Baxter that I don't know about?"

"You think Philip and I would ever do anything illegal?"

"Maybe not you. Philip, though…"

"I don't believe this. Of all the… I could sue. Give me my dog."

"Sarah has your dog," he said and stood aside, giving her no choice but to enter a house she'd vowed never to set foot in again.

He was standing on the top step of the veranda. He didn't move.

She would not let him make her feel like this. Like she'd felt as a kid.

But her arm brushed his as she passed him, so slightly that with anyone else she wouldn't have noticed.

She noticed. Her arm jerked as if she'd been burned. She glowered and stomped past and still he didn't move.

She pushed the screen door wide and let it bang behind her. She always had. It banged like it always banged and she got the same effect… From the depths of the house came the sound of hysterical barking. She braced.

When she'd been a kid and she'd come here, the Finns' dog pack would knock her over. She'd loved it. She'd be lying in the hall being licked all over, squirming and wriggling, a tadpole in a dog pond, giggling and giggling until Raff hauled the dogs off.

When she didn't end up knocked over she'd felt almost disappointed.

She was bigger now, she conceded. Not so likely to be knocked over by a pack of dogs.

But there weren't as many dogs, anyway. There was an ancient black Labrador, almost grey with age. There was a pug, and there was Kleppy bringing up the rear. Wagging his tail. Greeting her?

She knelt and hugged Kleppy. He licked her face. So did the old Labrador. The pug was young but this one… she even remembered the feel of his tongue. "Boris!"

"Abby!" Sarah burst out of the kitchen, her beam wide enough to split her face. She dived down onto the floor and hugged her friend with total lack of self-consciousness. "Abby, you're here. I've made you honey jumbles."

"I…great." Maybe she should get up. Lawyer on floor hugging dog…

Boris was licking her chin.

"Boris?" she said tentatively and she included him in the hug she was giving Kleppy.

"He is Boris," Raff said and she twisted and found Raff was watching them all from the doorway. "How old was he when you were last here, Abby?"

"I... Three?"

"He's fourteen now. Old for a Labrador. You've missed out on his whole life."

"That's not all I've missed out on," she whispered. "How could I ever come back?" She shook her head and hauled herself to her feet. Raff made an instinctive move to help, but then pulled away. Shook his head. Closed down.

"But you will stay for a bit," Sarah said, grabbing Abby's hand to pull herself up. Movement was still awkward for Sarah; it always would be. "I've told the dogs they can have a honey jumble each," she told Abby. "But they need to wait until they've cooled down. You can't take Kleppy home before he's had his."

"I could take it with me."

"Abby," Sarah said in a term of such reproach that Abby knew she was stuck.

How long did honey jumbles take to cool?

Apparently a while because, "I've just put them in the oven," Sarah said happily. "I made a lot after tea but Raff forgot to tell me to take them out. They went black. Even the dogs didn't want them. Raff never forgets," she said, heading back to the kitchen. "But he's funny tonight. Do you think it's because you're here?"

"I expect that's it," Abby said, trying desperately to find something to say. Babbling because of it? "Maybe it's because I'm a lawyer. Sometimes police don't like lawyers 'cos they ask too many questions."

"And sometimes they don't ask enough," Raff growled.

"Meaning..."

"Baxter…"

Oh, for heaven's sake… "Leave it, Raff," she said. "Just butt out of my life."

"I did that years ago."

"Well, don't stop now." She took a deep breath. "Sarah, love, I'm in a rush."

"I know you are," Sarah said and pushed her into a kitchen chair. "You sit down. Raff will make you a nice cup of tea and we'll talk until the honey jumbles are ready. But don't yell at Raff," she said disapprovingly. "Raff's nice."

Raff was nice? Okay, maybe a part of him was nice. She might want to hate Raff Finn—and a part of her couldn't help but hate him—but she had to concede he was caring for Sarah beautifully.

The twelve months after the crash had been appalling. Even her grief for Ben hadn't stopped Abby seeing the tragedy that was Sarah.

She'd lain unconscious for three weeks and everyone had mourned her as dead. At one time rumour had it that Raff and Gran were asked to stop life support.

At three weeks she'd woken, but it was a different Sarah.

She'd had to relearn everything. Her memory of childhood was patchy. Her recent memory was lost completely.

She'd learned to walk again, to talk. She coped now but her speech was slow, as was her movement. Gran and Raff had brought her home and worked with her, loved her, massaged, exercised, pleaded, cajoled, bullied…

When Gran died Raff had taken it on himself to keep on going. For over a year he hadn't been able to work. They'd lived on the smell of an oily rag, because, "She's not going into care."

With anyone else the community would have rallied, but not with the Finns. Not when Raff was seen as being the cause of so much tragedy.

How he'd managed…

If the accident happened now the community would help, she thought. Somehow, in the last years, Raff had redeemed himself. He was a fine cop. He'd cared for Sarah with such love and compassion that the worst of the nay-sayers had been silenced. She'd even thought… it was time she moved on. Time she learned to forgive.

But over and over… He'd killed Ben.

How could she ever be friends with him again?

She didn't need to be. She simply chose to be distant. So she sat in Raff's kitchen while Sarah chatted happily, showing her the guinea pigs, explaining they'd had too many babies and that Raff had told her they had to sell some but how could she choose?

Smelling honey jumbles in a kitchen she loved.

Knowing Raff was watching her.

She found her fingers were clenched on her knees. They were hidden by the table. She could clench them as much as she wanted.

It didn't help. This place was almost claustrophobic, the memories it evoked.

But Raff was watching her and how Raff was making her feel wasn't a memory. This was no childhood crush. It was like a wave of testosterone blasting across the table, assaulting her from every angle.

Sarah was laughing.

Raff wasn't laughing. He was simply watchful.

Judgemental? Because she was marrying Philip?

Why shouldn't she marry Philip? He was kind, thoughtful, clever.

Her fallback?

Um…no. He was her careful choice.

She'd gone out with Philip before Ben had died, just for a bit, when the boys had left home, Raff to the Police Training College, Ben to university.

Philip had left for university, too, but he'd caught glandular fever and come home for a term.

She'd needed a date for her debutante ball and was fed up with Raff being away, with the boys being obsessed with their junk-pile car when they did come home.

Philip had the most wonderful set of wheels. He had money even then. But he wasn't Raff.

She'd made her debut and she'd found an excuse to break up. The decision wasn't met with regret. Philip had immediately asked Sarah out.

Maybe if the accident hadn't happened... Maybe Sarah and Philip...

Where was she going? Don't even think it, she decided. They were different people now.

Philip especially was different. After the crash...he was so caring. Whenever she needed him, he was there. He'd encouraged her to take up law as well. "You can do it," he'd said. "You're bright, organised, meticulous. Do law and we'll set up the best law firm Banksia Bay's ever seen. We can care for our parents that way, Abby. Your parents miss Ben so much. We can be there for them."

And so they were. It was all working out. All she needed to do was avoid the judgement on Raff's face. And avoid the way Raff made her...feel.

How could he bear her here?
One night, one car crash.
And it stood between him and this woman for ever.
How could she marry Philip?
But he knew. It was even reasonable, he conceded. Philip was okay. Once he'd even been a friend. Yes,

the man made money and Raff did wonder how, but that was just his nasty cop mind. Yes, he took on cases Raff wouldn't touch with a bargepole. If he got Baxter off…

He would get him off, but Raff also knew a portion of Philip's fee would end up as a cheque to the pensioners Baxter had ripped off. Not all of it—Philip was careful, not stupid with his charity—but the town might end up being grateful. Baxter would think he was great as well.

It was only Raff who'd feel ill, and maybe that was part of ancient history as well. If Philip hadn't been there that night…

How unfair was that?

"Tell us about your wedding dress," he said, and Abby shot him a look that was both suspicious and angry.

"You want to know—why?"

"Sarah would like to know."

"I'm going to the wedding," Sarah said and pointed to the invitation stuck to the fridge. "You should come, too. Did you get an invitation? Where did you put it? Raff's coming, too, isn't he, Abby?"

"I'm on duty that day," Raff told her before Abby was forced to answer. "We talked about it, remember? Mrs Henderson's taking you."

"It'd be more fun if you were there."

No, it wouldn't, Raff thought, but he didn't say so. He glanced at his watch. "I reckon they'll be cooked, Sares."

"Ooh," Sarah said, happily distracted. "My honey jumbles. I could make you some more for your wedding present, Abby. Does Philip like honey jumbles?"

"Sure he does," Abby said. "Who wouldn't?"

Honey jumbles. A big cosy kitchen like this. Dogs. Would Philip like honey jumbles?

Maybe not.

* * *

Abby ate four honey jumbles and Sarah beamed the whole time, and how could a girl worry about how tight her wedding dress was going to be in the face of that beam?

Sarah wasn't the only one happy. This morning Kleppy had been due for the needle. Tonight he was lying under her chair licking the last of Sarah's honey jumbles from his chops.

And Sarah's beam, and Kleppy's satisfaction, and Raff's thoughtful, watchful gaze made her feel…made her feel…

Like she needed to leave before things got out of hand.

She needed to go home to Philip. To tell him she had a dog.

"What's wrong?" Raff asked and he sounded as if he cared. That scared her all by itself. She pushed her chair back so fast she scared Kleppy, which meant she had her dog in her arms and she was at the door before she meant to be.

She hadn't meant to look like she was rushing.

She was rushing.

"Will you take some jumbles in a bag?" Sarah asked and she managed to calm down a little and smile and agree. So Sarah bagged her some jumbles, but she was holding Kleppy, she didn't have a hand free, which meant Raff carried her jumbles down to the car while she carried her dog.

Kleppy was warm and fuzzy. His heart was beating against hers. He was a comfort, she thought, and even as she thought it he stretched up and licked her, throat to chin.

She giggled and Raff, who'd gone before and was

stowing her jumbles onto the back seat, turned and smiled in the moonlight.

"Dogs are great."

"They are," she said and felt happy.

"Philip will be okay with him?"

Why must he always butt into what wasn't his business? Why must he always spoil the moment?

"He will."

"So you'll tell him tonight."

"Of course."

"I wish you luck."

"I won't need it."

"No?"

"Butt out, Finn."

"You're always saying that," he said. "But it's not in my power to butt out. It's my job to intervene in domestic crises. Stopping them before they start is a life skill."

"You seriously think Philip and I would fight over a dog?"

"I'm thinking you might fight for a dog," he said softly. "The old Abby's still there somewhere. She'll fight for this dog to the death."

"And how melodramatic is that?"

"Melodramatic," he agreed. "Call the police emergency number if you need me."

"Why would I possibly need you?"

"Just offering." He was holding the passenger door wide so she could pop Kleppy in.

"You know Philip wouldn't…"

"Yeah, I know Philip wouldn't." He took Kleppy from her and laid him on the passenger seat. "You're giving him honey jumbles and Kleppy. Why wouldn't the man be delighted?"

"I don't know when I hate it most—when you're being offensive or you're being sarcastic."

"Maybe they're the same thing."

"Maybe they are. I wish you wouldn't."

"No, you don't," he said softly. "It helps you keep as far away from me as you want. Isn't that right, Abby?"

"Raff…"

"It's okay, I understand," he said. "How could I fail to understand? What you're doing is entirely reasonable. I only wish your second choice wasn't Philip."

"He's not my second choice. He's my first."

"That's right," he said, sounding suddenly thoughtful. "I forgot. You went out with Philip when you were seventeen. For two whole months and then you dumped him. Don't those reasons hold true now?"

"I can't believe you're asking me…"

"I'm a cop. I ask the hard questions."

"I don't have to answer."

"Meaning you can't."

"Meaning I don't need to. Why are you asking this now?"

"I've hardly had a chance until now. You back off every time you see me."

"And you know why."

"I do," he said harshly and she winced and thought she shouldn't have said it. It was too long ago. The whole thing… It was a nightmare to be put behind them.

"Yes, Philip and I broke up when I was seventeen," she managed. "But people change."

"I guess we do." He paused and then said, almost conversationally, "You know, once upon a time we had fun. We even decided we loved each other."

They had. Girlfriend and boyfriend. Inseparable. Raff had shared her first kiss. It had felt… It had felt…

No. "We were kids," she managed. "We were dumb in all sorts of ways."

He was too close, she decided. It was too dark. She should be back in her nice safe house waiting for Philip to come home. She shouldn't be remembering being kissed by her first boyfriend.

"I loved kissing you," he said and it wasn't just her remembering.

"It didn't mean…"

"Maybe it did. There's this thing," he said.

"What thing?" But she shouldn't have asked because, the moment she had, she knew what he was talking about. Or maybe she'd known all along.

This thing? This frisson, an electric current, an indefinable thing that was tugging her closer…

No. She had to go home. "Raff…"

"You really want to be Mrs Philip Dexter? What a waste."

"Leave it!"

"Choose someone else, Abby. Marrying him? You're burying yourself."

"I am not."

"Does he make you sizzle?"

"I don't…"

"Does he? You know, I can't imagine it. Good old Philip, knocking your socks off. Are you racing home now to have hot sex?"

"I don't believe I'm hearing this."

"You see, it's such a waste," he said, and suddenly he was even closer, big and bad and dangerous.

Big, bad and dangerous? Certainly dangerous. His hand came up and cupped her chin, forcing her to look up at him, and her sense of danger deepened. But she couldn't pull away.

"I wouldn't mind if it wasn't Philip," he told her and she wondered if he knew the effect he was having on her. She wondered if he could sense how her body was reacting. "I've known since Ben died that nothing could bring back what was between you and me. But there are men out there who could bring you alive again. Men who'd like Kleppy."

"Philip will like Kleppy."

"Liar."

He was gazing down into her eyes, holding her to truth.

She should break away. She *could* break away, she thought wildly. He was only holding her chin—nothing more. She could step back, get into the car and drive home.

To Philip.

She could. But he was gazing down into her eyes and he was still asking questions.

"So tell me he makes you sizzle."

"I…"

"He doesn't, does he?" Raff said in grim satisfaction. "But there are guys out there who could—who could find out what you're capable of—what's beneath your prissy lawyer uniform. Because you're still there, somewhere. The Abby I…"

He paused. There was a moment's loaded silence when the whole world stilled. *The Abby I…*

She should push away. She should…

She couldn't.

She tilted her face, just a little.

The moment stretched on. The darkness stretched on.

And then he kissed her. As inevitably as time itself, he kissed her.

She couldn't move. She didn't move. She froze. And then…

Heat. Fire. The contact, lips against lips, was a tiny point but that point sizzled, caught, burned and her whole body started heating. Her face was tilted to his but he had no need to hold her. It was as if she was melting against him—into him.

Raff...

He broke away, just a little, and his eyes blazed in the moonlight. "Abby," he said and it was a rough, angry whisper. "Abby."

"I..."

"Does he do this?" he demanded. He snagged her arms and held them behind her but this was no forceful hold. It was as if her arms might get in the way, could interfere, and nothing must. Nothing could.

She was paralysed, she was burning, but she couldn't escape. She didn't want to escape. What was between them... It sizzled. Tugged as if searching for oxygen.

He was watching her in the moonlight, his eyes questioning. She wouldn't answer. She couldn't.

She was being held by Raff. A man she'd once loved.

She found herself lifting herself, tiptoe.

So her mouth could meet his again.

This morning she'd fantasised about Raff Finn. Sex on legs. But this...

If she'd expected anything it was a kiss of anger, a kiss of sexual tension, passion, nothing more. And maybe it had started like that. But it was changing.

His kiss was tender, aching, even loving. It was as unexpected as ice within a fire, heating, cooling, sizzling all at once. She'd never felt anything like this—she'd never known sensations like this could exist.

Raff.

He'd released her hands and they were free to do as

she willed. Her will was that her hands were behind *his* back, drawing him closer, for how could she not want him close? Sense had flown. Thoughts had flown. There was only this man. There was only this need.

There was only now.

Raff.

Did she say his name?

Maybe she did, or maybe it was just a sigh, deep in her throat, a sound of pure sensual pleasure. Of taking something she'd never dreamed she could have. Of sinking into the forbidden, of the longed for, of a memory she'd have to put away quite soon but not yet, please, not yet.

Oh, but his mouth… Clever and warm and beguiling, it was coaxing her to places she had no business going, but she wanted, oh, she wanted to be there. She was helpless, melting into him, degree by achingly wonderful degree.

He was irresistible.

She was…appalled.

Somehow, she had to break this. Her head was screaming at her, neon danger signs flashing through her sensual need. No!

"No!" It came out a muffled whisper. If he didn't hear…if he ignored it, how could she say it again?

Did she want him to hear it?

But he did, he had, and the wrench as he put her away from him was indescribable. He let her go. He stepped back from her and his eyes in the moonlight were almost as dazed as hers.

But then his face hardened, tightened, and she knew he was moving on.

As she must.

Her mother's voice… *Keep away from the Finn boy. He's trouble.*

He surely was. She was kissing him nine days before her wedding. She was risking all—for the Finn boy?

"I…"

"Just go, Abby," he said and she didn't recognise his voice. It was harsh and raw and she could even imagine there was pain. "Get out of here. You know you don't want this."

"Of course I don't."

"Then take your dog and go. I'll see you in court."

Of course she would. She'd see him and he'd be back to being the local cop and she'd be a lawyer sitting beside her fiancé, trying to pretend tonight had never happened.

But it had happened. The feel of his mouth on hers was with her still.

She caught herself, gasped and thumped down into the driver's seat before she could change her mind.

"That was ridiculous," she managed. "How…how dare you…?"

"You wanted it as much as I did."

"Then we're both stupid."

"We are," he said gravely. "We were. But heaven help us, Abby, if we're stupid still."

Chapter 5

Abby drove home in a daze. She felt ill. The feel of Raff's mouth on hers wouldn't go—it felt as if her lips were surely bruised and yet she knew they couldn't be.

There had been tenderness in his kiss. It hadn't been one-sided. He hadn't been brutal.

It had been a kiss of...

No. Don't even think about it.

Kleppy put out his paw in a gesture she was starting to know. Giving comfort as well as taking it. The feel of him beside her was absurdly comforting.

Almost as if he was a little part of Raff...

And there was a dopey thing to think. The whole night had been dopey, she thought. Stupid, stupid, stupid. Imagine if she ever thought there could be anything between herself and Raff. Imagine the heartbreak.

Her heart clenched down. No! Just because the man

was a load of semi-controlled testosterone… Just because he had the ability to push her buttons…

She turned into her street and Philip's car was out the front. Her heart sank.

Philip, she told herself. Not a load of semi-controlled testosterone. A good, kind man who'd keep her happy—who'd keep her safe.

I might get tired of safe, she whispered to herself and then she let herself open her mind to the rush of memory that was Ben and she felt the concept of safe, the need for safe, close around her again. Safe was the only way.

"Hi," she said, climbing from the car. "The buck's night finished early, then?"

"Hardly a buck's night." He took her hands and kissed her and she had to stop herself from thinking *dry as dust.* "Just my dad and uncles and cousins."

"Why aren't you having a buck's night?"

"Tonight was enough," Philip said contentedly. "I'm busy right up to the honeymoon. Where have you…"

But then he paused. Inside the car, Kleppy had stirred and yawned and whimpered a little.

"What's that?"

Deep breath. "It's Kleppy."

"Kleppy?"

"He's my dog," she said and she had a really good shot at not sounding defensive. Maybe she even succeeded. "You know Raff gave me a dog this morning and asked me to take him to be put down? I couldn't. He's Isaac Abrahams' dog, he needs a new home and I've decided to keep him. Sarah's been looking after him for me."

There was no need to mention Raff again. "So we have a dog," she said and she surprised herself by sounding cheerful. "Philip, meet Kleppy. Kleppy, meet Philip. I just know you two are going to be best of friends."

He didn't like it, but she wouldn't budge; she didn't budge and finally he conceded.

"It'll have to sleep outside."

"*He,* not *it.*"

"He'll have to sleep outside," he conceded—no mean concession.

"Okay," she said with her fingers crossed behind her back. He could sleep outside for a little, she thought, until Philip got used to the idea and then she could sort of sneak him in. And for the next nine nights he could sleep inside at her place.

"And what about our honeymoon?"

"I'll get Mrs Sanderson to feed and walk him."

"She'll charge."

"We can afford it."

"I don't want Eileen Sanderson snooping in our back-yard."

"I'll figure something else out, then. But you'll love him."

"If you want a dog, then why don't we get a pure-bred?" he asked, checking Kleppy out with suspicion.

"I like Kleppy."

"And Finn dumped him on you."

"It was my decision to keep him."

"You're too soft-hearted."

"I can't do a thing about that," she admitted, knowing the hurdle had been leaped and she was over the other side. "You want to come in for coffee and get acquainted with our new pet?"

"I have work to do. I'm not confident about tomorrow."

He would be confident, Abby knew, but he'd still go over his notes until he knew them backwards. And once again she wondered—why had he come back to Banksia Bay? He was smart, he was ambitious, he could have made serious money in the city.

"I came back for you," he'd told her, over and over, but she knew it was more than that. He spent time with her parents. He worked at the yacht club where Ben had once sailed. Every time a challenge occurred that might draw him to the city, he looked at it with regret but he still turned back to Banksia Bay.

She kissed him goodnight and carried Kleppy inside, thinking every time she laid down an ultimatum Philip caved in.

This dog or no wedding?

This dog.

"He loves me," she told Kleppy, sitting down on the hearth rug and allowing her scruffy dog to settle contentedly on her knee. "He'll take you because he loves me."

But she'd seen Philip's ruthless behaviour in court. He could be ruthless. He'd never liked dogs.

Why didn't he just say no?

"I'm so lucky he didn't," she whispered and she hugged Kleppy a bit tighter and then gazed towards the spare room door. Her wedding dress lay behind.

She was lucky?

Of course she was.

She was gone and Raff stayed outside, staring sightlessly into the moonlit night.

Abby Callahan.

Right now there was nothing in the world he wanted but Abby Callahan.

Oh, but there was. Inside, Sarah would be snuggling into bed, surrounded by dogs and cats, dreaming of the day she'd just had—her animals, her honey jumbles. Her big brother.

He loved Sarah.

He also loved this place. He loved this town. But love or not, he'd leave if he could. To stay in this place with so many memories…

To stay in this place and watch Abby married…

But leaving wasn't an option. He'd stay and he wouldn't touch her again. Tonight had been an aberration, as stupid as it was potentially harmful. He didn't want to upset Abby. It wasn't her fault she was the way she was.

It was his.

He was thirty years old and he felt a hundred.

He hardly needed to see her again before the wedding. His participation in the Baxter trial was almost over. He'd given the prosecutor all the help he could manage, even if it wasn't enough to convict the guy. There might be another couple of times he was called to the stand, but otherwise he could steer well clear.

So… He'd drop Sarah off at the church next Saturday, pick her up afterwards and it'd be done.

Abby Callahan would be married to Philip Dexter.

Abby spent until midnight making Kleppy hers. She bathed him and blowed him dry with her hairdryer. He was never going to be a beautiful dog, but he was incredibly cute—in a shambolic kind of way. He was a very individual dog, she decided.

He tolerated the hairdryer.

He ate a decent dinner, despite his pre-dinner snack of honey jumbles.

He investigated her bedroom as she got ready for bed. And, curiously, he fell in love with her jewellery box.

It was a beautiful cedar box with inlaid Huon pine. Philip's grandfather had made it for her when she and Philip had announced their engagement. She loved its craftsmanship and she also loved the wood's faint and beautiful perfume, stronger whenever she opened it.

She also loved Philip's grandpa, she thought, as she removed Kleppy's paw from where it had been resting proprietorially on the box. His woodwork was his passion. He'd made these beautiful boxes for half the town. "It'll last for hundreds of years after I'm gone, girl," he'd told her and she suspected it would.

Philip's grandpa was part of this town. Philip's family. Her future.

More people's happiness than hers was tied up in next week's wedding. That should make her feel happy, but right now it was making her feel claustrophobic. Which was dumb.

"Do you like the box or the jewels?" she asked Kleppy, deliberately shifting her thoughts. She opened the lid so he could see he couldn't make millions with a jewel heist.

Kleppy nosed the trinkets with disinterest, but looked longingly at the box. He sniffed it again and she thought it was its faint scent he liked.

"No!" she said and put it further back on the chest.

Kleppy sighed and went back to his bra. The bra she'd paid for and given to him. Yes, he shouldn't benefit from crime but today was an exception.

He made a great little thief.

He slept on her bed, snuggled against her, and she loved it. He snored. She loved his snore. She didn't even mind that he slept with his bra tucked firmly under his left front paw.

"Whatever makes you happy, Klep," she told him, "but that's the last of your loot. You belong to a law-abiding citizen now."

One who needs to stay right away from the law.

From Raff.

Don't think of Raff. Think of the wedding.

Some hope. She slept, thinking of Raff.

She woke feeling light and happy. For the past few weeks she'd woken with the mammoth feeling that her wedding was bursting in on her from all sides. Her mother was determined to make it perfect.

It was starting to overwhelm her.

But not this morning. She loved that Kleppy woke at dawn and stuck his nose in her face and she woke to dog breath and a tail wagging.

It was lucky Philip wasn't here. He'd have forty fits.

He wouldn't mind being here. Or rather...he'd be happy if she was *there.* As far as Philip was concerned, she was wasting money having her own little house when he already had a wonderful house overlooking the sea.

Her parents had said that, too. When she'd moved back to Banksia Bay after university they'd welcomed her home and even had her bedroom repainted. Pink.

She had a choice. Philip's house or her old bedroom.

But her grandparents had left her a lovely legacy and this little house was her statement of independence. As she let Kleppy outside to inspect her tiny garden she thought how much she was going to miss it.

Philip's house was fabulous. She'd been blown away that he could afford to build it, and it had everything a woman could possibly want.

So get over it.

She left Kleppy to his own devices and went and checked on her wedding dress—just to reassure herself she really was getting married.

She should be excited.

She was excited. It was a gorgeous dress. It was exquisite.

It had taken her two years to make.

The pleasure was in making it. Not in wearing it.

This was dumb. She felt a cold spot on her leg and there was Kleppy, wagging his tail, bright-eyed and bushy-tailed. Looking hopefully at the front door.

Looking for adventure?

"I'll take you round the block before I go to work," she told him. "And I'll come home at lunch time. I'm sorry, Klep, but you might be bored this morning. I can't help it, though. It's the price you've paid for me bailing you out of death row.

"And I'm going to be in court this morning, too," she told him as he looked doleful. "You're a lawyer's dog and I'm a lawyer. I'm a lawyer with a gorgeous, hand-beaded wedding dress and you're a lawyer's dog with a new home. We need to be grateful for what we have. I'm sure we are."

She was grateful. It was just, as she left for work and Kleppy looked disconsolately after her, she knew how Kleppy felt.

Raff wasn't in court.

Of course he wasn't. He didn't need to be. He was a

cop, not a prosecutor, and he had work to do elsewhere. He'd given his evidence yesterday. Philip wouldn't call him back but she'd sort of hoped the Crown Prosecutor would.

There were things the Crown Prosecutor could ask…

It wasn't for her to know that or even think that—*she was lawyer for the defence*—and it also wasn't for her to have her heart twist because Raff wasn't here.

She slid into the chair beside Philip and he smiled and kissed her and then said, "Second thoughts about the dog? He really is unsuitable."

This was what would happen, she thought. He'd agree and then slowly work on her to come round to his way of thinking.

He wasn't all noble.

"No, and I won't be having any," she said.

"Where is he now?"

"Safely in my garden." Four-foot fence. Safe as houses.

"He'll make a mess."

"I walked him before I left. Walking's good. I'm going to do it every morning from now on. Maybe you can join us."

"Gym's far better aerobic exercise," he said. "You need a fully planned programme to get full cardiac advantage. Walking's…"

She was no longer listening.

Her morning had begun.

It was very, very boring.

The hands on the clock moved at a snail's pace.

How bored would Kleppy be?

How bored was she?

Malcolm, the Crown Prosecutor, should do something

about his voice, she thought. It was a voice designed to put a girl to sleep.

Ooh, Wallace looked smug.

Ooh, she was bored…

Lunch time. All rise. Hooray.

And then the door of the court swung open.

All eyes turned. As they would. Every person in the room, with the possible exception of Wallace and Philip, was probably as bored as she was.

And suddenly she wasn't bored at all. For standing in the doorway was… Raff.

Full cop uniform. Grim expression. Gun at his side, cop ready for action. At his side—only lower—was a white fluff ball attached to a pink diamanté lead. And in his arms he was carrying Kleppy.

"I'm sorry, Your Honour," he said, addressing the judge. "But I'm engaged in a criminal investigation. Is Abigail Callahan in court?"

Of course she was. Abby rose, her colour starting to rise as well. "K… Kleppy," she stammered.

"Could you come with me, please, Miss Callahan?" Raff said.

"She's not going anywhere," Philip snapped, rising and putting his hand on Abby's shoulder. "What the…"

"If she won't come willingly, I'm afraid I need to arrest her," Raff said. "Accessory after the fact." He looked down at his feet, to where the white fluff ball pranced on the end of her pink diamanté lead. A lead that led up to Kleppy's jaw. Kleppy had a very tight hold. "Abigail Callahan, your dog has stolen Mrs Fryer's peke. You need to come now and sort this out or I'll have to arrest you for theft."

The courtroom was quiet. So quiet you could have heard a pin drop.

Justice Weatherby's face was impassive. Almost impassive.

There was a tiny tic at the side of his mouth.

Raff's face was impassive, too. He stood with Kleppy in his arms, waiting for Abby to respond.

Kleppy looked disgusting. He was coated in thick black dust. His tail was wagging, nineteen to the dozen.

In his mouth he held the end of the pink lead and his jaw was clamped as if he wasn't going to let go any time soon.

On the other end of the lead, the white fluff ball was wagging her tail as well.

"He was locked in my backyard," Abby said, eyeing the two with dismay.

"My sharp investigative skills inform me that the dog can dig," Raff said, shaking Kleppy a little so a rain of dirt fell onto the polished wood of the courtroom door. "Will you come with me, please, ma'am?"

"Just give the dog back to whoever owns it," Philip snapped, his hand gripping Abby's shoulder tightly now. "Tie the other one up outside. Abigail's busy."

"Raff, please…" Abby said.

"Mrs Fryer's hopping mad," Raff said, unbending a little. "I've waited until court broke for lunch but I'm waiting no longer. You want to avoid charges, you come and placate her."

She glanced at Philip. Uh-oh. She glanced at Justice Weatherby. The tic at the corner of his mouth had turned into a grin. Someone was giggling at the back of the court.

Philip's face looked like thunder.

"Sort the dog, Abigail," he snapped, gathering his notes. "Just get it out of here and stop it interfering with our lives."

"Right this way, ma'am," Raff said amiably. "The solicitor for the defence will be right back, just as soon as she sorts her stolen property."

Abby walked out behind Raff, trying to look professional, but she didn't feel professional and when she reached the outside steps and the autumn sun hit her face she felt suddenly a wee bit hysterical. And also... a wee bit free?

As if Raff had sprung her from jail.

Which was a dumb thing to think. Raff had attempted to make her a laughing stock.

"I suppose you think you're funny," she said and Raff turned and looked at her, and once again she was hit by that wave of pure testosterone. He was in his cop uniform and my, it was sexy. The sun was glinting on his tanned face and his coppery hair. He was wearing short sleeves and his arms... They were twice as thick as Philip's, she thought, and then she thought that was a very inappropriate thing to think. As was the fact that his eyes held the most fabulous twinkle.

Her knees felt wobbly.

What was she doing? She was standing in the sun and lusting after Raff Finn. The man who'd destroyed her life...

She needed to get a grip, and fast.

"You're saying Kleppy dug all the way out of my garden?" she snapped, trying to sound disbelieving. She *was* disbelieving.

"You're implying I might have helped?" Raff said,

still with that twinkle. "You think I might have hiked round there and loaned him a spade?"

"No, I…" Of course not. "But the fence sits hard on the ground. He'd have had to go deep."

"He's a very determined dog. I did warn you, Abigail."

"Why don't you just call me ma'am and be done with it," she snapped. "What am I supposed to do now?"

"Apologise."

"To you?"

He grinned at that and his whole face lit up. She'd hardly seen that grin. Not since… Not since…

No. Avoid that grin at all costs.

"I can't imagine you apologising to me," he said. "But you might try Mrs Fryer. I imagine she's apoplectic by now. She rang an hour ago to say her dog had been stolen from outside the draper's. I did think we were looking at dog-napping—she'd definitely pay a ransom—but we have witnesses saying the napper was seen making a getaway. It seems Kleppy decided to go find another bra and found something better."

She closed her eyes. This was not good, on so many levels.

"You caught him?"

"I didn't have to catch him," he said, and his smile deepened, a slow, smouldering smile that had the power to heat as much as the sun. "I found the two of them on your front step."

"On my…"

"He seems to think of your place as home already. Home of Abby. Home of Kleppy. Or maybe he was just bringing this magnificent gift to you."

Oh, Kleppy.

She stared at her scruffy, kleptomaniac, mud-covered dog in Raff's arms. He stared back, gazing straight at her, quivering with hope. With happiness. A dog fulfilled.

Why did her eyes suddenly fill?

"Why…why didn't you just take Fluffy back to Mrs Fryer?" she managed, trying not to sniff. *She had a dog.*

"Watch this." He set Kleppy down and tugged the diamanté lead, trying to dislodge it from Kleppy's teeth.

Kleppy held on as if his life depended on it.

Raff tugged again.

Kleppy growled and gripped and glanced across at Abby—and his appeal was unmistakable. *Come and help. This guy's trying to steal your property.*

Her property.

Raff released him. The little dog turned towards her, his whole body quivering in delight. She stooped and held out her hand and he dropped the lead into it.

Oh, my…

She was having trouble making herself speak. She was having trouble making herself think. This disreputable mutt had laid claim to her.

She should be horrified.

She loved it.

"You could have just taken Fluffy off the other end of the lead," she managed.

"Hey, your dog growled at me," Raff said. "You heard him. He could have taken my hand off."

"He was wagging his tail at the same time."

"I'm not one to take chances," Raff said. "I might be armed but I'm not a fast draw. Too big a risk."

She looked up at him, big and brawny and absurdly incongruous. Cop with gun. He'd shoot to kill?

"You don't have capsicum spray?" she managed.

"Lady, you think this vicious mutt could be subdued by capsicum spray?"

She ran her fingers down the vicious mutt's spine. He arched and preened and waggled his tail in pleasure.

The fluff ball moved in for a back scratch as well.

She giggled.

"Abigail…" It was Philip, striding down the steps, looking furious.

Philip. Dignity. She scrambled to her feet and the dogs looked devastated at losing her.

"I'm just settling the dogs down," she managed. "Before Raff takes them away."

"Before *we* take them away," Raff said. He motioned to his patrol car.

"You can cope with this yourself, Finn," Philip snapped.

"No," Raff said, humour fading. He lifted Kleppy in one arm and Fluff Ball in the other. "You cope with getting Wallace off," he told Philip. "Abigail copes with the dogs."

"I need…"

"You're getting as little help as I can manage to get that low life off the hook," Raff snapped. "Abigail, come with me."

She went. Raff was not giving her a choice, and she knew Mrs Fryer would be furious.

Behind her, Philip was furious but right now that seemed the lesser of two evils.

She sat in the front of Raff's patrol car with two dogs on her knee and she tried to stare straight ahead; to think serious thoughts. She still wanted to giggle.

"Kleppy should be in the back," Raff said gravely. "A known criminal."

"You've accused me of being an accessory. Why don't you toss me in the back as well?"

"I like you up front," he said. "You do my image good."

"I need dark glasses," she said, glowering. "Carted round town in a police car."

"You will keep a kleptomaniac dog. It might well push you over to the dark side. Spoil that good-girl reputation. Send you into the shadowy side, like me."

Her bubble of laughter faded at that. He'd spoken lightly, but there was truth behind his words.

The shadowy side...

Raff's grandfather and then his mother had given the family a bad name. A drunk and then a woman who'd broken society's rules... If Raff's mother had had the strength to defend herself, to ride out community criticism, then maybe it would have been different but she'd been an easy target. The family had been an easy target.

Raff, though... He had defended himself. He'd come back here after the accident, he'd made a home for Sarah, he'd looked on community disdain with indifference.

Did it hurt?

It wasn't anything to do with her, she thought, but, as they pulled up outside Louise Fryer's, she watched the middle-aged matron greet Raff with only the barest degree of civility. It must still hurt.

After the accident... There'd been no trial.

She remembered the investigators talking to her parents. There'd been insufficient evidence to charge him.

"Is Raff denying it?" That had been Abby, whispering from the background. She barely remembered those appalling days after the crash but she did remember that. She did remember asking. "What does Raff say?"

"He can't remember a thing," the investigator told her. "His blood alcohol's come back zero and frankly that's a surprise. He was just a stupid kid doing stupid things."

"Our Ben wasn't stupid," her mother said hotly.

"Led astray, more like," the investigator said and the fair part of Abby, the reasonable part, thought no, Ben hadn't been wearing his seat belt. It wasn't all Raff's fault.

He'd been stupid. He had been on the wrong side of the dirt road and he'd been speeding.

He'd killed Ben and injured his sister.

Maybe that was enough punishment for anyone. The authorities seemed to think so. Even though her parents wanted him thrown in jail, it had simply been left as an accident.

Raff had come back as the town cop, he'd cared for his sister and he'd worked hard to rid himself of that bad boy reputation. For the most part he now had community respect, but there were those—her parents' friends... people with long memories... He was still condemned.

Louise Fryer, coming out now with her mouth pursed into a look of dislike, was one of the more vocal of the condemners.

"Haven't you found her yet?" Her voice was an accusation. "I've had five phone calls. People have seen her. Don't you know how valuable she is?"

Abby was trying to untangle leads to get out of the car.

"You don't care," Mrs Fryer said. "We need a decent police presence in this... Oh..."

For, finally, Abby was out. She set Fluff Ball on the ground. Fluff Ball headed over to Mrs Fryer.

But… Uh-oh. Kleppy was out of the car and after his prize. He grabbed the lead and Fluff Ball stopped in her tracks.

Fluff Ball looked at Mrs Fryer, then looked at Kleppy. She wagged her pompom and proceeded to check out Kleppy's rear.

"She'll catch something… Get it away…" Louise was practically screeching.

Abby sighed. She picked up both dogs and tucked them firmly under her arms. "Thank you, Kleppy, but no," she said severely. She took the lead from Kleppy and handed over Fluff Ball.

And finally Mrs Fryer realised who she was. "Abigail!"

"Hi, Mrs Fryer."

"What are you doing here?"

"My dog stole your dog."

"Your dog?" Louise's eyes were almost popping out of her head. "That's never your dog."

"He is. His name's Kleppy. He's lovely but I've only had him for a day so he's not exactly well trained. But he will be." Just as soon as she installed fences down to bedrock.

"Has this man foisted him onto you?" Her glare at Raff was poisonous.

"No." Not exactly. Or actually…yes. But that was what the woman was expecting her to say, she thought. Raff Finn—town's bad boy. One of *those Finns*.

Capable of anything.

Which was what she thought, too, she reminded herself, so why was she standing here figuring out how to defend him?

"He didn't foist…" she started.

"Yes, I did," Raff said before she could get any further. "Have you forgotten already? I definitely foisted. And that's exactly what you'd expect of someone like me, isn't it, Mrs Fryer? And here I am, messing up your front garden. But it's okay. Your dog's been restored. Justice has been done so I can step out of your life again. If you'll excuse me… Abby, when Mrs Fryer's given you a nice cup of tea so you can both recover from your Very Nasty Experience, could you walk back to court yourself, do you think?"

I…" She stared at him, speechless. He gave her his very blandest smile.

"I bet Louise wants to hear all about the wedding preparations. She'll be invited, though, won't she?"

"Yes," Louise said, a bit confused but mostly belligerent. Her dislike for Raff was unmistakable. "Of course I am. I'm a friend of dear Philip's mother."

"There you are; you're practically family." Raff's gaze met hers and there was laughter behind his eyes— pure trouble. "All it takes for you to be friends for life is for your two dogs to bond, which they're doing already. Me, I have other stuff to do. Murderers and rapists to chase."

"Or the police station lawn to mow," Abby snapped and then wished she hadn't.

"I was just saying that to Philip's mother the other night," Louise said. "Old Sergeant Troy used to keep the Station really nice."

"Yeah, but he wasn't a Finn," Raff said. "The place has gone to hell in a handbasket since I arrived. Did you think of the lawn yourself, Abigail, or did Philip mention it? A tidy man, our Philip. But enough. Murderers, rapists—and lawn!" He sighed. "A policeman's lot is indeed a tough one. See you ladies later. Have a nice cup of tea."

He turned and walked away. Louise put her hand on Abby's arm, holding her back.

The toad. Raff Finn knew she wouldn't be able to get away from here for an hour.

"Make sure you plant some petunias when you're finished," Abby called after him. "It'd be a pity if we saw our police force bored."

"Petunias it is," he said and gave her an airy wave. "Consider them planted. In between thefts. How long till the next snatch and grab?" He shook his head. "Keep off the streets, Abigail, and keep a tight hold on that felon of yours. Next time, I might have to put you up for a community corrections order. The pair of you might find yourself planting my petunias for me."

Chapter 6

Abby didn't go back to court. Philip phoned to find out where she was and she decided she had a headache. She did have a headache. Her headache was wagging his tail and watching as she dog-proofed her fence.

According to the Internet, to stop foxes digging into a poultry pen you had to run wire netting underground from the fence, but flattening outward and forward, surfacing about eighteen inches from the fence. The fox would then find itself digging into a U-shaped wire cavity.

That meant a lot of digging. Would it work when Kleppy The Fox was sitting there watching?

"Don't even think about it," she told him. "Philip's being very good. We can't expect his patience to last for ever."

Philip.

She was expecting him to explode. He didn't.

He arrived to see how she was just after she'd finished cleaning up after fence digging. They were supposed to be going out to dinner. Two of Philip's most affluent clients had invited them out to Banksia Bay's most prestigious restaurant as a pre-wedding celebration.

When Abby thought of it her headache was suddenly real—and, surprisingly, she didn't need to explain it to Philip.

"You look dreadful," he said, hugging her with real sympathy. "White as a sheet. You should be in bed."

"I…yes." Bed sounded a good idea.

"Where's the mutt?"

"Outside." Actually, on her bed, hoping she'd join him.

"You can't keep him," Philip said seriously. "He's trouble."

"This morning wasn't his fault."

"You don't need to tell me that," Philip said darkly. "The dog might be trouble but Finn's worse. It's my belief he set the whole thing up. Look, Abby, the best thing would just be for you to take the dog back to the Animal Shelter."

"No."

He sighed but he held his temper.

"We'll talk about it when you're feeling better. I'm sorry you can't make tonight."

"Will you cancel?"

"No," he said, surprised. "They'll understand."

Of course they would. They'd hardly notice her absence, she thought bitterly. They'd talk about their property portfolios all night. Make some more money.

"What will you eat?" he asked, solicitous, and she thought she wouldn't have to eat five courses and five different wines. Headaches had their uses.

"I'll make eggs on toast if I get hungry."

"Well, keep up your strength. You have a big week ahead of you."

He kissed her and he was off, happily going to a wedding celebration without her.

The moment the door shut behind him, her headache disappeared. Just like that.

Why was she marrying him?

Uh-oh.

The question had been hovering for months. Niggling. Shoved away with disbelief that she could think it. But, the closer the wedding grew, the bigger the question grew. Now it was the elephant in the room. Or the Tyrannosaurus Rex. What was the world's biggest dinosaur?

Whatever. The question was getting very large indeed. And very insistent.

Philip was heading to a dinner she'd been dreading. He was anticipating it with pleasure.

Worse. Philip's kiss meant absolutely nothing. Last night… Raff's kiss had shown her how little Philip's kisses did mean.

And worse still? She'd almost been wanting him to yell at her about Kleppy.

How had she got into this mess?

It had just…happened. The car crash. Philip, always here, supporting her parents, supporting her. Interested in everything she was doing. Throwing himself, heart and soul, into this town. Throwing himself, heart and soul, into her life.

She couldn't even remember when she'd first realised he intended to marry her. It was just sort of assumed.

She did remember the night he'd formally asked. He'd proposed at the Banksia Bay Private Golf Club, overlooking the bay. The setting had been perfect. A full moon. Moonbeams glinting on the sea. The terrace, a balmy night, stars. A dessert to die for—chocolate ganache in the shape of a heart, surrounded by strawberries and tiny meringues. A beautifully drawn line of strawberry coulis, spelling out the words "Marry Me'.

But there'd been more. Philip had left nothing to chance. The small town orchestra had appeared from nowhere, playing Pachelbel's *Canon*. The staff, not just from the restaurant but from the golf club as well, crowding into the doorways, applauding before she even got to answer.

"I've already asked your parents," Philip said as he lifted the lid of the crimson velvet box. "They couldn't be more pleased. We're going to be so happy."

He lifted the ring she now wore—a diamond so big it made her gasp—and slid it onto her finger before she realised what was happening. Then, just in case she thought he hadn't got it completely right, he'd tugged her to her feet, then dropped to his knees.

"Abigail Callahan, would you do me the honour of becoming my wife?"

She remembered thinking—hysterically, and only for the briefest of moments—what happens if I say no?

But how could she say no?

How could she say no now?

Why would she want to?

Because Rafferty Finn had kissed her?

Because Raff made her feel...

As he'd always made her feel. As if she was on the edge of a precipice and any minute she'd topple.

The night Ben died she'd toppled. Philip had held her up. To tell him now that she couldn't marry him...

What was she thinking? He was a good, kind man

and next Saturday she'd marry him and right now she was going to sit in front of the television and stitch a last row of lace onto the hem of her wedding gown. The gown should be finished but her mother and Philip's mother had looked at it and decreed one more row.

"To make everything perfect."

Fine. Lace. Perfect. She could do this.

She let Kleppy out of the bedroom. He seemed a bit subdued. She gave him a doggy chew and he snuggled onto the couch beside her.

She'd washed him again. He was clean. Or clean enough. So what if the occasional dog hair got on her dress? It didn't have to be that perfect. Life didn't have to be that perfect.

Marriage to Philip would be okay.

The doorbell rang. Kleppy was off the couch, turning wild circles, barking his head off at the door.

He hadn't stirred from his spot on her bed when Philip had rung the bell. Different bell technique?

She should tuck Kleppy back in her bedroom. This'd be her mother. Or Philip's mother. Philip would have reported the headache, gathered the troops. It was a wonder the chicken soup hadn't arrived before this.

Her mother would be horrified at the sight of Kleppy. She'd just have to get used to him, she decided. They'd all have to get used to him. The chicken soup brigade.

But it wasn't the chicken soup brigade.

She opened the door. Sarah was standing on her doorstep holding a gift, and Raff was right behind her.

See, that was just the problem. She had no idea why her heart did this weird leap at the sight of him. It didn't make sense. She should feel anger when she saw him. Betrayal and distress. She'd felt it for ten years but now... Somehow distress was harder to maintain, and there was also this extra layer. Of...hope?

She really didn't want to spend the rest of her life running into this man. Maybe she and Philip could move.

Maybe Raff should move. Why had he come back to Banksia Bay in the first place?

But Sarah was beaming a greeting—Raff's sister—Abby's friend—and Abby thought there were so many complexities in this equation she couldn't get her head around them. Raff was caught as well as she was, held by ties of family and love and commitment.

His teenage folly had killed his best mate. He was trapped in this judgemental town, looking after the sister he loved.

For ten years she'd felt betrayed by this man but she looked at him now and thought he'd been to hell and back. There were different forms of life sentence.

And he'd lost...her?

He'd never had her, she thought fiercely. She'd broken up with him before the crash. If she even started thinking of him that way again...

The problem was, she was thinking. But the nightmare if she kept thinking...

Her parents... Philip... The way she felt herself, the aching void where Ben had been...

She was dealing with it. She had been dealing with it. If only he hadn't kissed her...

"You're home," Sarah said. She was holding a silver box tied with an enormous red ribbon. "You took ages to answer. Raff said you probably weren't home. He said you'd be out gall...gall..."

"Gallivanting?"

"It's what I said but I guess that's the wrong word," Raff said. "You wouldn't gallivant with Philip."

She ignored him. She ignored that heart-stopping, dare-you twinkle. "Hi, Sarah. It's lovely to see you. What do you have there?"

"We're delivering your present," Sarah said. "But Raff said you'd be out with Philip. We were going to leave it on the doorstep and go. But I heard Kleppy. Why aren't you out with Philip?"

"I had a headache."

"Very wise," Raff said, the gleam of mischief intensifying in those dark, dangerous eyes. "Dinner with the Flanagans? I'd have a headache, too."

"How did you know we were going out with the Flanagans?" She sighed. "No. Don't tell me. This town."

"Sorry." Raff's mischief turned to a chuckle, deep and toe-curlingly sexy. "And sorry about the intrusion, but Sarah wrapped your gift and decided she needed to deliver it immediately."

"So can we come in while you open it?" Sarah was halfway in, scooping up a joyful Kleppy on the way. But then she faltered. "Do you still have a headache?" Sarah knew all about headaches—Abby could see her cringe at the thought.

"Abby said she *had* a headache," Raff said. "That's past tense, Sares. I reckon it was cured the minute Philip went to dinner without her."

"Will you cut it out?"

"Do you still have a headache?" he asked, not perturbed at all by her snap.

"No, but…"

"There you go. Sares, what if I leave you here for half an hour so you can watch the present-opening and play with Kleppy? I'll pick you up at eight. Is that okay with you, Abby?"

It wasn't okay with Sarah.

"No," she ordered. "You have to watch her open it. It was your idea. You'll really like it, Abby. Ooh, and I want to help you use it."

So they both came in. Abby was absurdly aware that she had a police car parked in her driveway. That'd be reported to Philip in about two minutes, she thought. And to her parents. And to everyone else in this claustrophobic little town.

What was wrong with her? She loved this town and she was old enough to ignore gossip. Raff was here helping Sarah deliver a wedding gift. What was wrong with that?

Ten minutes tops and she'd have him out of here.

But the gift took ten minutes to open. Sarah had wrapped it herself. She'd used about twenty layers of paper and about four rolls of tape.

"I should use you to design my police cells," Raff said, grinning, as Abby ploughed her way through layer after layer after layer. "This sucker's not getting out any time soon."

"It's exciting," Sarah said, wide-eyed with anticipation. "I wonder what it is?"

Uh-oh. Abby glanced up at Raff at that and saw a shaft of pain. Short-term memory… Sarah would have spent an hour happily wrapping this gift, but an hour was a long time. For her to remember what she'd actually wrapped…

There was no way Raff could leave this town, she conceded. Sarah operated on long-term memory, the things she'd had instilled as a child. A new environment…a new home, new city, new friends… Sarah would be lost.

Raff was as trapped here as she was.

But she wasn't trapped, she told herself sharply, scaring herself with the direction her thoughts were headed. She loved it here. She loved Philip.

She was almost at the end. One last snip and…

Ooooh…

She couldn't stop the sigh of pure pleasure.

This was no small gift. It was a thing she'd loved for ever.

It was Gran Finn's pasta maker.

Colleen Finn had been as Irish as her name suggested. She was one of thirteen children and she'd married a hard drinking bull of a man who'd come to Australia to make a new start with no intention of changing his ways.

As a young bride, Gran had simply got on with it. And she'd cooked. Every recipe she could get her hands on, Irish or otherwise.

Abby was about ten when the pasta maker had come into the house. Bright and shiny and a complete puzzle to them all.

"Greta Riccardo's having a yard sale, getting rid of all her mother's stuff." Gran was puffed up like a peahen in her indignation. "All Maria's recipes—books and books—and here's Greta saying she never liked Italian food. That's like me saying I don't like potatoes. How could I let the pasta maker go to someone who doesn't love it? In honour of my friend Maria, we'll learn to be Italian."

It was in the middle of the school holidays and the kids, en masse, were enchanted. They'd watched and helped, and within weeks they'd been making decent pasta. Abby remembered holding sheets of dough, stretching it out, competing to see who could make the longest spaghetti.

Pasta thus became a staple in the Finn house and it was only as she grew older she realised how cheap it must have been. With her own eggs and her home grown tomatoes, Gran had a new basic food. But now…

"Don't you use this any more?" she ventured, stunned they could give away this part of themselves, and Raff smiled, though his smile was a little wary.

And, with the wariness, Abby got it.

She remembered Sarah as a teenager, stretching dough, kneading it, easing it through the machine with care so it wouldn't rip, making angels' hair, every kind of the most delicate pasta varieties.

She thought of Sarah now, with fumbling fingers, knowing what she'd been able to do, knowing what she'd lost.

"We don't use it any more," Sarah said. "But we don't want to throw it away. So Raff said why don't we give it to you and I can come round and remind you how to do it."

"Will you and I make some now?" she asked Sarah before she could stop herself. "Can you remember how to make it?"

"I think so," Sarah said and looked doubtfully at her big brother. "Can I, Raff?"

"Maybe we could both give Abby a reminder lesson,"

Raff said. "As part of our wedding present. If your head-ache's indeed better, Abigail?"

Both? Whoa. No. Uh-uh.

This was really dumb.

The police car would be parked outside for a couple of hours.

"You want me to drive the car round the back?" he asked.

She stared at him and he gazed straight back. Impassive. Reading her mind?

This was up to her. All she had to do was say her headache had come back.

They were all looking at her. Sarah. Kleppy.

Raff.

Go away. You're complicating my life. My wedding dress is right behind that door. My fiancé is just over the far side of town.

Sarah's eyes were wide with hope.

"I guess it'll still get around that my car was round the back for a couple of hours," Raff said, watching the warring emotions on her face. "Will Dexter call me out at dawn?"

"Philip," she said automatically.

"Philip," he agreed. Neutral.

"He won't mind," she said.

"I'd mind if I was Philip."

"Just lucky you're not Philip," she said and she'd meant to sound snarky but she didn't quite manage it. "Why don't you go do what you need to do and come back in a couple of hours?"

"But Raff likes making pasta, too," Sarah said and Abby looked at his face and saw...and saw that he did.

There was a lot of this man to back away from. There

was a lot about this man to distrust. But watching him now… It was as if he was hungry, she thought. He was disguising it, with his smart tongue and his teasing and his blatant provocation, but still…

He'd just given away his grandmother's pasta maker. He'd given it to her.

She'd love it. She'd use it for ever. The memories… She and Sarah, Raff and Ben, messing round in Gran's kitchen.

If it wasn't for this man, Ben would still be here.

How long did hate last?

For the last ten years, every time she'd looked at Raff Finn she'd felt ill. Now… She looked at Sarah and at the pasta maker. She thought of Mrs Fryer's vitriol. She thought that Ben had been Raff's best friend. Ben had loved him.

She'd loved him.

She couldn't keep hating. She just…couldn't.

She felt sick and weary and desperately sad. She felt… wasted.

"Hey, Abby really isn't well," Raff said and maybe he'd read the emotions—maybe it was easy because she was having no luck disguising them from herself, much less from him. "Maybe we should go, Sares, and let her recover."

"Do you really have a headache?" Sarah put her hand on her arm, all concern. "Does it bang behind your eyes? It's really bad when it does that."

Did Sarah still have headaches? Did Raff cope with them, take care of her, ache for his little sister and all she'd lost?

Maybe she should have invited Raff to her wedding. Now there was a stupid thing to think. She might be coming out the other side of a decade of bitterness but her parents…they never would. They knew that Raff had killed their son, pure and simple.

Philip would never countenance him at their wedding. Her parents would always hate him.

Any bridges must be her own personal bridges, built of an understanding that she couldn't keep stoking this flame of bitterness for the rest of her life.

They were watching her. Sarah's hand was still on her arm. Concerned for her headache. Sarah, whose headaches had taken away so much…

"Not a headache," she whispered and then more strongly, "it's not a headache. It's just… I'm overwhelmed. I loved making pasta with you guys when I was a kid. I can't believe you're giving this to me. It's the most wonderful gift—a truly generous gift of the heart. It's made me feel all choked up."

And then, as Sarah was still looking unsure, she took her hands and tugged her close and kissed her. "Thank you," she whispered.

"Raff, too," Sarah said.

Raff, too. He was watching with eyes that were impassive. Giving nothing away.

He'd given her his grandmother's pasta maker.

He'd killed her brother.

No. An accident had killed Ben. A moment of stupidity that he'd have to pay for forever.

She took a deep breath, released Sarah, took Raff's hands in hers and kissed him, too. Lightly. As she'd kissed Sarah.

On the cheek and nothing more.

She went to release him but he didn't release her. His hands held for just a fraction of a second too long.

A fraction of a second that said he was as confused as she was.

A fraction of a second that said there could never be idle friendship between them.

No longer enemies? But what?

Not friends. Not when he looked at her like… Like he was seeing all the regret in the world.

She had to do something. They were all looking at her—Raff, Sarah and Kleppy. Wondering why her eyes were brimming—why she was standing like a dummy wishing the last ten years could disappear and she could be seventeen again and Raff could be gorgeous and young and free and…

And she needn't think anything of the kind. In eight days she was marrying Philip. Her direction was set.

Eight days was all very well, but what about now?

Now she closed her eyes for a fraction of a second, gave herself that tiny respite to haul herself together—and then she put on her very brightest smile.

"Let's make pasta," she said, and they did.

Chapter 7

He shouldn't have given the pasta maker away if it made him feel like this.

This was a bad idea and it was getting worse.

He was sitting at Abby's kitchen table watching Sarah hold one end of the pasta dough as Abby fed it through the machine. Watching it stretch. Watching Sarah hold her breath, gasp with pleasure, smile.

Watching Abby smile back.

He could help—Sarah kept offering him a turn—but he excused himself on the grounds that all Abby's aprons were frilly and there was no way Banksia Bay's cop could be caught in a rose-covered pinny.

But in reality he simply wanted to watch.

He'd forgotten how good it was to watch Abby Callahan.

Had she forgotten how to be Abby Callahan?

For years now, he'd never seen her with a hair out of

place. Now, though, she was wearing faded jeans, an old sweatshirt smudged with flour, bare feet.

He remembered her in bare feet.

Abby. Seventeen years old. She'd laugh and everyone laughed with her. She could tease a smile out of anyone. She was a laughing, loving girl.

She'd been his girlfriend and he'd loved it. They just seemed to…fit.

But then they'd grown up. Sort of.

One heated weekend. Angry words. The car. The debutante ball. Incredibly important to teenagers.

Abby had started dating Philip. She and Philip had broken up, and then Sarah had started going out with him.

He hadn't liked that, either. Maybe he'd acted like a jerk, making Abby pay. He'd assumed they'd make it up.

But then… The tragedy that turned Abby from a girl who'd dreamed of being a dress designer, who lived for colour and life, into a lawyer who represented the likes of Wallace Baxter.

A lawyer who was about to marry Philip Dexter.

No.

He came close to shouting it, to thumping his fist down on the flour-covered table.

He did no such thing. There was no reason why she shouldn't marry Philip. There was nothing Raff could put his finger on against the guy. Philip was a model citizen.

He didn't like him.

Jealous?

Yeah. But something else. A feeling?

A feeling he'd had at nineteen that had never gone away.

"Why did you and Dexter stop going out?" he asked as the pasta went through a third and final time.

She didn't lift her head but he saw the tiny furrow of concentration, the setting of her lips.

"Abby?"

"Just ease it in a little more, Sarah."

"Ten years ago. After your debut. Why did you break up?"

"That's none of your business. Now we put this attachment on to cut it into ribbons."

"I know," Sarah said, crowing in triumph as she found the right attachment. "This one."

"It's just I've always wondered," Raff said as Sarah tried to get the attachment in. They both let her be. It'd be easier to step in and do it for her—her fingers were fumbling badly—but she was a picture of intense concentration and to step in now…

They both knew not to.

"You know I only went out with Debbie Macallroy to get back at you," he said.

"So you did. Childhood romances, Raff. We were dumb."

Really dumb. Where had they all ended up?

"We did have fun before the crash," he said gently. "We were such good friends. But then Philip… First you and then Sarah. But you didn't fall in love with him then. You ditched him."

"I've changed. We both have."

"People don't change."

"Of course they do."

Of course people changed. She had, and so had Philip.

She didn't look up at Raff; she focused on the sheets of pasta, making sure they were dusted so they wouldn't stick in the final cutting process.

She thought back to Philip at nineteen.

He'd been rich, or rich compared to every other kid in Banksia Bay. He had his own car and it was a far cry from the bomb Ben and Raff were doing up. A purple Monaro V8. Cool.

Every girl in Abby's year group had wanted to go out with him. Abby didn't so much—she was trying hard not to think she was still in love with Raff—but she'd needed a partner for her debut, all Raff thought about was his stupid car, and Sarah had bet her she wouldn't be game to ask him.

For a few weeks she'd preened. Her friends were jealous. Philip danced really well and her debut was lovely.

But what followed…the drive-in movies… Sitting in the dark with Philip… Not so cool. Nothing she could put her finger on, though. It was just he wasn't Raff and that was no reason to break up with him.

But finally…

They'd gone for a drive one afternoon, heading up Black Mountain to the lookout. She hadn't wanted to go, she remembered, and when they'd had a tyre blowout she'd been relieved.

She hadn't been so relieved when they realised Philip's spare tyre was flat. Or when he thought she should walk back into town to fetch his father—because he had to look after the car.

"No way am I trudging back to town while you sit here in comfort," she retorted. "You're the dummy who didn't check his spare."

Not so tactful, even for a seventeen-year-old, but she was reaching the point where she wanted to end it.

Philip left her. Bored, she tried out the sound system. His tapes were boring, top ten stuff, nothing she enjoyed.

She flicked through his tape box—a box just like the one that graced her bedside table, beautiful cedar with slots for every cassette. His grandpa really was great.

Boring cassettes. Boring, boring. But, at the back, some unmarked ones. She slid one in and heard the voice of Christabelle Thomas, a girl in the same class as her at school.

"Philip, we shouldn't. My mum'd kill me. Philip…"

Enough. She met Philip and his father as she stomped down the mountain, fuming.

"You were supposed to stay with the car," Philip told her.

"I didn't like the music," she snapped, and held up the tape and threw it at him through his father's car window. "Put the ripped up tape in my letterbox tomorrow or I'm telling Christabelle."

Why think of that now?

Because of Raff?

She glanced up and he was watching her. Sarah was watching her.

"What's wrong?" Sarah asked, and she came back to the present and realised Sarah had successfully put the cutting tool in place.

"Hey, fantastic, let's cut," she said, and the moment had passed. The time had passed. The tapes had been an aberration.

Philip had brought the tape round the next morning, cut to shreds.

"Hey, Abby, I need to tell you I'm sorry. Christabelle and I only went out a couple of times, well before you and me. It's not what you think. I only asked to kiss her. And I hadn't realised the tape was on record. I record stuff in the car all the time on the trip between here and

Sydney—I try and recall study notes and then see how accurate I've been. I must have forgotten this was still on. I'm so sorry you found it."

It was okay, she conceded. It was a mistake. Kids did stupid things.

Like driving on the wrong side of the road?

"What's wrong?" Sarah asked again and Raff's eyes were asking the same question.

"Sorry," she said. "I just started thinking about all the things I had to do before the wedding."

"You want us to go home?" Sarah asked, and Abby winced and got a grip.

"No way. I'm hungry. Pasta, here we come. What setting shall we have it on? Do we want angels' hair or tagliatelle?"

"Angels' hair," Sarah said.

"My favourite," Raff said. "It always has been."

She glanced up and he was looking straight at her. He wasn't smiling.

Raff...

Don't, she told herself but she wasn't quite sure what she was saying *don't* to.

All she knew was that this man meant trouble. He was surely causing trouble now.

They left at nine, which gave her an hour to clean the kitchen and to get her thoughts in order before Philip arrived.

He arrived promptly at ten. Kleppy met him at the door and growled.

He hadn't growled at Raff and Sarah, but then he knew they were friends.

He didn't yet know Philip was a friend.

"If he bites…" Philip said.

"He won't bite. He's being a watchdog."

"I thought you had a headache," Philip said, wary and irritated. "I hear Finn and his sister have been here."

She sighed. She lived in Banksia Bay. She should be used to this.

"Sarah brought our wedding present. She wanted to demonstrate."

"Demonstrate what?"

"Her gran's pasta maker. You need to see it, Philip. It's cool."

"A second-hand pasta maker?"

"It's an heirloom."

"Pasta makers aren't heirlooms."

"This one is." She gestured to the battered silver pasta maker taking pride of place on her bench. "We'll make pasta once a week for the rest of our lives. When we're finally in our nursing home we'll discuss the virtues of each of our children and decide who most deserves our fantastic antique pasta maker. If our children are unworthy we'll donate it to the State Gallery as a National Treasure."

He didn't even smile. "You said you had a headache."

"I did have a headache."

"But you let them in."

"It was Sarah," she said, losing patience. "Her gran's pasta maker means a lot to her. She was desperate to see me using it."

"You weren't well enough to come out to dinner."

"If it was necessary I would have come," she snapped. "It wasn't. It was, however, absolutely necessary for me to show Sarah that her grandmother's pasta maker will be appreciated."

"And Finn?"

"You mean Raff?"

"Of course I mean Raff. Finn."

"He brought Sarah here. He watched."

"I don't see how you can bear that man to be in the house."

"I can bear a lot for Sarah."

"Even having a dog foisted onto you."

Kleppy growled again and Abby felt like growling herself. "Philip…"

And, just like that, he caved. He put his hands up in mock surrender, tossed his jacket over the back of a kitchen chair and hugged her. Kissed her on the forehead.

"Sorry. Sorry, sorry. I know you had no choice. I know you wouldn't let Finn in unless you had no choice."

Of course she wouldn't.

"Tell me about tonight," she said, and he sat and she made him coffee and he told her all about the fantastic business opportunities they'd discussed—projects of mutual benefit that needed careful legal input if they were to get past council.

And all the while… Things were changing.

Some time in the last twenty-four hours the buried question had surfaced in her head and it was getting louder and louder until it was almost a drumbeat.

Why am I marrying this man?

The question was making her feel dizzy.

A week on Saturday she'd be married to Philip.

Uh-oh.

This was Raff's fault, she thought, feeling desperate. Raff asking her…

Why did you and Dexter stop going out?

She'd shoved that memory away ten years ago, not

to be thought of again. Remembering it now... How she'd felt...

Underneath the logic, did she still feel like that?

This was like waking from a coma. A million emotions were crowding in. Memories. Stupid childhood snatches. Laughter, trouble, tears, adventure, fun...

Always with Raff.

"Philip, I..."

"You need to go to bed," he said, immediately contrite. He rose. "I'm sorry, I forgot the headache. You should have said. Just because Finn barges his way in, welcome or not... I have a bit more finesse. You sleep well and I'll see you in the morning. Breakfast at the yacht club? You want to come sailing afterwards?"

"Mum's organised the girls' lunch at midday."

"Of course. So much to plan..."

So much to plan? This wedding had been organised for years.

"Sleep well, sweetheart," he told her and stooped and kissed her. Dry. Dusty. He reached for his jacket...

And paused. Frowned. Felt the pockets. "My wallet."

"Your wallet?"

"It was in my side pocket."

"Could you have dropped it?"

"It was there when I got out of the car." He opened the front door and stared out at the path. The front light showed the path smooth and bare. "I always check I have my phone and my wallet when I get in and out of the car."

Of course. Caution was Philip's middle name.

"I'm sure I didn't drop it," he said.

Which left... She swivelled and looked for Kleppy.

Kleppy was at her bedroom door. He had something on the floor in front of him.

A wallet? Too big?

She walked over to see and he wagged his tail and beamed up at her. She was sure it was a beam. It might be the stupidest beam on the planet but it was strangely adorable.

"What have you got?"

It wasn't the wallet. It was her jewellery box, the cedar box Philip's grandfather had given her. Her heart sank. If he'd chewed it…

He hadn't.

How had he got it down from the bedside table?

There wasn't a mark on it. He had his paw resting proprietorially on its lid but when she bent down and took it he quivered all over with that stupid canine beam. *Aren't I fantastic? Look what I found for you!*

"That dog…" Philip said in a voice full of foreboding.

"He doesn't have it," she said. "But…"

She looked more closely at Kleppy. Then she looked at her bed.

Kleppy had retrieved the box via the bed. She had a pale green quilt on her bed. The coverlet was now patterned with footprints.

She bent down and looked at Kleppy's paws.

Dirt.

Uh-oh, uh-oh, uh-oh.

She looked out through the glass doors to the garden. To the fence. To where she'd dug in netting all the way along.

Lots of lovely loose soil. A great place to bury something.

Loose dirt was scattered over the grass in half a dozen places. Kleppy, it seemed, had been a little indecisive in his burial location.

"You're kidding me," Philip said, guessing exactly what had happened.

"Uh-oh." What else was a girl to say?

"You expect me to dig?"

"No." She'd had enough. She was waking from a bad dream and this was part of it.

"I'll find it," she told him. "I'll give it to you in the morning."

"Clean."

"Clean," she snapped. "Of course."

"It's not my fault the stupid…"

"It's not your fault," she said, cutting him off. It never was. Of all the childish…

No. She was being petulant herself. She needed to get a grip. She needed to find the wallet and then think through what was important here. She needed to decide how she could do the unimaginable.

"Of course it's not your fault," she said more gently and she headed outside to start sifting dirt. "I took Kleppy on. I'm responsible. Go home, Philip, and let me sort the damage my way."

"I can help…" he started, suddenly unsure, but she shook her head.

"My headache's come back," she said. "I can use a bit of quiet digging. And thinking."

"What do you need to think about?"

"Weddings," she said. "And pasta makers. And dogs."

And other stuff she wasn't even prepared to let into the corners of her mind until Philip was out of the door.

She dug.

She should have thought and dug, but she just dug.

Her mind felt as if it had been washed clear, emptied of everything.

What was happening? Everything she'd worked for over the last ten years was suddenly…nothing.

Stupid, stupid, stupid.

This is just pre-wedding nerves, she told herself. But she knew it was more.

She dug.

It was strangely soothing, delving into the soft loam, methodically sifting. She should be wearing gardening gloves. She'd worn gardening gloves this afternoon when she'd laid the netting, but that was when it mattered that she kept her nails nice. That was when she was going to get married.

There was a scary thought. She sat back on her heels and thought, *Did I just think that?*

How could she not get married?

Her dress. Two years in the making. Approximately two thousand beads.

Two hundred and thirty guests.

People were coming from England. People had already come from England.

Her spare room was already filling with gifts.

She'd have to give back the pasta maker.

And that was the thing that made her eyes suddenly fill with tears. It made her realise the impossibility of doing what she was thinking of.

Handing Raff Finn back the pasta maker and saying, *Here, I can't accept it—I'm not getting married.*

Why Raff? Why was his gift so special?

She knew why. She knew…

The impossibility of what she was thinking made her choke. This was stupid. Nostalgia. Childhood memories.

Not all childhood memories. Raff yesterday at the scene of the accident, standing in front of her car, giving orders.

Raff, caring about old Mrs Ford.

Raff...

"We always wish for what we can't have," she muttered to herself and shoved her hand deep into the loam so hard she hit the wire netting and scraped her knuckles.

She hauled her hand out and an edge of leather came with it.

She stared down at her skinned knuckle and Philip's wallet.

She needed a hug.

"Kleppy," she called. "I found it. You want to come lick it clean?"

Fat chance. It was a joke. She should be smiling.

She wasn't smiling.

"Kleppy?"

He'd be back on her bed, she thought. How long till he came when she called?

"Kleppy?" She really did want a hug. She wiped away the dirt and headed inside.

No Kleppy.

How many hiding places were there? Where was he?

Not here.

Not in the house.

The front door was closed. He could hardly have opened it and walked out. He was clever but not...

Memory flooded back. Philip, throwing open the door to stare at the front path. She'd gone to look for Kleppy, then she'd headed straight out to the garden.

Philip leaving. Slamming the door behind him.

The door had been open all the time they'd talked.

Her heart sank. She should have checked. She'd been too caught up with her own stupid crisis, her own stupid pre-wedding jitters.

Kleppy was gone.

Chapter 8

Abby searched block by block, first on foot and then fetching the car and broadening her search area.

How far could one dog get in what—half an hour? More? How long had she sat out in the garden angsting about what she should or shouldn't be doing with her life?

How had one dog made her question herself?

Where was he?

She wanted to wake up the town and make them search, but even her friends… To wake them at midnight and say, *Please, can you help me find a stray dog?* was unthinkable.

They'd think she was nuts.

Sarah wouldn't think she was nuts. Or Raff.

Her friends…

She thought of the kids she'd messed around with

when she was a kid. They'd dropped away as she was seen as Philip's girl. Philip's partner. Philip's wife?

Those who remained… She winced, wondering how she'd isolated herself. She'd done it without thinking. How many years had she simply been moving forward with no direction? Or in Philip's direction. So now, who did she call when she was in the kind of trouble Philip disapproved of?

She knew who.

No.

She searched for another hour.

One o'clock.

This was crazy. She couldn't do it by herself.

Do not go near Raff Finn. That man is trouble. It had been a mantra in her head for years but now it had changed. Trouble had taken on a new dimension—a dimension she wasn't brave enough to think about.

She pushed the thought of Raff away and kept searching. Wider and wider circles. A small dog. He'd be safe until morning, she told herself. He had street smarts. He was a stray.

He wasn't a stray. He was Isaac Abrahams' loved dog. He wore his owner's medal of valour on his collar.

He was *her* Kleppy.

She drove on. Round the town. She walked through the deserted mall. She walked out onto the wharves at the harbour.

And then? There was only one place left to search. Isaac's.

Up the mountain in the dark? To Isaac's? She hated that place. She couldn't.

He had to be somewhere. After this time, logic said that was where he'd be.

She couldn't make herself go alone. She just... couldn't.

Don't do it.

Do it.

At two in the morning she phoned the police. The police singular.

Raff's patrol car pulled up outside her front door ten minutes after she called. He had the lights flashing.

He swung out of the car, six feet two inches of lethal cop. Ready for action.

She'd been parked, waiting for him. In the dark. Not wanting to wake the neighbours. His flashing lights lit the street and curtains were being pulled.

"Turn the lights off," she begged.

"This is Kleppy," he said seriously. "I thought about sirens."

"You want to wake the town?"

"How much do you want to find him?"

"A lot," she snapped and then caught herself. "I mean...please."

"So how did you lose him? You let him out?"

"I...yes."

He looked at her face and got an answer. "Dexter let him out."

"By mistake."

"I'm sure."

"By mistake," she snapped.

"How long ago?"

"Three hours."

"Three hours? You've only just discovered he's missing?" There was a whole gamut of accusation in his tone.

Like what had she and Philip been doing for three hours that they hadn't noticed they'd lost a dog?

"I've been searching," she said through gritted teeth. "Can we just... I don't know..."

"Find him?" he suggested, and suddenly his voice was gentle. The switch was nearly her undoing. She was so close to tears.

"Yes. Please."

"Where have you looked?"

"Everywhere."

"That just about covers it. You sure he's not under your bed?"

"I'm sure."

"That's where we find most missing kids," he said. "Within two hundred yards of the family refrigerator."

"You want to look again?"

"I trust you. Is Dexter out hunting?"

Silence. She wasn't going to answer. She didn't need to answer.

"I'm... I'm sorry to call you out," she ventured.

"This is what I do."

"Hunt for lost dogs when you should be home with Sarah?"

"Sarah's used to me being out in the night. She has her dogs."

"Are you on duty?"

"This is a two cop town. When there's an emergency, Keith and I are both on."

"This is an emergency?"

"Kleppy's definitely an emergency," he said. "He's a loved dog with an owner. I was never more relieved than when you said you'd take him on. For all sorts of reasons," he said enigmatically, but then kept right on.

"You want to ride with me? We'll check out Main Street. Morrisy Drapers is his favourite spot."

"I've been there. It's all locked up. The bargain bins are inside. No Kleppy."

"You've what?" he demanded, brow snapping. "You walked the mall alone?"

"This is Kleppy."

"At two on a Saturday morning? There's the odd drunk and nothing else in the mall."

"Yeah, and no Kleppy."

His mouth tightened but he said nothing, turning the car towards the waterfront. "He likes the harbour, our Kleppy. Isaac's been presented with a live lobster before now. Isaac had to get Kleppy's nose stitched but he got him home, live and fighting."

"Oh," she said and choked on a bubble of laughter that was close to hysteria. "A lobster?"

"Almost bigger than he was. Cost Isaac a hundred and thirty dollars for the lobster and another three hundred at the vet's. They had a great dinner that night."

He had his flashing lights on again now. He hit another switch and floodlights lit both sides of the road.

The law on the hunt.

"I've checked the harbour," she said in a small voice, already knowing the reaction she'd get.

And she did.

"Also by yourself." His tone was suddenly angry. "Hell, woman, you know the dropkicks go down there at night."

"They haven't seen Kleppy."

"You asked?"

"This is Kleppy."

"You asked. You approached the low life that crawl round that place at night? Where the hell is Dexter?"

"In bed," she snapped. She caught herself, fighting back anger in response. "I know I should have phoned him but he's not...he's not quite reconciled to having a dog."

"Which is why he left the door open."

"He did not do it deliberately."

"You make one stubborn defence lawyer," he said more mildly and went back to concentrating on the sides of the road.

She fumed. Or she tried to fume. She was too tired and too worried to fume.

"Have you tried up the mountain?" Raff asked and she caught her breath.

The mountain.

Isaac's place.

"N... No." She swallowed. Time to confess. "That's why...that's why I called you."

"You didn't go up there?"

"I haven't. Not since..." She paused. Tried to go on. Couldn't.

Tonight she'd walked a deserted shopping mall. Tonight she'd fronted a group of very drunk youths down at the harbour to ask if they'd seen her dog.

But the place with the most fears was Kleppy's home. Isaac's place.

Up the mountain where Ben had been killed. To go there at night...

The last night she'd been there would stay in her mind for ever. The phone call. The rain, the dark, the smell of spilled gasoline, the sight of...

"It's just a place, Abby," Raff said gently. "You want to stay home while I check?"

"I...no." She had to get over this. Ten years. She was stuck in a time warp, an aching void of loss. "I'm sorry. You must hate going up there, too."

"There's lots of things I hate," he said softly. "But going up the mountain's not one of them. It's Isaac's home. He was a great old guy."

He was. She remembered Isaac the night of the accident. Of course he'd heard the crash; he'd been first on the scene. He'd been cradling Ben when she'd got there.

All the more reason to love his dog. All the more reason to face down her hatred of the place.

"You know, you can't block it out for ever," Raff said. "Work it through and move on."

"Like you have." She heard the anger in her words and flinched.

"Like I try to," Raff said evenly. "It always hurts but limbo's not my idea of a great time. You want to spend the rest of your life there?"

"What's that supposed to mean?"

"Meaning you've never come back," he said. "You're as damaged as Sarah is in your own way."

She shook her head. "No. No, I'm not. I'm fine. Just find my dog, Raff."

"I'll do my best," he said gravely. "You know, taking Kleppy's a great start. Kleppy's forcing chinks in your lawyerish armour and I'm not so sure you can seal them up again. Let's see if we can find him so he can go the whole way."

Isaac's place was locked and deserted, a ramshackle homestead hidden in bushland. Through the fence, they could see Isaac's garden, beautiful in the moonlight, but they couldn't get in the front gate. The gate was padlocked and a cyclone fence had been erected around the rickety pickets.

"Isaac's daughter's worried about vandalism before she can get the place on the market," Raff said. "She sacked the gardener, hired a security firm and put the fence up." Raff headed off, striding around the boundary, searching the ground with his flashlight as well as through the fence. Abby had to run to catch up with him.

The ground was unsteady. Raff's hand was suddenly holding hers. She should pull away—but she didn't.

"Call him," Raff said.

She called, her voice ringing out across the bushland, eerie in the dark.

"Keep calling." Raff's hand held hers, strong and warm and pushing her to keep going.

"We'll call from the other side," he said. "If he's down nearer the road..."

Near the road where Ben was killed?

Move on. She did move on, and Raff's hand gave her the strength to do it. How inappropriate was that?

But she called. And she called. And then, unbelievably...

Out through the bush, tearing like his life depended on it, Kleppy came flying. Straight to her.

She gasped and stooped to catch him and the little dog was in her arms, wriggling with joy. She was on her knees in the undergrowth, hugging. Maybe even weeping.

"Hey, Klep," Raff said, and she could hear his relief. "Where have you been hiding?"

She hugged him tight and he licked her...then suddenly he wrenched out of her arms, backed off and barked—and tore back into the bush.

Raff made a lunge for him but he was too fast.

He disappeared back into the darkness.

"You could have held his collar," Raff said, but he didn't sound annoyed. He sounded resigned.

"Oh, my…" She started to run, but Raff put his hand out and stopped her.

"We walk. We don't run. Wombat holes, logs, all sorts of traps for the unwary in the dark."

"But Kleppy…"

"Won't have gone far," he said, taking her hand firmly back into his. "You saw him—he was joyful to see you. This is Isaac's place, Kleppy's territory, but I reckon you're his now. It seems you're his person to replace Isaac. That's a fair responsibility, Abby Callahan. I hope you're up to it."

"Just find him for me," she muttered.

Kleppy's person?

She didn't want to think about where that was taking her.

She didn't actually want to think at all.

Kleppy had headed back down the hill. Towards the road. They were now within two hundred yards of where the cars had crashed.

It had rained this week. The undergrowth smelled of wet eucalypt, scents of the night, scents she hated.

She'd never wanted to come back here.

"Move on," Raff said, holding her hand tightly. "You can."

She couldn't.

The thought that it had been Raff, the man holding her hand right now…

Raff…

She could not depend on this man. This man was dangerous; he always had been. He'd been dangerous to Ben. Now suddenly he seemed dangerous in an entirely different way.

But he was the one searching for Kleppy, not Philip.

That would have to be thought about tomorrow. For now…just get through tonight.

"If he's gone back down to the town…"

"Why would he do that? This is Isaac's place. You're here. Everything he knows is here." And then, before she could respond, his flashlight stopped moving and focused.

Kleppy was fifty yards from the road. Digging? He was nosing his way through the undergrowth, pawing at the damp earth, wagging, wriggling, digging…

"Kleppy…" she called and started towards him.

Kleppy looked up at her—and headed back in the direction he'd come from. Back to Isaac's.

Raff sighed.

"You don't make a very good cop," he said. "Letting the suspect go. Sneaking up and then breaking into a run at the last minute."

"What's he doing?" They were following him again, back through the undergrowth. Once more, Raff had her hand. She absolutely should let it go.

She didn't.

"I suspect he's one very confused dog," Raff said. "He knows where Isaac lived but he can't get in. He's forming new bonds to you but his allegiance will be torn— he'll still want Isaac. And what's back there buried… who knows? Some long hidden loot, or a wombat hole, or something he sniffed on the way past and thought was worth investigating. But now… He's weighed everything up—you, wombats, Isaac—and decided he needs to go back to his first love."

And Raff was right. They emerged from the bush and Kleppy was waiting for them—or rather he was waiting for someone to open the gate.

His nose was pressed hard against the cyclone fencing and he whimpered as they approached. He was no longer running. He was no longer joyful to see them.

Abby knelt and scooped him up and he looked longingly at the darkened house.

"He's not there any more," she whispered, burying her nose into his scruffy coat. "I'm sorry, Kleppy, but I'm it. Will I do?"

"He'll grow accustomed," Raff said, and his voice was a bit rough—a bit emotional? "You want me to take you both home?"

She looked at the darkened house, then turned and looked out towards the road, to where Ben had been snatched from her.

He'll grow accustomed.

Ten years…

Her parents would never forgive Raff Finn. How could she?

"It's okay, Kleppy," she whispered. "We'll manage, you and I. Thank you, Raff. We'd appreciate it if you took us home."

He drove them down from the mountain, a woman and her dog, and he felt closer to her tonight than he had for ten years.

Maybe it was what she was wearing. The normally immaculate lawyer-cum-Abby was wearing old jeans, a faded sweatshirt and her hair had long come loose from its normally elegant chignon. She still had flour on her face from pasta making. There were twigs in her hair.

Her face was tear-streaked and she was holding her dog as if she were drowning.

She made him feel…

Like he'd felt at nineteen, when Abby had started dating Philip.

He and Abby had been girlfriend and boyfriend since they were fourteen and sixteen. Kid stuff. Not serious.

She hung round with Sarah so she was always in and out of the house. She was pretty and she laughed at his jokes. She was always…there.

Then he'd come home and she was dating Philip and the sense of loss had him gutted.

He should have told her how he felt then, only he'd been too proud to say, *Okay, Abby, wise choice, I know at seventeen you need to date a few people, see the world.*

He'd been too proud to say that seeing her and Philip together had made him wake up to himself. Had made him realise that the sexiest, loveliest, funniest, happiest, most desirable woman in the world was Abby.

He had known it. It was just… He thought he'd punish her a little. He and Ben had even been a bit cool to her—Ben had hated her dating Dexter as well.

They'd backed off. The night of the crash, where was Abby? Home, washing her hair?

Home, being angry with all of them.

That probably saved her life, but what was left afterwards…?

The sexiest, loveliest, funniest, happiest, most desirable woman in the entire world had been hidden under a load of grief so great it overwhelmed them all. Then she was hidden by layers of her parents' hopes, their fixation that Abby could make up for Ben, and their belief that Philip was the Ben they couldn't have.

He'd watched for ten years as the layers had built up, until the Abby he'd once known, once loved, had been almost totally subsumed.

And there was nothing he could do about it because he was the one who'd caused it.

He felt his fists harden on the steering wheel, so tight his knuckles showed white. One stupid moment and so many worlds shot to pieces. Ben and Sarah. And Abby, condemned to live for the rest of her life making up for his criminal stupidity.

"You know I once loved you," he said into the night and she gasped and hugged Kleppy tighter.

"Don't."

"I won't," he said gently. "I can't. But, Abby, if I could wipe away that night…"

"As if anyone could do that."

"No," he said grimly. "And I know I have to live with it for the rest of my life. But you don't."

"I don't know what you mean."

"I mean you lost Ben that night," he said. "For which I'm responsible and I'll live with that for ever. But Ben was my mate and if he could see what's happening to you now he'd be sick at heart."

There was a long silence. She wasn't talking. He was trying to figure out what exactly to say.

He had no right to say anything. He'd forfeited that for sure, but then…

Forget himself, he thought. Forget everything except the fact that Ben had been his best friend and maybe he needed to put what he was feeling himself aside.

Make it about Ben, he told himself. Abby hated him already. Saying what he thought Ben would say couldn't make things worse.

"Abby, your parents and Dexter's parents are thick as thieves," he told her. "They always have been. After the accident, your families practically combined. The Dexters had Philip. The Callahans were left only with Abby. Two families, a son and a daughter. When Ben died you were about to go to university and study creative arts. Afterwards, Philip told you how sensible law was. Your mother told you how happy it'd make her to see you at the same law school as Philip. Philip's dad told you he'd welcome you into his law firm. And you just…rolled."

"I did not roll," she said but it was a whisper he knew didn't even convince herself.

"You used to wear sweaters with stripes. You used to wear purple leggings. I loved those purple leggings."

Silence.

"I never saw you wear purple leggings after Ben died."

"So I grew up."

"We all did that night," he said gravely. "But, Abby, you didn't just leave behind childhood. You left behind… Abby."

"If you mean I left behind stupidity, yes, I did," she snapped. "How could I not? All those years… *Keep away from the Finn boy. He's trouble.* That's what my mother said but I never listened. Not once did I listen and neither did Ben, and now he's dead."

He couldn't answer that.

The car nosed its way down the mountain. He could drive faster. He didn't.

Keep away from the Finn boy.

He knew Ben and Abby had been given those orders. He even knew why.

His grandfather's drunkenness. His mother's lack of a wedding ring. His family's poverty.

The prissiness of Abby's parents, secure in their middle class home, with their neat front lawn and their nice children.

"I dunno about the Callahan kids." He remembered Gran saying it when he was small as she tucked him into bed. "You be careful, Raff, love. They don't fit with the likes of us."

"They're my friends."

"And they're nice kids," his gran had said. "But one day they'll move on. Don't let "em break your heart."

As a kid, he didn't have a clue what she was talking about. He'd figured it out as he got older, but Ben and Abby never let it happen. They simply ignored their parents' disapproval and he was a friend regardless.

But for how long? If Ben hadn't died...would Abby have gone out with him again?

And now she was a defence lawyer and he was a cop. Never the twain shall meet.

Except she was staring ahead with eyes that were blind with misery and she was heading into a marriage with Dexter and he couldn't bear it.

"I'm not talking about us now," he said, and it was hard to keep his voice even. "As you say, we've both grown up and there's so much baggage between us there's never going to be a bridge to friendship. But I'm not talking about me either, Abby. I'm talking about you. You and Dexter. He's burying you."

"He's not."

"Mrs Philip Dexter. Where's the Abby in that equation?"

"Leave it."

"You know it's true. Would Mrs Philip Dexter ever spend the night trawling Banksia Bay looking for a dog?"

"Of course she would." She gulped. "No. That is… I'll hang onto Kleppy from now on."

"And if Dexter leaves the door open?"

"He won't."

"Don't do it, Abby."

"Butt out." They were pulling up outside her house. She shoved the door open and hauled Kleppy out. She staggered a little, but straight away he was beside her, steadying her.

She was so…so…

She was Abby. All he wanted to do was fold her into his arms and hold her. Dog and all.

He'd had ten years to stop feeling like this. He thought he had.

One stupid night hunting a kleptomaniac dog and he was feeling just what he'd felt ten years ago. As if here was the half to his whole. As if something had been ripped out of him ten years back and this woman was the key to getting his life back.

This wasn't about him. It couldn't be.

"There are lots of guys out there, Abby," he said in a voice that was none too steady. "Guys who'd marry you in a heartbeat. Guys who'd love Kleppy. Don't marry Dexter."

"Get out of my way."

"You're better than this, Abby."

"We've had this conversation before. Philip's better than any of us. He wasn't stupid. He's dependable."

"He's boring. He doesn't like this town."

"How can you say that? He lives for this town."

"He spends his life criticising it. Making reasons why he should go to conferences far away. Where are you going on your honeymoon?"

"You're suggesting we should honeymoon at Mrs Mac's Banksia Bay's Big Breakfast?"

"No, but…"

"That's what I'd have done if I'd married you."

Her words shocked them both.

If I'd married you…

The unsayable had just been said.

The unthinkable had just been put out there.

"Abby…"

"Don't," she said and pushed and Kleppy got caught in the middle and yelped his indignation. "Now see what you've done."

Kleppy wagged his tail. Wounded to the core.

"Think about it," he said, but softly, knowing he'd gone too far; he'd pushed into places neither of them could contemplate going.

"I've thought about it. Thank you very much for your help tonight."

"Any time, Abby, and I mean that."

"I've accepted all the help from you I'll ever accept."

"You can't say that. What if you need help over the street in your old age? There I'll be in my fading cop uniform, all ready to hold up the traffic, and there you'll be with your pride and your walking frame. *Don't you stop the traffic for me, young man…*"

She gasped and choked, laughter suddenly surfacing at the image.

"That's better," he said. "Abby, can we be friends?"

Friends. She looked at him and the laughter faded. Her eyes were indescribably bleak.

"No."

"Because of Ben?"

"Because of much, much more than that."

"Don't go near the Finn boy. He's trouble?" he said.

"More than that, too," she whispered. "You know I… You know we…"

He didn't know anything, and he couldn't bear it. She was looking at him with eyes that were so bleak the end of the world must be around the corner, not the marriage of the year, Banksia Bay's answer to a royal couple—a wedding that had been planned almost since she was a baby.

She hesitated for just a fraction of a second too long and logic and reason and everything else he should be thinking flew straight out of the window.

He took her shoulders in his hands. He tugged her to him—dog included—and he kissed her.

One minute she was angry and confused, intending to wheel away and stalk into the house, dignity intact.

The next minute she was being kissed by Raff Finn and her dignity was nowhere.

Second time in two days? She felt as if her body had opened to this two days ago and she'd been waiting for a repeat performance ever since.

Only this wasn't a repeat performance. Tonight she'd been scared and lonely and emotional, remembering so much stuff that her head was close to exploding even before Raff's mouth met hers.

It was no wonder that when it did she couldn't handle it.

She liked control. She was a control girl. Her emotional wiring was neat and orderly.

His mouth touched hers and every single fuse blew, just like that.

Her circuits closed down and every one of the emotions she'd been feeling during the night was replaced, overridden by one gigantic wire that sizzled and sparked and threatened to blow her tidy existence right out of the water.

Raff Finn was kissing her.

She was kissing Raff Finn.

Or…maybe she wasn't kissing. She was simply dissolving into him.

Ten long years of control, ten years of carefully recreating her life, was forgotten. All she could feel was this man. His hands. His mouth. The taste of him, the smell, the sheer testosterone-laden charge of him.

Raff. The man who was kissing her totally, unutterably, mind-blowingly senseless.

She had sensations within her right now that she didn't know existed. She didn't know feeling like this was possible. If she had…

If she had, she'd have gone hunting for them with elephant guns.

Oh…

Did she gasp? Did she moan?

Who knew? All she knew was that her mouth was locked on his and the kiss went on and on and she didn't care. She didn't care that it was three in the morning and she was engaged to Philip Dexter and Raff Finn was a man her family hated. Raff Finn, six foot two, was holding her and kissing her until her toes curled, until her mind was empty of anything but the taste of him.

This was a pure primeval need. It had nothing to do with logic. It had everything to do with here and now. And Raff—a man she'd wanted since she was eight years old.

Here, now and…and…

"Is that you? Abigail?"

Uh-oh.

This was Banksia Bay.

It was three in the morning.

She lived next door to Ambrose Kittelty and Ambrose watched American sports television all night on Pay TV—as well as watching out of his front window.

Banksia Bay. Where her life was never her own. Could never be her own.

"It's Abby all right." Somehow, Finn was putting her away from him and she could have wept. To have him so close… To know she could never… Must never…

"Is she kissing you?" Mr Kittelty sounded almost apoplectic.

"Bit of trouble with a dog," Raff said smoothly. "I'm helping the lady get him under control."

"You looked like…"

"Took two of us to get him settled. Seems okay now. You right, ma'am?"

"That's Abrahams' dog," Ambrose said.

"Yes, sir, the same dog that took your boot from the bowling club," Finn said. "Still causing trouble."

"Get him put down," Ambrose said and slammed down the window.

"I didn't know Ambrose and Phil were related," Raff said and any last vestige of passion disappeared, just like that.

She felt cold and tired and stupid. Very, very stupid.

"Thank you for tonight," she said, and she couldn't keep the weariness from her voice. "Don't..."

"Come near you any more?"

"That's right," she whispered. "There's too much at stake."

"Your marriage to Philip?"

"You know it's much more than that."

"First things first, Abby," he said softly. "Figure the marriage thing out and everything else can come later."

"Not with you, it can't."

"I know that."

"So goodnight," she said and she hugged her dog close—a wild dog this, he hadn't even wriggled while her brain had been short-circuiting—and she walked inside with as much dignity as she could muster.

She closed the door as if she was trying not to wake a household.

There was no household. Just Abby and Kleppy and one magnificent wedding dress.

"What will I do?" she whispered and she leaned back against the closed door. "Kleppy, help me out here."

Kleppy's butt wriggled until she set him on the floor. He headed into the bedroom while she stood motionless, trying not to think.

Kleppy headed straight back to her. Carrying her jewellery box.

He set it down at her feet and wriggled all over.

See? She had a guy who'd steal for her.

What more did a girl want?

* * *

Raff drove half a mile before he pulled over to the side of the road. He needed time to think.

He didn't have the head space to think.

Abby, Abby, Abby.

Ten years…

He'd been busy telling Abby she should move on. Could he?

He'd dated other women—of course he had. He'd set himself up with a life, of sorts. Living in this town. Keith, his partner, was getting long in the tooth. Keith was senior sergeant but, for all intents and purposes, Raff was in charge of the policing in this town. When Keith retired, Raff would be it.

Not bad for a Boy Who Meant Trouble.

He was still judged by some in this town, but only as someone whose background made people sniff, who'd been stupid in his youth. He was accepted as a decent cop. Sarah had friends, support groups, the farm she loved.

He had everything he needed in life, right there.

Except Abby.

How did you tell a woman you loved her?

He couldn't. To lay that on her… There was no way she could take it anywhere. They both knew that.

This thing between them…

He shouldn't have kissed her. It reminded him that it was more than a kid's dreaming. It was as real today as it had been the first time he'd kissed her. Life had been ahead of them, exciting, wonderful. Anything had been possible.

But to love Abby now…

She'd closed herself off. After Ben's death she'd simply shut down, retired into her parents' world, into Philip's world, and she'd never emerged. She was junior partner in Banksia Bay's legal firm. She was Philip's fiancée. Next Saturday she'd be Philip's wife.

The waste…

Do you want to marry her yourself?

The thought was enough to make him smile, only it wasn't a happy smile. He'd faced facts years ago. Even if she could shake off the past, to live with her parents' condemnation, with the knowledge that every time she looked at him she was seeing Ben…

They'd destroy each other.

A couple of kids drove past—Lexy Netherland driving his dad's new Ford. He bet Old Man Netherland didn't know Lexy was out on the tear. He had Milly Parker in the passenger seat. They'd be going up the mountain, to the lookout. Only not to look out.

Kids, falling in love.

He could put the sirens on, pull 'em over, send 'em home with their tails between their legs.

No way could he do that. It wasn't long before they'd be adults. The world would catch up with them and they'd be accepting life as it had to be.

As he had.

Loving Abby. Then Ben's death. Then the other side, where the woman he loved could never find the courage to move on.

He knew she was having doubts—how could he kiss her and not sense it? Maybe if he pushed harder he could stop this marriage. But then what? What would he be doing to her?

He'd pushed her already to look seriously at the life

she was facing. There was nothing else he could do. For Ben. For himself.

He put his head on the steering wheel and thumped it. Hard. Three times.

The third time he hit the horn and the dogs in Muriel Blake's backyard started barking to wake the dead.

Time to move on, then?

Back to Sarah.

Back home.

Where to move forward in this town?

There was never a forward.

Chapter 9

How to sleep after a night like this? She did at last, but not until dawn. She woke and it was ten o'clock and she'd been meant to meet Philip for breakfast at the yacht club.

She phoned and he was fine.

"No problem. I have three newspapers and Don's here with his plans for the new supermarket. As long as it's safe and clean, I can do without my wallet until later. I've hardly realised you weren't here."

That was supposed to make her feel better?

She showered slowly, washed her hair, took a long time drying it.

Kleppy watched, looking anxious.

"I'm not going anywhere today where I can't take you," she told him. "It's the weekend."

He still looked anxious. He climbed onto her bed, and then onto the dressing table. Wriggled himself a spot next to her cedar box. His new favourite thing.

"I guess last night upset you," she told him, abandoning her hairdryer to give him a hug. "I'm so sorry about Isaac. It's horrid loving someone and losing them."

Like she had.

Like Raff had.

It was Raff's fault.

But that mantra, said over and over in her head for ten years, sounded hollow and sad and bleak as death—a sentence stretched into the future as far as the horizon.

Could she put it away? Find the Raff she'd once loved?

Whoa. What was she thinking?

"It's wedding nerves," she told Kleppy and on impulse she carried him into her spare room where her wedding gown hung in all its glory.

Two years of love had gone into making this dress.

She set Kleppy down. The little dog nosed his way around the hem, ducked under the full-circle skirt, poked his nose out again and headed back to her. She smiled and held him and stared at her dress some more.

She'd loved making this dress. Loved, loved, loved.

Once upon a time, this was what she was going to do. Sew for a living. Make beautiful things. Make people happy.

Now she was employed getting a low life off the hook. She was going to be Philip's wife.

But to draw back now...

The morning stretched on. She sat on the floor of her second bedroom and thought and thought and thought.

Her mother rang close to midday. "You ready, darling?"

"Ready?"

"Sweetheart, don't joke," her mother said sharply. "This is your afternoon, like Thursday night was Philip's night. Philip's mother and I will be by to collect you in half an hour. Don't wear any of your silly dresses now, will you, dear. You know I hate them."

Her silly dresses.

She meant the ones she'd made herself. The ones that weren't grey or black or cream.

This was a wedding celebration. Why not wear something silly? Polka dots. Her gorgeous swing skirt with Elvis prints all over?

"I'll drive myself," she told her mother. "I'll meet you at the golf club."

"You won't be late?"

"When am I ever? Oh, and Mum?"

"What?"

"I'm bringing my dog."

There was a moment's grim silence. Her mother would know what she was talking about. The whole town would know. She'd expected her mother to have vented her disapproval by now.

"Hasn't Philip talked some sense into you about that yet?"

"About that?"

"Abrahams' dog. Of all the stupid…"

"I'm keeping him."

"Well." Her mother's breath hissed in and Abby waited for the eruption. But then suddenly Abby could hear her smile. There was even a tinkling laugh. "That's okay," she said and Abby realised she was on speaker phone, and her mother was also talking to her father. "Philip will cope with this." Then, back to her… "They don't let dogs in the club house."

"They do on the terrace as long as I keep him leashed. It's a gorgeous day. I'm bringing him."

"This is between you and Philip, not you and us," her

mother said serenely. "Philip will talk you into sense, and we can cope with a dog for one afternoon. But don't be late. Isn't this exciting? So many plans, finally come together."

She disconnected.

So many plans, finally come together.

Abby stood and stared at the phone. How could she do the unthinkable?

How could she not?

"I'm ready."

Sarah looked beautiful. Hippy beautiful. There was a shop behind the main street catering for little girls who wanted to be fairies or butterflies and adults who wanted to be colourful. It suited Sarah exactly.

The woman who ran it thought Sarah was lovely. She rang Raff whenever a new consignment arrived and he'd wave goodbye to half his weekly salary. It was worth it. Sarah's joy in her pretty dresses and scarves and her psychedelic boots made up...well, made up in some measure for the rest.

She'd woken with another of her appalling headaches. It had finally eased but she was still looking wan, despite her smile. Pretty clothes were the least he could give her.

"Can you drive me to the golf club now? I don't want to be late," she said, anxious. She'd been looking forward to this week for months. Abby's pre-wedding parties. Abby's wedding itself.

"My car is at your disposal," he said and pulled on his policeman's cap, tipping it like a chauffeur. She smiled.

"Tell me again why you're not coming."

At least that was easy. "It's girls only. I'd look a bit silly in a skirt."

Sarah giggled, but her smile was fleeting. "If it wasn't only girls, would you want to come?"

Sometimes she did this, shooting him serious, insightful questions, right when he didn't need them.

"Abby's mother doesn't like me," he said, deciding to be honest. "It makes things uncomfortable."

"Because of the accident?"

"Yes."

"Oh, Raff," she said and walked over and hugged him. "It's not fair."

"There's not a lot we can do about it, Sares," he told her and kissed her and put her away from him. "Except be happy ourselves. Which we are. How can we help but be happy when you're wearing a bright pink and yellow and purple and blue skirt—and your purple boots have tassels?"

"Do you like them?" she said, giggling and twirling.

"I love them."

He was making Sarah happy, he thought as they headed to the golf club to Abby's pre-wedding party. At least he could do that.

No one else?

No one else.

Philip was sailing. He'd gone out with his supermarket-planning mates. Even now he was cruising round Banksia Bay, discussing the pros and cons of investment opportunities.

How did you tell a guy you'd made the biggest mistake of your life when he was out at sea?

How did you go calmly to your pre-wedding party when you'd made a decision like this?

How did you call it off—when you hadn't told your fiancé first?

All those wedding gifts, coming her way. She'd be expected to unwrap them. Aargh.

But by now the gifts would already be in cars heading towards the golf club. It didn't make any difference if she said, *Don't give them to me today,* or if on Monday she re-wrapped them and sent them all back.

That'd be her penance. Sending gifts back.

That and a whole lot else.

She drove towards the golf club slowly. Very slowly. Kleppy lay beside her and even he seemed subdued. She turned into the car park. She sat and stared out through the windscreen, seeing nothing.

Someone tapped on her window. She raised her head and dredged up a smile. Sarah was peering in at her, looking worried.

"What's wrong? You look sad. Do you have another headache? Oh, Abby, and on your party day."

Raff was right behind his sister. In civvies. Faded jeans and black T-shirt, stretched a bit too tight.

"No, I… I just didn't want to be the first to arrive." She climbed from the car and sent Raff what she hoped was a bright smile, a smile that said she knew exactly what she was doing.

"Collywobbles?" he asked and it was just what she needed. It was the sort of word that made a woman gird her loins and stiffen her spine and send him a look that was pure defiance.

"Why on earth would I have collywobbles?"

"I'd have collywobbles if I was marrying Philip."

"Go jump."

"Philip's really handsome," Sarah said. "Almost as handsome as Lionel."

"Lionel?" They said it in unison, distracted. They looked at each other. Looked back at Sarah.

"Lionel's cute," Sarah said. "So's your dress, Abby. I love the Elvises."

"So do I," Abby said, thinking she had one vote at least. She loved this dress—a tiny bustier, a full-circle skirt covered with Elvises—black and white print with crimson tulle underneath to make it flare. It was a party dress. A celebration dress.

What was she celebrating?

"And you've made Kleppy a matching bow." Sarah scooped up the little dog and hugged him. "He's adorable. He's even more adorable than Lionel."

"Who's Lionel?" Abby asked.

"Kleppy's friend," Sarah said simply. "Ooh, there's Margy." Abby's next door neighbour was pulling up on the far side of the car park, a dumpy little woman whose looks belied the fact that she ran the most efficient disability services organisation in the State. "Hi, Margy. Can I sit next to you?" And she dived off, carrying Kleppy, leaving Abby and Raff together.

"Lionel?" she said, because that seemed the safest way to go.

"There's Lionel who was Isaac's gardener," Raff said, frowning. "I didn't realise he and Sarah knew each other, but Sarah gets around more than I think. Okay, have a great hen's party. I'll pick Sarah up at four."

"Raff?"

"Yes?" He sounded testy.

She'd said his name. She needed to add something on the back of it. Something sensible.

But how to say what she needed to say? How to think about saying what she needed to say? How to get over the impossibility of even thinking about thinking about…?

Maybe she should stop thinking. Her head was about to fall off.

People were arriving all around them. Her friends. Her mother's friends. Every woman in this little community who'd come into contact with her over the years seemed to be getting out of cars, carrying gifts into the golf club.

How many women had her mother invited?

How many gifts would she need to return?

"Abigail?" That was her mother calling. She was standing on the terrace, shielding her eyes from the sun, trying to see who her daughter was talking to. "Your guests are here. You should be receiving them."

"There you go," Raff said and eased himself back into his car. "By the way, I'm with Sarah. That's a cute dress. Really cute. You should try wearing that in court some time."

"Raff?" She didn't want him to go. She didn't want…

"See you later," he said.

He drove away. She stood there in her Elvis dress, staring after him like a dummy.

"Abigail." Her mother's voice was sharp. "What are you thinking? You're being discourteous to our guests. And what on earth are you wearing?"

A cute dress, she thought, as she headed up to her mother, to her waiting guests.

Abigail, what are you thinking?

What was he thinking?

Nothing. He'd better not think anything because if

he did there was a chasm yawning and it was so big he couldn't see the bottom.

He needed some work. He needed a few kids to do something stupid so he could lay down the law, vent a bit of spleen, feel in control.

Abby in an Elvis dress.

Abby, who was marrying Philip.

Any minute now the steering wheel was going to break.

"Raff?" His radio crackled into life and he grabbed it as if it were a lifeline.

It was Keith. "Yeah?"

"There's a bit of trouble down on the wharf. Couple of kids chucking craypots into the water, and Joe Paxton's threatening to do "em damage. I'm stuck up on the ridge "cos John Anderson's locked himself out. Can you deal?"

"Absolutely," Raff said, feeling a whole heap better.

Trouble, he could deal with.

Just not how he was feeling about Abby.

The afternoon was interminable. She smiled and smiled, and thought she should have run. What was she thinking, letting this afternoon go ahead? Just because she needed to tell Philip first.

"You'll make such a lovely couple. A credit to the town." That was Mrs Alderson, one of her mother's bridge partners. "We're so looking forward to next Saturday."

"Thank you," she said and then realised that Mrs Alderson was carrying a rather long shoulder bag and something had peeped from the edge and Kleppy had just...just...

He was heading under the table, to the full length of his lead, looking satisfied.

She stooped to retrieve it. It was a romance novel, a brand she recognised. A really... Goodness, what was that on the front? She snatched it from her dog and handed it back, apologising.

Margot Alderson turned beet-red and stuffed it back into her bag.

"I don't know what you're doing with that dog," she snapped. "He's trouble. If you must get yourself a dog, get a nice one. I have a friend who breeds pekes."

Kleppy looked up at her from under the table and wagged his tail. He'd done what he wanted. He'd had his snatch and he'd given it to his mistress.

"I kinda like Kleppy," Abby said. "And you know... I don't even mind a bit of trouble."

Her mother's friend departed, still indignant. Abby stared after her, thinking—of all things—about the cover of the romance novel. The cover showed a truly fabulous hero, bare from the waist up.

I don't mind pecs, either, she added silently. *Or a bit of hot romance.*

He had two kids in the cells waiting for their parents to come and collect them. "Take your time," he'd told them. "It'll do 'em good to sweat.

Which meant he was stuck at the station, babysitting two drunken adolescents. Forced to do nothing but think.

Abby.

A man could go quietly nuts.

It wasn't fair to interfere more than he already had.

He wasn't feeling fair.

"If I was a Neanderthal I'd go find me a club and a cave," he muttered.

He wasn't. He was Banksia Bay's cop and Abby was a modern non-Neanderthal woman who knew her own mind. He had to respect it.

"I miss the old days," he said morosely. "It'd be so much easier to go set up a cave."

It was over. The last gift was in her father's van, being taken home to their spare room, Abby's old bedroom, pink, pretty.

"I wish you'd come home for your last week," her mother said, hugging her. "It's where you belong."

Abby said no, as she always said no. They left, leaving Abby sitting on the terrace with Kleppy.

Philip was coming by to meet her. She had to tell him.

Her mother's words… *It's where you belong.*

Where did she belong?

She didn't know.

"What do you mean you don't want to get married?"

To say Philip was gobsmacked would be an understatement. He was staring at her as if she'd lost her mind.

Maybe she had.

"I can't," she muttered, miserable. She'd tried to get him to go for a walk with her, to get away from the people in the bar. He wouldn't. They were out on the terrace but they were still in full view.

Philip was tired from sailing. He didn't want a walk. He wanted to go home, have a shower, take a nap, then take his fiancée out to Banksia Bay's newest restaurant. That was what he'd planned.

He hadn't planned on Abby being difficult.

He hadn't planned on a broken engagement.

"It's just… Kleppy," she said in a small voice and Philip stared at her as if she were demented.

"The dog."

"He's made me…"

"What?"

What, indeed? She hardly understood it herself. How one dog could wake her from a ten-year fog. "You don't like him," she said.

"Of course I don't like him," Philip snapped. "He's a mutt. But I'm prepared to put up with him."

"I don't want you to put up with him." She took a deep breath. Tried to say what she scarcely understood herself. The thing in the middle of the fog. "I don't want you to put up with me."

"What are you saying?"

"You don't like me, Philip."

He looked at her as if she'd lost her mind. "Of course I like you. I love you. Haven't I shown you that, over and over? This is craziness. Pre-wedding nerves. To say…"

"You don't like this dress, do you?"

He stared down at the Elvises and he couldn't quite repress a wince. "No, but…"

"And you painted your living room…our living room when I move in…beige. I don't like beige."

"Then we'll paint it something else. I can cope."

"See, that's exactly what I mean. You'll put up with something else. Like you put up with me."

"This is nonsense."

They were sitting at the table right on the edge of the terrace, with a view running all the way down the valley to the coast below. It was the most beautiful view in the world. If anyone looked out from the bar right now they'd see a man and a woman having a tête à tête, she flashing a diamond almost as wide as her finger, he taking her hand in his. Visibly calming down.

"Mum said this was bound to happen," Philip said. "She felt like this when she married my father. A week before the wedding. Pre-wedding jitters."

Philip's mother. A mouse, totally dominated by Philip's father—and by Philip himself.

She'd seen Philip's mother looking at her dress today. Not brave enough to say she liked it. But just…looking.

"I don't want to be beige," she whispered.

"You won't be beige. You'll be very happy. There's nothing you want that I can't give you."

"I want you to like my dog." She felt as if she was backed into a corner, trying to find reasons for the unreasonable. Trying to explain the unexplainable.

"I'll try and like your dog."

"But why?" she said. "There are women out there who like beige. There are women out there who don't like mutts. Why do you want to marry me?"

"I was always going to marry you."

"That's just it," she said and it was practically a wail. "We've just drifted into this."

"We did not drift. I made a decision ten years ago…"

"You wanted to marry me ten years ago?"

"Of course I did." He sighed, exasperated. "It's okay. I understand. One week of pre-wedding nerves isn't going to mess with ten years of plans."

"Philip, I don't want to," she said and, before she could think about being sensible, she hauled the diamond from her finger and laid it on the table in front of him. "I can't. I know… I know it's sensible to marry you. You're a good man. I know you've been unfailingly good to me.

I know you'll even put up with my dog and paint your living room sunbeam-yellow if I really want. But, you know what? I want someone who likes sunbeam-yellow."

"What the…? Is there someone else?"

Someone else. At the thought of who that someone else was…at the sheer impossibility of saying his name, voicing the thought, her courage failed her. Her courage to say *Raff*.

But not her courage to do what she must, right now.

"I can't," she said quietly. "No matter what. This isn't about someone else, Philip. It's about what I'm feeling. Finding Kleppy… Yeah, it's crazy, but he makes me laugh. He's a little bit nuts and I love it. I wish you loved it. You don't, and it's made me see that I don't want to be Mrs Philip Dexter. You've been wonderful to me, Philip. You deserve a woman who thinks you're wonderful in return. You deserve a woman who'll love the life you want to live instead of putting up with it, and you deserve a woman who you'll think is wonderful instead of putting up with her."

"Abby…" He was truly shocked now, ashen, and she felt dreadful. Appalling.

She had to do this.

She pushed the diamond closer to him, so close it nearly fell off the edge of the table.

Philip was a sensible man. This diamond was worth a fortune. He didn't let it fall. He took it, looked down at it for a long moment and then carefully zipped it into the pocket of his sailing anorak.

He rose.

"I'm damp in these clothes," he said, pale and angry. "I need to get changed. And you… You need to think about what you're throwing away. You're being foolish beyond belief. Insulting, even. I know it's pre-wedding nerves and I'll make allowances. Think about it overnight. I'll come and see you in the morning when you've had time to reconsider."

"I won't reconsider."

"You have twenty-four hours to see sense," he snapped. "After all I've done for you... I can't believe you'd be so ungrateful. To walk away from me... Of all the crazy... Why don't you just get on a slow boat to China and be done with it?"

A slow boat to China? Right now, the concept had enormous merit, but she wasn't going anywhere.

She couldn't move. She sat and stared sightlessly over the golf course and she thought...nothing.

Someone came and cleared her glass. Asked if she'd like another drink. Asked if she and Philip were going to China for their honeymoon.

Finally let her be.

They'd be muttering in the bar. Wondering what she was doing, just sitting.

Expecting Philip to come back?

Maybe they'd seen his anger, his tight lips, his rigid stance as he'd stalked to his car.

Maybe the town already knew.

She wouldn't tell anyone. She couldn't. Philip had given her twenty-four hours to come to her senses. She owed it to him to wait, to make him see it was a measured, sensible decision.

Is there someone else?

She thought of Philip's demand. Was there?

Raff had kissed her. Twice. He'd made her feel...

She couldn't afford to acknowledge how he made her feel.

"Klep!" The call jolted her out of her misery, an unfamiliar voice filled with joy. It was one of the golf course groundsmen, striding up from the first tee. She looked closer and recognised him.

Lionel. Isaac's gardener. A big, burly man in his mid-thirties. Slow and sleepy and quiet.

He reached her and knelt on the terrace and Kleppy was licking his face with joy. "Klep!"

"Lionel," she said, hauling herself out of her introspection. "What are you doing here?"

"Working," he said, briefly extricating himself from Kleppy's licking. "Gotta job mowing. Not as good as Mr Abrahams'. S'okay."

"You and Kleppy are friends?"

"Yeah."

Oh, help. She looked at the two of them and thought… and thought…

Thought they were greeting each other with a joy born of love.

"Did you want him?" It nearly killed her to say it. To lose Kleppy and Philip in the one afternoon…

She knew what would hurt most.

But… "Can't," Lionel said briefly. "I live in a rooming house now. I had to sell the house when Baxter pinched Mum's money. Lost the house, then lost me job when Mr Abrahams died. Someone said the Finns had Klep. Went up there to see and Sarah said he were yours. Sarah said he were happy. You're looking after "im?"

"I…yes."

"He's a great dog, Klep," Lionel said. "Makes a man happy."

"I… He'll make me happy."

"Goodo," Lionel said. "That man… Dexter… They said you're getting married."

"I…"

"He's the lawyer." It wasn't a question.

"Yes."

"He don't like dogs," Lionel said. "He come up to Mr Abrahams' when he made a will. Kleppy jumped up and it were like he was touching dirt. You and he…" He stopped, the question unasked. *You and he…*

"We'll sort it out," Abby said. "I love Kleppy enough for both of us."

"That's good," Lionel said. "You've made me feel better. And you're a lucky woman. Kleppy's the best mate you could have." He gave Kleppy a farewell hug and went back to mowing.

Abby kept on staring at nothing.

Like he was touching dirt…

She'd done the right thing. She didn't need twenty-four hours. *She was a lucky woman?*

Maybe she was. She had Kleppy and she was… *free?*

Chapter 10

Abby told no one but it was all over town by morning.

Abigail Callahan and Philip Dexter had had a row. She'd flung his ring back in his face. He'd accused her of having an affair. She'd accused him of having an affair. The wedding would cost squillions to cancel. Abby was threatening to go to China.

Abby was threatening to take the dog to China.

Why, oh, why, did she live in a small town?

The phone rang at seven-thirty and it was her mother. Hysterical.

"Sam Bolte said he saw you at the golf club and you weren't wearing your ring. I've just had a call from Ingrid. Ingrid says Sam says Philip was rigid with anger, and he said it's all about that stupid dog. Are you out of your mind?"

She laid back on the pillows and listened to her mother's hysteria and thought about it.

Was she out of her mind?

Kleppy was asleep on her feet.

She could sleep with Kleppy for ever. If she didn't do something about Raff.

She couldn't do something about Raff. There was nothing to do.

"It's okay, Mum, I'll sort it," she said.

"Sort it? Tell Philip it's all a ghastly mistake? You know, if it means the difference between whether you marry or not, your father and I will even keep the creature."

The creature nuzzled her left foot and she scratched his ear with her toe.

"That's really generous, but…"

"You can't cancel the wedding. It'll cost…"

"No, it won't." This, at least, she could do. She'd figured it out, looked at the contract with the golf club, had it nailed. "I lose my deposit, which is tiny. None of the food's been ordered. Nothing's final. I can do this."

"You're never serious?"

"Mum, I don't want to marry Philip."

There was a long, long silence. Then… "Why not?" It was practically a wail.

"Because I don't want to be sensible. I like being a dog owner. I like that my dog's a thief." She thought about it and decided, why not go for broke; her mother could hardly be any more upset than she was now. "I might as well tell you… I don't think I want to be a lawyer, either."

"You've lost your mind," her mother moaned. "John, come and tell your daughter she's lost her mind. Darling, we'll take you to the doctor. Dr Paterson's known you since you were little. He can give you something."

"I'm not sure he can give me what I want."

"What do you want?"

"My dog, for now," she said, shoving another thought firmly away. "My independence. My life."

"Abigail…"

"I'm hanging up now, Mum," she said. "I love you very much, but I'm not marrying Philip and I'm not mad. Or I don't think I'm mad. I'm not actually sure who I am any more, but I think I need to find out, and I can't do that as Mrs Philip Dexter."

"Rumour is she's thrown him over. Rumour is she met some guy at that conference she went to in Sydney last month. Chinese. Millionaire. Loaded. Couple of kids by a past marriage but that's not worrying her. Rumour is she wants to take the dog…"

Raff spent the morning feeling…

Surprised?

"Go away. I'm not home."

She was pretending not to be home. The first couple of times the doorbell rang Kleppy barked, which might be a giveaway, but she fixed that. She tucked him firmly under the duvet, and she put her jewellery box down there with him. Which reminded her…

Should she give the box back to Philip's grandfather? He'd given it to her as a labour of love, on the premise she was marrying his grandson.

Maybe he was one of those out there ringing her doorbell, sent by her mother to tell her to be sensible.

It couldn't matter. Go away, go away, go away.

How long could she stay under the duvet? She started working out how much food she had in the place; when she'd be forced to do a grocery run. She thought of the impossibility of facing shopping in Banksia Bay. Maybe she and Kleppy could leave town for a bit.

Where could she go?

Somewhere Raff could find her. If he wanted to find her.

Don't think of that. Don't think of Raff. Get this awfulness out of the way, and then look forward. Please…

The doorbell rang again.

Go away.

It rang again, more insistent, and it was followed by a knock, too loud to be her mother. Philip?

Go away!

"Abigail Callahan?" The voice was stern with authority and it made her jump.

Raff.

Raff was right outside her front door.

Panic.

What did he think he was doing, hiking up to her front door as bold as brass? She peeked past the curtains and his patrol car was parked out front. With its lights flashing.

She practically moaned. This was all she needed. Who knew what the town was saying about her, but she did not need Raff in the mix. It was all too complicated.

Kleppy whined, sensing her confusion, and she hugged him and held her breath and willed Raff to go away.

But Raff Finn wasn't a man to calmly turn away.

"Abigail Callahan, I know you're in there. Answer the door, please, or I'll be forced to come back with a warrant."

A warrant? What the…?

"Go away." She yelled it to the front door and there

was a moment's silence. And then a response, deep and serious, and only someone who knew him well could hear the laughter behind it.

"Miss Callahan, I'm here to inform you that your dog is suspected of petty larceny. I have information that stolen property may be being stored on your premises. Open the door now, please, or I'll be forced to take further action."

Her dog…

Petty larceny…

She lifted the duvet and stared at Kleppy. Who gazed back, innocent as you please. What the…? He hadn't been out. How could he have stolen anything?

She'd given back her mother's friend's romance novel. Kleppy was clean.

"He hasn't done anything," she yelled, and then had to try again because the first yell came out more like a squeak. "Go find some other dog to pin it to. Kleppy's innocent."

"There speaks a defence lawyer. Sorry, ma'am, but the evidence points to Kleppy."

"What evidence?"

"Mrs Fryer's diamanté glasses case, given to her by her late husband. It's said to be worth a fortune, plus it has sentimental value. It's alleged it was stolen from her bag, which was parked underneath the table you were sitting at yesterday. I have reason to believe your dog was tied under that very table. Circumstantial, I'll grant you, but evidence enough for a warrant."

Uh-oh.

She thought about it. Kleppy lying innocently at her feet through yesterday's lunch. A big table, twelve or so women. Twelve or so handbags at their respective owners' feet.

Uh-oh, uh-oh, uh-oh.

"I have more serious things to think about this morning than glasses cases," she managed and she heard the laughter intensify.

"You're saying there's something more serious than grand theft?"

"I thought it was petty larceny."

"That depends whether the diamantés are real. Mrs Fryer swears they are. I knew old Jack Fryer and I'm thinking otherwise but I need to give the lady the benefit of the doubt."

"He hasn't got them," she wailed. "He'd have given them to me by now."

"I need to search."

"Go away."

"Let me in, Abigail," he said, stern again. "The neighbours are looking."

Oh, for heaven's sake. Raff walking in here... If anyone in this town got even the vaguest sniff of what she was feeling...of why she'd been jerked out of her miserable life into something resembling a future...

Her future.

The word somehow steadied her. She wasn't marrying Philip. She had a future. Okay, maybe she needed to step into it rather than hiding under the duvet.

She climbed out of bed and shrugged on her brand new honeymoon wrap. Where was her shabby pink chenille? She'd got rid of it. Of course she had. That was what a girl did when she was getting married.

So now she was stuck with pure silk. Pure silk and Raff. She shoved her toes into elegant white slippers, pasted a glower on her face and stomped through to the front door. Hauled it open.

Raff was there in his cop uniform. He looked…he looked…

Maybe how *he* looked wasn't the issue. "Whoa," he said, his gaze raking her from the toes up, and she felt herself start to burn. She'd had fun buying herself wedding lingerie. She'd never owned silk before. It was making her body feel…

Well, something was making her body feel—as if it had been a really bad idea to give all her shabby stuff to the welfare store. The way Raff was looking…

Stop it. She practically stamped her foot. Raff was a cop. He was here to search the place. What she was thinking?

She knew what she was thinking, and she'd better stop thinking it right now. Instead, she concentrated on keeping her glower at high beam and stood aside as he came in.

"I don't want you here." What a lie.

"Needs must. You say you don't have a glasses case, ma'am?"

"If you say *ma'am* once more I may be up for copicide."

"Copicide?"

"Whatever. Justifiable homicide. Kleppy didn't pinch anything."

"Are you sure?"

She winced at that. "Um… No."

He grinned. "Not such a good defence lawyer, then. So what's with the millionaire?"

"The millionaire?"

"The guy you've thrown Philip over for."

The millionaire. If he only knew. "I hate this town," she muttered, and she didn't need to try and glower.

"So it's all a lie."

"What's a lie?"

"That you've tossed Philip aside and found another."

"Yes. No. I mean…"

He caught her hand and held it up for them both to see. She'd been wearing Philip's ring for two years now. A stark white band showed where the ring had been.

"Proof?" Raff said softly.

"If I ran off with someone else I wouldn't be here now," she snapped. "And if he was a millionaire I'd have a rock to match."

"But you've given Philip the flick."

"Philip and I are taking time to reassess our positions."

He surveyed her thoughtfully, once more taking in the silk. "That's lawyer speak for a ripper of a fight and no one's speaking. Does this mean Sarah and I get our pasta maker back?"

That was a punch below the belt. But still… The pasta maker and Philip, or no pasta maker and no Philip.

No choice.

How had she changed so much? This time last week she'd been the perfect bride. Now, here she was, standing in the hall with her criminal dog behind her, with Raff right here. Right in her hall. Big, sexy, smiling.

Raff.

"I'll check my bag," she muttered but he put her aside quite gently.

"No, ma'am. I'll check your bag. I don't want evidence tampered with."

"You're thinking of taking paw prints?"

He chuckled, a lovely rich sound that filled the hall;

that made her feel…like there might be something on the far side of this awfulness.

Her bag was by the front door where she'd tossed it when she'd come in yesterday. Big, bright, covered with Elvises. She'd made it as a picnic bag, thinking wistfully her Elvis dress would look cute on picnics. As if Mrs Philip Dexter would ever go on picnics.

Now the bag was stuffed with legally gathered loot—all the small gifts she'd been given yesterday. These were the gifts she'd have to sort and send back, with a note saying very sorry, she wasn't marrying Philip.

She'd have to reword that. She wasn't sorry at all. Especially now Raff was here.

He squatted beside the bag and started laying gifts out on the floor.

"Candle holders—very tasteful. Place mats—a girl can't have too many place mats. What's with the Scent-O-Pine Air Freshener? Oh, that's from Mrs Fryer. She really doesn't like your Kleppy. Hey, His and Her key rings—very useful. Oh, and what's this?"

This was a glasses case. Exceedingly tasteful. Pink and purple, studded with huge diamantés.

"Worth a billion," Raff said appreciatively. "Every diamond over a carat, but not a one out of place. Lovely soft mouth, our villain."

The villain had come to investigate, pushing his way through the crack in the bedroom door, nosing his way to the crime scene. Checking out the glasses case. Putting his paw on it, then looking back to Abby and wagging his tail.

"Don't say a thing, Klep," Abby said. "No admissions."

"His DNA's all over it."

"He put it on just now. He's as horrified as I am. And

you…you've let the suspect himself contaminate the crime scene. I'm appalled."

He grinned and rubbed Kleppy under the ear and Kleppy wriggled his tail, lifted the glasses case delicately from his hand and headed back into the bedroom. Straight under the duvet with the rest of his loot.

Raff looked through to the bedroom, thoughtful. "Maybe I should search in there, too."

"Don't you dare," she said, suddenly panicking, and he straightened and his smile faded.

"I won't. You okay?"

"I'll live."

"You have a hard few days ahead. I hope your millionaire's going to take care of you."

"Raff…"

"Mmm?" He was watching her. Just…watching. The laughter had gone now. He was intense and caring and big and male and… and…

"I think I can put Ben behind me," she said and his face stilled.

"Sorry?"

"I…"

How to say the unsayable? How to get it out? She'd never intended… In a few months, maybe, when the dust had settled… But now? Here?

"I think I might love you," she whispered and the thought was out there—huge, filling the house with its danger.

Danger? That was what it felt like, she thought. A sword, hanging over her head, threatening to fall.

Falling in love with the bad boy.

"I know…this is dumb." She was stammering, stupid with confusion. "It's not the time to say it. I shouldn't…

I mean, I don't know whether you want it. I'm not sure even that I want it, but I fell in love with you twenty years ago, Raff Finn, and I can't stop. This week…it's jolted me out of everything. It's made me see… Your craziness broke my heart but it hasn't changed anything. I can't… I can't stop loving you. If I can forgive what happened with Ben, is there a chance for us?"

"For us?" His face was emotionless. Still. Wary?

"Once upon a time we were boyfriend and girlfriend." She hadn't got this right. She knew it but she didn't know how to get it right. "I was hoping…"

"We might get together again?"

"Yes."

"Now you've forgiven me."

"I…yes. But…"

"There's no chance at all," he said and suddenly there was no trace of laughter, no trace of gentleness, nothing at all. His voice was rough and cold and harsh. He looked stunned—and, unbelievably, he looked as if she'd just struck him. "*If I can forgive what happened to Ben…* What sort of statement is that?"

"It's what I need to do."

"What do you mean?" he demanded.

"If I'm to love you. I need to forgive you if I'm to love you. All I'm saying is that I can. All I'm saying is that I think I have."

Silence. Silence, silence and more silence.

She couldn't bear it. She wanted to dive back under the duvet and hide. Hide from the look on Raff's face.

But there was no escaping that look. There was such pain…

"There's no such thing as forgiveness for Ben," he said at last, and the harshness was gone. It had been replaced with an emptiness that was even more dreadful. "If you have to say it… It's still there."

"Of course it's still there."

"Of course," he repeated. "How can it not? And it always will be." He took a deep breath. Another.

The silence was killing her.

She had this wrong. She didn't know how. She didn't know what she could do to repair it.

Would it ever be possible to repair it?

"Abby, ten years ago, I was crazily, criminally stupid," he said at last, speaking slowly, emphasising each word as if it were being dragged out of him. "I can't think about it without hating myself. But you know what? I've moved on."

"You've…"

"If I hadn't, then I'd go insane," he said. "How do you think I felt? My best friend dead, my sister irreparably injured, and me with no memory of it at all. I was gutted by Ben's death—I still am. To lose such a friend… To inflict such pain on everyone who loved him… And more, every time I look at Sarah I know what I've done. But after ten years…"

Another deep breath. Another silence.

"After ten years, I have it in perspective," he said. "I've seen a lot of stupid kids. A lot of appalling accidents. There's always a driver; it's always someone's fault. But in those situations, you know what? There are other things, too. Kids egging other kids on. Being dumb themselves. That night Ben wasn't wearing a seat belt. We had "em fitted—my gran insisted on it. Sarah wasn't wearing a seat belt, either—she was wearing a cute new dress she knew would crush. None of us should have been up there on that track in the rain. It was totally dumb. Yes, I was driving. Yes, I must have veered to the wrong side of the road and Philip says I was speeding. I've taken that on board. I've convicted myself and I've received my sentence. I've lost Ben as you've lost Ben. I've lost parts of Sarah, and my actions hurt so many, had so many repercussions, they can never be repaired. That's what I live with, Abby, every day of my life, and I'm not adding to it."

"I don't... I don't know what you mean."

"If we took this further... Waking up every morning beside a woman who says she forgives me? What sort of sentence it that? This week...okay, I've kissed you and yes, I've wanted you. I've given you a hard time about marrying Philip. And you know what? Last night, when the whispers went round that you'd given back his ring, for one breathtaking moment I thought maybe we could figure out some sort of future. But now... You forgive me? Graciously? Lovingly? Thanks, but no thanks. I can't live with that, Abby. You do what you need to do, but don't factor me in. Fetch Mrs Fryer's glasses case, please. I need to go."

"Raff..."

"Don't push this any further," he snapped. "Figure it out for yourself. It's your life. I've done what I need to survive and forgiveness doesn't come into it. Acceptance...that's a much harder call."

She stared up at him, confused. Shattered. Knowing, though...knowing in the back of her mind that he was right.

She forgave him?

Where was a future in that?

Raff returned the glasses case to Mrs Fryer, who took it with suspicion and examined it from all angles for damage. She glared at him and he thought that if it had been his dog that had taken the case, he'd be up on charges by now. Even though the case was worth zip.

Diamonds? He'd seen a diamond that big and he knew what a real one looked like. That diamond was sitting in Philip's security safe by now, he thought. That it wasn't sitting on Abby's finger...

He couldn't afford to go there.

"Did you see her?" Mrs Fryer hissed.

"See who, ma'am?"

"Abigail."

"I did. She's extremely apologetic. I believe she may come round later and apologise in person."

"Was there anyone with her?"

"Her dog," Raff said neutrally and Mrs Fryer sighed in exasperation.

"No, dummy. I mean a man. Is there anyone else?"

"I believe the crime was the dog's own work," Raff said, and turned and left before Mrs Fryer could slap him.

Anyone else...

No. Only him. She'd tossed Philip's ring back at him because she loved...*him?*

I think I might love you.

The words echoed over and over in his head. Where did a man go with that?

Without thinking, he found himself driving past his little farm, further up the mountain, up near Isaac's place, to the road where one night ten years ago his world had been blasted to bits.

How long did a man suffer for one moment's stupidity?

He'd stopped suffering. Almost. He'd almost found peace. Until Abby had said...

I think I might love you.

He couldn't afford to let her words rip him apart. He had his life to get on with and she had hers.

It might be a good idea if she did go to China.

Chapter 11

On Sunday afternoon Abby decided that she did need to speak to Philip. It was only fair. What followed was a very stilted phone call. Philip sounded appalled and angry and confused. She crept back under her duvet and hugged Kleppy and decided she didn't need milk or bread; she could live on baked beans for a while.

The whole town was judging her.

On Monday she decided she couldn't hide under her duvet for ever. She had to pull herself together. She was not a whimpering mess. She was not hiding a millionaire under her bed. She needed to get on with her life.

That meant getting out of bed, dressing as she always dressed, smart and corporate for the last time. Today she'd wind up this court case with Philip and then she'd resign. She'd talk reasonably to her parents. She'd start sending gifts back and then figure, slowly and sensibly, where she wanted to take her life from here.

She did need to be sensible. She no longer wanted to be a lawyer, but that didn't mean stranding Philip or stranding her clients without reasonable notice. That was the sort of thing an hysterical ex-bride would do—the sort of woman who'd throw Philip over for some crazy, unreasonable love.

She wasn't that woman. She'd ended an unsuitable engagement for totally sensible reasons and she was totally in control. She entered court with her head held high. She sat in court and concentrated on looking...normal.

She was aware that the courthouse held more people than it had on Friday. That'd be because people were looking at her. The woman who ditched Philip Dexter.

No matter. She was in control. Kleppy was safely locked up. She looked neat and respectable, and her court notes were beautifully filed in her lovely Italian briefcase in the order they were needed.

As the morning stretched on, she decided she hated her briefcase. She'd give it back to Philip, she thought. That was sensible. He might find a use for a matching pair.

Back home, her wedding dress was packed in tissue, waiting for someone to make another sensible decision.

What to do with two thousand beads?

Decisions, decisions, decisions.

She concentrated on taking notes for Philip, handing him the papers he needed, keeping on her sensible face—but it was really hard, and when Raff entered the courtroom she thought her face might crack. Quite soon.

Philip had called Raff back on a point of law. Just clarifying the prosecution case. Just decimating the case Raff had put together with such care.

Raff wasn't a lawyer and he had no help. The Crown

Prosecutor was hopeless. She wanted to cross the room and shake him, but Malcolm was eighty and he looked like if she shook him his teeth would fall out or he'd die of a coronary.

Wallace Baxter would get off. She could hear it in Philip's voice.

Philip might not have had a very good weekend—yes, his fiancée had jilted him—but there was nothing of the destroyed lover in his bearing. As the morning wore on he started sounding smug.

He was winning.

He sat down beside her after pulling the last of Raff's evidence apart and he gave her a conspiratorial smile.

He didn't mind, she thought incredulously. He didn't mind that she'd thrown back his ring—or not so much that it stopped him enjoying winning.

Her sensible face was slipping.

"This is brilliant," Wallace hissed beside her. "Philip's great. The stuff he's done to get me off… But what's this I hear about your engagement being off? You'd be a fool to walk away from a guy this great."

A guy this great. Wallace was beaming.

She felt sick.

She stared around to the back of the court where Bert and Gwen Mackervale looked close to tears. Because of Wallace Baxter's deception they'd had to sell their house. They were living in their daughter's spare bedroom.

She thought of Lionel, a lovely, gentle man who'd live in a rooming house for ever. Because of Wallace.

And because of Philip's skill in defending him.

She looked at Wallace and Philip and the smile between them was almost conspiratorial. The vague suspicions she'd been having about this case cemented into a tight knot of certainty. *The stuff he's done to get me off...*

She was lawyer for the defence. Sensible defence lawyers did not question their own cases.

She'd stopped being sensible on Saturday afternoon. Or she thought she had. Maybe there was more *sensible* she had to discard.

She looked at Wallace—a guy who'd systematically cheated for all his life. She looked at Philip, smug and sure.

She looked at Raff, who'd lost control of a car one dark night when he was nineteen years old.

Forgive?

"It's nailed," Philip said. "Let's see Finn get out of this."

Finn get out of this?

Wallace, surely.

But she looked at Philip and she knew he hadn't made a mistake. Morality didn't come into it. Raff was on the other side, therefore Raff had to be defeated.

How could she ever have thought she could marry Philip? How could her life have ended up here?

Her head was spinning. Define sensible? Sitting in a Banksia Bay courtroom defending Wallace Baxter?

Wallace and Philip...smug. Winning.

Wallace and Philip... *The stuff he's done to get me off...*

Her thoughts were racing, suspicions surfacing everywhere. She didn't know for sure, but in Philip's briefcase... The briefcase that matched hers...

What was she thinking?

Raff was leaving now, his evidence finished. She could see by the set of his shoulders that he knew exactly what would happen.

He'd done his best for the town—for a town that judged him.

Wallace was smiling. Philip was smiling. There were only a couple of minor defence witnesses to go and then summing up. Unless…unless…

She couldn't bear it.

Philip. Smiling. The model citizen.

Raff. Grim and stoic. The bad boy.

She was a mess of conflicting emotion. She was trying to get things clear but it was like wading into custard. All she knew was that she couldn't stay here a moment longer.

"Excuse me," she said to the men beside her. "I need to go."

"Where?" Philip said, astounded.

"To check on Kleppy. He gets into trouble alone."

"You can't walk out—to check on a dog."

"No," she said. "Not just to check a dog. Much, much more."

She rose and the eyes of the court were on her. Too bad. She wasn't sure what she was doing, but there was no way in the world she could sit here any longer.

"Bye," she said, to the courtroom in general.

"Don't be stupid," Philip snapped, and she looked at him for a long moment and then she shook her head.

"I won't. Not any more. Bye, Philip."

She lifted up the glossy Italian briefcase from under the desk, swiftly checking she had the right discreet initials, and she strode out of the court. Her pert black shoes clicked on the floor as she walked, and she didn't look back once.

Raff paused in the entrance, to take a few deep breaths, to think there was no one to punch.

He'd wanted to punch Dexter for maybe ten years.

He couldn't. Good cops didn't punch defence lawyers. Dexter was just doing his job.

Another deep breath.

"Raff."

He turned and Abby was closing the courtroom door. Leaning against it. Closing her eyes.

"Hey," he said and she opened her eyes and met his gaze. Full on.

"Hey." She sounded like someone just waking up.

"You taking a break?"

"I need to go home and check Kleppy."

"Fair enough." He hesitated. Thought about offering her a ride. Thought that might be a bad idea.

Her sports car was close, in the place marked *Abigail Callahan, Solicitor.* Her spot was closer than the one marked *Police.* It wasn't as close as Dexter's though. Dexter and the Judge had parking spaces side by side.

Dexter's Porsche was the most expensive car in the car park.

Get through the other side of anger, he told himself harshly. Was there another side?

Abby had passed him now, walking into the sunlight to her car. She raised her briefcase to lay it in the passenger seat.

Hesitated.

She lowered her briefcase. Fiddled with the catch.

Raised it again. Tipped.

Papers went everywhere, a sprawl of legal paperwork fluttering in the sunlight. And tapes. A score of tiny audio cassettes.

"Whoops," she said as tapes went flying.

The Abigail Callahan he'd known for the last ten years would never say *whoops*.

But she didn't look fussed. She didn't move. She didn't begin to pick anything up.

He didn't move either. He wasn't sure what was going on.

"You know, these should probably be picked up," she said. "They might be important."

Might they?

"I'm sorry to trouble you, but I seem to have taken the wrong briefcase," she said, sounding carefully neutral. "But I'm in such a hurry… Would you mind putting the stuff back in and returning it to Philip?"

What the…?

"There's no rush," she continued. "Philip has his notes on the desk so he won't miss these for a while. Maybe you could go back to the station to sort them into order before you give them back. I'm sure Philip would think that was a kindness."

She sighed then, looking at the mess of tapes and paperwork. "This is what comes of having matching briefcases," she said. "They're so easy to mix up. I told Philip it was a bad idea—I did want a blue one. But at least I do know this is Philip's—because of the tapes. Philip always records his client appointments. He's a stickler for recording…everything. He always has. My briefcase holds files for submission to court. Philip's files and tapes are always in much more detail."

They stood staring at each other in the sunlight. Abby…

"The tapes, Raff," she said gently, and she gave him a wide, impudent smile. It was a smile he hadn't seen for years. It made him feel… It made him feel…

As if Abby was back.

"You'll take care of them?" she asked.

"I...yes." What else was a man to say?

"Have fun, then," she said and she climbed into her car. "I'm sure you will."

He collected the tapes with speed—something told him it might be important to have them collected and be gone before Dexter realised the mix-up.

He thought about Abby.

He headed back to the station thinking about Abby.

Life was getting...interesting.

Have fun?

He should be thinking about tapes.

He was, but he was also thinking about Abby.

She went home, but only briefly. She changed into jeans, collected Kleppy and headed up the mountain.

She had some hard thinking to do, and it seemed the mountain was the place to do it. For a little bit she thought about Philip's briefcase but by the time she reached the mountain she'd forgotten all about Philip. She'd moved on.

She parked out the front of Isaac's place—the safest place to park. Kleppy whined against the fence and she cuddled him and thought...

Ben was here.

That was why she'd come. Ben had died up here, in the thick bushland on the mountain, a place that had magically been spared logging, where the gums were vast and the scenery was breathtaking. After all these years, suddenly it felt right that she was here with him. Her brother.

For the last ten years Ben had been lost, and she'd been empty.

With Kleppy carefully on the lead—who knew what he'd find here?—she walked along the side of the road where the crash had happened. The smells were driving Kleppy wild. He tugged to the place he'd been digging the night she and Raff had been here, but she pulled him away.

"No wombat holes," she told him. "Sorry, Klep, but this trip is about me."

She reached the foot of the crest. The road was incredibly narrow. The trees were huge—they were so close to the road.

Two cars colliding at speed… They'd never stood a chance.

She thought of that night. Of how they'd been before. Five kids. Fledgling love affairs. The things they'd all done.

Stupid kids, trying their wings. They'd been so sure they could fly. The only unknown was how far.

They'd been kids who thought they were invincible. One stupid night.

She sank onto the verge at the side of the road and hugged her dog. "Raff's right," she whispered, the emotions of the past two days kaleidoscoping and merging into one clear vision. "To forgive… That means he was wrong; the rest of us were right. That's how we've acted and that's what he's worn. He's accepted total blame."

How hard must that have been?

A truck was approaching, slowly, a rattler. It came over the crest and slowed and stopped.

Lionel. Climbing out. Looking worried. "Are you okay?" he asked.

Then he saw Kleppy and Kleppy saw him. It was

hard to say who was most delighted and it took a while before Lionel finally told her why he was here.

"I keep coming up hoping she's left the gate open," Lionel told her. "Mr Isaac's daughter. She's locked the place and I can't water the spuds. We were growing blue ones this year, just to see what they're like."

"It's a lovely garden."

"It was a lovely garden," he said, sad again, and he gave Kleppy a final hug and rose. "The gate's still shut?"

"Yes."

"I'd better slope off then," he said sadly. "Back to the golf course." He sighed and glanced towards the garden. "You gotta put stuff behind you. I'll be good at growing grass."

"You will, too."

"I might go out to see Sarah some time," he said diffidently. "You be out there, too?"

"I…probably not. I'm not sure."

"You're Sarah's friend?"

"I am."

"And the copper's friend? Raff?"

"I hope so."

"He's good," Lionel said. "When I wanted to keep Kleppy he came to see my landlady; told her how much I wanted him. Didn't make any difference but he tried. I reckon a man like that's a friend."

"He…he is."

"And I bet he's pleased Kleppy's found you," Lionel said, and he hugged Kleppy one last time and headed off back to his golf course.

She sat on the verge with her dog for a while longer. Letting her thoughts go where they willed.

She fiddled with the medal on Kleppy's collar. Thought about Lionel. Thought about Isaac.

Isaac Abrahams was a brave man, she thought. He'd been through so much—and he'd gone through more for his dog.

And Raff?

He'd faced condemnation from this community from the time he was a kid, and after Ben's death it had been overwhelming. He'd been based in Sydney at the Police Training College when the accident happened. All he'd needed to do to escape censure was move Sarah into a Sydney apartment and never come back.

He'd come back and faced condemnation because this was the place Sarah loved.

What you did for love...

She hugged her dog and looked at his collar and thought about what brave meant.

And what forgiveness was.

Tears were slipping down her cheeks now and she didn't care. These tears should have been cried out years ago, only she'd shut them out, shut herself down, turned into someone who couldn't face pain.

Turned into someone she didn't like.

Could Raff like her?

In time. Maybe. If she changed and waited for a while.

But then she thought about the expression on his face as she'd told him.

If I can forgive what happened with Ben...

How could she have said it? How could she be so hurtful?

Kleppy whined and squirmed and she hugged him tighter than he approved. She let him loose a little and he licked her from throat to chin. She chuckled.

"Oh, Kleppy, I love you."

Love.

The word hung out there, four letters, a concept huge in what it meant.

Love.

She whispered it again, trying it out for size. Thinking of all its implications.

Love.

"I love Raff," she told Kleppy, and Kleppy tried the tongue thing again.

"No." She set him down and rose, staring along the track where Ben had died. "I love you, Kleppy, but I love Raff more. Ben, I love Raff."

Was it stupid to talk to a brother who'd been dead for ten years? Who knew, and it was probably her imagination that a breeze rustled through the trees right then, a soft, embracing breeze that warmed her, that told her it was okay, that told her to follow her heart.

"Just as well," she told her big brother in a tone she hadn't used for ten years. "You always were bossy but you can't boss me out of this one. I love Rafferty Finn. I love Banksia Bay's bad boy, and there's nothing you or anyone else can do to change my mind."

Chapter 12

The sight of Wallace Baxter's face as the Crown Prosecutor asked a seemingly insignificant question about a bank account in the Seychelles was priceless.

As Crown Prosecutor, Malcolm might be too tired to do hard research, but when something was handed to him on a plate he shed twenty years in twenty seconds. Raff slipped him a question with a matching document, and suddenly Malcolm was the incisive legal machine he'd once been.

Wallace Baxter was heading for jail. The people he'd ripped off might even be headed for compensation.

And there'd be more, Raff thought with grim satisfaction. Raff had spent half an hour with Keith, poring through documents, listening to snatches of conversation, before Raff found the Seychelles document and they knew they had enough to pin Baxter.

They also suspected this was the tip of an iceberg.

Philip's tapes might have been intended for blackmail, or maybe they were simply a product of an obsessive mind, but they covered this case only, and there'd been murky cases in the past. By the time Philip finished in court there'd be forensic investigators on his doorstep, Raff thought with satisfaction. With search warrants.

Keith, though, was in charge at that end. He was calling for backup. Raff's role was to return to court, focusing on this case only. So he listened to Malcolm ask his question and wave bank statements. He saw the moment Philip realised Abby had taken the wrong briefcase, and he watched his face turn ashen.

What had Philip been thinking, to record everything? Who knew? All he knew was that he was very, very pleased Abby was no longer marrying him.

He wanted to find her, but that was stupid. Wanting Abby had been stupid last night and it was stupid now.

He could leave the case to Malcolm now. He left. He should go back to help Keith—but he didn't. Instead, he stopped at the baker's to buy lamingtons. Sarah's favourite. They'd sit in the sun and eat them, he thought. He needed to settle.

But when he got home he remembered Sarah was at the sheltered workshop on Mondays. What was he thinking, to forget that?

Maybe he'd been thinking about why he couldn't go find Abby.

Stupid, stupid, stupid.

Should he go back and help Keith?

Keith would do just fine without him—and for some reason he didn't want to see the grubby details of Philip's profit-making. He didn't want to think about Philip.

Instead, he turned his attention to the garden. There

was plenty here that needed doing. His grandmother would break her heart if she could see how he'd let it run down.

This was a gorgeous old house, but huge. There were four bedrooms in the main house and there was another smaller house at the rear where he and Sarah had lived with their mother before her death, to give them some measure of independence.

Sarah would like to live there now. She hankered for independence but she couldn't quite manage. She loved it here, though. To move away…

He couldn't, even if it meant spending his spare time mending and mowing and tending animals and feeling guilty because his grandmother's garden was now mostly grass.

And he was too close to Abby.

Do not go there, he told himself. He started tugging weeds, but then…

The sound of a car approaching tugged him out of his introspection.

Abby.

The car door opened and Kleppy flew to greet him as if he was his long lost friend, missing at sea for years, feared dead, miraculously restored to life. This was the new, renewed Kleppy, sure again of his importance in the world, greeting friends as they ought to be greeted.

He grinned and scratched Kleppy's stomach as he rolled, and Kleppy moaned and wriggled and moaned some more.

"I wish someone was that pleased to see me," Abby said.

She was right by her car. She was smiling.

He couldn't roll on his back and wriggle but the feeling was similar.

She'd been crying. He could see it. He wanted…he wanted…

To back off. What she'd said… *If I can forgive what happened with Ben*… He'd gone over it in his mind a hundred times and he couldn't get away from it.

He could not afford to love this woman.

"I came to apologise," she said.

He stilled. Thought about it. Thought where it might be going and thought a man would be wise to be cautious.

"Why would you want to apologise?" He rose. Kleppy gave a yelp of indignation. He grinned and scooped Kleppy up with him. Got his face licked. Didn't mind.

Abby was apologising?

"The forgiveness thing," she said, and he could see it was an effort to make her voice steady. "I didn't get it."

"And now you do?"

She was standing beside her little red sports car and she wasn't moving. He didn't move either. He held her dog and he didn't go near.

Neutral territory between them. A chasm…

"I've…changed," she said.

He nodded, still cautious. "You got rid of the diamond. That's got to be a start."

"It wasn't the diamond. It was Kleppy. One dog and my life turns upside down."

"He hasn't ended you in jail."

"Not yet."

"How much did you know about what was in Dexter's briefcase?"

"Was there anything?" She couldn't disguise the eagerness. She didn't know, he thought with a rush of relief, though he'd already felt it. The Abby he once knew could never have collaborated with dishonesty. She hadn't changed so much.

Maybe she hadn't changed very much at all. This was the Abby he once knew, right here.

"There's enough to convict Baxter," he said mildly—there was no need to go into the rest of it yet—and he watched the rush of relief.

"I'm so glad."

"So are a lot of people. Me included. Is that why you're here? To find out?"

"No. I told you. I came to say sorry."

Sorry. What did that mean?

He couldn't help her. He knew she was struggling, but she had to figure for herself where she was going.

Abby.

He wanted to walk towards her and gather her up and claim her, right now. He ached to kiss away the tracks of those tears.

But he had to wait, to see if the figuring would come out on his side.

"Kleppy and I have been up at Isaac's," she said. "We've been sitting on the road where Ben was killed."

"Mmm." Nothing more was possible.

"We were all dumb that night."

"We were." Still he was neutral. He was having trouble getting a breath here. Abby took a deep breath for him.

"Sarah and I were seventeen. You and Ben and Philip were nineteen. I'd made my debut with Philip and you were mad at me. Sarah was mad at you, so she accepted a date with Philip to make you madder still. Ben was fed up with all of us—I think he wanted to go out with Sarah so he was fuming. Then the car... The rain... It would have been far more sensible to wait till the next weekend but Ben had to go back to uni so he was aching to try the car."

"Abby..."

"Let me say it," she said. "I'm still trying to figure this out for myself so let me say it as I see it now."

"Okay." What else was a man to say?

"My dad came up here that afternoon and he was angry with Ben for spending the weekend here and not sitting in our living room giving Mum and Dad a minute by minute description of life at uni. So Dad didn't take any interest. He should have said, *Don't try the car until next weekend.* Or even offered to go with you and watch. And Sarah... I remember her trying on the dress I'd just finished making for her, and your gran saying, "Don't you crush that dress, Sarah, after all the time I spent ironing it." And I was home, fed up with the lot of you."

"So..."

"So it was all just...there," she said. "Pressure on you to drive on a night that wasn't safe. Excitement. Knowledge that no one used that track except loggers and no loggers worked over the weekend. Stupid kids and unsafe decisions and a slippery road, and pure bad luck. Sarah not wanting to crush her dress. Ben being too macho to wear a seat belt. Philip wanting to show off his car, his girlfriend. You weren't charged with culpable driving, Raff, and there was a reason. My parents took their grief out in anger. Their anger soured...lots of things. It enveloped me and I've been too much of a wuss to fight my way out the other side."

"And now you have?" It was a hard question to ask. It was a hard question to wait for an answer.

But it seemed she had an answer ready. "You kissed me," she said simply. "And it made me realise that I want you. I always have. That want, that need, got all mixed up, buried, subsumed by grief, by shock, by obligation. I've been a king-sized dope, Raff. It took one crazy dog to shake me out of it."

The dog in question was passive now, shrugged against Raff's chest. Raff set him down with care. It seemed suddenly important to have his arms free. "So you're saying…"

"I'm saying I love you," she said, steadily and surely. "I know it seems fast. We've been apart for ten years so maybe I should gradually show you I've changed. But you know what? I can't wait. I've messed the last ten years up. Do I need to mess any more?"

He didn't move. He didn't let himself move. Not yet. There were things that needed to be said.

"Your parents hate me," he said at last, because it was important. Hate always was.

"They have a choice," she said steadily now, and certain. Her eyes not leaving his. "They can accept the man I love or not. It's up to them but it won't stop me loving you. I'll try and explain but if they won't listen…" She took a deep breath. "I can't live with hate any more, Raff, or with grief. I can't live under the shadow of a ten-year-old tragedy. You and me…" She gazed round the disreputable farmyard. "You and me, and Sarah…"

And Sarah? She was going there?

She'd accept Sarah. He knew she would.

He could never leave Sarah. That fact had coloured every relationship he'd had since the accident, but this was the old Abby emerging, and it was no longer an issue. This was the Abby who held to her friendships no matter what, who'd never stopped loving Sarah, the Abby with a heart so big…

So big she could ignore her parents' hatred?

So big she could take on the Finn boy?

And then he paused. Another vehicle was approaching, travelling fast. Its speed gave it a sense of urgency and he and Abby paused and waited.

It was a silver Porsche.

Philip.

For ten years Abby had never seen Philip angry. She'd seen him irritated, frustrated, condescending. She'd always felt there was an edge of anger held back but she'd never seen it.

She was seeing it now. His car skidded to a halt in a spray of gravel, and the hens clucking round the yard squawked and flew for cover. Kleppy dived behind her legs and stayed there.

Philip didn't notice the hens or Kleppy. He was out of the car, crashing the door closed, staring at her as if she were an alien species.

Raff was suddenly beside her. Taking her hand in his. Holding her against him.

Uh-oh.

She should pull away. Holding hands with Raff would inflame the situation.

She tugged but Raff didn't let her go. Instead, he tugged her tighter. His body language was unmistakable. My woman, Dexter. Threaten her at your peril.

How had it come to this?

"So that's it," Philip snarled, staring at the pair of

them as if they'd crawled from under Raff's pile of weeds. "You slut."

"It's not polite to call a lady a slut," Raff said and his body shifted imperceptibly between them. "You want to take a cold shower and come back when you're cooler?"

"You sabotaged the case," Philip said incredulously, ignoring Raff. "The bank accounts… Suddenly you leave, and my briefcase's gone and in comes Finn and the Prosecutor has a whole list of new evidence. *You gave it to Finn.*"

"Baxter's a maw-worm," Abby said, trying to shove Raff aside so she could face him. This was her business, not Raff's. "I didn't know there was anything in your briefcase to convict him, but if there was we shouldn't have been defending him."

"It's what we do. Do you know how much his fee was?"

"We can afford to lose it."

"You might." He was practically apoplectic, and she knew why. She'd had the temerity to get between him and his money. Philip and his reputation. Philip and his carefully planned life.

"So what about this?" He hauled the diamond out of his top pocket and thrust it towards her, but he was holding it tight at the same time. "Do you know how much this cost? Do you know how much I've done for you?"

"You've been…" How to say he'd been wonderful? He had, but right now it didn't seem like it.

"I've sacrificed everything," he yelled. "Everything. Do you think I wanted to practice in a dump like Banksia Bay? Do you know how much money I could have earned if I'd stayed in Sydney? But here I am, doing the books of the Banksia Bay yacht club, stuck here, seeing the same people over and over, even mowing your parents' lawn."

"I could never figure out why you offered to do that," she whispered, but he wasn't listening.

"I've done everything, and you throw it all away. For this?" His tone was incredulous. He was staring at Raff as if he were pond scum. "A Finn."

"There's some pretty nice Finns," she said mildly and Raff grinned and tugged her a little closer. Just a little, but Philip noticed.

"You'd leave me for this…this…"

"For Raff," she said and she gazed steadily at Philip and she even found it in her to feel sorry for him. "I'm sorry, Philip, but I'm not who you think I am. I've tried… really hard…to be what everyone wants me to be, but I've figured it out. I'm not that person. I'm Abby and I love bright clothes and sleeping in on Sunday and I hate business dinners and I don't like spending my whole life in legal chambers. I like dogs and…"

"Dogs," Philip snarled. The new, brave Kleppy with his brave new life had emerged from behind Abby's legs and was nosing round Philip's feet, checking him out for smells. Philip looked down at him with loathing. "That's what this is about. A dog."

"I know you don't like dogs," Abby said. "It was generous of you to say you'd take him…"

"Generous?" He gave a laugh that made her wince. "Yeah. I'd even put up with *that*." The word made her know exactly what he thought of Kleppy.

"Because you love me?" she asked in a small voice and Raff's hand tightened around hers.

"Love." Philip was staring at her as if she'd lost her mind. "What's love got to do with it?"

"I...everything."

"You have no clue. Not one single clue. Enough. You and your parents have messed with my life for ten years. That's it. I've paid a thousandfold. I'm out of here, and if I never see this place again I'll be delighted."

He turned away, fast, only Kleppy was in the way. He tripped and almost fell. Kleppy yelped.

Philip regained his feet but Kleppy was still between him and his car. And suddenly...

"No," Raff snapped, but it was too late. They were both too late.

Philip's foot swung back and he kicked. All the frustration and rage of the last two days was in that kick and Kleppy copped it all.

The little dog flew about eight feet, squealing in pain and shock.

"Kleppy!" Abby screamed and ran for him, but Philip moved, too, heading for another kick. Abby launched herself at him, throwing herself down between boot and dog.

Philip grabbed her by the hair and hauled her back... And then suddenly he wasn't there any more. Raff's body was between hers and Philip's. Raff's fist came into contact with Philip—she didn't know where; she couldn't see—but she heard a sickening thud, she saw Philip lurch backwards, stumble, and she saw Raff follow him down.

He had him on the ground, on his stomach, his arm twisted up behind his back, and Philip was screaming...

"Lie still or I'll really hurt you," Raff said in a voice she didn't recognise. "Abby, the dog..."

She turned back to Kleppy but Kleppy was no longer there.

He'd backed away in terror. Whining. Horrified, she saw him bolt under the fence and into the undergrowth beyond.

He was yelping in pain and fear and he ran until he was out of sight.

She couldn't catch him. Beyond Raff's fence was Black Mountain. Wilderness.

"Kleppy," she yelled uselessly into the bushland, but he was gone.

She turned and stared back at Philip with loathing and distress. "You kicked him."

"He's a stray."

"He's mine. I can't believe…" She gulped and turned back to the fence, knowing to try and follow the little dog into the bush would be futile.

"He was running," Raff said. He was hauling Philip to his feet, none too gentle. "If he's running, he can't be too badly injured."

"More's the pity," Philip snarled, and Raff wrenched him over to the Porsche with a ruthlessness Abby had never seen before. He shoved him into his driver's seat like she'd seen cops put villains into squad cars, only this was Philip's car and he was sending him away.

Or not. Before Philip could guess what he intended, Raff grabbed the keys to Philip's car and tossed them as far as he could, out into the bush.

"You've lost your keys," he said conversationally. "Abby, get the handcuffs. They're in the compartment on the passenger side of the patrol car."

"What…?" she said, and Raff sighed.

"You want to hold your fiancé or get the cuffs."

"He's not my fiancé." It seemed important.

"Sorry," he said. "Get the cuffs, Abby." Then, as she glanced despairingly at the fence, he softened. "Cuffs first. Kleppy second. Move."

She moved and thirty seconds later Philip was cuffed to his own steering wheel.

"You can't do this," he snarled.

"Watch me," Raff said. Then he lifted his radio. "Keith? You know we were getting a search warrant for Dexter, thinking it might be better to do it when he wasn't home? I have another suggestion. You come up to my place and pick him up. He's cuffed to the car in the driveway. He kicked a dog, pulled Abby's hair. Take him to the station, charge him with aggravated cruelty to animals, plus assault. I'll be there with details when I can but meanwhile he stays in the cells. The paperwork could take quite some time."

"You…"

"Talk among yourself, Dexter," he said. "Abby and I have things to do. Dogs to rescue. And if I find he's badly hurt…" His look said it all. "Come on, Abby, let's go. He'll be headed for Isaac's and I hope for all our sakes we find him."

They drove in silence. There was so much to say. On top of her fear for Kleppy, there was so much to think about. Philip's invective…

Philip's words.

I've paid a thousandfold. It was a statement that made her foundations shift from under her.

She cast a look at Raff and his face was set and grim. Had he heard? Was he thinking about it?

Philip… But her thoughts kaleidoscoped back to Kleppy.

"He can't be too badly hurt."

"No," Raff said. "He can't be. He's a dog who's given me my life back. I owe him more than putting Dexter behind bars."

Where? Where?

They reached Isaac's place and it was fenced and padlocked as it had been fenced and padlocked since Isaac's death.

All the way up the mountain she'd held her breath, hoping Kleppy would be standing at the gate, his nose pressed against the wire. He wasn't.

She called. They both called.

No Kleppy.

"We've come fast on the track," Raff said. "Kleppy's having to manage undergrowth."

"He could be lost."

"Not Kleppy. Our farm is on his route down to town from here, his route to his source of stolen goods. He'll know every inch."

"If he's hurt he could creep into the undergrowth and…"

Raff tugged her tight and held her close. "He was running," he said. "If he's not here in ten minutes I'll start bush bashing." He tugged her tighter still and kissed her, hard and fast. Enormously comforting. Enormously… right. "If we don't have him in an hour I'll organise a posse," he said. "We'll have an army of volunteers up here before nightfall."

"For Kleppy?"

"We have two things going for us," Raff said, and his smile was designed to reassure. "First, Kleppy's one of Henrietta's dogs. She hates having them put down.

She's over the moon that you're taking him, and she has a team of volunteers she'll have searching in a heartbeat. Second, if I happen to mention to about half this town that if we find an injured dog we'll put Dexter behind bars... How many raised hands do you reckon we'd get?"

"Is he that bad?" she said in a small voice.

"You know he is."

She did know it. The thought made her feel...appalled.

What had she been thinking, to drift towards marriage? She'd been in a bad dream that had lasted for years. Of all the stupid...

"Don't kick yourself," Raff said. "We all have dumb youthful romances."

She tried to laugh. She couldn't. A youthful romance that lasted for ten years?

"I seem to remember I did have a youthful romance."

"Yeah," he said. They were walking the perimeter now, checking. "I should have come home and been your partner at the deb ball."

She did choke on that one. Her debutante ball. The source of all the trouble.

She'd been seventeen years old. A girl had to have a really cool partner for that.

Raff had been in Sydney. She'd been annoyed that he couldn't drive home twice a week to practice, two hours here, two hours back, just to be her partner. Of all the selfish...

"Don't kick yourself," he said again. "Dexter does the kicking. Not us."

"But why?" It was practically a wail. Why?

She'd always assumed Philip loved her. He'd given

up Sydney, he'd come home, he'd been the devoted boy-friend, the devoted fiancé for ten years.

Why, if he didn't love her?

"Let's walk down to the road," Raff said, taking her hand. He held her close, not letting her go for a moment as they walked down the driveway to the gravel road where their world had turned upside down ten years ago.

"Kleppy?" she yelled and then paused. "Did you hear?"

"Call again."

She did and there was no mistaking it. A tiny yelp, and then the sound of scuffling.

She was off the road and into the bush, with Raff close behind. Through the undergrowth. Pushing through…

And there he was. Kleppy.

Digging.

Philip's kick had hit his side. She could see grazed skin and blood on his wiry coat.

He looked up from where he'd been digging and wagged his tail and she came close to bursting into tears.

"Klep…"

But he was back digging, dirt going in all directions. His whole body was practically disappearing into the hole he was creating.

"You don't need a wombat," she told him, feeling almost ill with relief. She reached him and knelt, not caring about the spray of dirt that showered her. "Klep…"

He tugged back from inside his hole. He had something. He was trying to hold it in his mouth and front paws, tugging it up as he tried to find purchase with his back legs.

She didn't care if it was a dead wombat, buried for

years. She gathered him into her arms, mindful of his injured side, and lifted him from the hole.

He snuffled against her, a grubby, bleeding rapscallion of a dog, quivering with delight that she'd found him and, better still, he had something to give her. He wiggled around in her arms and dropped his treasure onto the ground in front of her.

Raff was with her then, ruffling Kleppy's head, smiling his gorgeous, loving smile that made her heart twist inside. How could she have ever walked away from this man for Philip? Like Kleppy's buried treasure, his smile had been waiting for her to rediscover it.

She had rediscovered it.

She wasn't going to marry Philip. Raff was smiling at her. The thought made her feel giddy with happiness.

"Hey," Raff said in a voice that was none too steady and he gathered them both into his arms. He held them, just held them. His woman, with dog in between.

Happiness was right now.

But there was only so much happiness a small dog could submit to. He submitted for a whole minute before wriggling his nose free and then the rest of him. He started barking, indignation personified, because Abby hadn't taken any interest in his treasure.

Too bad. Raff was kissing her. She had treasure of her own to be finding.

But Kleppy was nothing if not insistent. He was hauling his loot up onto her knees. It was a dirt-covered box, a little damaged at one corner, but not much. It was pencil-box sized, or maybe a little bigger.

She took it and brushed the worst of the dirt off—and then she stilled.

This box.

Philip's box.

No. Philip's grandfather's box. He made boxes like this for all his relations, for all his friends.

This one, though… The shape…

Slowly now, with a lot more care, she dusted the thing off. It was almost totally intact. Cedar did that. It lasted for generations. Something had nibbled at the corner but had given up in disgust.

Cedar was pretty much bug-proof. Obviously it tasted bad. Except to Kleppy.

It would have been the smell, she thought, the distinctive scent, showing him that something was buried here, something like the box he loved back at her place.

"What is it?" Raff was watching her face, figuring this was important.

"I'm not sure," she said, hardly daring to breathe. A box. Made by Philip's grandfather. Buried not fifty yards from where Ben had been killed.

A box she might just know.

Her fingers were suddenly trembling. Raff took the box from her. "A bomb?" There was the beginning of a smile in his voice.

"No," she whispered and then thought about it. "Maybe."

"You want me to open it?"

"I think we must."

There were four brass clips holding it sealed. Raff flicked open each clip in turn.

He opened the box, but she knew before she saw it what its contents would be. And she was right. She'd seen it before. It held cassette tapes, filed neatly, slotted against each other in the ridged sections of Huon pine that Philip's grandpa had carved with such skill.

She didn't need to take them out to know what they were. Music tapes, with a couple of blank ones at the back.

There was an odd one. Not slotted into place. The ribbon had been ripped from its base and the tape looked as if it had been tossed into the box in a hurry. It wasn't labelled.

Her mind was in overdrive.

What do you do when you're panicking?

You grab the tape from the player, rip the ribbon out, throw it into the box with the others that might point to the fact that this tape might exist, and then you head into the bush. You bury it fast, deep in the undergrowth.

And then you come back to the car and you face the fact that a friend is dead and two others injured...

Even if you tried to find it later, you might not. It'd take Kleppy's sense of smell...

But why?

"I'm guessing what this might be," she said bleakly, and she knew she had to take this further. She was feeling sick. "Do you think we could still play it?"

"It looks like it's just a matter of reattaching the ribbon. Is it important?"

"I think it might be."

Chapter 13

They took Kleppy to the vet and Fred declared he'd live. While he did, Raff made a quick call to Keith.

"Dexter's nicely locked up and he's staying that way," Keith said. "I have a team organised to swarm through his files. You look after Abby."

"How did he know you and I…?" Abby said and Raff grinned and shook his head.

"Banksia Bay. Don't ask."

With his wound cleaned and dressed, they took Kleppy back to Raff's. An hour later, a hearty meal demolished, Kleppy was watching television with Sarah. Lionel was with them. He'd just sort of turned up.

"Heard Kleppy got kicked," he muttered, and Abby thought, *How does this town do it?*

Abby and Raff were in the back room, standing over Gran's ancient tape player. Waiting for a repaired cassette to start.

Abby felt sick.

Raff was curious. Worried. Watching her. She hadn't told him what to expect. It might not be anything.

But why was it buried there if it wasn't anything?

And as soon as it started she knew she was right, at least in thinking she knew what it was.

She'd watched Philip over the years as he'd recorded his client discussions—"in case I miss something'. She'd attributed it to his meticulous preparation.

She'd believed him, all those years ago when she'd found the Christabelle tape. She'd used it as a reason to break up with him, but had hardly thought any more of it. But in the box buried by the roadside where Ben died...there was more evidence.

Maybe Philip taped all his girlfriends.

For this was Sarah, ten years younger but still unmistakably herself. Young and excited and a little bit nervous.

It had been set to record as soon as Philip picked her up, and they knew immediately it was the night of the crash. They listened to Sarah asking if they could go up the mountain and see if the boys had their car going.

"Sure." Philip was amenable. "I wouldn't count on it going, though. Let's show "em what a real car can do. You like my wheels?"

"Your car's great." But even from the distance of ten years they could hear Sarah's increasing nervousness, from almost as soon as they started driving. "Philip, slow down. These curves are dangerous."

"I can handle them. It's Raff and Ben who should worry. They can hardly drive."

More talk. Sarah asked if he liked her dress. Even then, Philip wasn't into bright dresses.

"Not so much. Why'd it have to be red?"

A terse response. Sarah sounded peeved.

"Movies afterwards?" Philip asked.

"I'm not sure. If you don't like my dress sense…"

"There's no need to be touchy."

Silence. An offended huff? Then Sarah again…

"Phil, be careful. That was a wallaby."

"It's fine. Wallabies are practically plague round here, anyway. Why are they using the fire track?"

"They can't go on the roads. Their car isn't registered."

"That hunk of junk'll never get registered. Not like this baby. Watch it go."

"Philip, no. Slow down. You're scaring me. There'll be more wallabies—it's getting dark."

"There's nothing to be scared of. You reckon they're on this track?"

"Philip… Philip, no. You nearly hit it…" And then… "You're on the wrong side of the…"

"There's ruts on the other side. No one uses this."

"But it's a crest." Her voice rose. "Philip, it's a crest. No…"

Then…awfulness.

Then nothing. Nothing, nothing and nothing.

The tape spun on into silence.

Dear God…

Raff changed colour. Held onto the back of the nearest chair.

She moved then, closing the distance between them in a heartbeat, linking her arms around his chest and tugging him to her. She held him and held him and held him. She'd had some inkling, the moment she'd seen the buried box. But Raff… This was a lightning bolt.

Raff…

He'd been her hero since she was eight years old. He was her wonderful Raff.

Her love.

"I didn't…" he said, and it was as if he was waking from a nightmare. "I believed Philip. He said I was on the wrong side."

"That's why there was never a court case," she whispered. "The storm hit just as the crash happened. There was only Philip's word."

They'd believed him. They'd all believed him. It had been so hard—so unthinkable—to do anything else.

She saw it all.

Philip's stupidity had killed Ben; had desperately injured Sarah. He couldn't admit it, but what followed…

Some part of Philip was still decent. He was a kid raised in Banksia Bay, and he'd been their friend in childhood. His parents were friends with her parents. They'd loved Ben to bits.

He'd have been truly appalled.

So a part of him had obviously decided to do the "right thing', and in his eyes he had. He'd come back here to practice law, playing the son to her parents, devoting himself to Banksia Bay as Ben would have.

"He's been making amends for Ben," she said, and she was trying hard to hold back the anger. Raff didn't need her anger now. He just needed…her? "He came back and tried to make amends to us all."

And then, despite what she'd intended, anger hit, a wave so great it threatened to overwhelm her. "No. Not to us all. He tried to make amends to me and to my parents. He would have married me, as if that somehow made up for Ben's life. But to you… For ten years he's let you think you were responsible. For ten years he's let you hold the blame."

Tears were coursing down her cheeks now. She'd thought she was comforting Raff but her rage was so great there was no comfort she could give. If Philip walked in the door right now...

"I'll tear his heart out," she stammered. "If he has a heart. I can't bear it. He's lost you years."

"No."

Raff put her back from him then, holding her hard by each shoulder. He'd regained his colour and, unbelievably, he was smiling. "I believe you told me you loved me before you found this tape."

"Yes, but..."

"Then it's Philip who's lost the ten years. I've faced it and come out the other side." He took a deep breath. "Whew. This takes some getting used to."

"We can tell the world. Oh, Raff... I can't bear anyone thinking a moment longer that you..."

"That I was dumb as a teenager? I *was* dumb," he said gently. "I shouldn't have been up there that night. None of us should. I believe I might even cut Philip slack on this one."

"No!"

"He's lost you," Raff said and he tugged her against him and let his chin rest on her hair. "Winner takes all. That'd be me. And I need to think things through before I do anything rash—like spreading this far and wide."

She stared at him as if he were out of his mind. "Why on earth...?"

"You know, my reputation does no end of good for my street cred," he said, thoughtful now. "How many local kids know the local cop was dumb and someone died because of it? You get experts lecturing kids on speed and they shrug it off. They see how Mrs Fryer treats me? For a cop, that's gold. I reckon it's even saved lives."

"Raff…"

"Don't think it's not important," he said, laughter fading. He was holding her at arm's length and meeting her gaze with gravity and truth. "To look at Sarah now and know I wasn't responsible for her pain… To look at you and know it wasn't me who hurt you… I can't tell you what that means. But Philip has some pretty heavy stuff coming to him anyway. I can cope without my own pound of flesh. Believe me, I can cope.

"All I need I have right here. This tape is a great gift, Abby, but the greatest gift of all is you."

He tugged her to him then, and he held her, close enough so their heartbeats merged. She was dissolving into him, she thought. She loved this man with all her heart. No matter what he decided to do about this tape, they could go forward from this moment.

"Marry me," he said and the world stood still.

"Marry?" She could barely get the word out.

"I hear on the grapevine you have a perfectly good wedding dress. I'm a man who hates waste."

"Raff…"

"Don't quibble," he said sternly. "Just say yes."

"You're in shock. You're emotional. You need time to think."

He put her away from him again. Held her at arm's length. Smiled.

"I've thought," he said. "Marry me."

"Okay."

* * *

Okay? As an acceptance of a marriage proposal it lacked a certain finesse but it was a great start. For a lawyer. He found himself laughing, a great explosion of happiness that came from so far within he'd never known that place existed. He lifted her up in his arms and whirled her round as if she weighed nothing.

She did weigh nothing. She was part of him—his Abby, his love.

His…wife?

He set her down, laughter fading. Joy was taking its place, a joy so great he felt he was shedding an old skin and bursting into something new.

She tilted her chin and he kissed her, so slowly, so thoroughly satisfactorily, that words weren't possible. Words weren't needed for a very long time.

She held him tight, she kissed him and she placed her future in his hands. She loved him so much she felt her heart could burst.

He was Banksia Bay's bad boy no longer. He was just… Raff.

If he insisted, then maybe she wouldn't tell the town about Philip, she conceded—but she would tell her parents. And she would tell Philip that she knew. And then… This was Banksia Bay. If things got around… Things always got around.

But right now it was becoming incredibly hard to care. All she cared about was that Raff was holding her as if he'd never let her go. He was kissing her as he'd kissed her when she was sixteen, only more so. A lot more so. He was grown into her man. He was her love, for ever and ever.

"I can't believe this is happening," he said at last in a voice that was changed, different. It was the voice of a man who was walking into a future he'd never dreamed of. "Abby, are you sure?" And then he hesitated. "I do need to care for Sarah." There was sudden doubt.

"I believe there's room enough here for all of us," she said, deeply contented. She pulled back enough to peep through to the next room, where Lionel and Sarah were watching television. They were covered in three dogs, two cats and a vast bowl of popcorn. They were looking…self-conscious. On closer inspection… They were holding hands.

"There must be something in the water," she said and grinned, and Raff tugged her close again, smiling wide enough to make her dissolve in the happiness of his smile.

"So you'd take us all on? This place. And Sarah's dogs and guinea pigs and hens and ponies and…"

"And whoever else comes along," she said, and chuckled at the look on his face.

He caught his breath. "You'd…"

"I think I would," she said, a bubble of joy rising so fast it was threatening to overwhelm her. "It might be fun."

"You're talking babies," he said, feeling his way.

"I believe I am. You know," she said thoughtfully, "if we sold my place we could even do up your other house as well as this one."

He took a deep breath. Looked through to the sitting room. Saw what she was seeing. Sarah and Lionel…

"We might just have found ourselves a gardener," Abby said, smiling and smiling.

Enough. This was going so fast he was being left behind. A man had to take a stand some time, so he took his stand right there. Right then. A simple *okay* was not satisfactory for what he had in mind. He dropped to one knee. "Abigail Callahan, will you marry me?"

"I've already said…" she started.

"You said *okay*. I don't think *okay*'s legally binding."

"You want me to prepare contracts?"

"In triplicate."

She smiled down at him, for how could she help it? She smiled and smiled. And then she thought this moment called for gravitas. It was a Very Serious Moment. It was the beginning of the rest of her life.

She stepped back and stood a little way away, looking down at him. At all of him.

At this man who'd be her husband.

She could still see him, she thought. The spiky-haired ten-year-old who her eight-year-old self had fallen in love with. That dangerous twinkle…

Her bad boy.

Her love.

"If I turn out to be a sewing mistress instead of a lawyer…" she ventured.

"Suits me."

"If I'm not struck off the professional roll for this morning's unprofessional conduct I might help out the Crown Prosecutor from time to time."

"You can't get struck off for dropping a briefcase— and Malcolm surely needs some help. You know, I'm feeling a bit dumb, kneeling over here when you're over there."

She hadn't finished. "I do want babies."

"How many?" he asked and there was a trace of unease in his voice.

"Six," she said, and laughed at the look on his face.

"Can we try one out for size first?"

"Sounds a plan. Raff…"

"Yes, my love?"

"That's just it," she said, feeling suddenly…shy. "My love. Let me say… I need to explain. Only once and then it's over, but I do need to get it out. Raff, I've loved you all the time without stopping but my pain stopped me thinking with my heart. I forced myself to think with my head. That's done. I'm so, so sorry that I can't take back those ten years."

"Hush," he said.

"I have to say it."

"You've said it," he murmured. "I don't like to mention it but there's no carpet here. I'm kneeling on wood. I didn't have the forethought to use a cushion. Any more quibbles?"

"No, but…"

He sighed. "Then how about saying you'll marry me and taking me out of my pain?"

"Okay."

"Abigail!"

She laughed, and she hardly felt herself cross the distance between them. She knelt to join him and he tugged her close.

He kissed her again, so thoroughly, so wonderfully that doubts, unhappiness, emptiness were gone and she knew they were gone for ever.

"We can't take back those ten years," he whispered into her hair as the kiss paused before restarting. "How about we give ourselves the next ten instead?"

"Ten…"

"And the ten after that. And after that, too. Decades and decades of love and family and…"

And something was bumping against her leg.

Kleppy. He was tugging the popcorn bowl to his mistress with care.

She giggled and lifted him up and popcorn went flying. He'd tugged it with such care and she'd spilled it.

Who cared? A lawyer might. Not Abigail Callahan. Not the wife of Banksia Bay's Bad Boy.

"Decades and decades of love and family and dogs," she said, and Raff took Kleppy firmly from her and set him down so he could kiss her again.

"Definitely, my love. Definitely family, definitely dogs, definitely love. For now and for ever. For as long as we both shall live. So now, Abigail Callahan, for the third and final time, will you marry me? I want more than *okay*. I want properly, soberly, legally, and with all your heart."

"Why, yes, Rafferty Finn," she managed between love and laughter. "Where would you like me to sign?"

Abby didn't wear two thousand beads to her wedding.

For a start, it didn't seem right that she wear a dress she'd prepared for her marriage to Philip. Almost as soon as Raff put a ring on her finger she was planning an alternative.

Rainbows.

So Sarah wore her dress—Sarah, who'd looked at her dress of two thousand beads and burst into tears. "It's the most beautiful thing I've ever seen." And Sarah needed a wedding gown.

For: "Lionel's not staying in that horrid boarding house a minute longer," she declared, but Lionel was old-fashioned. He was delighted to move to Raff's farm; he was incredibly happy to start renovating the little house at the rear, but he'd marry his Sarah first.

They were even thinking…if Lionel got his money back from Philip… Isaac's place wasn't so far from the farm. Maybe they could be even more independent.

So Raff gave his sister away. Abby was maid of honour and if she was as weepy as any mother of the bride then who could blame her? Her gown of two thousand beads had found a use she could hardly have dreamed of.

And then it was Abby's turn for her wedding, a month later, but on a day just as wonderful. They were to be married in the church—the church she'd been baptised in, the church Ben had been buried from.

Half Banksia Bay came to see. Even Mrs Fryer.

For things had shifted for the town's bad boy.

Rumours were flying. True to his word, Raff refused to make public the contents of the tape, but the people of Banksia Bay never let lack of evidence get in the way of a good rumour. And there were plenty of pointers saying Raff might well have been misjudged.

For a start, Abby's parents were trying their best to get to know Raff, and suddenly they wouldn't hear a bad word against him. They even offered to move into Raff's house while Raff and Abby went on their honeymoon, in case Lionel needed help with Sarah.

And people remembered. Raff had been judged on Philip's word and nothing else. But now… Philip had abandoned the town and moved to Sydney. He was facing malpractice charges and more.

Philip's parents were appalled. They owned an apartment in Bondi and rumour said they were thinking of moving themselves, leaving Banksia Bay to be with their son.

They were the only ones behind Philip, though. Even Philip's grandpa was right here at the wedding. What was more, at Abby's tentative request he'd made a beautiful box for the ring bearer.

The ring bearer...

Raff stood before the altar waiting for his bride and he couldn't help thinking the choice of ring bearer might be a mistake.

Abby swore it'd be okay. She'd spent hours training him. The plan was for her mother to hold Kleppy, and then, when Raff called, he'd trot across, bearing the ring. What could possibly go wrong?

Who knew, but Raff organised for Keith to carry a backup ring in his pocket. It wasn't that he didn't trust Kleppy.

Um...yes, it was. He stood in the church waiting for his bride and he thought he definitely didn't trust Kleppy.

But suddenly he could no longer focus on Abby's dog. The doors of the church swung open and Abby was right there. Holding her father's hand. Looking along the aisle to find him.

His bride. His Abby.

She'd wanted rainbows, and that was what she was to be married in. She'd made this herself as well, and it was as individual as she was. The gown was soft white silk, almost transparent, floating over panels of pastel hues, every shade a man could imagine. Her tight-fitting bodice clung to her lovely figure and the skirt flared out in clouds of shimmering colour, with the soft-coloured silk shimmering from underneath.

She was so beautiful…

She wore her hair simply, no longer in the elegant chignon he'd hated for years, but dropping in tendrils to her bare shoulders. She wore a simple halo of fresh flowers in her hair—and she took his breath away.

Sarah followed her in, proud fit to burst. Matron of honour. She wore a matching dress, also rainbow-coloured but without the translucent overskirt that made Abby seem to float.

Sarah was also supposed to be wearing a ring of flowers in her hair, but that had been the one hiccup of the morning. "It might give me a headache," she'd said, doubtful.

"Why don't you take it and leave it in the car?" Raff had suggested. "That way, you can wear it for the official photographs and take it off if it starts hurting."

She'd approved his suggestion. She was happy now, bareheaded, beautiful, a married woman, fussing over her best friend's gown.

She wasn't as happy as Raff. Not possible. His Abby was smiling at him. His Abby was about to be his wife.

What could be more perfect?

The music filled the church. Abby's father led her forward, beaming with pride, and Raff stepped forward to receive his bride.

His Abby.

What could go wrong with today?

Kleppy could go wrong.

There was a scuffle in the front pew. Abby's mother had retired behind her handkerchief and forgotten her Kleppy-clutching duty. She made a wild grab but it was too late: he was free.

Kleppy was groomed to an inch of his life. He was

wearing a bow of the same rainbow-coloured fabric lining Abby's gown.

He was off and running.

He trotted straight up the aisle, tail high, a dog on a mission—and he disappeared out of the door.

Uh-oh. What was a cop supposed to do now? What was a groom supposed to do?

"Leave him to me," Keith growled, setting a hand firmly on Raff's shoulder. "Lights and sirens. Handcuffs. Padded cell if necessary. I'll pull him in no time."

"Kleppy," Abby faltered.

"You two get on with your wedding," Keith told them, and they looked at each other and knew they must. A hundred people were watching them. These people loved them and they were waiting to see them married.

"But he has the ring," Abby faltered.

"We have backup," Keith said and handed Raff the spare.

"Oh, Raff…" He could tell she didn't know whether to be thankful or indignant.

"It's not that I didn't trust him," Raff said—unconvincingly—and then he paused.

Kleppy was back. With a ring.

He had two rings now, the plain band of gold in the tiny box hanging round his neck—and Sarah's halo of flowers, left on the front seat of the bridal carriage.

It was a ring of fresh flowers to match Abby's.

He carried it straight to Abby and sat and wagged his tail and waited to be told how good he was.

"He's brought us a ring," Abby said and choked.

The congregation was choking as well—or laughing out loud. Kleppy's reputation had grown considerably in the last couple of months.

But Raff had his priorities in order now. There were things to be done before he acknowledged his soon-to-be wife's dog. He took her hands in his, tugged her to face him and lightly kissed her. "You," he told her, "are the most beautiful woman in the world."

"You make my toes curl," she said.

There was a light "harrumph' from before them. They were, after all, here to get married.

Raff smiled and stooped and held out his hand, and Kleppy laid his ring of flowers into his palm. He lifted it up and gave it to Abby.

"I guess this is Kleppy's wedding gift."

"I'll treasure it for always," she managed.

"You should. For with this ring, I thee wed," he said softly. "With this dog, I thee marry. Before this community, with these friends, I pledge you my troth."

There was a murmur of delighted approval.

Abby was looking…in love.

Kleppy, however, was still looking expectant.

Raff knelt and lifted the small gold band from the box around Kleppy's neck. He pocketed it carefully—and then he placed the ring of flowers around Kleppy's neck.

"Sarah," he said to his sister. "Can you hold Kleppy? I have things to do."

"Sure," Sarah said, beaming. "Lionel will help me."

So Sarah and Lionel held Kleppy. Raff took Abby's hands in his and he faced her—a man facing his woman on their wedding day.

"Enough," he said softly, for her ears alone. "Dogs have their place, as do sisters and friends and flowers. But for now… Are you ready to marry me?"

"If you'll take me. And my crazy dog."

"We'll take whatever comes with both of us," he told her, strongly and firmly. "As long as we have each other."

"Oh, yes." She smiled at him mistily through tears. He kissed her again, lightly on the lips—and then the ceremony began as it was meant to begin. As Rafferty Finn and Abigail Callahan stood together, in peace and in love, to become one.

* * * * *

Tracy Madison is an award-winning author who makes her home in northwestern Ohio. As a wife and a mother, her days are filled with love, laughter and many cups of coffee. She often spends her nights awake and at the keyboard, bringing her characters to life and leading them toward their well-deserved happily-ever-afters one word at a time. Tracy loves to hear from readers. You can reach her at tracy@tracymadison.com.

Books by Tracy Madison

Harlequin Special Edition

The Colorado Fosters

A Bride for the Mountain Man
From Good Guy to Groom
Rock-a-Bye Bride
Dylan's Daddy Dilemma
Reid's Runaway Bride
Haley's Mountain Man
Cole's Christmas Wish

The Foster Brothers

An Officer, a Baby and a Bride
A Match Made by Cupid
Miracle Under the Mistletoe

Visit the Author Profile page
at Harlequin.com for more titles.

A BRIDE FOR THE
MOUNTAIN MAN

Tracy Madison

To the canine loves of my life:
Roxie, Max and Maggie, Sadie, and Holly.

Chapter 1

There were many ways a person could die. Before this moment, Meredith Jensen had never given much thought to how her life might come to an end.

Why would she? She had youth, good health and a rather safe existence on her side.

Other than her penchant for over-easy eggs paired with buttered toast every Sunday morning, she didn't participate in dangerous activities. Her weekends weren't spent skydiving or bungee jumping, she drove a Volvo S60 and not a sports car and most nights, she was tucked securely into bed with a book no later than ten. As far as her career went, until two weeks ago, she'd worked as a stager for a high-end, prestigious construction and realty company in the San Francisco Bay area. Dressing up the interiors of spectacular houses, apartments and condos to make them more desirable for prospective buyers held very little risk.

And oh, how she'd loved her job.

The creativity involved, the process of designing each room around the architecture and the lighting and the scavenger hunt in locating the perfect accompaniments to bring her vision to reality. She supposed something unfortunate could have occurred if she'd been on a job-site at the wrong moment, but truly, the vast majority of her time was either spent in her office or canvassing the city in search of the right furniture, artwork, rugs and anything else she had deemed necessary.

If Meredith had spent any amount of time consider-ing her demise, a whopper of an earthquake would've topped the list, due to where she lived. Everyday trag-edies, such as car accidents, house fires and random acts of violence would have been noted, as well. To be complete, she would've included illness as an additional possibility.

But getting lost in the mountains of Colorado while the heavens unleashed a torrential, icy downpour out-side her rental car? In the middle of October, no less? Nope. The predicament she currently found herself in wouldn't have landed a spot on her personal scenarios-of-death list. This trip was meant to be an opportunity to catch up with an old friend, relax, indulge in some skiing and most important…make peace with her past and reassess her future.

If everything had gone according to plan, she would have arrived at her friend Rachel Foster's house over an hour ago and would certainly be enjoying a glass of wine this very second. Naturally, Rachel had offered to pick her up from the airport, but Meredith wanted to have a car at her disposal. She had GPS, Rachel's address and her phone number. That and the Honda Accord she rented was all she needed.

Except the weather had turned on a dime shortly after she'd left the airport, going from cold to freezing temperatures and drizzling rain to an icy mess, as if Mother Nature had flipped the "storm switch" out of boredom or anger.

She shouldn't be surprised, really. While the vast majority of Meredith's life had gone precisely according to plan, recently fate seemed determined to push her off course onto one bumpy, twisty road after another.

A small, semihysterical laugh, born from desperation and fear, escaped her. No, maybe she hadn't sensed disaster looming when she'd boarded her plane in San Francisco earlier that afternoon, but all things being considered, she should have.

Squinting her eyes in an attempt to focus on the narrow mountain road, Meredith looked for a clearing to turn the car around. Obviously, she'd gone left when she should've gone right or vice versa. Not that she had any idea of exactly where she'd erred. Because of her location, the weather or a combination of both, her phone had lost its signal thirty-plus minutes ago.

No GPS. No way to search for directions from her current location. No way to call or text Rachel or to reach out for help. She was on her own.

And didn't that feel like some type of a sick joke?

To make matters worse, as late afternoon crawled its way toward dusk, snowflakes had joined the wintry mix and now whipped through the air, their numbers seemingly multiplying by the minute. They fell hard and fast, covering the ground in a growing sheath of white. She was, as her much loved and dearly departed grandmother used to say, in quite the pretty pickle.

Meredith drew her bottom lip into her mouth and tried to hold back the panic rippling through her blood. Barely able to see through the windshield, driving as slow as she could manage in deference to the slick, icy road, she said a silent prayer for her safety. Then, right on the heels of that, she gave herself a swift, mental kick in the butt.

"Be smart," she said. "Stop feeling and start thinking. There will be plenty of time to fall apart later."

Right. Assuming she lived, she could give in to hysterics as much as she wanted once she got out of this mess. And the first step had to be reversing her direction, so she could attempt to find one of the houses she'd driven past and hope for a kind Samaritan who would be willing to take her in until the weather cleared. Locating Rachel's house at this point was akin to finding a solitary needle in a hundred—no, make that a thousand—haystacks.

Leaning forward in her seat and completely removing her foot from the gas pedal, Meredith peered through the windshield. The sky was darkening quickly, the sun's already dimming glow further diminished by clouds and snow, rain and ice.

She couldn't even see far enough in front of her to know if she was approaching a bend in the road or a cross street she could use for a U-turn. Other than her headlights, there weren't any lights to be seen, whether from oncoming cars, houses or businesses that might be tucked off the road.

The terror that Meredith had worked so hard to contain engulfed her in a rush, sending a tremor of shivers through her body.

Where the hell was she?

How had she managed to find what had to be one of the very few mountain roads in a tourist town filled with skiers that wasn't populated with residences, hotels or any other signs of human existence?

She couldn't see a damn thing, so she braked to a full stop, the tires sliding precariously on the icy road before obeying her command. With the car engaged in Park, she switched on the emergency lights—just in case she was fortunate enough for another vehicle to come along—opened the door and stepped outside.

Okay, yeah, it was cold. The type of cold that hurt.

Edging to the side of the road, she walked forward, looking for what she hadn't been able to see from the car: a wide, relatively flat and clear space she could use to turn the car around.

In mere seconds, her hands were tingling from the frigid temperature and the slashing wintry mix. She hadn't been thinking clearly. She should have grabbed her coat from the back seat before leaving the car. She didn't bother turning back. She wouldn't be out here for long.

Tugging down her sleeves to use as makeshift gloves, eyes downcast, she trudged forward. In careful, small steps, she navigated a path through the thickening snow and around the outer layer of trees—a mix of deciduous and coniferous, mainly aspen, pine, spruce and fir—that blanketed this section of the mountainside.

Earlier, before the drastic change in the weather and becoming hopelessly lost, she'd marveled at the natural beauty of these trees, of their rich and varied shades of green and gold, with splashes of red, atop a canopy of pure white leftover from a prior snowfall. Now, they were nothing more than another set of obstacles, blocking her route and her vision. Still beautiful, without doubt, but entirely unhelpful.

Her arms, legs and feet were already numb. Her cheeks already raw, her lips chapped and her hair a mass of wet, frozen strands.

She couldn't have traveled more than twenty feet from the car, but what would've been an inconsequential distance in the full light of day and under normal circumstances might as well have been two hundred miles. It was just too cold, too gray and shadowed, too windy, too…everything. Each step she took away from the car increased her brewing panic. She kept at it for a few more minutes, without any luck, before deciding she'd gone far enough.

If there was an easy spot to turn around, she couldn't see it.

Okay. No biggie. She'd just keep driving in the same direction and hope she'd come across a house, a hotel, a gas station or a restaurant. An igloo. Somewhere, anywhere, that would offer safety until the storm passed.

"Please, please let there be shelter just up the road," she whispered into the frigid air as she stumbled in retreat toward her waiting car. Somewhere with food would be a tremendous bonus, as she hadn't eaten anything that day. She never did before getting on a plane.

A burger dripping with melted cheese would taste like heaven. Or a large pepperoni and mushroom pizza. Or…her stomach grumbled in response to her thoughts, which made the entire situation seem even worse. She'd never had to ignore her body's natural reminder for sustenance.

If she was hungry, she ate. It had always been that simple.

Back in the Accord, Meredith aimed the vents in her direction and cranked up the heat. She closed her eyes and breathed through her shivers and chattering teeth, letting the solid stream of warm air soak into her skin and begin to dry her hair and clothes. Just that fast, she regained some of her optimism. She might be hungry, but she certainly wouldn't starve. She had shelter and warmth right here. Even if she was stuck in the car until morning, she would survive.

She would be fine.

With that mantra running through her head, she rebuckled her seat belt, put the car into Drive and cautiously pressed on the gas pedal. The car rocked as the tires fought for traction on the icy layer of snow but didn't actually move forward.

Biting her lip, Meredith applied a miniscule amount of more pressure to the gas pedal and, when that didn't work, a little more yet. The tires spun uselessly for another instant—no more than a second or two—before the car lurched into actual motion. Without conscious thought, she gripped the steering wheel tighter and drove, using the brakes far more often than the gas to retain some semblance of control.

And even her current speed of a sleepy, lazy tortoise felt too fast, too reckless.

She drove slowly, not so much following the road as the dense line of dark trees along either side of the car. As she did, the sun continued its unrelenting descent and the snow kept falling, faster and thicker, decreasing her scant visibility to the point of near blindness. The gusting, rushing gales of wind battered against the car with such ferocious strength that being swept off the road ranked as a real possibility. Terrifying, yes, but also…lonely.

Not in the "oh, I wish I had someone to talk to" sense of lonely, but in the "if this goes bad, I could legitimately die out here, by myself, and no one would know."

Her parents wouldn't have a clue, nor would her brothers or friends or prior coworkers. No one, except for Rachel and her husband, Cole, would even think to try to contact her for days, if not for weeks. She was supposed to be on vacation, after all.

More than that, though. This trip was about a lot more than a simple getaway.

After an inferno of an exchange with her father, Arthur Jensen had made it clear that for the next year, no matter the circumstance she found herself in, he would not intervene. The rest of the family wouldn't, either.

It was what she had wanted, had asked for and then demanded when he'd initially taken her request as a joke. But she hadn't guessed how upset her father would become, the awful truth that slipped out in his anger, which further upset *her* or, when he finally capitulated, the strict set of rules he put in place. She recognized why. He didn't believe she'd agree, but oh, she had. Because really, what else was she to do?

But she certainly hadn't foreseen a freak autumn snowstorm, losing her way in a wholly unfamiliar and apparently remote location or the possibility of death on the horizon. And even if her father could somehow know of her predicament and even if he hadn't declared her as, for all intents and purposes, an orphan for the next year, he couldn't help her now anyway.

No one could.

"Stop it," she said, loud and clear. "I am not going to die out here."

She'd no sooner spoken the words than the faint-est shimmer of light appeared ahead and to the right. So faint, she almost wondered if her eyes were playing tricks on her, and what she thought she saw was nothing more than a panic-induced mirage…her personal oasis in the desert. Could be that, she thought, or it could be just as it appeared: a sanctuary. She wouldn't know for sure until she got closer, but hope and relief tempered the rapid beat of her heart.

Neither lasted long. Seemingly out of nowhere, the narrow, uphill road curved sharply to the right and Mer-edith, in an instinctive attempt to correct her direction, yanked the steering wheel too hard. The car whiplashed to the side before settling into a spin and, now facing the opposite direction, picked up speed and careened downhill.

Gripping the steering wheel even tighter, she worked to keep the car on the road while pumping on the brakes. She couldn't regain control. She closed her eyes, tensed her body and readied herself for whatever came next. Damn it! This should not be happening. She should be with Rachel, sipping wine and trying to let go of the past while deciding on a new and improved future. She was *not* supposed to be lost, scared and…

The impact came hard and swift, jarring her body and ending her inner tirade.

In sync with the crash, a loud noise, almost like a gunshot, rang in Meredith's ears as the airbag deployed and slammed against her chest. An acrid smell, strong and pungent, consumed the interior of the car, along with a powdery dust that coated her face and hair. She might have screamed, if she'd been able to breathe.

Keeping her eyes closed for a minute and then another, she waited for her lungs to kick into gear and her shivers to fade, for her heart to regain its normal rhythm and her stomach to stop sloshing. Finally, when her breathing returned and the starkest edge of her fear ebbed, she opened her eyes. She clenched and unclenched her hands, wiggled her toes and moved her legs.

Okay. Good. All seemed in working order. She hadn't died yet.

Where had those dogs gotten off to? Liam Daly swore under his breath and hollered their names—Max and Maggie—uselessly into the wind tunnel the night had become. They didn't come running, nor could he hear their boisterous barking. Not good.

Not good at all.

It was unusual for them to leave his side in the middle of a storm. Even more unusual for them to do so after he'd been gone for so long.

He'd just returned home after an extended stay in the Aleutian Islands, where he'd photographed a variety of wildlife, including those that lived on the land, flew in the air and swam in the sea. It was a good trip and as always he was thankful for the work, but Lord, he was happy to be back home in Colorado.

He'd be happier if his dogs would show themselves. Max and Maggie were Belgian Tervurens, a shepherding breed closely related to Belgian sheepdogs. They were smart, intuitive, active and more often than not, positioned themselves so close to Liam's legs that he was lucky not to trip over them. They'd done so when they'd first arrived home, after Liam had picked them up from his sister's place in Steamboat Springs proper. Fiona always looked after Max and Maggie when Liam was away, and they loved her almost as much as they loved him.

Fiona had asked him to stay in her guest room for the night, to relax and spend some time with her and her foster daughter, Cassie, due to the oncoming storm. He'd thought about it, because he'd missed them both, but the storm could last for days. Frankly, he'd been away long enough, and he knew the mountains like the back of his own hand.

So, he'd promised his sister and niece—because that was how he thought of Cassie—that he'd visit them soon, and as he'd thought, he didn't have a lick of trouble on the drive home. He'd even made a quick but necessary stop for groceries and still managed to roll into his drive-way a solid thirty minutes before the spitting rain had fully turned to sheets of snow-drenched ice.

Knowing his sister would worry, he tried to check in using his mobile, but without a signal, that proved fruitless. And his satellite phone—a necessary piece of technology for assignments in certain remote locations—was pretty much useless with all the trees. Fortunately, and surprisingly, the landline still had service. Wouldn't last much longer, he'd expect, but he was able to reassure Fiona that he'd made it home in one piece.

The dogs had followed as he'd brought in the groceries, turned on the lights and jacked up the heat. They'd gobbled their kibble lightning fast and had then run in circles outside as he lugged in wood for the fireplace.

He'd gotten the fire going before heading out to make sure everything was in order with the generator, because before the night was through, he'd likely lose power. All was good. He had plenty of firewood, propane and food to outlast a storm of mega proportions. He could last a couple of weeks without issue. Good thing, too.

He had that bone-deep intuition that this storm would be one for the history books.

Trying not to worry about the dogs—they knew this part of the mountains as well as Liam did—he hollered their names again while deciding on his next course of action. Likely, the dogs were fine. Wouldn't hurt to give them a bit more time to stretch their legs and find their way home before allowing his concern to rule his judgment.

He'd unpack his equipment, get everything set straight and orderly, so that he could buckle in and work for the next long while. He had hundreds upon hundreds of digital photographs to sort through, analyze, decide which were gold and which were not, in addition to the many rolls of film he had to develop in his darkroom.

It was, perhaps, one of Liam's favorite aspects of his job: the meticulous process of bringing a captured image to life. Oh, he wasn't opposed to technology. Hell, he friggin' loved what technology could do and had done for his profession, both in the practical and artistic sense.

He was, however, a stalwart follower in the church of film photography. He would never want to give up either for the other, but if forced to choose…well, he'd say goodbye to technology and every one of his digital cameras, even his newest Canon, in a nanosecond.

And yeah, he'd be sorry to see them go, but everything about film photography—from the cameras themselves, to how they worked and how to coax the best possible shot out of them, to the art of developing the prints—was what had drawn Liam to this profession to begin with. His want for solitude and exploration drove him toward the obvious niche: nature and wildlife.

Well, also that he tended to understand animals far easier than people. Typically, he liked them better, too. And he would always choose just about any remote location over a city. Cities had too many people, and people liked to talk. Something Liam wasn't all that fond of.

His sister teased him, liked to say that Liam was allergic to other human beings outside of their family network. In a way, he supposed there was some truth to that statement, but his "allergy" was by choice. He was just a guy who did better on his own and had long ago recognized that fact. Other than Fiona and a few friends who didn't annoy him every time they opened their mouths, he had Max and Maggie. Along with his job, that was all he needed.

Calling out their names once again, he waited to see if they'd show. When they didn't, Liam shoved his worry to the back burner and returned to his cabin.

He'd built it close to five years ago now, on a secluded plot of land that was situated on an equally secluded area of the mountain. He didn't have neighbors. He had trees and streams, wildlife and tons of privacy.

Just as he liked it.

Inside, he shrugged off his coat and boots. If the two shepherds weren't back by the time he was done unpacking his gear, he'd put on his layers of arctic wear and try to track them down. Difficult, maybe impossible, with the current state of the weather, but he would have to try. He wouldn't be able to relax, otherwise.

Making quick work of the job, Liam hauled the equipment to his office at the back of the cabin, taking care to unpack and organize in his standard methodical fashion.

His rolls of exposed film were in airtight, labeled canisters, which he stacked in the refrigerator he kept in this room for just that purpose. A set of customized shelves sat against the back wall that held moisture-proof containers for his various cameras, along with those meant for other necessary items, such as lenses, straps and memory cards. The longest wall of the room held his desk, computers, monitors and an array of additional storage. Everything had a place.

Liam's darkroom was attached to the office, but for the moment, he left that door closed. No reason to go in there until he was ready to begin developing his film, which wouldn't be for another day or two.

With everything more or less put away, he took the stairs two at a time to his bedroom—the only room on the second floor—where he put on the layers of clothing and outerwear appropriate for the howling storm, which was turning into one hell of a blizzard.

Yeah, he had to go after his dogs.

Downstairs, he grabbed a flashlight before opening the front door. Then, having second thoughts, closed it against the torrential slam of wind and snow.

Max and Maggie's favorite roaming grounds were in the dense cluster of trees directly behind the cabin. They'd go round and round, sniffing out squirrels or rabbits, roughhousing with each other and in warmer temperatures, cooling themselves off in the stream that twisted through the trees. He'd go that route first and hope he could outlast the storm long enough to find them and bring them home.

Exiting through the back door, Liam did his best to ignore the worry gnawing at his gut. This just wasn't like them. Unless one of them had gotten hurt somehow, maybe a soft spot in the icy stream held one of them captive or…no. He wouldn't assume worst-case scenario.

They were smart, agile dogs. Excitable and full of energy. Probably, they were happy to be home and, in their canine glee, were ignoring the cold and snow in favor of a frozen romp. Sounded good. Plausible even, to anyone who didn't know Max and Maggie. Problem was, Liam did know them, and that sort of behavior in this type of weather didn't ring true.

He'd find them. He had to. They were as much his family as Fiona and Cassie.

Chapter 2

Within minutes of slamming into a cluster of trees, Meredith realized she no longer heard the comforting hum of the car's engine or felt the warm flow of heat blowing from the vents. She almost turned the key in the ignition to see if the engine would fire again, but had second thoughts. Better to first check out her surroundings and the car's condition.

Shoving the now-deflated airbag off of her body, she unclasped her seat belt, opened the driver's side door and stumbled to her feet. Wind-propelled snow slapped at her face, stinging her skin and making her eyes water. The early evening hung in complete darkness, without so much as a single star shining through to offer even the slimmest ray of light.

In her entire life, she had never felt so alone or unprepared.

She walked the perimeter of where she crashed. Since

she couldn't see more than a foot in front of her, she sniffed the air for signs of a fuel leak. Fortunately, if she could trust her nose, she didn't smell any gas fumes. Assuming the car would start, would she be able to get it back on the road? Maybe. She'd have to be lucky, though. The path out would need to be fairly straightforward, and the car would have to power through the snowy, icy uphill terrain in reverse.

The wall of never-ending wind almost knocked her over, and she had to brace herself to keep standing, had to force her frozen legs to slog through the snow. Again, she was stunned by the saturating, painful depth of the cold. She swore her bones were shivering.

Reaching the back of the car, Meredith tried to gauge how far off the road she'd gone. She couldn't tell, not from where she stood. But with so many trees, she couldn't be too far in. Probably, in the light of day, with or without a storm, she'd be able to see the road from here. As it was, however, attempting to blindly maneuver the car seemed a very bad idea.

Okay, then. Her best course of action was huddling in the Accord for the night. So long as the engine would start, she'd have heat. She had plenty of dry clothes in her suitcase. Oh! She even had a bottle of water and a roll of butter rum–flavored Life Savers. Not the most enjoyable way to spend a night, but it could be worse. A lot worse.

She would be fine.

As she fought her way toward the driver's side door, she suddenly recalled hearing of a woman who—a year or two ago—had died from carbon monoxide poisoning while waiting out a storm in her car. The tailpipes had become clogged with snow, cutting off oxygen. That poor woman had likely also thought she would be safe and sound in the shelter of her car.

Great. Yet another way that Meredith could die tonight.

She retreated again to check the tailpipes. For the moment, the snow wasn't quite high enough to reach them, thank God. Though, at this rate, with the direction the wind was blowing, it wouldn't take too much longer. Then what? She'd have to keep checking.

Satisfied that she'd be safe for the next little while, at least, she finally pushed her frozen, wet and shivering body into the driver's seat. The dry, still somewhat warm interior, even without blowing heat, immediately offered a blessed reprieve. But she'd feel much better with running heat. So, inhaling a large, hopeful breath, she twisted the key in the ignition.

The engine did not rumble to life. Heck, it didn't even squawk. Or whimper. It did nothing. She squeezed her eyes shut and prayed as fervently as she knew how and tried again. Nope. Still nothing. Tears of frustration and fear filled her eyes, but she ignored them.

The good news, she supposed, was that she could cross off carbon monoxide poisoning from tonight's worry list. But the possibility of freezing to death moved up to number one.

Grabbing her iPhone, Meredith pressed the Home button, hoping that between the crash and now, a miracle had somehow occurred and she'd have a signal. And… no to that, as well. She bit her lip hard to stop the fear from taking complete control and leaving her useless.

"Talk through this," she said, finding comfort in the sound of her voice. "What are the options?" There weren't many, so they were easy to count off. "I can stay here, inside the car, out of the storm. Or I can leave and try to find whatever shelter is attached to that light."

Remaining in the car, shielded from the elements, felt the safer of the two options. She would even bet that was the recommended advice for such a situation. But she didn't fool herself into thinking another motorist would fatefully come along the exact same path, realize she'd crashed, find her and rescue her or that Rachel would send out help—which, okay, she probably already had, but they wouldn't begin to know where to look—or even that she could make it until morning if she hung tight. The hours between now and then seemed endless.

If the storm continued with this force, she could be stuck here for longer than overnight. It could be days. Her car could become buried, the brutal winds could cause a tree to fall, shattering her windshield or trapping her inside.

Or worse.

Beyond all those horrific possibilities, the idea of sitting here, merely waiting for the storm to pass and hoping that nothing dire would occur, did not resonate well. It left too much to chance. It took too much out of her control.

Of course, on the other hand, she really did not relish the thought of going back outside.

Leaving the security of the car, no matter how temporary, required her to fight through the storm, that awful cold, the wind and the mounting snow, with the hope of locating a true shelter. She could fall and hit her head or twist an ankle or become even more lost. Even if she escaped those disasters, she would have to be strong enough to keep moving for however long it took to get somewhere safe. Could she do it? Was she that strong?

With a firmness that surprised her, she came to a decision. Her gut insisted that staying in the car would prove to be a mistake, and really, what else could she trust in but her instincts?

She'd find that light, which had to be connected to a house. And it couldn't be too far away for the glow, as faint as it was, to have made it through the thick, blinding haze of snow.

If she was wrong…no, she wasn't wrong. She *couldn't* be wrong.

In a flurry of adrenaline, Meredith climbed into the back seat and opened her suitcase. She needed dry clothes, layered, something to cover her face, ears and hands. She needed her hiking boots, which would offer a good deal more protection than her perfect-for-traveling, oh-so-cute clogs. And her coat, naturally. On the plus side, she had not packed light.

Sloughing off her wet jeans and sweater—quite the arduous process in the small constraints of the back seat—she put on a pair of leggings she'd planned on sleeping in, followed by one pair of jeans and then another. Over her head, she pulled on a T-shirt, a turtleneck sweater and finally, a long, roomy, extra-thick sweatshirt. Wet socks were replaced with two pairs of warm, dry socks, over which went her hiking boots. Along with her coat, she grabbed another turtleneck, a button-down flannel shirt and two additional pairs of socks.

Before leaving the car, she wrapped the turtleneck around her head and tied the sleeves under her chin. The flannel shirt, she folded and used as a scarf. She hung her purse diagonally over her neck and shoulder, slipped her hands into both pairs of socks and then on top of it all went her coat, which was a struggle of mega proportions to zip.

When all was said and done, she was hot, bulky and uncomfortable, but she thought she'd done a fairly decent job in protecting herself from the elements. Fingers crossed, anyway. As ready as she was going to get, she closed her eyes and breathed. Deeply.

"I will not die out there," she whispered. Opening her eyes, she stepped once again into the icy maelstrom. "I will be strong. I will find the light, which will be attached to a warm and occupied house, and someday in the future this entire night will be nothing more than an awful, distant memory. A story I will tell over drinks."

Right. A story and not the end of her life.

Hunching her shoulders against the wind, Meredith trudged away from the car, keeping her head angled downward and focusing on staying upright.

Her pace was slow, almost sluggish, due to the snow and the wind and the layers of clothing she wore weighing her down. While she had no actual sensation of time, it seemed to take forever to break through the trees and reach the road. So long, in fact, she had a moment of chilling fear that perhaps the car had spun again before the collision and she was walking in the exact wrong direction.

Relief centered in the pool of her stomach that this wasn't the case. Shoving her hands in the pockets of her coat—the socks she'd used as mittens were already wet, leaving her with frozen fingers—she paused to get her bearings. Here, at least, there was zero doubt as to which route to take. Uphill, the way she'd been driving. She'd continue along until she saw that light again. That light would lead her through the storm to safe ground.

Okay. She could do this.

"I am woman, hear me roar," she said into the wind. Silly, maybe, but the words gave her another bolt of strength, of courage. Of belief in herself. Whatever worked, right?

She started the trek, walking smack-dab in the middle of the road, using every muscle in her body to stay upright, all the while pretending that she didn't notice how the cold was seeping through her multiple layers of clothing. Or how her thighs were burning from the exertion. Or how her heart pumped faster, harder, with every labored breath. She kept her gaze glued in the direction she'd seen the light, praying she'd see it again with every step.

So far, just unforgivable darkness.

Had she made a mistake in leaving the car? *No. Don't think like that.* If she had made a mistake, there wasn't a darn thing she could do about that now. What she had to do, all she could do, was keep moving. That was her only job, the only "rule" she needed to follow.

"Don't stop, don't stop, don't stop," she said.

Time melted into a black hole of nothingness. She could've been walking for five hours or five days...she no longer knew. For a good while, her mind remained clear and her focus unfettered by the still-worsening weather or the effect it was having on her body.

But when she realized that it seemed she had gone a farther distance uphill on foot than she had in her car, still with no sign of the glowing light, fear and desperation rode in and took control.

Tears that she'd held back rushed her eyes and clogged her throat. Her legs, frozen and unwieldy, gave in to the demands of the wind and buckled at the knees. She tried to catch herself but couldn't.

Losing her balance, she toppled backward and landed in a heap in the thick, icy snow. She instantly went to stand, but between the weight of her clothes, the ferocious, sharp bite of the wind, the gales of stinging, slashing snow and the unexpected unresponsiveness of her numb limbs, her attempt was met with failure. As were the next three.

She breathed deeply, searched for and found an inner kernel of strength amidst the fear. Of course she could stand. She'd been able to stand for most of her life. It was second nature. It was easy.

She breathed in again, rolled to her knees and planted her hands deep into the snow, until she felt the ground and then, after counting to three, shoved herself up.

She didn't waste time feeling relief or in congratulating herself. This was bad. Worse, even, than she'd let herself believe when she'd ventured from the Honda. Yes, she quite possibly had erred in judgment.

Now, her decision to tread through the storm instead of staying put, where she would have had protection from the wind and snow, felt ludicrous and shortsighted and…well, stupid. Because no, she still did not see that light.

She had been so sure, but could she have imagined it? Perhaps. Especially with her deep desire to locate shelter, yeah, it was possible.

Meredith stopped. Should she turn around and try to find the car? Did that even make sense? The return trip was sure to be easier, since the wind would blow against her back and push her forward, but she wasn't positive she'd be able to locate the car again. Confusion swept in, mixing with her exhaustion and panic, making it nearly impossible to form any decision other than to do just as she was: stand in place. And that…well, that would seal her fate.

Right. Keep moving.

She started to walk again, forcing her body through the unyielding storm, her vision once again aimed in the direction she'd seen the light. If it hadn't been a mirage, she would see it eventually. But she couldn't stop again. No matter what, she couldn't stop.

One step. Two steps. Three, four, five and six.

When she reached ten steps, she started over with one. Anything to keep walking. If she stopped again, that would be that. And she was pretty sure if she fell again, she'd curl up in a ball and close her eyes. Because oh, every ounce of her body yearned for rest.

On her third set of ten steps, acceptance that, yes, she might be facing the last moments of her life seeped in.

How was that possible? How could *this* be it? How could she be *done*? What had she accomplished and what would she be remembered for? What dreams had she fulfilled? Did even one person on the face of the earth really know her?

The answer to that last part came swiftly. How could anyone else really know her when she didn't yet know herself? This trip was supposed to be the official, if belated, start of that journey. A time to make sense of all she'd learned, of what she'd thought was true balanced against the real truth. And then, over the next year, the rest of the pieces would fall into place.

That had been the plan. Not this fight for survival.

Until her early twenties, she hadn't had to fight for much of anything of importance. She and her two brothers were raised in an affluent household. Their parents were strict but attentive. Her childhood was filled with private schools, extensive travel and chauffeur-driven cars. Extracurricular activities were carefully chosen by her parents, and success in school was demanded more than encouraged.

Meredith's grades were always exemplary. She liked to learn, so that part of the equation came naturally. And yes, there were moments she wished her parents would loosen their will in favor of hers, but mostly she towed the line. She went to the college of their choosing, majoring in business as they expected. She fed her love of art with a class here and there, trips to various museums and devoting hours of nonstudy time to sketching and painting.

During her final year of college, she fell head over heels for a man who did not fit in her parents' neat and tidy box of expectations for their only daughter.

Alarico—Rico—Lucio worked as a mechanic, but he had big dreams and, she believed, the will to fulfill them. He drew her into his world quickly, so fast her head spun. He came from a large and boisterous family that had made Meredith feel at home the second she met them. They accepted her without question, as one of their own, simply because she was Rico's girlfriend.

And with love, everything changed. For the first time in Meredith's life, she had something to fight for. A future she wanted with a man she adored. She hoped that given enough time, her parents would come around and embrace her relationship with Rico, just as his family had.

There was a short period where she believed they tried and that they wanted her to be happy. Rico saw it differently, though, and he worried that eventually, their relationship would cause irreparable harm between her and her parents. He refused to separate Meredith from her family, and he refused to be viewed as a second-class citizen. Two strikes, not three.

But they were brutal strikes.

He ended their relationship, swearing that he would love her forever, and that someday, he would return to her as a man her family would respect and honor. His words were heartfelt, his voice sincere…his decision final.

The best year of her life ended in her greatest heart-break. She blamed her parents and their unrealistic ideals of perfection for pushing Rico away. She blamed her brothers for their choice in "acceptable" mates, and she blamed the universe.

She missed Rico. Her heart ached for him, but she respected his decision and did not try to contact him. There was some pride there, as well. She'd hoped he'd miss her as much as she missed him, give up on his insistence to wait and come to her. He did not.

After graduation, she found some backbone and instead of going to work for her father as had been the original plan, landed the stager position with little trouble. Surprising, really, since she had a degree in business, but oh, had she been happy. The job paid more than the going rate, which pleased her, and she found a small but nice apartment to live in.

For the next handful of years, she'd worked hard to create a life that she believed was of her own making. She'd been happy, except for missing Rico. She never stopped hoping that one day he would reach whatever level of success he needed and come back to her as he'd promised.

She had *waited* for him, day in and day out, for... years. Her heart held hostage, her hopes in limbo. And all for nothing. Absolutely nothing. None of it was real.

As it turned out, her job wasn't real, either. Well, the work was, she supposed, but she hadn't gotten the job on her own accord. The great and mighty Arthur Jensen had paved the way and was even "helping" with Meredith's salary. Tidbits of information that a tipsy coworker with loose lips had accidentally slipped at a company get-together less than three weeks ago.

She hadn't aced the job interview to win the job. She hadn't *earned* her bonuses over the years. All she was, all she'd ever been, was the privileged daughter of a successful man who had the leverage and the will to pull the right strings at the right time.

The second she confirmed the information was true, she quit her job. Then, humiliated and angry, resentful, too, she confronted her father. Initially, he'd tried to pacify her, but as their argument grew more heated, he called her "soft and sheltered" and stated that if he hadn't stepped in, she wouldn't have survived a year.

In a burst of emotion, she told her father that she was tired of living a life that he deemed appropriate and that due to him, she'd lost Rico. The best man she'd ever known. That it was his fault. Because her father had been blind to her happiness, because all he saw was a man with a blue-collar job who came from a blue-collar family, and wouldn't that be embarrassing, to have to introduce Rico—a mechanic—as his daughter's boyfriend? Or worse, as his son-in-law?

Her father wasn't a warm and cuddly man, but he

wasn't a cruel man, either. No, Arthur Jensen was a decisive man. He formed decisions quickly, based on all available information combined with a high-functioning intuition, and he rarely backed down. Meredith's words, along with her emotional state, must have hit a nerve. After years of staying silent, her father told her the truth about the man she claimed to love.

Rather than accepting an entry-level position at one of Arthur's companies—which Meredith hadn't known was even offered at the time—Rico turned the tables. He promised he would walk out of Meredith's life, never to return, for the sum of $50,000. Otherwise, he would marry her and within a year, she'd have one child and be pregnant with another.

Disgusted with Rico but seeing the man spoke the truth, her father paid the money, and Rico did exactly as he'd promised. Broke off their relationship and disappeared.

Her father had proof in his safe—the cashed check and a signed statement from Rico—but Meredith did not require that confirmation. Her father wouldn't lie about something so terrible. Her heart had cracked in agony again as she realized all the emotion, time and energy she'd wasted on Alarico and her ridiculous dreams for the future.

The only love she'd ever known had been false. The job she'd worked hard at for years, had believed she'd earned on her own merits, ranked as another false belief. On their own, these two were enough to swing the pendulum, but when she considered how often she'd followed her parents' wishes over her own, she was... done. Done being the privileged daughter of a successful man. Done living her life by someone else's set of expectations and rules.

More arguing ensued before she got what she wanted: zero interference. She also got what she hadn't asked for in the way of zero contact with her family. For a period of one year. She hadn't expected that stipulation, and it hurt, but she held her chin high and agreed.

It was time—more than time—to build a life she could trust in.

The following seven days were a mix of self-recrimination, doubts and insecurities as she attempted to pull herself out of the muck and consider her options for the future. That was when she contacted Rachel, a close friend who had grown up in the same affluent world as Meredith. Of all her friends, Rachel was the only one who was sure to understand the importance of Meredith's decision. And why she absolutely had to succeed.

It was decided that Meredith would use some of her savings to spend a few weeks vising Rachel in Steamboat Springs, Colorado. In addition to rest and relaxation and letting her brewing emotions settle, the reprieve would offer the opportunity to come up with an achievable plan. Where to live? Where to work? What dreams to chase?

To think she'd put so much energy into proving that she could make it on her own. An idealistic notion that, while important in a lot of ways, felt ridiculous and meaningless now that her life hung in the balance. *This* was the only fight that mattered. Survival.

And it was all on her.

Her thoughts ended when her knees buckled against the strong wind for a second time. She managed to stay standing, but it was by the skin of her teeth. Still no sign of that light, and she knew—in the way a person *knows*—that she did not have much left in her.

Lord. She was really going to die out here. Alone.

Why bother trying for another step, let alone ten, when her body, heart and brain all knew the truth? She wouldn't find that light. She wouldn't reach safety. She didn't know how long it would take, but yes, death was pounding on her door. Soon, not much longer, she guessed, he'd kick down the door and that would be that. And she would take her last breath. Have her last thought. Perhaps, if she had the strength, she'd cry her last tear.

So why bother? Why not just drop to the ground and…no. No!

She wasn't about to give up until she was left with no other choice. And no matter how close that moment might be, she wasn't there yet. She'd fight for as long as she could. Simple as that.

"Help me," she whispered the prayer. "Send an angel to guide me. Please?"

A sound other than the howling wind made it to her ears. What was that? She stopped, listened harder and heard the sharp, abrupt noise again and then again. It sounded like barking.

A dog? Yes. Had to be a dog.

More barking, and it seemed to be growing closer. Where there was a dog, there was probably a human. An actual person! Meredith turned in a circle, trying to gauge which direction the sounds were coming from. Close, she thought, but…where?

Oh, God, show me where.

"Help!" she called out, hoping her voice would cut

through the storm as cleanly as the dog's continuous series of barks. "Help me, please! I'm—"

Through the darkness a dog emerged, followed by another, both barking and moving far swifter than she would've thought possible. And then, they were at her side. *Two* dogs, not one. They were covered in snow, whining now instead of barking, and one started nipping at her ankles while the other mouthed her sock-covered hand and tugged.

"Hello?" she yelled. "Your dogs are with me! Hello?"

No response other than the dogs, who were still whining and nipping and tugging. Were they out here alone? She hollered into the wind again and waited, watched to see if anyone would answer or a human figure would emerge from the same direction the dogs had.

And...no.

Okay. Okay. Her salvation wasn't right around the corner. The dogs had probably gotten loose and were trying to find their own way back home. She could barely keep herself standing. What was she to do with two dogs who were likely just as lost as she was?

Still. They were company. She was no longer alone.

"Hey, guys," she said, her voice weak. "I'm happy to see you, but I'm afraid I'm not going to be of much help. I have no idea where I am or where you two came from."

The dog that was nipping at her heels stopped for a second to growl. Softly, not menacingly, and then returned to gently prodding at her heels. The dog who had her hand tugged harder and whined plaintively. As if to say, "Come on! Pay attention to what we're doing! Don't just stand there. Get moving! Lead us to safety, why don't you?"

"I don't know where safety is," she said. Tears flooded her eyes. "I wish I did."

Dropping her hand, the dog barked and ran ahead a few feet. Faced her and barked again. The other dog barked, too, and then shoved its head against the back of her legs, toward dog number one.

She stumbled from the pressure, almost fell, but the pooch pushed to her side and she grabbed onto its fur for stability and managed to keep herself standing.

Her numb brain clicked into gear. Were they trying to get her to move? Were they trying to lead *her* to safety? That was how it seemed, and because she needed something to believe in, to propel her into action, she chose to accept that these dogs were her saviors and all she had to do was follow them. Trust in them to get her out of this mess.

So she did.

Once the dogs saw she was walking, one stayed at her side while the other would run up a few feet, stop and bark until she made her way to that position. Over and over, this pattern was repeated. She almost fell a few times, but by the grace of God and the dog beneath her hand, she didn't. The storm wailed on, the cold grew even more bitter, and she knew that if not for these dogs—angels, they were angels—she wouldn't have made it this long.

She would have fallen. And this time, she would not have gotten back up.

Suddenly, Dog A—the one setting their direction—started barking even more exuberantly, and that was when Meredith saw the light.

She hadn't imagined it!

With tremendous effort, she pushed herself forward,

watched the dog run ahead a few more feet, and she pushed herself again. A house! An actual house. She could see the outline now.

She was so close that she was almost on top of it.

The storm had grown increasingly worse since she'd first seen the porch light, before her accident. She should have realized that by the time she returned to approximately the same position on foot, the snow would've fully camouflaged the glow. She wouldn't have seen it again. Not on her own, not without these dogs. But here it was. Just a few more feet.

That was all she had to walk, all she had to find enough power for. A few more feet.

They were, without doubt, the most difficult, exhausting few feet that Meredith had ever walked. But she made it to the porch, up the few steps and to the door.

The dogs were on either side of her now, pressing their bodies against her legs, sharing their strength. Keeping her standing. She knocked on the door, but her fist barely made a sound. She tried again and then, knowing she was this close to collapse, turned the doorknob and pushed open the door.

She called out a feeble "Hello?" but received no response. The room—the blessedly warm room—was empty. The dogs left her side to run in, barked at her to follow and so…well, she did. Unless the owner of this house was heartless, he or she would most certainly understand. And if they didn't? Well, that was the last worry on Meredith's mind.

Closing the door behind her, she tried for another "Hello" before half stumbling her way across the room. A low-burning, welcoming fire glowed brightly from the fireplace, and a long, inviting couch was right there along the wall. She went to the sofa, knowing she should take off her coat and outer layers of clothing, but...she couldn't.

As in, she was unable to.

All she could do was sit down, and then stretch out, on the thick, comfortable cushions and stare at the fire. Oddly, she did not feel awkward at being in a stranger's home without permission. She wasn't worried if the owner would understand or be angry when he or she walked in. All she felt, through and through, was a deep, abiding sense of relief.

Just relief. But it was profound.

Meredith fought to stay awake so that when the mystery owner appeared, she could try to explain her presence. Probably, she should sit up. Thought again that she should take off her coat, the shirts wrapped around her head, the socks on her hands. But doing so seemed impossible. Doing so would require considerably more energy than she currently had available.

So she closed her eyes, breathed in the deliciously warm air, and thanked the good Lord for getting her this far. She was alive. Freezing, exhausted, shivering and numb...but *alive*.

A miracle had occurred. She was not going to die tonight.

Vaguely, she felt the pressure of the dogs—her angels—as they jumped onto the sofa and snuggled their bodies around her, again offering what protection, what help they could. And that was enough to put an end to her feeble resistance. She stopped trying to find energy where there was none, stopped thinking altogether and allowed her body to do what it demanded.

She slept.

Chapter 3

For a solid hour and a half, Liam searched for Max and Maggie. They weren't behind the house, nor were they at the stream. He branched out in an ever-widening circle around the cabin while keeping track of his own position. At the forty-five-minute mark, he promised himself he'd only give it another fifteen before returning home, even though he flat-out hated the idea of stopping.

The dogs had gotten stuck somewhere, or one of them was injured. There just wasn't another logical explanation for their absence. And he had no doubt that if something had happened to one, the other would stand sentry. His dogs were loyal beyond belief, to each other, to him, to Fiona and Cassie. Hell, they'd probably be loyal to a stranger, so long as that stranger wasn't causing them or their family harm. They were those sorts of dogs.

So when he hit an hour without any sign of them, he

gave himself another thirty minutes. Due to the storm and all it brought with it, it was slowgoing despite his knowledge of the terrain and his attempts to move quickly. Didn't matter where he looked, though. They had seemingly vanished.

It was possible they'd returned to the cabin while he was trekking over the mountainside and even now were waiting for *his* return. He hoped so.

But yeah, another half an hour before turning back.

At one point, through the wind, he thought he heard barking, but it was so faint and so distant, he couldn't determine the direction. He called out their names repeatedly and listened closely.

Nothing.

Just the noisy storm playing tricks with his ears, fueled by his desperate hope to locate his dogs. Sighing, Liam pushed forward for the allotted thirty more minutes before turning on his heel and heading back toward the cabin with that awful, sick sloshing in his gut.

If they weren't there, he'd do the smart thing and warm up, get some food in him, rest for an hour or so, before beginning the search anew. And he'd rinse and repeat those actions for as long as it took or until his body gave out on him and he required more than an hour rest in between. Experience had taught him that he could go a real long time with minimal rest.

As he approached the house, he kept his eyes peeled for signs of Max and Maggie, willing them to appear. They did not. Nor were they waiting for him near the back door.

Damn it!

It was difficult to not turn around and retrace every one of his steps, but he knew better. This storm was fierce. As much as he wanted to get his dogs, he needed intermittent breaks in order to keep going throughout the night. Otherwise, he faced the possibility of wearing himself out too soon, which wouldn't do Max or Maggie a lick of good.

Sighing, feeling the weight of the world upon his shoulders, Liam entered through the back door, stopping in the heated mudroom. Piece by piece, he removed his outerwear, starting with his insulated gloves, coat and pants and ending with his heavy-duty hiking boots. Next came the wool hat and the midlayer, which was basically a fleece track suit. He hung each item separately, so all would be dry and ready to wear when he ventured back out.

Wearing only his socks, thermal-compressed long johns and a long-sleeved shirt, he walked into the kitchen, his plan to start a pot of coffee. While that brewed, he'd go upstairs, put on a fresh base layer and then prepare a meal. He wasn't tired yet, so he didn't need a nap. No more than an hour's reprieve should do the trick, less if he could get away with it.

He measured the coffee, filled the pot's reservoir with water, clicked the power button, and as he completed each step, he considered where to start his next foray. If the dogs were stuck or hurt anywhere nearby, he felt sure he would've found them. So, they were either farther out than seemed reasonable or, somehow, they'd been picked up by a passing motorist who just happened to be driving through this remote area in the middle of a friggin' storm.

Doubtful, though not impossible.

Running his hands over his eyes, Liam released a worried sigh. When he woke that morning, all had been right with the world—his world, anyhow—and now, because of two lost dogs, every last thing felt slightly skewed, just enough off balance to be completely wrong. If he'd accepted Fiona's offer of staying at her place through the storm, he'd still have his dogs.

All would have remained right in his world.

He stomped out that thought good and fast. One of the many lessons he'd learned over the years was not to dwell on what couldn't be changed. What-ifs did not yield results. All what-ifs did was fill a person with regret, making them wish for the impossible. And that right there was a huge waste of brainpower, energy, and productivity.

Smarter, better to learn from where you've already walked, but focus on the ground ahead of you that has not yet been covered.

Fifteen minutes gone. Liam strode from the kitchen into the living room, his vision planted directly on the stairs. Change clothes. Eat. Drink coffee. Get back out there, and…whoa.

Halting with one foot half raised in the air in front of the first step, he pivoted toward the sofa. There were his dogs, safe and sleeping so soundly that neither raised their sharp, pointed noses in his direction.

For a fraction of a second, all Liam could do was stare in shock. How the hell had they gotten into the house? Had they somehow followed him in earlier and he hadn't noticed? In another millisecond, as his shock faded into relief, he realized they were not alone.

A slight, huddled figure—a woman, he thought— was curled tight against the back of the sofa. Maggie rested at the tips of a pair of petite hiking books and

Max stretched out on his stomach along the length of the stranger's body.

Liam went to the couch, knelt down and patted Max's head before reaching over to gently shake the woman's dark-gray-coat-covered shoulder. She didn't budge or make a sound. He tried again with the same result.

Sizing up the situation and not liking what he saw— wet coat and jeans, pale skin, slight shivers rippling through the woman's body—Liam muffled a curse. Max, hearing Liam, opened his eyes and scooted to join his sister at the end of the sofa. He whined in an imploring fashion, pushed his nose into the woman's denim-clad leg and whined again.

"I know, boy," Liam said. "I know."

There were a few scenarios that came to mind, but the precise details of how this woman got to his couch escaped him. He also did not know how long she'd been roaming in the bitter cold before finding her way here. Neither of those mattered at that moment. What did was determining the state of her health, along with that of his dogs.

Questions could be answered later.

"Max. Maggie," he said sharply. "Down!" Max obeyed instantly, but Maggie kept sleeping, so Liam gently tugged her ear. She shifted, opened her eyes and yawned. He repeated his command, and she slid to the floor, where she stood next to Max and added her canine voice to his in a whine equally as imploring. "I got her," Liam said. "Promise."

The tense lines of the dogs' bodies relaxed as they plopped their butts on the floor, both sets of eyes now bright and alert, focused on the prone woman. Apparently relieved to pass on the caretaking duty to Liam but unwilling to drop their protective vigil until whatever danger they sensed had passed.

"I got her," Liam repeated. The dogs retreated to the thick rug in front of the fireplace, where they landed on their bellies. Both sets of eyes continued to watch, assess.

He gently rolled the woman to her back and tried to wake her again. Her eyes remained firmly shut, her breathing a little too fast for his comfort. He also wasn't fond of the whiter-than-milk shade of her skin.

Hypothermia? Quite possibly, and if so, hopefully not too far advanced. And yeah, he knew what he had to do, he just didn't want to without her permission. Which she couldn't give unless she woke the hell up.

"Hey, there," he said, squeezing her hand as he spoke. "I'm Liam and my dogs are Max and Maggie. We're… ah…happy you're here, safe. And I'm guessing this is the most comfortable you've been in a good long while, but I would greatly appreciate it if you'd open those eyes of yours. Maybe talk to me for a few minutes, answer some of my questions."

She did not even flinch.

He set his discomfort aside and, moving quickly, unzipped her coat. "Okay, I get it. You don't want to be disturbed. No problem for the moment, but if you can hear me," he said, keeping his voice at an even, calm keel, "I need to get all of these wet clothes off of you. I'm sorry about this, but don't be scared. I'm trying to help, not hurt."

Doubtful she heard him, but it seemed better somehow, saying the words.

He took off the wet socks covering her hands, removed her coat, unlaced and yanked her boots from her feet and—feeling like a peeping tom, even knowing he had to do it—unclasped and unzipped her cold, wet jeans.

Ah. Smart woman, she had on another pair underneath. Also cold, also wet. When both pairs were tugged from her body, leaving her in a pair of thin black leggings—they would also have to come off, but not yet—he pushed out a strangled breath.

Turning his attention to the rest of her body, ignoring the rapid beat of his heart—she hadn't moved a muscle, even as her jeans were removed—he untied the shirts she'd wrapped around her head and face, exposing a tumble of long, curly, matted blond hair. And he had that weird déjà vu sensation that he'd been here, done this before.

She, this, reminded him of… "Goldilocks," he muttered. "Asleep on my couch, rather than my bed, but close enough. Guess that means I'm one of the three bears."

Of course, his sister would say he was grumpy enough to be all three bears in one.

Trying not to jar Goldi too much, he lifted her upper body with one arm and unhooked her purse from her shoulder, taking it over her head. Her black sweatshirt and the turtleneck she wore under it were both wet. It took some doing, but he got those off, too. Now, Miss Goldilocks was down to a T-shirt, leggings and socks. And she still hadn't moved.

A thick, soft blanket was folded over the back of the sofa. Covering her with it, he said, "I need to get a few things, darlin', but I'll only be a couple of minutes. Why don't you try to open your eyes while I'm gone? Would make me and the dogs very, very happy."

Upstairs first, for dry clothes—she'd drown in them, as they were his, but he figured she wouldn't mind—and next, the linen closet for several more blankets. As expected, when he returned, Max and Maggie had jumped on the sofa, taking their prior positions at her feet and alongside her. And the sight of this, for some unknown reason, made his heart pound a mite harder. Warmed it a little, too.

"Down," he said, motioning his arm toward the floor. They didn't obey instantly, just whined and gave him *that* look. Not a surprise, really. Now that they'd shaken off their tundra expedition and had warmed themselves by the fire, their stubborn streak had intensified. "Down," Liam repeated, in a firm, don't-argue-with-me tone. They complied.

But they didn't return to the fire. They stood as close to the sofa as possible without actually being on it, watching Goldi with acute alertness. In some way Liam did not yet understand, his dogs had bonded with this woman. She was theirs now. One of the pack.

Unexpected. Curious, too.

Liam sighed and finished what he had started. Reminding himself that he was taking *care* of her and not taking advantage, he used the blanket that was already covering her as a privacy tent of sorts.

He reached underneath and slipped off her leggings, replacing them with a pair of his drawstring pajama bottoms, which he tied at her waist. Rinse and repeat with her T-shirt and one of his sweatshirts, although this switcheroo proved a bit more complex. He did the same with her feet, shucking off her wet socks—two pairs—and covering them with a single pair of his thick, wool socks. Finally, he gathered the blankets he'd brought downstairs, and one by one, layered them on top of her, using one to tuck around her head.

Now that she was dry, clothed and covered, he tried once again to rouse her to awareness. While she did not fully open her eyes, her lashes fluttered slightly and a soft moan fell from her lips.

That seemed positive, and far better than complete unresponsiveness. But she was still shivering. Her breathing remained rapid, though perhaps less so than earlier, and when he checked her pulse, he found it steady if a bit fast. She was also still too pale for his peace of mind.

She needed hydration. Something warm, sweet, and caffeine free. Liam wasn't much for sweet or caffeine free, but Fiona kept a few boxes of herbal teas here for when she visited. He'd brew a cup of that, add a little sugar, and spoon it into Goldi's mouth. He couldn't give her much, as she was still unconscious, but even a little would help. He'd take it slow. Which meant that he had one long night ahead of him, because—much like his dogs—he wouldn't leave his surprise houseguest's side until he knew she was okay or, he supposed, was on the definite road to being okay.

Max woofed a soft, impatient bark. A whine from Maggie followed. Looking at his anxiously waiting dogs, Liam nodded toward the sofa. They seemed fine physically, but after the tea, he'd give them a thorough once-over to reassure himself.

"Go ahead," he said. "I won't stop you now. Your body warmth will do her good."

That was all they needed to hear. Thirty seconds later, Maggie was curled around Goldi's feet and Max was stretched out beside her. In almost perfect unison, they heaved breaths of relief while giving Liam a look that seemed to say, "Okay! Good! What's next?"

Great question. "We need her to wake up. Work on that, while I make the tea."

She'd been cold. So very cold, yet her exhaustion had overpowered the need to find warmth. Sleeping was easier, made her forget about the cold.

A voice, soothing and rich, layered and evocative, had chiseled into her brain, asking her to wake up. And oh, she tried to do as the voice asked, tried to find the will to rouse herself and talk, because it seemed of utmost importance to whomever spoke that she do so.

But try as she might, she couldn't. It was as impossible as taking flight, using her arms as wings. So, she fell deeper into the realm of the unconscious, where her mind concocted a fairy tale to explain all she felt, all she heard.

In her dream, there wasn't a blizzard raging outside. It was the middle of summer, one of those perfect balmy days that smelled of coconuts and lime, with fluffy cotton clouds floating in a robin's-egg-blue sky. She was on a boat, drifting aimlessly, listening to the lapping waves and enjoying the luxurious rays of the sun as they coated her naked body in the most delectable warmth. Hands, also warm and soothing, brushed gently against her skin—her legs, her arms, her face—and every now and then, stroked her hair.

She hadn't felt safe in so long. Why? She couldn't remember the details, but tendrils of nausea swirled in her belly. *Now*, though, she felt safe and protected and so gloriously, wonderfully warm.

Again, the stranger's tenor sifted into the smoky film

of her dreams, where it sparked and sizzled in her soul. Her brain decided that this deep and evocative voice must belong to the man who loved her and that he was, in some form or fashion, taking care of her.

Had she been ill? Her stomach rocked with another bout of nausea. Seasick, she determined. While the softly bobbing boat spoke of calm waters now, it must have been rough going earlier. And this man with his delicious voice had seen her through the worst of it. So, yes, he loved her.

Did she love him? She couldn't see his face, recall his name or even how they had met, but for her to feel so absolutely safe and cared for, love had to exist on both sides.

She continued to sleep, continued to dream. Lost to reality. There was nothing to worry about, not a reason on earth to force herself awake.

Slipping deeper into this magnificent dream world, her subconscious manufactured the type of love only found in the most romantic of movies, with her and the man behind the gentle touches and seductive voice as the leads. She still couldn't remember his face, which was odd, yes, but somehow, this lack of knowledge didn't cause her a moment's concern. He was hers. She was his. That was enough.

But suddenly, she saw his eyes. And oh, were they gorgeous. Sensual and vivid and striking. Distinctive. Irises rimmed in dark olive green that gradually lightened to the color of moss near his pupils, glinted with shots of burnished gold and warm brown. Eyes she *knew*.

They belonged to the man she loved.

And with this man at her side, her brain continued to weave a story for her alone to experience. There was laughter and passion. Long talks and handheld walks. A proposal and then a wedding. Children, a boy and a girl named Max and Maggie.

Years upon years passed while she slept, years filled with the purest form of happiness she'd ever known. Satiating, complete, fulfilling and robust. Ever changing, ever growing, ever stronger…day in and day out.

This fantasy was so intense, so real, so exhilarating and breathtaking, so *beautiful* a life her mind had created, that even as she started to come around, to realize she was merely dreaming, she staunchly resisted the pull of awareness. She wanted, yearned for more of this.

Precisely, *this* life. And she wasn't ready to leave it behind.

The sad truth was that even with Rico, before learning that all of his words had been bald-faced lies, she hadn't known such depths of emotion existed. So, she stubbornly held on to her dream world and tried—oh, how she tried—to quiet her thoughts, relax her body, to return to the fantasy. But with conscious thought of Rico, her fog-filled brain cleared and the rest of the facts from the past several weeks engulfed her in a rush.

Her job. The argument with her father. Deciding to visit Rachel and flying to Colorado. Her decision to rent a car and then losing her way in the mountains. The storm. The accident. Her loneliness and consuming fear, the acceptance that she would die…and then, those dogs.

Those astounding dogs who'd found her and led her to shelter. Had led her…here.

No. She did not want to think about any of that, had no desire to do anything other than fall back into a coma-like sleep and return to that oh-so-beautiful life. Pretend or not, it didn't matter. She yearned to be there again, even if every speck of it was only her imagination.

But the voice that had started it all was becoming more insistent that she wake. *Now.* That she'd been sleeping for too long and enough was enough. That she open her mouth and drink, because she needed more than a spoonful or two of tea every hour. He was tired. He was worried.

"Open your eyes, Goldi," he said, his voice loud and commanding. "Now!"

She did *not* obey his command. Eventually, she would have to, but at the moment, she didn't need to look into this man's eyes and see they weren't green with golden flecks. They were probably brown. And while she did not have a thing in the world against brown eyes, she wasn't ready to give up her fantasy. This man's voice— his deliciously rich voice—was, in her mind, a matching set to the green eyes she'd imagined.

To see otherwise would only make it more difficult to jump into her dream life when she was able to sleep again, and she believed she'd be able to soon. If only he would stop *talking.*

"Goldilocks, you're killing me here," the man said in a lower volume. "Wake. Up."

She still would not have responded except for the identifiable set of canine whines that followed his plea. *Her dogs.*

Sighing, unwilling to ignore her angels, she capitulated enough to say, "I'm awake." A tail thumped near her leg as she spoke. A warm nose pressed against her cheek, giving her a lavish lick. "Kind of."

Ouch. His voice might be a melody fit for a concert,

but hers sounded rough and raspy. Thick. Nothing like normal. As if she hadn't spoken aloud in days.

"Thank God," he half whispered. Then, "Great! I knew you could do it. How about opening your eyes and trying to sit up? Move slowly, though. You've been out for a while."

Those words acted as a catalyst, and suddenly, she realized how heavy and cumbersome her body—as in, every inch of it—felt. Tipping her head in the opposite direction of the man's voice, because no, she still wasn't ready to see him, she did as he asked and waited for her blurry vision to sharpen. She stared at the back of a couch, at the thick stripes of deep burgundy, gold and forest green on the cushion. She remembered how she'd stumbled across the room on unwieldy legs, frozen and exhausted, with this piece of furniture as her singular goal.

She had almost died. *Almost.*

"You said I have been out for a while," she said. "How long is that, exactly?"

"I don't know the precise moment you found your way here and collapsed." Muted frustration, perhaps some concern, echoed in his speech. "When I came home, you were already down for the count, but we're going on close to twenty-four hours since then."

How was that possible? In reality, an entire night and another day had elapsed, yet in her dreams, that same amount of time had equaled years. She thought about the picture she must have presented to this man, a stranger, as he'd walked into his living room with her passed out on his couch. She was lucky. So very lucky. He could've been a monster.

"I'm sorry about letting myself in and...well, I

mean, I knocked first and I tried to stay awake, but...
I should've tried harder." Though, even as she said the
words, she knew there wasn't any *trying harder*. She'd
barely made it this far. "So, um, I'm sorry."

With each word, her voice grew in strength, became
more sure, but still held that rough and raspy edge.
Thirsty. Lord, she was thirsty. And she had to pee, too.
Badly, though not as desperately as one would think
after sleeping for a full twenty-four hours.

He snorted. "You're forgiven for saving your life. I'd
have done the same."

"You...took care of me, too." She knew he'd stripped
off her clothes, redressed her in something else, had
dribbled tea into her mouth. It was a lot to do for a
stranger. "Thank you."

"Didn't have much choice," he said in a brusque but
not unkind manner. "There's no way to get help out
here until the storm is over and the roads are cleared.
From the looks of it, we'll be stuck together for another
handful of days. Maybe a week. But you're welcome."

"A week?"

"Unlikely, but possible. So, if you hadn't found your
way here, well..."

Right. She would have died. She'd already figured
that one out. Pretending she felt better than she did,
she said, "If we're going to be stuck together, I'd like to
know your name."

"Oh, sorry. It's Liam. And it will be fine. Number
one priority is your health."

So far, he hadn't pushed her to do *anything* now that
she was awake and talking. He had to be exhausted, but
he was giving her the opportunity to orient herself. To
figure out how she felt and how to find some comfort

in this strange situation. Unless, of course, he often had strangers stumbling to his house in the middle of a storm and passing out on his sofa.

For some reason, the thought made her laugh.

"What's so funny, Goldilocks?"

"Meredith," she corrected, "And…" Oh. Okay. That small, barely there laugh had magnified the pressure on her bladder tenfold.

Saying a mental goodbye to that beautiful, love-filled—and not to mention, pretend—life she'd concocted, Meredith planted her hands on the couch and slowly pushed into a sitting position. The dog who had been squashed against her side jumped off the couch but not before gracing her with another doting lick to her cheek. "This is awkward," she said, "but I need to use the bathroom."

"No need to feel awkward, and of course you do," he said, his voice reasonable. "I'll show you where it is, but be careful when you stand. Take it slow."

"Right." Her head swam for a minute, maybe two, before she regained her equilibrium. Time to face the music, time to look into this man's real eyes.

She turned to face him. And her breath caught in her throat, her heart ramped up in speed and a tremble of surprise rolled through her weakened limbs as she stared into Liam's eyes.

Green and gold, sensual and vivid, striking and distinctive. The same eyes she'd dreamed about. But they were real, not imaginary, and they belonged to Liam-with-the-rich-and-layered-voice.

And oh, the rest of what she saw lived up to those eyes. Wavy black hair, somewhat tousled at the moment, framed a strongly featured face that all but begged to be touched. The chiseled, powerful line of his cheekbones was a work of freaking art, as was the firm, somewhat generous stretch of his lips. His nose was mostly straight, neither too large nor too small, and a square, powerful jaw that suggested inherent stubbornness completed the picture. Her fingers itched to sketch this man, to bring his likeness to life on the page.

Without doubt, though, it was Liam's eyes that resonated with her soul. They brought to the surface how, in her dreams, this man had been *hers*, and she had been his.

"I dreamed you," she blurted, lost as their "life" came back to her in waves. "I dreamed us. And you're going to think I'm crazy, but I'm supposed to be here, with you. Because this is how we meet, and there must be a meeting before anything else can happen. And a lot is going to happen for us." Great. She had to sound like a nutcase. "Or…um… I meant to say that in my dream, a lot happened. But you know, not until after we met. Which makes sense!"

Confusion darted into those stunning eyes of his, followed quickly by concern. "Is that so?" he asked lightly. "Well, before you explain any more of that, how about we get you to the bathroom? Once you're set there, your body needs sustenance. I'll whip up something that resembles a meal. After that, you'll probably feel a lot better. More like yourself."

Ha. He thought she was delirious. And okay, she probably shouldn't rule out that possibility. But if there was any chance at all that she'd dreamed about a life—an incredible, beautiful life—with this man for a reason, then she had to consider what that reason could be. The pull to do so was strong. Stronger than she thought she could, or even should, resist.

Though, he was right on one front: she'd wait and see how she felt about everything later, once she'd shaken off more of the dream world in favor of the real world.

This world. The one she was apparently stuck in for... oh, maybe a week. With a man whose eyes seared her soul.

It would prove interesting, to say the least. It might even be life changing.

Chapter 4

Liam needed to sleep. Soon. The grouch in him was crawling to the surface, and the last thing he wanted to do was bite this poor woman's head off. She'd already been through enough. Before he could give into his body's demand for rest, though, he had to be certain Goldi—*Meredith*—wasn't about to pass out again. She required food far more than he did sleep.

Even if his body declared otherwise.

He waited outside the bathroom door, listening for signs of distress or cries for assistance. So far, all he heard was the full blast of the water faucet as she, presumably, tended to some hygiene matters. After she ate, he'd get her another set of clothes and show her where the bath towels were, as he imagined she'd like a shower. Hell, he'd like one of those, too.

She had dreams about him, she'd said, and that she was supposed to be here, that a meeting had to happen before anything else could, and that a lot was going to happen. Made him worry she'd bonked her head, though he hadn't noticed any bruising or, for that matter, lumps or bumps.

What if she was delusional? Dealing with an extra person with their sanity intact, stuck in the same space— *his* space—would prove challenging enough for a guy like him, but if she kept rambling on about dreams? Well, he'd rather not deal with any of that nonsense, thank you very much.

Not that he had any other option, he supposed. She was here for the next good while, and there wasn't a damn thing he could do about it.

Combing his fingers through his hair, Liam tried to keep his impatience under wraps. Wasn't her fault she ended up in his vicinity during a freakishly early storm. Wasn't her fault that she'd dreamed whatever she had. More than likely, once she ate and rested again, she'd be closer to her normal self. Which, hopefully, would be defined as the non-annoying type.

That, he could handle. He'd been dealing with that most of his life.

Finally, the water turned off, and a few seconds later, the door creaked open. Lord, she was pale. And the purple smudges under her eyes spoke of her exhaustion. Maybe she'd eat, take that shower, and sleep for another twelve hours. A likely scenario. Hell, she'd probably sleep most of the next week, which meant they'd barely have to exchange words.

He felt a whole lot better at that thought. It would be almost as if she wasn't even here.

Until she slept again, though, this would be awkward as hell. Sighing, Liam gestured toward the sofa. "You're going to be weak for a while. Rest. I'll bring you some food and…ah…more tea. Unless you'd rather have something cold? I have grape juice or—"

"Yes, please." She leaned into the wall for support and a shudder rolled through her slight frame. He wanted to pick her up and cart her to the couch, but he managed to restrain that instinct. "Grape juice sounds fantastic," she said. "But I'm not ready to lie down again when I've barely opened my eyes. I'll join you in the kitchen. We can…talk. I'll fill you in how your dogs recued me."

He waited a beat and then another, to see if her body would give in to its obvious weakness. If she sagged to the floor, he could legitimately refuse her offer and insist she rest—without coming off as a Class A jerk—but no. She remained standing, albeit somewhat crookedly propped against the wall, with a hopeful smile. How could she want to talk? If she already wanted to talk, he was done for.

"Tell ya what," he said, swallowing another sigh. "If you can make it to the kitchen without falling, then sure. We can…chat it up while I put together some food."

The second—as in the *very* second—the words came out of his mouth, Maggie pulled herself off the floor and went to Goldi's side. Rather, Meredith's side. Standing straight, the woman put her hand on the top of Maggie's head for balance and, with a determined set to her jaw, said, "Lead the way!"

Hrmph. He should've added "on your own" to his prior statement. As in, "If you can make it to the kitchen *on your own* without falling, then sure." Regrettable error, but an understandable one. He was, after all, beyond exhausted.

Nodding sharply, he turned and strode to the kitchen,

shoving his concern for a stranger's well-being *and* his grumpy attitude as far down as possible. It wasn't as if he planned on preparing a feast. He'd open a can of soup, which would take all of five minutes, and slap a slice of bread in the toaster. In less than ten minutes, she'd be eating. She couldn't talk his ear off with food in her mouth, and by the time she was done, she should be ready to collapse.

Ten minutes should be a cinch.

In the kitchen, he pulled out one of the chairs and waited for her and Maggie. She entered a minute later, Maggie still by her side with Max following. Yup. Whether he understood why or not, his dogs had declared Goldi—damn it, *Meredith*—to be one of theirs. Perhaps hearing about how they'd rescued her would clue him in as to why. And yeah, he'd like to know the details of how his dogs had brought her to his couch.

How bad could it be? It was her story, since the dogs—amazing as they were—had yet to learn how to speak the English language, so she would do most of the talking. Realizing that all he had to do was cook and listen, maybe nod every now and then, utter an "ah" or an "is that so?" the tension between his shoulder blades relaxed.

"Here," he said, his voice gruffer than he'd intended, "sit down before you keel over." Now, under the bright, overhead light in the kitchen, her pale skin appeared almost translucent. Those dark circles beneath her eyes could've been the result of being on the losing side of a bar fight. "Last thing you need is to cause more damage to yourself. I'll get you that juice."

Lips stretched into a faint smile as she lowered herself to the chair. "That would be fantastic. And I'm okay. A little weak, yes, but really, not so bad considering."

She was probably the type of person who refused to admit when she was sick, too. He supposed he couldn't give her grief over that, at least not if his sister was anywhere close to hearing distance. He didn't get sick. Or so he told Fiona whenever she tried to coddle him over a cold or what-have-you. He didn't need coddling. Despised coddling.

After handing her the juice, he said, "Drink it nice and slow. There's a lot of sugar in that, and it is ice cold. I guarantee if you chug it down, no matter how thirsty you feel, you will throw up all over my floor, and I don't really feel like cleaning that up."

She nodded and took a grateful sip. "How is it that…" she trailed off. At his confused expression, she said, "Sorry. I forgot to speak my words and just thought the rest of the question. Let me try again…how is it that you have electricity? I mean, with the weather like it is, and that wind, and being so deep in the mountains, I would've guessed you'd have lost power ages ago."

"We did. Or I did." Opening the pantry, he grabbed a can of chicken noodle soup and the loaf of bread. "Yesterday, actually. Not long after I came home and found you."

"Oh." Turning her head, she glanced out the window, at the still-raging storm. "They already got the power back on? In this?"

"Nope." He opened a drawer and retrieved the can opener. "They can't do anything while it's still snowing like that, and even if the snow stopped now, it will take days—if not a week—for the power to be reestablished. I'm used to it, though admittedly, not this early in the season."

"You have power," she said. "Unless I am imagining the lights and the heat, which would mean that I really am delusional."

"I'd say the delusional part remains to be seen, but your observation skills are not in question. Yes, I have power."

She snickered, showing she had a functioning sense of humor. "How?"

"Magic," he said, surprising himself.

"Magic?"

"Yup. You, my dear, were lucky enough to become snowbound with a wizard." Now, where had that come from? Liam wasn't the teasing sort. Never had been, anyway. It didn't feel awful. Actually, he somewhat liked this moment. Dumping the can of soup into a saucepan, he turned the burner on low. "Why do you think I choose to live up here, alone and in complete seclusion? People, even in today's world, tend to become fearful of what they don't understand."

"Afraid you'll be burned at the stake?"

"Nah. I'm a wizard, not a witch."

"Doesn't really matter what you call yourself, if you have magic and people are afraid of magic," she said in a dry manner. "I rather like the idea of it, myself."

"You do, huh?"

"Sure. Why wouldn't I? Magic could ease so many discomforts in life." She took another careful sip of her juice. No puking yet, thank goodness. "And I would be willing to buy into the implausible tale you tell, except for one small detail that has left me confused."

"And that would be?"

She grinned and wrinkled her nose. It was…well, the word *adorable* came to mind. "I don't quite understand how you are able to use magic for electricity, yet… you're heating up a can of soup and toasting bread the old-fashioned way. Why not just wave your hand and have a bowl of homemade soup appear? Along with… hmm, a basket filled with artisan breads?"

"Simple. I didn't say I was a good wizard. Electricity is one thing, but food is quite another. Food takes a lot more skill than turning on the lights. Magically speaking."

"Is that so?" Her lips twitched again. Yup. Adorable. "I would think it would be quite the opposite."

"You would, huh? I agree, but alas, the world of magic isn't based in logic." He felt himself smiling. Whoa. He must be on the edge of collapse if this conversation was amusing him, rather than annoying him. Stirring the soup, he said, "But consider everything that goes into a bowl of soup. It's really quite difficult."

"Huh. I guess that makes a weird sort of sense." Again, she sipped her juice. He was pleased she didn't appear to be having problems with it. "Oh," she said, "I got it. A generator?"

"Yeah. Up here, you pretty much need one." The soup was hot and the toast was done and thanks to his out-of-character whimsy, he'd done all of the talking. Quickly, he buttered the toast and ladled the soup into two over-size mugs, grabbed a couple of spoons and napkins. "Here you go," he said as he set her food in front of her. "Eat up. But…slowly."

"Is that your advice for everything? Go slowly?"

"For a woman who has just gone through what you have? Yup."

"I'm actually doing…okay."

"Good." He sat down across from her and waited for the dogs to sidle next to him, as they did whenever he ate. They didn't. They stayed planted at Goldi's feet, looking up at her with what could only be described as utter devotion.

He knew that look. He'd seen it on his own face a grand total of once. A little over a decade ago, which seemed unbelievable. So much time had passed. An entire lifetime, plus one or two more.

But he hadn't forgotten that look. His dogs were besotted.

"Tell me the story," he said, "of how you met Max and Maggie."

Sky-blue eyes widened in shock. She dropped her spoon, which clattered on the table and sent sprays of broth, along with a few noodles and chunks of chicken, flying into the air. Blinking, she asked, "How I met who?"

"Max and Maggie," he said. She blinked again, obviously still confused. "My dogs? You were going to tell me how they found you, rescued you?"

"Max and Maggie are your dogs! Right. Of course."

"Are you okay? Feeling dizzy or sick to your stomach?" he asked. "We can put this off until later, after we've both slept some."

"No, no. Not that. I just didn't know the dogs' names, so it took a minute for the pieces to connect." Her words came out in a jumble, one on top of another, and a smattering of pink blossomed on her cheeks. "You are correct, though! I promised you the story, and really, it won't take that long to tell."

"If you're sure, then go ahead."

"Yes, I am," she said as she sopped up the soup spill with her napkin. "I'm supposed to be on…vacation. I'm from San Francisco, and I have a friend who lives in Steamboat Springs. Rachel. Who is probably frantic with worry right about now. The last time we spoke was right after my plane landed. I checked in, told her I'd be there soon, and then the storm hit. I got lost."

"She probably is worried, but there isn't anything we can do about that just yet. Once we have phone service again, you can call her." She nodded, but didn't speak. He waited a few more seconds before saying, "Go on. Eat as you talk. Your body needs the nourishment."

Dragging in a deep breath, she nodded again and started to talk. Bit by bit, as she slowly ate her soup and toast, drank her juice, the entire story came out. With each word spoken, he easily heard the remnants of fear, desperation, loneliness in her voice. Saw it in her eyes, whenever she looked in his direction, and in her body, as she shivered in remembrance.

He felt for her, deeply. In a manner that held zero logic. She wasn't a part of his life. Could not be described as either family or friend. That he knew her at all boiled down to a simple coincidence of timing and location. Yet, he *felt* for her, and had the inane wish that he could step backward in time and meet her at the airport, warn her…lead her in the correct direction, so she'd never have to go through what she had.

So she could escape this haunting fear, stark loneliness and sheer desperation that would likely forever live in her memory.

It would take more effort than she realized at this moment to find peace and acceptance for what had occurred, for all she'd experienced. He knew this with absolute fact. Hell, it had taken him close to five years to free his soul, his heart, from his darkest memory. Some days, he still struggled more than he thought he should, even now, even after almost a decade.

Well, perhaps that right there was the foundation, the reason…the *logic* of feeling so much for a stranger. It was based on pure compassion for another human being's struggle that, while vastly different in the actual facts from his most personal battle, held enough emotional nuances to strike a chord.

Demons. They looked alike, felt alike, despite their origin.

Liam pushed out a breath, set the past aside and focused on this minute with this woman. No matter the reason, he was damn glad his dogs had found her and brought her here, to him. Was glad the coincidence of timing and location had led to her arriving when he was actually in the state and not off on assignment. Was glad he hadn't chosen to stay at his sister's place for the duration of the storm. He was just…glad.

And he didn't need to decipher all the reasons why.

"That had to be absolutely terrifying," he said when she'd finished speaking, when he'd finished thinking. "Draining. But you persevered. You didn't give up and now, you're safe. In another day or two, you'll feel more yourself. And you will know, for the rest of your life, that you are formed of steel. Don't forget that part. Steel. Many people never gain that knowledge."

"Maybe. But really, without your dogs, I don't know how much longer I would've made it." She shrugged as if attempting to lighten her words. Or maybe the fatalistic meaning behind them? Could be either, he supposed. Half collapsing in her chair, she reached one hand down to pat Max's head and said, "I've decided that your dogs are my guardian angels. They saved me."

"You were working on rescuing yourself before they found you. Don't forget that, Meredith." Points to him for speaking her actual name. "Yes, they led you here, but don't minimize your part in saving your own hide. Okay?"

"Okay. Right. I won't. But I can also be ever grateful for Max and Maggie's abilities. They're incredible," she said, smiling. "They're also gorgeous, sort of like a cross between a German shepherd and a fox. What breed are they?"

"You won't get an argument from me on their abilities or their looks," he said. "But to answer your question, they're Belgian Tervurens, herding dogs, and incredibly smart. There isn't a lot they can't do when they set their minds to it, but they've never had the opportunity to rescue a damsel in distress before."

He almost told her about the time, when they were puppies, they managed to open a sealed container of frosted sugar cookies Fiona had baked, without so much as leaving a bite mark on the lid. He'd been outside, had returned to find an empty container and the pups snoozing by the fire. Hell, he hadn't eaten even one of those cookies. And even though he did not have a sweet tooth, they'd looked delicious.

He chose to keep his mouth shut. Yes, he felt for this woman, was relieved she was safe and sound, but he wasn't the type to swap stories. Even about his beloved dogs.

Besides which, she was seriously starting to droop. He guessed she wouldn't be able to keep those blue eyes open that much longer. And hallelujah, when she slept, he'd sleep. *Finally.* His bed was calling to him something fierce.

"Who is who?" she asked over another spoonful of soup. "I'd hate to call Max by Maggie's name or vice versa. Miracle dogs should be correctly identified!"

Miracle dogs, eh? He sort of liked that description. "Maggie is a little shorter than Max, and her coloring is lighter. Less russet and black, more tawny and chestnut. And," he said, feeling a mite foolish, "if you watch them move, Maggie is more graceful. Softer in her gait, though no less agile. Max is brute strength, through and through."

Scooting out her chair a few inches, Meredith leaned over and patted the dogs on their heads. "It is very nice to finally have a proper introduction. Thank you for saving me."

Those words, as few as they were, held the power of a sledgehammer against a marshmallow. His heart being the friggin' marshmallow. He shook off the ludicrous image and focused on the brass tacks. Most of her soup was gone, about half of her toast and she'd drained her juice. Good. "How are you doing?" he asked. "Had enough to eat?"

"Yes," she said, sitting straight. "Plenty. Thank you."

"Welcome." Only one item remained on the list. "Think you have enough energy for a shower? I don't have a bathtub, but if you're worried about standing that long, the shower's big enough for a stool. Can move one in there easy. Don't want you fainting or anything."

The pink returned to her cheeks, darker than before. "A shower is exactly what I need. Thank you," she said with a cute-as-a-button lift to her chin, "but I am fairly sure I can handle standing without passing out. What about my clothes? Are they dry?"

"Dry, yes, but not washed yet." Standing, Liam gathered the dishes and cups. "I'll loan you something else of mine until we get yours taken care of."

"Okay. Yes. Thank you."

Suddenly aggravated and not knowing why, Liam dumped the dishes in the sink, to be cleaned later. "Come on, then. Let's get you situated so you can rest. Once you're settled, I plan on doing the same."

She didn't object or thank him again, just nodded. Together, with the dogs glued to her side, they left the kitchen.

He brought her another pair of drawstring pajama bottoms, along with a sweatshirt and fresh socks, showed her where the towels were and when she closed the door to the bathroom, he breathed in relief. Now that she was out of his sight, his aggravation lessened.

She didn't seem crazy and hadn't mentioned her strange dreams about him again. In fact, she seemed nice and smart, grateful and easygoing, with a good dash of quirky humor embedded in her personality. He might, though it was much too soon to say, actually like her.

Just that fast, his sour mood returned.

Oh, no. Nope. He didn't want to like her. He didn't want to get to know her any better than he already did. All he wanted was for the damn snow to stop falling, the wind to cease blowing and the roads to clear. So he could go back to his solitary lifestyle.

The life he'd chosen.

Closing her eyes, relishing the feel of being clean and warm and fed, Meredith snuggled under the blanket on the sofa. Liam had gallantly waited for her to shower—and yes, she'd managed to keep standing, barely—and had brought her another glass of juice before taking the stairs to where she assumed his bedroom was. He'd stopped at the top of the stairs, turned around and somewhat sheepishly offered her the use of his bed, saying he could take the couch.

A sweet offer, but no. She didn't think her legs were strong enough for the stairs, and frankly, she preferred this room, this sofa, where she had dreamed a life that she'd adored. If she had any hope of falling back into her dream, she figured she had the best chance of it happening here. And she did want to dream again.

The sound of rumbling footsteps on the stairs forced her eyes open. Max and Maggie, not Liam. Dogs, not children.

Easily explained. She must have heard him call them by name while she slept, even if she didn't recall doing so. Weird, how her brain had taken that scrap of information and turned these two amazing dogs into her children. *Their* children.

Interesting, but really of little consequence. She'd had a dream. A wonderful dream, yes, and one she very much hoped she would have again, but she didn't fool herself into thinking the dream itself meant anything. Now that she was fully awake and able to think logically.

Her guardian angels padded to the side of the couch and whined.

"Come on," she said, "there's plenty of room, as you both well know. Though, I kind of think even if there wasn't enough room, you'd find a way to fit anyway."

Within seconds, both were tucked tight around her body. Max laid his head on her hip and instantly fell asleep. Maggie wrapped herself in a curve at Meredith's feet and did the same. And never, in her entire life, had she felt quite so secure. So…at peace with herself and her surroundings. How was that?

Why was that? She should be uncomfortable, frantic for the storm to end so she could contact Rachel, let her know that she was alive and continue with what she had originally planned. She should be desperate to touch base with her parents, because despite everything else, they remained her family. She should feel awkward in this house, hidden away with a man she did not know, like any other normal woman would. She should feel… pensive and concerned for her well-being. She should feel a million and one ways that she did not, in any manner whatsoever, feel.

That, too, probably fell firmly on the inconsequential side of things.

Rather than dwell on how she didn't feel, Meredith chose to focus on the truths of her situation. And right now, those facts were pretty darn awesome. She was alive. And yes, she was clean, warm and fed. She was safe. And even without her dream as a backdrop, she couldn't deny that Liam, the real man and not the imaginary one, fully intrigued her.

Yes, he intrigued her…with his quiet, bordering-on-brusque attitude one second, and then stating he was a wizard in that firm, no-argument tone, with the slightest lift to the corners of his mouth the next. With the love he obviously felt for his dogs and how he'd cared for her, a stranger. The concern he showed. His constant "take it slow" advice, and…and *oh*.

The way he'd looked at her as she'd told him her story, with intensity and interest, almost as if he could see straight into her soul…well, that was something new. Yet another first.

In addition to all of that, she believed, regardless of how little sense the believing made, that she was here with this particular man at this particular time because she was supposed to be. Not because of her dream or the fantasy her brain had concocted, but due to where she was at in her life and the uniqueness, the suddenness of this situation.

She had walked—no, make that *stumbled*—into Liam's life for a reason. It had to be a good reason.

Probably not the lifetime of love she'd dreamed about, but something worthwhile. Something positive and fulfilling and valid. Something that maybe, just maybe, both she and Liam had been lacking their entire lives thus far. Something they might learn from each other, that they wouldn't be able to learn any other way.

It was a good thought.

And if it was correct, she couldn't wait to see what that something turned out to be, to discover the precise reason that fate had tossed her into a series of cataclysmic events only to end up precisely *here*.

For now, though, she chose to sleep. To regain more energy. Because she had a feeling that Liam the wizard was sure to keep her on her toes, for however long her "visit" lasted. Hopefully, this storm would rage for… weeks.

Chapter 5

Music? Liam opened his dry, scratchy eyes and sat up in bed, instantly on the alert. His mind thick from sleep, he tried to make sense of what he heard. Why was music—ABBA, he thought—blasting through his house? Strike that. *Blasting* was an inaccurate description, as the volume wasn't quite that loud, but there shouldn't be any music. He lived alone. Unless his dogs had figured out how to—oh. *Goldi*. "Meredith," he mumbled, tossing off his blankets.

He threw on a T-shirt and looked outside the window. Snowing. Still. Though, not quite as violently as before he fell asleep. Or perhaps that was only wishful thinking. Next, he picked up his watch—which had once belonged to his father—and frowned.

Eight o'clock? Morning, based on the hazy light suffusing his room and the fact that he could see more than two feet outside of his window, so he'd slept…twelve hours? Twice his typical amount? Well, hell.

He hadn't done that in almost ten years. In the days after the tragedy that had forever changed his life, that for too long had filled him with regret.

He'd fallen in love in a whirlwind romance, had proposed and within a year was married and expecting his first child. They'd only known each other three months before they tied the knot, six before she had gotten pregnant.

Sure, he'd had his concerns and she'd had hers, but they were in love and believed that was enough to buffer them through any storm. They were wrong.

Home base was in Denver then, since that was where Christy had been born and raised, where her family lived. Seemed only fair to keep her in familiar surroundings where she had support, since his job took him out of the country so often. They lived in a typical house in a typical neighborhood, with too many people for Liam's comfort, but for Christy…well, he'd put up with just about anything. Even living in the middle of suburbia.

She'd been almost seven months pregnant when he'd gone to parts of the Amazon Basin to photograph birds for *National Geographic*.

It was a long assignment—six weeks—and Christy hadn't wanted him to go. She'd almost pleaded with him to stay, but he'd convinced her that by accepting the job, he'd be able to pass on any other assignments for a good long while afterward. So that he'd be close at hand for their baby's birth and through the first year.

That had been the plan. Privately, he'd hated the idea of turning down the opportunity, because he figured it would be the last extended assignment he'd take for… well, years.

After some discussion, Christy had agreed. Of course she had. She was a sweetheart and tended to look after his needs more often than her own, and she'd seen the logic in his argument.

The morning he left, he'd kissed her and her baby belly, promised to touch base as regularly as he could, reminded her of how very much he loved her and he… walked out of their house. When he'd returned four weeks later, rather than six, it was to bury his wife and unborn child.

Carbon-monoxide poisoning had stolen them away while she slept, while he was thousands of miles away taking photographs of birds.

Didn't matter what he knew—that it wasn't his fault, and if he'd been at home, he would've been sleeping right beside her. The guilt had nearly consumed him, the loss had nearly destroyed him.

It had taken far too much time to locate stable ground once again. To find any peace within himself and, eventually, forgiveness. This house, the mountains, his career, his solitary existence—save for his sister and niece and his dogs—had, bit by bit, returned him to a state of near normalcy. He was better now, for the most part. Scarred, sure. How could he not be? But time did have a way with healing whatever wounds it could, and those that couldn't be healed…well, they hardened and quit hurting so damn much. So a man could breathe, accept and carry on.

Liam forcibly shook himself out of his memories, shoved the entirety of that particular past into the recesses of his mind and took the stairs two at a time.

Where were Max and Maggie? Not with him, as they normally were. They would need to go out. They needed to be fed. And he'd have to deal with this woman who, for whatever reason, thought it was appropriate to listen to "Mamma Mia" at a higher-than-reasonable volume in a stranger's house, while that stranger slept, at eight in the freaking morning.

A stranger who'd saved her butt, no less.

Nope, his inner Jiminy Cricket proclaimed, *your dogs saved her butt, you just...ah, warmed it up some, along with the rest of her body.* True story there, but these facts did not alter Liam's annoyance one iota. *His* house. *His* part of the mountain.

He should be able to sleep all damn day if he chose, without worry that some woman and her love of a Swedish pop group would wake him from a near-dead sleep. It was, at the very least, inconsiderate. Bordering on rude. And something that required discussion, now, so that it did not happen again for however long he was stuck in these walls with Miss Goldilocks.

Moving through the living room, he noted that she'd folded the blankets on the sofa into a nice, neat pile, and that she'd fed the fire at some point, so that it still burned warmly, gently. That was decent of her, thoughtful.

This realization, however, did not cool his frustration. Here, the music was louder, more annoying and the last damn thing he wanted to hear. He wanted quiet. Silence. He wanted the normalcy of returning home from assignment and not having to deal with another human being until he was good and ready.

At the entrance to the kitchen, he stopped. Bubbling annoyance melted into a pool of nothingness as he stared.

The small oak table, which his grandfather had made with his own hands, was set for two. The dishes from last night were washed and drying in the stainless steel counter rack. And Goldi was standing in front of the stove, whipping up what looked to be a breakfast for a king. Eggs. Bacon. Pancakes.

And as she cooked, her hips swayed to the beat of the music, and her mane of curly blond hair all but bounced on her shoulders.

His dogs…his *traitorous* dogs…were sitting on their haunches near the door to the mudroom, watching Goldi with that adoring gaze. Of course, she was frying a panful of bacon. That could account for the love pouring from their eyes.

But he didn't think so. Based on the quickening of his pulse and the tightening in his gut just at the very sight of this woman, he couldn't really blame them, either. She had a way. A way that tended to appeal just as much, if not more, than frustrate. And they'd barely spent any time awake together. Didn't seem to bode well for him.

"Morning," he said, his tone sounding rough to his own ears. "You seem to be feeling…ah, let's go with spirited. Slept well, did you?"

"Yes, Yoda, I slept quite well, and before you ask… I am feeling much better today," she said, turning on her heel to face him. A quirky, almost mischievous grin lifted her lips. She reached over and picked up her phone, which she'd plugged into an outlet, slid her finger across the screen and the music stopped. Blissful silence filled the room. "Hungry? I hope so, because I seem to have gone a bit overboard here."

With those simply stated words, his inner grouch quit fighting to resurface and disappeared into the nether, smothered by another person's—this specific person's—kindness.

Nope, he wasn't hungry. Liam rarely ate breakfast, but no way and no how was he prepared to dim the glow in Meredith's beautiful blue eyes. Today, he didn't see any of the fear or loneliness he'd witnessed last night.

"Starving," he said, rubbing his stomach for emphasis. "And preparing breakfast was unnecessary, but thank you. I'm unaccustomed to people cooking my meals. Unless I am at my sister's place for dinner or I have to eat at a restaurant. It's very thoughtful of you, and…well, very much appreciated."

"I like to cook," she said simply. "Can't do a lot else for you at the moment, so…"

Her words trailed off, she shrugged and returned her focus to the stove. The silence went from blissful to a heavy type of awkwardness. Why?

Frowning, unable to think of anything else to say but needing to say something, he went with, "Looks as if breakfast is about ready. I'll let the dogs out. If there's anything I can do to help when I get back, I'll—"

"Oh! No need," she said over her shoulder. "I let them out earlier. We had to go through the front door. The snowdrifts in the back are piled ridiculously high. They did their thing and came right back in without any trouble. It's nasty out there."

"Okay, then. Thank you." There went that idea. And he doubted that he'd ever expressed his thanks so often in so short of a time in his entire life. "I'll just get them fed, so they're not begging at the table while we eat. After breakfast, I'll clear some of that snow in the back before it gets any higher. It looks as if we might be nearing the tail end of the storm."

Thank God.

"Tail end, huh?"

"Think so. Hope so." He stepped fully into the kitchen and whistled to the dogs. Both snapped their gazes to his for all of half a second. "Bet you two are hungry, huh?"

"I actually fed them, too." Goldi tossed him an apologetic look before flipping two pancakes onto a plate and pouring another large spoonful of batter into the pan. "I wasn't sure if that would be okay, since I don't know their schedule, but they were adamant."

Straightened the living room, added logs to the fire, took care of his dogs and was in the process of making him breakfast. Twenty-four hours ago, this woman lay unconscious on his couch and here she stood, apparently with every last thing under control. "Thank you," he repeated, instantly wincing. "I'm all yours, then. Anything you need help with?"

"Coffee, I guess? I meant to start that earlier."

Coffee! Hell yes. Caffeine was his ambrosia. Caffeine should jumpstart his brain, so he could think and regain control. Because right now, his world was spinning off its axis and he didn't know how to stop the spinning. "I can do that. Not a problem."

He grabbed the bag of coffee from the freezer and tried—oh, how he tried—to pretend that his entire being wasn't centered on the tiny blonde in front of his stove. Or how adorable she looked wearing his navy plaid pajama bottoms—far too large for her small frame and rolled up at the ankles so she wouldn't trip—and his forest green sweatshirt that just about hung to her knees.

Her curves were well hidden by the oversize clothing, and frankly there shouldn't be one damn thing about her current appearance that could account for the tight ball of heat in the pit of his stomach. But she appealed to him, nonetheless. Made him want what he hadn't wanted in… forever. Caused sweat to form on the back of his neck.

Sweat! How could she do that?

All of this was uncomfortable. Jarring. And a state of affairs he needed to get under control. Fast. But Lord, she made it difficult. Not only due to his nonsensical attraction, but…well, damn it all, she *fit* somehow.

In the way she jockeyed around him while he filled the pot with water, reached in front of him for a plate she'd left on the counter, tossed him a grin when they went for the dishtowel at the same time. It—*this*—felt familiar. It resonated. Her being here seemed easy, comfortable and…like the normal way of things.

Except, of course, none of this was normal. Distance was called for. Walls required building. *Rules* needed to be set. Because whatever was happening here couldn't be allowed to continue. He'd traveled the yellow-brick road of following his heart instead of his common sense before, and that had not turned out well by *anyone's* standards. He would not err again.

He was a man meant to be on his own. He did not need to be taught that lesson again.

"Once we're done with breakfast, I'll spend a couple hours outside, clearing the snow around the back door and shoveling a path to the shed. I need to check the generator, make sure we're good still. And then, well, then I need to get some work done." He said all of this lightning fast, in a no-room-for-argument tone, just as the coffee started to brew. "You're welcome to make yourself at home. Feel free to poke around and do whatever you want to pass the time, but I will be busy. All day. Sorry about that, but a storm doesn't negate my responsibilities."

"Oh. I see. Okay. And of course it doesn't." Disappointment rang in her words, which made him feel like a heel, but he didn't backtrack.

She transferred the bacon—what appeared to be an entire pound, perfectly cooked—to a plate. Then, with the skillet of scrambled eggs in hand, she dished them each a serving at the table and asked, "You work at home, I take it?"

His mule-headed nature kicked in, fierce. A normal question to ask, but he refused to be dragged into a conversation he did not want to have. General conversation? No problem. But anything deeper seemed a very bad idea, considering the current set of circumstances. He couldn't outright ignore her question, either. *That* would be rude. He went with, "Partially."

"Let me guess," she said, her teasing humor returning. "Donning your wizard hat and casting spells? What is on today's agenda, creating havoc or harmony or something in between?"

He liked her. Damn it. He *liked* her. "Perhaps a little of both."

"Hmm. Well, if you could use your sorcery to get the phones working, even for a few minutes, that would be very much appreciated. I keep thinking about Rachel and how worried she must be. And if she contacted my family, they'll also be worried." She flinched and her chin lifted. "I mean, I think they'd be worried. They'll probably be worried."

Think? What kind of family did she have that she couldn't state with unequivocal certainty that they would be worried? There was a story there, and yup, he was curious.

But he kept his questions to himself. Even so, her statement bothered him. That it did managed to bother him more. The fact she had the power to bounce his thoughts around like a basketball bothered him the most. He did not know her. She meant nothing to him. Yet, here they were.

"Wish I could do that for you," he said about the phones. "But as we surmised last night, I'm not a wizard. The most I can do is get you out of here the second the weather and the roads allow. Besides which, chances are high that your friend doesn't have phone service, either. Or power."

"Right. Of course. I was just teasing. And I figured I'd call her mobile, but who knows. I should quit worrying. I'll contact her when I can, as soon as I can."

"I know you were teasing, and somehow I doubt you'll stop worrying. But," he said, "give it a shot. Worrying won't solve a damn thing."

Neither spoke for a few seconds, but then, as she set the plate of pancakes and the syrup bottle on the table, she asked, "So you're not a wizard. What are you then? A butcher, baker or candlestick maker? King of some country I've never heard of?"

He grinned. He couldn't help himself, and the answer slipped out. "Photographer."

"What type? Wedding, babies, families…that sort of thing?"

Flinching at the idea of being around so many people so often, especially crying babies, he asked, "Since when did we start playing a game of twenty questions?"

He retrieved two extra-large coffee mugs from the cupboard. "How do you take your coffee?"

"No sugar. Cream if you have it, but if you don't, milk is good. And we might as well get to know each other a little since we're cooped up together. Don't you think?"

"Ah." No, he did not think. Yet, he couldn't say so without hurting her feelings. A thought he despised. "I guess that makes sense."

"So…what type of photographer?"

"The type that uses cameras." She was a persistent one, he'd give her that. Well, he could be more so. "I have the powdered version of cream…want that or prefer the milk?"

"Powdered is fine." She tapped her sock-covered foot in mock impatience. Or he thought so, anyway. "I'm waiting. Who do you photograph? Babies, families, brides and grooms, or…?"

"Wildlife, mostly." He filled the mugs with coffee, preparing hers as she'd asked. And that, too, felt familiar. Normal and comfortable, even if the questions weren't. More so than he often felt when Fiona and Cassie were visiting, and they were his family. Now that was something that *didn't* make a lick of sense. He hated when he couldn't logic out a solution. "What about you? Butcher, baker or candlestick maker?"

Once breakfast was done, he'd make darn sure he stayed far away from Goldi until she was, hopefully, conked out on the sofa tonight. With his dogs, since they now seemed to prefer her over him. He couldn't fault them for their good taste.

"At the moment, I am in between jobs. But I worked as a stager for several years." She sat down at the table in the same chair she used the night before. "I liked it.

Quite a bit, actually, but your job sounds so much more interesting. What type of wildlife?"

"Any type. All types." He wasn't quite sure what a stager was, but didn't much feel like asking, so he didn't.

Sitting down at the table, he took a large gulp of his coffee. He had to admit that the spread on the table was impressive, in sight and smell. His stomach rumbled in response, which shocked him. Typically, he didn't get hungry until lunch. "Everything looks amazing."

"Well, enjoy." She served herself a pancake and a few strips of bacon. "I'm a master in the kitchen at breakfast, but that's the extent of my culinary knowledge. Other than sandwiches."

"Nothing wrong with a good sandwich," he managed to say.

"No, I guess there isn't." Darting her gaze downward, she concentrated on her food, on slowly and methodically taking one bite at a time.

Following her lead, he filled his plate and tried to ignore the guilt gnawing his gut to shreds.

It was *not* his job to entertain this woman. She was his guest, but only by…well, force seemed too harsh a word, but it wasn't far off. And worse, much worse, he didn't feel himself around her, which further complicated the situation. What he wanted was for them to exist in their separate corners until she could leave, in order to preserve his sanity.

There were a few problems there. His place wasn't tiny, but it wasn't built for two people to stay out of each other's way. It seemed selfish. Mostly, though, he didn't want her to feel bad.

He'd go for some honesty, see where that took them. "I'm sorry," he said. "I can see you're trying here, and

I appreciate your intent. I really do. I'm just not much of a socializer."

"It's okay," she said, her voice quiet. She looked at him and smiled. "Really. I get it. You wish I wasn't here. You're used to being by yourself, and in from the storm, here I am, and now you're stuck with me. I'm sorry about that, and I'll try to be less...sociable."

Lie through his teeth or go for more honesty? Liam pushed his eggs around on his plate before choosing the careful answer of, "It isn't that I wish you were gone. Don't think that. I'm glad you're here, relieved my dogs found you and brought you to safety. But you're not wrong in everything else you said. I am not a people person, by anyone's definition."

"So you're the guy at parties who hides in the corner, sipping his drink, hoping no one talks to you and watching the clock, waiting for the polite time to leave."

"Nope. I'm the guy who doesn't go to parties. Or barbecues or picnics or family reunions, unless I have absolutely no other choice. If I could figure out how, I wouldn't even go to the grocery store," he said. "Unfortunately, I've yet to train the dogs to shop for me."

"I bet they could learn," she said with a laugh. "And this might surprise you, but I'm not a people person, either. I can force it, though. Most people who meet me think I'm an extrovert, when the complete opposite is the truth. I tend to need lots of time after expending that type of energy to regroup, to find my bearings again, so I really do get it."

"You have one up on me. I barely get by in any social situation. Usually, when I'm forced to attend one," he said, surprised at his willingness to share even this, "I stand there, trying to find the right thing to say and counting the seconds until I can make my escape. I've always been that way."

Well, in most circumstances. He didn't feel that way with his sister or a few of his longtime friends or when the topic of conversation surrounded an area of interest. He could talk about photography and some of his favorite locales around the world forever.

Tipping her chin, so their eyes met, she nodded. "I hate that feeling. You wish the floor would open up and suck you away. My family attended a lot of social occasions when I was growing up, and I used to hate them. But my dad taught me a trick that made it easier."

"Oh, yeah?" He might just be able to stare into this woman's eyes for hours on end. They called to him, somehow. Soothed him. Made him feel…enough. "What would that be?"

"When you don't know what to say to another person, ask them a question. Any question. Doesn't much matter what it is because the attention is diverted back to them, and all you have to do is listen…and then ask another question based on whatever they said." She shrugged. "You can even avoid answering their questions that way. Just keep asking your own."

Was that why she'd been asking him so many questions? "That works for you, huh?"

She picked up a slice of bacon, broke it in half and gave a piece to each of his dogs, who were on their haunches right next to her chair. Maggie licked her palm. Lucky dog. "It really does. With most people." She shot him a grin. "Try it…ask me a question. Anything at all."

Giving in to her charm, her rather easygoing nature, her innate appeal, he nodded. "Oh, all right. What is a stager? I have the impression it does not involve an actual stage in a theater."

"No, it doesn't, but wouldn't that be fun? And that is a great question." Another piece of bacon, which she split in half and again fed to the dogs. He should tell her that was enough, as he didn't give Max and Maggie table food all that often, but hey…bacon wasn't going to hurt them. "I staged houses to look their best, keeping in mind the area and the targeted pool of buyers, to make them more appealing, so they'd sell fast and hopefully at top dollar."

"Furniture, artwork, knickknacks, that sort of thing?"

"That's it, exactly. If there were special architectural details or an interesting design element to a room, I'd play that up. The goal," she said, popping a bite of bacon into her mouth, "was for a buyer to walk into the home and think, 'I could live here. I want to live here.'"

"Were you good at it?"

"I think so. I enjoyed the creative elements of the job. I loved conceptualizing how a room should look and then putting all the pieces together to achieve that vision."

He nodded. "I can see how that would be rewarding."

Silence kicked into being once again, which he filled by eating a few forkfuls of his eggs. No longer feeling the consuming need to finish eating and make his escape, but disliking the quiet, Liam took Goldi's advice and asked another question. "How did you meet Rachel if she lives here and you live in San Francisco?"

"Through some of those various social events I mentioned earlier. Rachel grew up in New York, but over the years, we were at the same place at the same time often enough, and we're the same age." Goldi shrugged. "I guess it was natural we became friends."

She hadn't said much, but Liam was struck with the image of two young girls stuck in places they didn't want to be, had found each other and a bond formed. "Tell me about the first time you met. How old were you? What was the social event?"

Long lashes blinked. "You're getting pretty good at this question thing."

"I'm a fast learner. Or," he said with a grin, "maybe you're a great teacher."

Cupping her coffee mug in her hands, she said, "Either or both. But to answer, we were twelve. Our fathers are both businessmen, so even though they don't work directly with each other, they have numerous connections. I met Rachel in the lobby of a hotel." A quick grin flitted across her face. "We were at a charity fund raiser. It involved dinner and endless speeches, and it was one of those things where our fathers wanted to show off their families. We both sneaked away out of sheer boredom, bumped into each other and… I don't know, we just clicked."

There were so many more questions he could ask, but eventually, she'd volley a few his way. Since she'd answered his, he'd have to answer hers, which would open another entire field of curiosity on both sides. They could be stuck at this table for hours.

Not an entirely distasteful thought. Perhaps even an enjoyable one, depending on where their conversation led. The danger existed in the possibility of exposing areas of himself he just did not talk about. With anyone. Even a charming blonde with beautiful blue eyes.

"I'm glad you two met," he said, putting an end to the questions. "My guess is the rest of that night was much more enjoyable for the both of you."

"Oh, it was. As were any of the functions we attended together after that. For a while, I even hoped she'd manage to fall in love with one of my brothers, so we could be sisters."

"Brothers? How many? Older or younger?" Damn it. There he went, asking more questions. Giving into his curiosity when he should be outside, clearing a path and making sure everything was in order. "It's okay, you don't have to—"

"Two. Both older. Both married now, with kids." She finished eating the last of her pancake before asking, "You mentioned a sister. Is she your only sibling?"

"Yup." Standing before he asked something else, he started clearing off the table. "You cooked, so I'll clean. Shower if you want, and there are a ton of books in the living room. A few decks of playing cards, too, if you like solitaire. Make yourself at home."

"Sure," she said. "I appreciate that! We'll get done quicker in here if I help, though."

"It isn't necessary. I can take care of this."

"I know. I'd like to help. Besides which," she said, filling the sink with soapy water, "you've already stated you'll be busy for the entire day. I have plenty of time to shower, look through your books and play solitaire. Or whatever else I can come up with."

He didn't argue further even though he wanted to. It would prove fruitless, and her point held validity. Together, they tidied the kitchen and again, the way they moved around each other seemed effortless. As if they were accustomed to doing so. Comfortable. Easy. *Familiar.*

A state of being that landed squarely in the irrational range.

Chapter 6

Make herself at home, huh? Meredith sighed and thumbed through the books on the shelf for the third time. Liam's selection of books was rather narrowly focused, most of them nonfiction, either about photography, remote locations around the world, different species of animals or—big surprise here—filled with photographs of remote locations around the world and different species of animals.

The handful of novels he owned were, by and large, of the action-and-adventure type. Spies and private detectives and mystery thrillers, none of which appealed. She wanted to lose herself in something light and easy. Frivolous and fun.

Biting her lip, she stared at Liam's closed office door, which was next to the stairs going up to his bedroom.

Earlier, he'd dashed in after clearing some of the snow, took a shower and after a small, tight smile directed at her and a reminder to make herself at home, had disappeared into that room with the dogs. She hadn't seen nor heard from him since.

Which was perfectly fine. It wasn't as if he'd invited her to visit and then had chosen to make himself inaccessible. The guy had a life. Responsibilities. But geez, was she ever bored.

She could, she supposed, play another three dozen rounds of solitaire. Or try to take a nap. Or braid her hair or count to one million or…it was after three o'clock, and she hadn't eaten lunch.

Liam hadn't, either, unless he had a picnic basket tucked away in his office, which she doubted. He'd expended a ton of physical energy dealing with the snow, and now she had to assume he was expending a ton of mental energy. Doing whatever he was doing.

How could it hurt to make him a plate of food, a fresh cup of coffee, leave them outside of his door with a quick knock? She'd walk away so he wouldn't feel forced to talk, and he could get right back to work. And maybe after she ate, she'd fall into a food coma and be able to take that nap. A long one, please, so by the time she woke, there wouldn't be so many hours to fill. Surely, tonight at some point, he'd sit here with her by the fire, and they could talk.

Get to know each other a little more. Get to know *him* a little more.

Making lunch might not be the best plan, but at least it gave her a task in this moment and, really, that was about as positive as it was going to get. And if she couldn't sleep afterward, she'd give in and read one of those spy novels or find another way to spend the next many hours.

In the kitchen, Meredith grilled two ham-and-cheese

sandwiches, added a handful of salt-and-vinegar chips and some green grapes to the plate, looked for and didn't find anything dessert-like—not even a single box of cookies—and after giving up on that, poured him a mug of coffee and called the job done. It wasn't much of a meal, but it was sustenance.

A small pad of paper sat on the counter, next to the useless phone. After a small amount of deliberation, she jotted a note that said, "Thought you might be hungry!" and drew a smiley face with a wizard hat.

There. Done. Her stomach sloshed with nerves, which was just silly. Pushing her apprehension to the side, Meredith returned to the living room and quickly placed his lunch and the note on the floor. Rapping on the door once, she turned on her heel and made her escape, feeling very much as if she were involved in a game of Ding Dong Ditch.

Her heart regained its normal rhythm the second she returned to the cozy, comfortable kitchen. She liked this room, liked the simplicity of the decor, the natural wood cupboards and the concrete countertops, the way that everything fit without overtaking the small space.

She took her own plate to the table and sat down, wondering if she'd be able to hear him open the door. She hoped he wouldn't think she was trying to get his attention or time—because, really, she understood their situation, and if he had to work, he had to work. She hoped he'd appreciate the makeshift lunch. She hoped it wouldn't be seen as an intrusion.

She'd already intruded into this man's life enough.

Picking through her meal halfheartedly, she ate most of what she'd served herself before sighing in frustration. Clean up, and then she'd try that nap.

As the kitchen was compact and well organized to begin with, tidying the area took no time at all. And she felt weak more than tired, which pointed to the fact that she probably needed the rest. So, okay. She'd choose a book, snuggle into the sofa with a couple of blankets and read. Maybe she'd sleep.

When she entered the living room, though, and saw Liam's lunch sitting on the floor untouched, unwanted emotion swam to the surface.

Really? He couldn't even be bothered to pick up the damn plate? Or take it to the kitchen and say, "Hey, thanks for this, but I'm not hungry"?

Though, even as she thought the words, they didn't seem to fit the man. Oh, she knew full well they were mostly strangers, but he had tried to talk to her last night and this morning. He'd taken care of her. He had definitely shown concern for her well-being.

Just that fast, her brewing emotions settled. He hadn't heard her knock. He didn't know she'd made him lunch. He was, as his sister called him, a hermit, but he wasn't rude or inconsiderate, so…yes, he just hadn't heard the knock. Well, she'd take care of that.

She walked over, raised her fist to knock and the door opened. Another millisecond and she'd have clocked the poor man on his chest. Startled, she stepped to the side and managed to kick over the rapidly cooling cup of coffee, which—naturally—spilled onto the plate of food.

"Well, hi there," he said with an amused expression. "Whatcha doing?"

"Apparently, I am ruining your lunch." Heat touched her cheeks. Not only due to the circumstances, but due to his physical presence. He only wore a pair of jeans and a T-shirt, but on him, they looked…*he* looked almost too good to be real. "Which I left here for you, and I knocked but…it doesn't actually matter. If you're hungry, I can make you another sandwich. And of course, I'll deal with the mess I just made. Sorry about that."

"You're sorry for making me lunch?" His forehead creased into furrows. "Then why, pray tell, did you go to the trouble? Seems counterproductive."

"No, I'm not sorry I brought you lunch. I'm sorry for spilling coffee all over your floor and ruining your lunch," she explained. He grinned and she realized he was teasing her. She liked this side of him, so she gave some back. "Though, really, I shouldn't be sorry. It's more your fault than mine that it even happened. For opening the door at that precise second."

"Ah, yes. I would have to agree. That was an extraordinarily thoughtless move on my part." Bending at his knees, he picked up the note, read it and grinned again. Her heart sort of did a spinning dive at the sight of that smile. "Love the wizard hat. Nicely done and don't worry about the mess. We agreed it was my fault. I'll take care of it."

"You always insist on doing everything on your own?" The dogs made their appearance then, pushing their bodies around Liam and all but drooling over the coffee-saturated lunch. "Or does that trait only appear with women you find unconscious on your sofa?"

"I don't insist on doing everything on my own," he said. "It's just how I am. And seeing how I live alone, it's good I'm that way. Otherwise, nothing would ever get done."

Well, that was true. But, "Not while I'm here, you don't live alone. And I can't sit around and just wait. I'll be bored out of my skull, so I might as well be helpful. If you'll let me?"

His eyes narrowed, causing them to crinkle at the corners and his jaw hardened. One quick shake of his head and, "Just take it easy while you're here. You went through something extraordinarily difficult, and I... well." He rubbed his free hand over his face. "I don't need help, Meredith, with anything, but I appreciate your offer. And your willingness. Just take it easy, read, relax."

"Making you a meal when I have to make one for myself anyway is not a hardship," she said, raising her chin a notch. She could out-stubborn just about anyone, being the daughter of the most stubborn man alive. "Maybe you don't mean it this way, but when you tell me to 'just take it easy, read, relax,' I hear, 'sit in the corner and be quiet, so I forget you're here.'"

"That is on you, because that is not what I said."

"I would bet that is what you thought, though," she said, lifting her chin another inch. "You said I should make myself at home, correct?"

"Yes."

"Did you mean those words?"

He sighed, ran his hand over his jaw. "Yes."

"Well, then I win. I get to help out, as that is part of the definition of making myself at home." She pointed toward his office. "So you can go back to work and I will take care of this mess and make you a new lunch. Listen for the knock. I'll just leave it out here."

With that, she picked up the plate and the now-empty coffee mug and took off before he could offer more objections. She was about two steps from the kitchen when his deep, rolling laugh hit her ears. It was a good sound, that laugh.

"Stop, Meredith. I'm done with work," he said from behind her. "I was on my way to find you. I thought you might want some company, seeing how I abandoned you for most of the day. And the dogs were whining at the door, probably because they missed you."

"Company would be nice," she said, smiling from ear to ear. Something, fortunately, that Liam could not see since her back was still facing him. Who cared if he made this choice out of guilt? She was lonely. She did want his company. And regardless of the reason, it was still *his* decision. "I missed them, too. Did you have anything in particular in mind, or just want to sit and talk some more? I'd love to—"

"Sit and talk? More?" She heard a sigh and had to swallow a laugh. "Sitting and talking is one idea, I suppose. I was thinking more along the lines of…well, see, I have a few board games for when my sister and niece visit. Monopoly, Scrabble…um, a few others. Can't think what they are right now. Feel up to something like that?"

"Sure. That works." She took a breath and pivoted, so she could see his face. "I'll clean this up and get you something else to eat and I'll be all set. You can choose the game."

"Nope. I'm not all that hungry, and I want you to rest. I'll deal with clean-up." He approached her and removed the dishes from her hands. "No arguing for once, okay?"

Their eyes met and heat flashed, for just a second, between them. On her side, at least. And it felt…good. Reminded her that she was alive. That she wasn't done. That she still had time to follow her dreams, figure out who she was—who she could become—and to open herself to possibilities she never truly had before. She had time. Thanks to this man and his dogs.

Thanks to herself, too. She'd persevered.

"Okay," she said, knowing when she was beat. "I'll take it easy until you're ready to lose at whatever game we play."

"Perfect." He whistled at the dogs. "I'm just going to let them out and then I'm yours for the night. You should know, though, I rarely lose at Monopoly or Scrabble."

Hers for the night? She liked the sound of that, too. Probably a bit more than she should, but right now a world of possibilities beckoned and she welcomed them all. Especially those that might include this man. He intrigued her. Deeply. And his eyes did something to her soul.

Warmth whooshed through her, from head to toe, and she fought the temptation to fan herself. "Oh, yeah?" she managed to ask. "Well, neither do I."

One eyebrow raised. "Is that so? Is that a challenge, Goldi?"

"Meredith," she corrected instantly, though she didn't know why. She liked that he called her Goldi. "And yes, you can take it that way. So, let out the dogs and…we'll see who wins."

He nodded and whistled at the dogs again, leading them past her and through the kitchen to the back door.

She stood there motionless for another minute, waiting for her skin to cool and her heart to stop racing. Why this man, when there was so very much she didn't know about him? Why now, when her primary goal should be focusing on creating the life she yearned for?

She didn't know the answer to those questions, but she knew one thing for sure: she was done allowing the "should nots" to clutter her brain. They had never done her any good in the past, so it was time to try something different. Something new. Something courageous.

And just…live.

They were, Liam noted, evenly matched. So far, they'd played Monopoly—he'd won—followed by a game of Scrabble—she'd won—and they'd just finished their second round of Crazy Eights, and yup, one win for each. Throughout each game, they'd kept up a steady stream of chatter that stayed solidly within the impersonal range of topics.

Her last name…his. How much longer until the storm ended—by morning, he guessed—and other miscellaneous topics that included his dogs, where she went to college and not much else other than general conversation, a little teasing here and there about whatever game they were in the midst of.

All of this should have relieved Liam to no end, and through the first couple of games, it did. But now, he was dismayed to realize his curiosity was building.

He found he wanted to know more about the woman. About Meredith. Why she wasn't sure if her family would be worried. Why she left a job she'd apparently liked and was good at.

What made her smile? What made her sad? Why did she, every now and then, seem to look at him as if she knew him, knew what was in his head…in his heart? Of course, she didn't. Couldn't, even. But that look seemed to state otherwise and raised his curiosity another notch.

Made him wonder what it would be like to really let someone—particularly her—in. He'd gone down that road before, to a disastrous and heartbreaking result, and he was a fool to revisit the idea. But there it was, front and center in his thoughts.

Did that make him a sucker for punishment? Perhaps. Probably. Or at the very least, proved that he wasn't as content with his life as he'd believed. A sobering realization and not one he wanted to give credence to just yet.

Also, though he'd never verbally admit it, he wondered about that dream she'd had, even though she hadn't mentioned it again. A lot happened in that dream, she had said. And that a meeting had to occur before anything else. What was *anything else*? What exactly had she dreamed?

Asinine to have his thoughts so fully occupied by another person's dream. Especially a person who had gone through what she had in the hours before collapsing. Exhausted. Freezing. Scared. From what she had said, hopeless by the time his dogs had led her to safety.

She'd heard his voice, had maybe caught a glimpse of his face when she'd opened her eyes for that brief second and in her exhaustion and fear, her hopelessness, had a dream about him...*them*? Seemed that way, and he couldn't blame her for that, couldn't call her crazy.

She'd obviously forgotten all about it, so why couldn't he?

It went back to that look, which she happened to be giving him right now, as if she was thinking about her dream if not outright talking about it. Worse, though, as if she could read his friggin' thoughts. He wasn't sure he liked that.

Wasn't altogether sure he didn't like it, either.

"We have to play one more game," he said quickly, both to wipe out her expression and to distract his oddball thoughts. "To determine the…ah, Blizzard Gaming Championship."

She raised an eyebrow and grinned. "What does the winner get?"

"Pride and a boost to their ego?" he said. "Need more than that?"

"Seeing how I am planning on taking that championship, yes, I do." Her voice held a teasing quality, and her eyes were bright. Happy. He liked that. "There needs to be a prize."

"Ah. I could order a trophy. If you win, that is. I'm happy enough with the title." Shrugging, he put the playing cards back in their respective boxes. "As big and ostentatious a trophy as you want. Can be taller than you, if that will make you happy."

Hell. He'd buy her a trophy as big as a house to keep that smile on her face.

"Oh, I have no need for a trophy, but thank you for the offer," she said in a sweet-as-sugar sort of way. He liked that, too. "I think the winner should be able to choose their prize. But it has to involve the loser. So, if you win, your prize involves me doing something for you or with you. Whatever you want, within reason. And I get the same choice if I win."

Hmm. Well, then. He wasn't so sure what would be better, being on the winning or losing end of that deal. It would prove interesting to see what she'd choose as her "prize" if she won and, okay, if he won? He might just ask her about the details of that dream, so long as he could figure out a way to do so without sounding as corny as a lovestruck teenager.

"You have a deal," he said, scratching his jaw. "I've been thinking for a while now of having the house painted. Think you could handle that? I'd buy all the supplies, of course, and even some how-to books if you were to need them. Might go that direction, supposing I win."

She scrunched her nose. "I would say that painting your house does not fall in the 'within reason' category, so nope, you'll have to come up with something else. Supposing you win."

"Okay, sure, I can come up with something else." He grinned, enjoying this exchange more than any of their other conversations thus far. "Only question that remains is…what game should be the tie breaker? One we've already played or something different?"

"Something different, of course." Walking to the pile of games he'd brought out earlier, she looked through them, one by one. "Lots of choices here. Do you have a preference?"

He narrowed his eyes, took stock of the various games—some meant for families, some for adults and some bought with his niece in mind—and considered a few of the strategy games. He excelled in those. But really, he was far more curious to see what Goldi would choose, so in the end, he shook his head. "Nope. No preference. You pick, I'll play."

She laughed, instantly reaching for a game, and damn it, why did the glow from the fireplace have to send a shimmer of light through her hair, making it resemble spun gold? Or what he assumed spun gold would look like. And what was wrong with him to notice such a thing, anyway? It took every ounce of willpower to stay seated, to not walk over and…well, hell, touch her hair. Like a kid reaching for a piece of chocolate he should *not* have.

Swallowing hard, he forced his attention from the shimmering spectacle of her hair to the box in her hands, and all comparisons to spun gold evaporated.

"Really?" he said. Hell. He'd never even played that game. He'd bought it last year as a gift for Cassie's birthday, but she already had it. He'd brought it back home for when she visited, but they'd yet to actually play. "All those choices and you think that should be the game that decides the championship?"

Returning to the couch, she set the game on the coffee table. "I picked it, didn't I? But I have an excellent reason why. Neither of us have ever played this game, so we're starting at ground zero. No one has an advantage. That seems appropriate for a tie breaker."

"Excellent point, but how do you know I haven't played it before?"

She reached over and picked at the plastic still coating the box. "Original packaging, never been opened," she said, grinning. "And I seriously doubt you've sat around with your, um—photographer buddies?—with beer and munchies over a game of Hedbanz."

"More excellent points," he admitted. "And you're right on every one of them."

Except for the photographer buddy thing. Oh, he had a few close friends, but they didn't exactly hang out over beer or munchies playing anything. Only reason he had all these games was for Fiona and Cassie. They tended to get bored real fast when visiting. Didn't stop them from showing up at least once a week when he was around. His sister insisted on family togetherness, on being *present*.

He knew why. Their parents had died when they were young, and she'd gone to live with their aunt while he'd lived with his grandfather. They'd missed a lot of years together, and Fiona had never really gotten over that, never stopped longing for what they hadn't had.

Well, that and her stubbornness. The woman never gave in on a damn thing, even when doing so would be easier. "Why don't you read the rules while I grab us some of those munchies you mentioned?" he asked. "You can fill me in when I get back."

"Sure thing," she said, already picking open the plastic covering. Lifting her eyes to his, she smiled. "Bring lots of sustenance. You'll need it to survive the loss."

"Is that so?"

"That is so."

"We'll see about that," he said, heading toward the kitchen and keeping his smile to himself.

Tough talk. With the way she'd invaded his brain, she probably would win. And that was fine. Surely, she'd smile again then, which should further lessen the awkwardness between them from earlier.

She'd made him lunch. She hadn't wanted to disturb him, but she'd thought about his welfare. It made the memory of that morning's Swedish pop group alarm, and his grumpiness about it, extinguish as if it had never occurred. Funny. Thoughtful. Caring. Sweet. All words that described this…stranger. Beautiful, too, without doubt.

Strikingly so, even without makeup and clothes that properly fit.

Liam put together a plate of cheese, crackers and grapes and poured them each a fresh cup of coffee.

Before returning to the living room, he went through the back door and stepped outside. The storm had calmed considerably. The wind still blew strong, but there wasn't nearly as much snow falling.

Yup. The storm was gearing down. Very likely by tomorrow afternoon, the roads would start to get cleared and within another twenty-four hours he'd be able to cart Miss Goldilocks to her friend's house. He'd have his space again. His quiet.

And that would be that.

Chapter 7

Hedbanz, as it turned out, was insanely easy. Guess "what" or "who" you were by asking questions to the other players—in this case, Liam—for a yes or no response. The "who" or "what" was displayed on a card bound to your forehead with a headband. You couldn't see it, but those you were playing with could.

Meredith won, but only by a single point and only due to the fact that after several rounds of being an animal—how unfair was that, seeing that he earned his living by photographing wildlife?—Liam had the misfortune of choosing the "I am a flashlight" card. He was stuck with being a flashlight for several rounds, his questions not getting him close enough for a correct guess, which allowed her ample opportunity to move ahead and win.

Which she did, with the "I am bacon" card. She'd narrowed it down to being a food, asked if it was mostly eaten at breakfast, if it fell into the meat category and finally, if she'd made it that morning. With a sigh and a quick roll of his eyes, she had the answer. She'd never loved bacon quite so much as she did at that moment, because now...*now*...she'd earned the right to request something from Liam without feeling guilty.

She hadn't yet decided what that something should be, but she'd figure that out soon. She'd have to. It looked as if tomorrow would be the last full day she'd be here alone with Liam. Unless fortune truly shone on her shoulders and another storm swept in while they slept. Unlikely, but hey, that she was even here at all was even more so.

"Sure you wouldn't prefer a trophy?" Liam asked as they picked up the game and put the various pieces back in the box. "Or...a Harry & David gift basket? Fruit-of-the-month club?" He winked and her heart dropped to her stomach. Over a wink. That had never happened to her before, with anyone. Even Rico. "I know! A year's supply of bacon. That seems fitting."

"None of those ideas include you," she said. "Remember the deal?"

"They do include me, since I would be the one supplying you with a trophy, gift basket, a fruit-of-the-month subscription or a year's supply of bacon." Another wink, followed by a semisarcastic grin. "Not sure how you can state otherwise!"

"They do not include you in the way I would like," she said, surprised by her forthrightness. But hey, it was time to start living, right? "And before you ask, no, I don't know what exactly I'm going to ask for my prize yet. But when I know I will let you in on it."

Leaning over the coffee table so they were mere inches apart, he said, "And will your prize fall within the reasonable range? I mean, you're not going to ask me to drive you to New York or take you on a vacation to Hawaii or anything of that nature, are you?"

"Um…no. Nothing like that." Lord, he smelled good. It wasn't the scent of a cologne or aftershave or even his soap or shampoo. He didn't smell like trees or the air after a drenching rain or anything so defined. It was just him. And it was good. Welcoming and appealing and sexy all rolled into one package.

She drew in a breath, a rather large one, and worked to modulate her voice, saying, "And of course it will be reasonable. Probably fun, too. I just have to think some on the actual specifics of what that will entail."

A whisper of a wish slipped into being. A kiss. She could ask for a kiss. That would be fun. Reasonable, however? Not so much.

Besides which, if this man ever kissed her, it needed to be of his own free will. Because he just *had* to. Because the thought of not kissing her would be unbearable. Unthinkable.

Heat rushed her cheeks, soaked into her skin and swept through her limbs until her fingers and toes tingled. Great. Now all she could think of was kissing this man, of what his mouth would feel like on hers, of how her body would respond to his touch. And he was so close. If she pushed herself forward a few more inches, if she were courageous enough, she could kiss him before he even realized what was happening.

Quickly, before the wish fueled a type of courage she didn't really want to have—at least not yet—she stood and picked up the game. "I suppose we should put everything away and…and…" What? It was too soon for sleep, they'd eaten enough snacks to not need dinner, there wasn't a television that she'd seen and even if there was, she doubted they'd have reception. Even a generator couldn't fix that. "I guess I don't know what we should do then."

"Now you sound like my niece," Liam said, also standing. "We could play a few more games, or...well, would you be interested in seeing some of my photographs?" He blinked as he asked the question, as if he'd surprised himself. "Or...let's just go with another game."

"Oh, no you don't. Once an offer like that is made, there is no taking it back!" Before he could argue further, she stacked several of the games in her arms. "These go in the mudroom?"

"Yeah. I can put them away. I need to let out the dogs anyway."

"And I can help."

"Stubborn," he said, half under his breath. "And really, I don't expect you to want to look at photographs. I'm not sure why I suggested it, but—"

"Liam," she said, interrupting him, her voice soft. "I already asked you questions about your work this morning, remember? I am very interested in seeing what you do, and I am honored you're willing to show me. Please don't take that away. Okay?"

His gaze dropped to the floor, which surprised her, but he nodded. "Okay. On both accounts, but as soon as you want to do something else, just say the word."

"Oh, I doubt that will happen. But yeah, you have a deal." Surely, he was accustomed to people viewing his photographs if this was his profession. Yet, he seemed shy at the idea, even though he was the one who'd broached it. Another interesting facet of this man she'd dreamed about. Another tidbit of information to store with the rest.

So far, she very much liked what she knew.

"Well, then," he said, that gruff tone returning to his voice. "I guess I can't argue."

"No, you really can't."

They put away the games, he let out Max and Maggie and less than twenty minutes later, he was opening the door to his office.

And she felt privileged, somehow, to be let into the wizard's inner sanctum. A place, she was sure, not many people had entered. She didn't take this lightly. She knew, in the way a person really knows something, that Liam didn't easily share his privacy.

The room was larger than she'd imagined, rectangle in shape. Windows that almost went from floor to ceiling occupied the wall directly across from the door. Against this wall of windows was his desk—long and sturdy—upon which sat three oversize monitors, boxes in various shapes and sizes that she assumed held...well, photography odds and ends, a couple of framed photos that must be of his sister and niece and an impressive stack of notebooks, sketch pads and file folders.

The back wall seemed to be formed from shelves from the ground up and storage containers, so many that she couldn't even see the wall behind them, along with camera cases and other paraphernalia of one sort or another. The bottommost shelf held several oversize duffel bags that appeared to be full. What he stored in those, she couldn't say.

There was also a large refrigerator to her right and next to that, another door. A second bathroom, maybe? Or a darkroom. The latter of those two possibilities made the most sense.

While there were a lot of items in this room, everything appeared neat and orderly—save for the tottering stack of files, notebooks and sketchbooks on his desk—which didn't surprise her. She'd already noticed Liam's preference for tidiness. Oh, he didn't seem obsessive about it, but to her, he was obviously a man who believed that everything had its place.

Meredith believed in the same, but she also didn't mind a little clutter every now and again. Her grandmother used to say that the messy bits were where real life happened. Meredith tended to agree with that assessment, more so today than ever before.

Clearing his throat, Liam gently took hold of her arm and guided her to the center of the room. He turned her toward the long wall across from his desk and said, "There. Some of my photographs. My personal favorites, I guess you could say."

And oh. Just...oh.

She blinked at the display, let out a breath and blinked again. If someone had blindfolded her and led her to this precise spot with this precise view, she would've stated with unequivocal certainty that she was standing in an art gallery and that these photographs were taken by someone at the top of his or her career.

There were large photographs, small ones and those that fell in a myriad of sizes in between. And all were... well, she didn't have a word that could capture every one.

Some were beautiful. Some were striking. Some, to her, were melancholy...almost sad. There were those that evoked the sensation of joy and togetherness and those that resonated of loneliness. There were close-ups and distance shots, those captured in a hazy, dreamlike manner and those that were so crisp and clear, she could have been there in the moment, rather than simply looking at a photograph of one.

All of them, though, were breathtaking and rich with emotion.

She saw pride and focus in the loyal stance of a muscled lion, giggling, playful mirth in the gazes of chubby, tumbling wolf pups and fierce love in the mama wolf standing sentry. In another, three multicolored birds—she didn't know their type—were perched on a long, curvy branch, their eyes curious and intent on the camera, and she knew they were but a millisecond from taking off in flight. She saw a pile of sleepy monkeys, so entwined with each other that it was difficult to see which limbs belonged to which monkey, a herd of elephants studiously guiding their young and a rather large lizard that might have been a Komodo dragon surrounded by green foliage, staring upward at a vibrant purple butterfly.

While she looked, while she thought and felt, Liam stood silently next to her, waiting, without expression, his body tense.

Still uncomfortable? Why? Obviously, this man wasn't merely a talented photographer, he was successful. His home and the equipment in this room told her that much. Success in a creative career typically meant that others viewed your work on a consistent basis. Surely, he'd had plenty of experience in this by now?

Though, perhaps he wasn't used to standing in the same room while someone looked over his work. Especially in this room, in his house where he lived with his two dogs and no one else on the side of a mountain. A private man. A quiet man. So, okay, his discomfort made sense.

The sudden want to comfort, to be there for him, had Meredith reaching for Liam's hand. He jerked slightly as she wove her fingers through his, but he didn't pull away.

"Thank you," she said. "So very much."

"For what?"

"Letting me in here. Showing me what you do. I know this isn't easy for you."

"You're welcome." He cleared his throat a second time. "Truth is, I wanted to or I wouldn't have offered and...it's easier than I thought it would be."

"Good." And then, "Your pictures are in magazines, aren't they?"

"Yes."

"Has one ever been on the cover of *National Geographic*?"

"Yes."

"Have several made it to the cover?"

"Yes," he said.

"How many?" The minute she could, she would be scouring her local library's magazine collection, hoping to find those covers. He didn't answer, so she repeated, "How many?"

"Enough of them."

"That isn't an appropriate answer! But okay, where else are your photographs?"

"Framed prints. Posters. Calendars. A few books." Tugging on her hand, he started to lead her out of the room, but she planted her heels and stayed put. "Come on, Miss Nosy. If you're done with the questions, we should—"

"Oh, I'm far from done," she said, interrupting him before he could suggest they return to more board games. "I've barely had a chance to really look. And I don't know the stories."

He inhaled a breath, gave her hand a gentle squeeze. "The goal is for the audience to create their own story, from what they see. From what they feel. That job is yours, my dear."

"I already have, but… I want to know yours." She turned, faced Liam and forced herself to meet his eyes with hers. Never easy. Not when his eyes beckoned and pulled her in, made her want more than she should. "Will you tell me your story behind them? Where you were, what you were you feeling? Why these particular shots and why they made it to this wall when I'm sure you have thousands of other photographs that are equally beautiful? Please?"

Dark, ridiculously long lashes fluttered as he blinked. If only she could have those lashes, she'd never have a need for mascara again.

He let go of her hand and shook his head, his mouth already forming the word *no*. She was ready for this, had another slew of arguments all set to go because she did not want to leave this room without hearing Liam's voice adding depth to his work. It felt necessary, somehow. As necessary as food and water and air.

But then he surprised her again. He closed his mouth, shook his head a second time and said, "If this is what you want, then okay, I will tell you…my stories."

"It is what I want." Oh. Did he think this was her prize for winning Hedbanz? If it had to be to get him to talk, she'd absolutely go that route, but she kept that information to herself. "And thank you for your willingness to share. I'm guessing it isn't something you're used to?"

"It's happened before, but no… I tend to keep to myself."

"Shocker," she said lightly. "That seems so out of character."

A brow lifted and his lips split into a grin. "Any more sarcasm and I'll take back my offer and you'll never know any of my stories, Miss Goldilocks." Another long-lashed blink. "Ah… Meredith. Sorry about that, but in my head, you're Goldi."

"I don't mind." Until this moment, she hadn't realized that Goldi was a nickname for Goldilocks. She wasn't sure if that was a compliment or something less. "I am curious, however. Why Goldilocks?"

"Really? You have to ask?" Tugging on a strand of her long, blond hair, he said, "Well, there's the hair and the fact that you invaded my home and passed out on my couch."

"But I did not eat your porridge or break anything!"

"Well, you haven't broken anything yet," he said. "Though, you did manage to make quite a mess earlier. I'd say that's close enough."

"We already agreed that wasn't my fault," she said with a toss of her head. "And I had no real choice but to invade your home, but you and your two dogs could absolutely be the three bears…and wasn't the papa bear really, really grumpy?"

"Grumpy? Nah. He was just misunderstood."

She laughed. "Is that what they're calling it nowadays?"

"Yes, Miss Sass, it is."

"Well, in my book, that isn't—" The room spun as a sudden wave of dizziness overtook her, forcing her to blindly reach out for something to grab onto.

Liam's arms came around her and he pulled her close to keep her standing. And he didn't let go.

"Now, see," he said, his voice soft, "this is what I was worried about. You should've rested today. I should have insisted you rest. But instead—"

"I'm fine, and I did rest. I sat on my butt and played games most of the afternoon and evening. You were with me, so you should know I didn't do anything strenuous." But okay, in this second, she felt as if she'd run a marathon at full throttle without eating for days. Not that she would tell Liam that. He'd drag her to the sofa and she wouldn't hear any of his stories.

Worse, this lovely moment would end. She didn't want that.

"You're not fine. You're pale and trembling." A long sigh emerged. "Come on, let me help you to the living room. We'll get you settled and—"

"Oh, no you don't, mister," she said with every ounce of strength she could muster. "You were about to tell me about your photographs. You're not getting off that easy."

Another sigh, longer and deeper than the one before. "Don't ask me to ignore your well-being in favor of more talking. Because it isn't going to happen."

He started to tug her toward the door, so she did the only thing she could by pulling herself loose and dropping to the floor. Before he could think that she'd fainted or something and pick her up and carry her away, she tossed him a satisfied grin. "See what I did here? Now I can rest and listen to your stories at the same time. We both get what we want."

A third sigh emerged. "Sitting on the floor is not the same as lying down. You know this as well as I do." She didn't respond, just continued to smile up at him while he stared at her with…incredulity? Humor? She wasn't sure, but she didn't see annoyance. "Fine," he said after a short pause. "You win. Kind of, but you're not sitting on the floor."

He pulled his chair out from his desk and rolled it her way. Well, that was fine. She wouldn't argue about sitting in a chair over the floor. "Thank you, Liam," she said, carefully standing. "I think this works quite well as a compromise."

"Compromise, hmm?" he said. "We can call it that if you wish."

She sat down and waited a second for her head to stop spinning before asking, "What else would you call it?"

"That I recognize mule-headed stubbornness when I see it and that I would have to bodily carry you to the couch to get my way." He ran his hand over his jaw. "And don't think I didn't consider that idea, because I did. I'm just fairly sure you'd stomp back in here, and we'd be right where we started. Figured I'd save us a few steps."

"Right. A compromise."

Between them, the air simmered with unsaid words. Again, she asked herself how this man could feel so familiar to her. Solely because of her dream? Maybe. Or maybe she'd had the dream due to this sense of *knowing*. What came first, the chicken or the egg?

A laugh almost broke free, but she held it in. "You should get a chair, too," she said. "So you can sit next to me."

"I'm good," he said. "Let's just…"

"Get this over with?"

"Something like that." Walking forward, he pointed to the photograph of the three multicolored birds, inhaled a breath and, a second later, shook his head. "There isn't really anything to tell with this one," he said after a rather long pause. "Just three pretty birds."

Shadows existed there in his voice, and a bolt of tension ripped through his body. Meredith's senses went on alert, and she wondered—worried a little, too—about the reason for whatever darkness existed and how a photograph of three birds could be the cause. Should she say anything? Stay quiet? In the end, she went with her instincts and said, "Oh, I doubt that. I mean, they're on your wall of fame, right? There has to be a reason?"

Another inhale and he turned just enough away that she could no longer see his face. But then, he nodded and started talking. "The paradise tanager is an outgoing, social breed of bird found in the Amazon Basin. They're songbirds, restless and active, and don't tend to stay in any one place for very long. They group together, typically in clusters of five or more. Like a…um…family, I suppose you could say. Traveling together, protecting each other."

He went on to describe how they foraged for food, their nesting habits, along with a variety of other information one could find on the internet or in a book. The darkness was no longer evident, and in fact he spoke easily, with knowledge, but now his tone reminded Meredith of a school teacher giving a lesson.

She listened quietly, mostly watching his body language and wishing she could see his eyes. Even if only for a heartbeat.

What he didn't talk about—what she guessed he was purposely leaving out—were the personal details she'd asked for. What was in his head when he took this photograph, how did he feel, what was going on for him in that moment and why had this particular photograph made it to this wall?

Even so, she remained silent and listened, hoping something—anything—personal would creep into his verbiage. She yearned to know more about this man, from the smallest detail to the largest. She ached to know what had caused his change in demeanor.

But she couldn't ask those questions. They were too private, given the darkness she'd heard, which meant that he likely wouldn't answer them anyway.

One by one, Liam went through the photographs in the same manner as he had with the paradise tanager shot, his voice calm and smooth, knowledgeable and yeah…impersonal. Not quite flat, but without offering anything to connect the man behind the camera with these incredible works of art.

Whatever memories those "three pretty birds" evoked seemed to have stuck around for the duration. She hated that, but despite how much she wished he'd open up a little and despite the questions circling in her brain, she still didn't interrupt.

There wasn't any reason to. She had the sense that no matter what she might say in this moment, her questions wouldn't achieve the desired result. He'd have to get there on his own, due to a want to share with *her*. That was something you couldn't push a person into doing. All she could do was listen to what he chose to share. Even if that amounted to nothing more than a bunch of basic facts.

So, she listened. And she wondered. And she worried. Tomorrow was possibly her last full day to spend here, in this house that was hidden in the mountains, with a man like no one she'd ever known before. What if, when she left here, she never saw Liam again?

The thought sobered her further and weighed heavier than it should. Quickly, before the heaviness could take root, she shoved practical, reasonable thoughts into her head. Life would go on. She'd visit with Rachel and figure out where to go from here.

Her original plan still existed. Nothing had changed. And the honest truth of the matter was that nothing *should* change. There was a lot of rocky, uneven ground to cover before she would be ready to truly consider the wishes and wants that now swam in her heart.

Right. Because how could she have the life she'd dreamed about—whether with Liam or another man she'd yet to meet—before she realized some of her own goals? How could she really know someone else or let anyone fully into her world before she really knew herself and what she was made of?

So, okay. Nothing had changed. Her focus remained the same, on her future and creating a life of her own making. That goal needed to come to fruition, and none of what she felt—or thought she felt—toward Liam held any bearing.

But that didn't mean she could erase her concern or her curiosity, and that didn't mean that she wouldn't enjoy the rest of her time here with him. And there was no chance that she would walk away and forget.

Because she wouldn't. Couldn't.

If her dream held any true importance, if fate had brought her here for a reason, she would eventually know that as surely as she knew her own name. She wouldn't have to question or guess or push or prod. All she had to do was follow her path and see where it led. See if

Liam's path merged with hers again at some point in the future. She hoped it would.

She returned her attention to him, to the steady, calm beat of his voice as he spoke about the wolf cubs and the mama standing sentry. His body was still angled away from hers, but she would guess he wore a serious expression and a hooded gaze. The unnamed darkness still had its hold, and she felt for him. Wanted and wished for lightness to enter his speech, for a rolling laugh to emerge, for a ray of sunlight to overtake that darkness and send it scurrying for cover.

All at once, an idea of what she would ask for as her "prize" blossomed into being.

Maybe she only had one more day with this man. Maybe she couldn't offer the light he seemed to need at this moment, but she could use her prize to elicit some frivolity. And he'd have to say yes, because her request absolutely fell into the reasonable range.

They would have fun. There would hopefully be laughter. And perhaps that would be a gift to Liam, as well as to herself. If nothing else, they would create another memory she would carry with her, along with the rest, as she forged a future she could call her own.

Leaving Liam and his sanctuary didn't have to be sad. Not if she could help it.

Chapter 8

For the second day in a row, Liam woke up grumpy. Today, though, he couldn't place blame on a Swedish pop group or Meredith's choice to play "Mamma Mia" at a louder than decent volume. The house was whisper silent when he opened his eyes, still more dark than light outside and as had already become the norm, his dogs were nowhere to be seen.

They were, without a doubt, curled up with Goldilocks. And even the absence of his traitorous dogs didn't account for his sour mood. If anything, he figured Max and Maggie had the better end of the sleeping deal. How could he fault them for that?

Punching his pillow, Liam rolled over and closed his eyes. He tried to force his body to relax and his brain to stop its incessant thinking in the hope that maybe, just maybe, he could catch a tad more sleep.

He hadn't slept well. Every hour or so, he'd wake and

thoughts of the woman downstairs would be merged with Christy, with that god-awful loss, and he'd toss and turn for another thirty minutes before drifting off again. He hated that.

It had taken so long to come to terms with losing his wife and child. So damn long he'd worked to make peace with what couldn't be changed. And now, a few days with Meredith and all that muck had churned to the surface.

That accounted for his bad mood. He never wanted to return to those days of barely being able to breathe without feeling that sharp, incapacitating pain.

Very purposefully, Liam turned his thoughts away from Christy, away from Meredith and instead focused on the day ahead. The activities that required his attention.

He couldn't really do a lot more workwise until power was restored. The generator kept the house livable, but the PCs were a major power drain and he wouldn't risk developing prints. Yesterday, when he'd sequestered himself in his office, he'd spent the majority of his time organizing the digital photographs on his laptop until the battery had gotten too low to continue. And then, he'd spent another solid hour dozing in his chair. That was why he hadn't heard Meredith's knock, why he hadn't known she'd left him a meal outside his door.

And that was all it took for his mind to once again focus on what he did *not* want to focus on. Which also meant that any additional sleep was out of the question. He was up for the duration, which meant he might as well—

Music.

ABBA again interrupted his thoughts, and he felt his

mouth stretch into a smile. A wide enough one that his cheeks hurt from the effort. And the fact that the smile came on its own accord, so quickly and so naturally, didn't escape his analytical brain.

This woman was something special. Someone special.

And that made her even more dangerous. To his peace of mind, to the lifestyle that had saved him from being buried alive, to holding on to his sanity and every other damn thing he'd worked so hard to achieve since losing Christy, their baby and the future he'd believed was theirs for the taking. The future that would've existed, if not for the winds of fate. An unstoppable force, one you couldn't predict or, in any true fashion, protect yourself from.

But that very same force had brought Goldi to his couch.

Standing, Liam strode to his bedroom window and pulled back the curtain. The snow had stopped. Not so much as a flurry whisked through the early morning air. It would take a full day, he knew from prior experience, before he'd have any possibility of safely escorting Meredith into Steamboat Springs. So, fate had brought her to him, and now with the end of the storm, fate was allowing—encouraging?—her departure? Possibly.

And maybe, just maybe, a twinge of regret lived alongside his relief.

"Of the many, many possibilities you could ask for as a prize, this is what you're going with?" Liam asked Meredith later that day.

His expression was a solid mix of shock and good humor. The good humor appealed obviously, but Meredith kind of enjoyed surprising him, too. She had the feeling he wasn't used to being surprised.

"Didn't you spend enough time outside in the snow the other night? One would think that experience would be enough to last a lifetime."

Ha. If he thought that would change her mind, he was very much wrong. "That was different, which you know full well." She avoided looking him straight in the eye. Every time she did that, she fell a little more. A little harder. "I won fair and square."

They were dressed similarly, in jeans and sweatshirts. Her clothes hadn't yet been washed, but they were dry and serviceable enough for a couple of hours outside. And okay, she maybe felt a little bad at making him spend more time outside—he'd been out there most of the morning, clearing snow from the porch and pathways—but not bad enough to give in on her prize.

They were going to build a snowman together. And darn it all, one way or another, she planned on eliciting at least one laugh from him before they were done. Somehow.

"That's a point." He gave her one of those long, searching looks before asking, "You're sure you're up for it? You weren't doing all that well last night."

"I'm feeling great. So we're agreed?"

"Sure, if this is really what you want." He gave his head a quick shake. "But I don't know, if I were you, I'd definitely be going for the Harry & David fruit-of-the-month club."

"Good thing you're not me, then! But...um, I will need some gloves. And maybe a hat and a scarf? If you have any extras I could borrow." And then, before he could use that as an excuse to weasel out of her plan, she continued with, "If you don't, I'll just use socks again."

"Uh-huh, as if I'd allow such a thing." He went upstairs and returned a scant minute later with a pair of gloves. "There are a few extra hats and scarves in the mudroom. What else do we need? I have never actually constructed a person made of snow before."

Meredith had been in the process of putting on her coat, but Liam's words stopped her midzip. "Are you joking?" she asked. "Because I have never met a person over the age of four who hasn't built a snowman."

"I spent most of my childhood years in Florida, with my grandfather."

She waited for him to say more, but he didn't. There were so many obvious questions, but how could she ask them? Why he grew up "mostly" with his grandfather wasn't her business.

"I was hoping you'd give me an answer I could use as fodder for picking on you," she said in a teasing sort of way. "But no, you had to go with a perfectly logical response."

Shrugging, he tossed her the gloves, which she—surprisingly—managed to catch. "Just the facts, ma'am, just the facts. So are we ready?"

"Well, we need a carrot and…you wouldn't happen to have a bag of coal lying around, would you? Maybe a handful of buttons?" She finished zipping her coat and slid on the gloves. They were meant for Liam's hands, so they were loose, but she didn't mind. "Oh, another scarf!"

"You take this snowman stuff pretty seriously, huh? I don't know what I have lying around, but I'll see what I can come up with."

Did she hear a hint of frustration? Maybe. "Or, you know, it doesn't really matter," she said. "We can use sticks and stones and whatever else we can find. The goal is to have fun."

"Right. Fun," he said over his shoulder as he headed toward the kitchen. "Let's go do this, before it gets any colder out there."

Yup. Definitely frustration. Due to her and her choice of a prize—which was supposed to be silly and light-hearted—or due to the admission that he'd been raised by his grandfather and the unspoken story behind the statement? Or something else entirely?

This, like so many other aspects of Liam's personality, she couldn't hazard a guess. The man just did not give enough away for any shot at an accurate prediction. She thought he was that way with everybody, so the short time they had known each other didn't really come into play.

Her goal hadn't changed, though. One laugh, that was all she needed to coax from him. Come hell or high water, another freak snowstorm, or some other out-of-the-ordinary event, she would get that laugh. It seemed of the utmost importance, even if she didn't know why.

"Goldi?" Liam's voice, the volume of which was just shy of a bona fide shout, hit her ears. "Do you want to build this damn snowman or not?"

"You bet I do," she said under her breath. *One* laugh. How hard could that be? Following the same path he'd taken less than a minute ago, she called out, "On my way!"

She found him standing in the mudroom, holding a long, purple scarf and a matching knit hat. His sister's or an old girlfriend's? Or hell, maybe he had a current girlfriend. Who knew, and yup, that was yet another series of questions she refused to ask, albeit for different reasons than all the others she'd smothered so far.

Accepting the scarf and hat, she quickly put them on and then, offering him a grin, said, "Well, what are we waiting for? I'm ready. Are you?"

"Sure. Ready enough anyway," he said in a sandpaper-dry voice. He whistled and Max and Maggie ran to the door, tails wagging. Well, at least they were excited. "You're in charge of this expedition, by the way. Tell me what you want me to do and I'll do it."

Finally, because she had to say *something* even if it wasn't what she really wanted to say, she said, "Are you okay? I mean, if you really don't want to do this, that's fine."

Those ridiculously beautiful eyes of his found hers, and there it was again…that spark of attraction that sizzled and popped in her blood.

"I'm fine," he said. "Just feeling antsy today, ready for everything to get back to normal. But I suppose every man should build a snowman once in his lifetime, and I likely never would have without prodding."

Not an enthusiastic response, but she'd take it. Happily, even.

He held the door open, allowing Max and Maggie to take off in an exuberant run. Meredith went next, stepping carefully onto the recently cleared path, and waited for Liam.

The snow was piled in uneven slopes brought on by the high winds, and the trees were weighted and almost completely white. It was beautiful and quiet and deeply spiritual in its serenity. She had the out-there realization that she could live here, in this silent sanctuary, without any trouble whatsoever.

She might even be happier here than she'd ever been before in her life.

A nice thought, but not exactly a feasible one. Forcing a smile, she turned toward Liam. "I think we should make our snowman over there," she said, pointing toward a relatively flat section of snow in front of a cluster of fir trees and a single towering aspen. "He'll look good over there and easily visible from the house. What do you think?"

"Ah… I'm not sure that's a good idea, Meredith. Consider—"

"It's a great idea, Mr. Grump," she interrupted. If this continued, she might have to smack him with a snowball or two. "My prize, right? I should get to choose."

A brow raised, but he nodded. "Mr. Grump, is it?" Shielding his gaze with one hand, he looked toward the area she'd already pointed out. "Perhaps I am simply confused and incorrectly identifying the spot you're after. Why don't you walk over there and show me where you mean? I'm quite sure that will help me visualize what you've so easily seen."

"I can do that." Pleased he'd shown any interest, she walked off the shoveled path toward the section of trees she'd chosen. Initially, she didn't have too much trouble, as the snow directly around the path wasn't that high, probably because Liam had leveled it out some. But as she continued her forward motion, that quickly changed.

She stopped and looked down, saw the snow had already reached about midcalf and she wasn't even at the deepest portion yet. Reconsidering, she turned around, only to see Liam watching her with his arms crossed over his chest and wearing a smart-ass grin. The brat! He'd known and hadn't said a thing.

Well. He'd tried to. She'd interrupted him, sure he was hip-deep in grump mode. Of course, she should've considered the snow obstacle on her own.

"Problem?" Liam asked, his smile widening another notch. "That can't be the spot you meant, is it? I really misunderstood, then. I thought you wanted it nearer the trees?"

"Well, I did."

"But?"

"It seems as if I—"

"Yes? Do tell. Is there a problem? Something you want to share?" His lips twitched in an almost laugh. "Having second thoughts, are you?"

"Nope. No problem. No second thoughts." Narrowing her eyes, she shrugged. "I...ah... I just wanted to be sure you were paying attention and not playing with the dogs."

"Never fear, Goldi. At this moment, you have my undivided attention."

Yeah. She bet she did. "Good!" And with that, she turned around again, dead-set on getting herself through the snow and to those trees.

To prove what, exactly? And why? She didn't have an answer for either question other than pure stubbornness. In her book, that was more than enough reason. Even if the stance fell on the slightly childish side.

She pushed through another few feet, the level of the snow creeping upward as she slogged forward. Another few feet and she just about had to climb out of the snow for each step as it had almost reached her knees. No amount of sheer stubbornness would get her the rest of the way without tumbling face-first into the snow. And if that happened, she had zero doubt that Liam would insist she go inside and change into another pair of his pajamas and rest.

So maybe this hadn't been a true battle of wills, but she sort of felt as if he had won. Which was fine, she supposed. Maybe that would put him in a better mood for the rest of the day. Giving up, she faced Liam and shrugged. "Can't get there," she said. "Snow is too high."

"Reason over stubbornness, eh? I wondered how far you'd take it."

"Just enjoying the view, huh?"

"Something like that, but another step or two and I would've stopped you. I don't want you to fall again," he said. "Be careful coming back, okay?"

His words soothed. Warmed her heart, too. "I'll be fine. Just have to follow the same—" And naturally, because she was focused on talking and not her movement, she didn't lift her right leg high enough to clear the ledge she'd created on her way in, and yup, she fell. Face-first.

The heavy snow surrounded her body, almost sucking her in as she imagined quicksand would, burying her face and leaving her without the ability to breathe. A now familiar terror, one she'd sincerely hoped she'd never experience again, erupted into being. Really? She'd survived being lost in the middle of a snowstorm, but she couldn't pick herself up out of this?

Pressing her arms downward, she pushed with all her might, and just as she did, Liam's arms came around her and pulled her up. To him. To safety and oxygen and a pair of green eyes filled with fear that mirrored her own. Suddenly, the very last thing she cared about was building a damn snowman.

"You okay?" Liam asked, his hold on her secure, his gaze glued to hers.

She could barely breathe, let alone talk, but she managed an "I am now, yes."

"Okay. Good." He picked her up as if she weighed little more than a can of beans and carried her in the direction of the house. "I'm sorry, Goldi. I shouldn't have let you walk out here, but I really didn't think you'd go so far. Of course, if you had let me talk to begin with," he said with teasing candor, "we'd be halfway done with that snowman by now."

He smelled good. He felt good. She still couldn't breathe correctly, but that had zip to do with her tumble in the snow. It had everything to do with the man holding her. "You're right. But you were so grouchy! So, really, the fault is on both of our shoulders."

"Hmm. I wonder if there is ever a time you're not stubborn?"

"Hmm," she mimicked, "I wonder the same about you."

He kept carrying her as he treaded through the thick snow. The fact he could with so little effort astounded her. Made her feel…feminine and fragile and as if his primary goal was to protect her, which okay, at this moment that was the case. And strangely, as much as she'd pushed against her father's various ways of protecting her, in this scenario with Liam, she found she didn't mind at all. He…well, he made her feel safe, rather than little more than a porcelain doll.

"You…ah…can probably put me down now. I'm guessing I can walk the rest of the way without falling."

"I'll put you down when we're inside and not a second before." He let out a sigh. "Sorry, but you're going to have to cross that snowman off your list, because it's not happening."

Oh. The snowman. She'd already forgotten, because now, there was only one thought in her head. Just one. And it had nothing to do with making Liam laugh.

She wanted a kiss. Yearned for a kiss. The possibility bopped around in her head a bit, and unlike last night, she determined it was a reasonable request. They were both consenting adults. She'd won fair and square and had earned herself a prize. He might object, but she could certainly ask.

And now, the thought of not kissing Liam, of not knowing what his lips felt like on hers seemed…impossible. She had to know.

Would he reject her request? She had the belief that he wouldn't. Or that he wouldn't, at the very least, outright refuse the proposition. "I'm in total agreement," she said. "We can nix the snowman in lieu of another prize."

"Giving up that easily? Did you conk your head on a rock when you fell?"

"I did not! But there is something else, something… better, that I'd like for my prize. Now that you've vetoed my snowman." It was one thing to decide the asking made sense; it was another to actually verbalize the question. "I'm pretty sure it will make me far happier than the snowman would've. No. Not pretty sure. Absolutely sure."

She could still back out if she lost her courage. She hadn't given anything away yet.

"That was quick." He paused at the door, looked down at her and said, "Let me guess. More talking? I suppose— under great duress, mind you—I can agree to that."

If a kiss hadn't become her goal, she might've agreed.

Mostly due to Liam's pained expression at the possibility of exposing more of himself via a conversation. It was vulnerable and disarming, and the fact that he was willing to go there if that was what she wanted showed her a lot about the man behind that expression. Maybe more than she'd seen before.

"No worries. I'm not going to ask you to talk."

Relief etched his face, easing the lines around his mouth. "Really? Gotta say, Goldi, that's surprising. You've barely stopped talking since you've been here."

"Right. Because a near-comatose woman has so much to say," she fired back.

"All right, you have a point. I will amend my statement to reflect that you've barely stopped talking since we officially met." He winked and her heart spun. It was that simple. That powerful. "How's that? Better?"

"Much. But no, what I'm thinking of requires very little talking. If any at all. In fact, no talking would probably be best, because, well…"

Lovely. Now she was rambling. But how could she not while this man held her smelling like he did? Looking at her as he did? Sounding like he did? With the image of them kissing now solidly planted in her brain?

Impossible.

She breathed. Blinked a half dozen times or so. Her skin warmed even though she hadn't yet uttered the word *kiss*. Hell. There was not one portion of her being that didn't feel warm, from the inside out.

"Um. So, yeah. No snowman. No talking. And for the record, you might not initially think my request falls within the reasonable range, and I didn't think so last night when I first thought of it, but now I do. You…um… should know that."

He paused seconds before opening the door, stared down at her again and those green and amber eyes of his darkened to a burnished moss. The change wasn't fueled by anger or frustration or even confusion, because she saw desire looming in the depths of his gaze. As if he already knew what she was about to ask. As if he'd considered the very same.

Maybe he did know. Maybe he had.

"You're trouble," he said. "I knew it the second I saw you."

"Yeah? Well, you're trouble, too. But… I like it." Oh! Where had that come from? She blinked another half dozen times, breathed again. "I *might* like it."

"Tell me, Goldi," he said. "If I have to guess, I might guess wrong."

It was now or never. So, now please. "A kiss. I want you to kiss me."

His eyes darkened another full shade. She didn't know the word to describe their color now, but they pulled at her, made her want so much more than a kiss. But…she'd take the kiss and be happy with it. Maybe for the rest of her life.

A low growl emerged from the back of his throat. And that sound? The heat in her belly grew hotter, her shivers grew stronger.

"A kiss," she repeated firmly, with far more bravado than she felt. "A real kiss, Liam. Not just a peck on my cheek or forehead, but a full-blown, sweep-me-away type of a kiss." Oh, wow. She was both proud and shocked she'd said that so clearly.

His arms tightened around her at these words, and hunger entered his gaze.

That seemed so very positive, so she continued with,

"I think a kiss is fair compensation for winning the Blizzard Championship and for almost dying for the second time in the span of a few days. Don't you?"

"Damn it, Goldi, I'm not made of stone," he said half under his breath. "Be careful what you ask for. I'm not a man to…have fantasies about or tie yourself to."

"I don't see a problem with a fantasy or two," she said, "and I'm not asking you for a diamond ring. Just a simple kiss." Her heart slammed against her breastbone and her mouth went dry. She was out of her mind. Absolutely so. But now that she'd started this, now that she saw and heard the same desire from Liam, she wasn't about to back off. "Well, maybe not a *simple* kiss. One amazing, toe-curling kiss. I think you might like it, too."

A glimmer of amusement swept over his features. "Toe-curling? Who talks like that?" He shoved open the door and carted her to the living room. But he did not set her down. He kept holding her, staring into her eyes, and yeah, that seemed positive, too. Very much so.

"My grandma did, so I guess I do, too."

"A kiss. You're asking for a kiss."

"Yes, please," she said. "Just make it—"

"Toe-curling, yeah." He closed his eyes, let out a sigh. "Can't say I'm entirely sure I know what that is, but it is your prize, after all. But who determines if it's toe-curling?"

"Well, me, of course," she said, further emboldened by his seeming acceptance of her proposal. "I'll have to be the judge. I mean, it's my toes you have to curl."

"Sounds painful. But okay, I'll…ah…"

"You'll what?" she prodded.

Another sigh. "This is a very bad idea. You know that, right?"

Oh, no. She couldn't let him think that through. Because, yes, it was a very bad idea. It was, at the exact same time, the best idea in the entire world. "Well, we could bet on that, as well," she said, her voice low. Breathless. And so unlike her normal voice. "If you're right and it turns out to be a bad idea, you can choose a prize. If I am right, then I get anoth—"

"Stop. No more talking." He carried her to the couch. "No more prizes."

"But I get this one, right?" Realizing he was about to deposit her on the sofa like an invalid, she stiffened in his arms. Nope. That was not going to happen. At least not before she got her kiss.

"Oh, no you don't, mister. I don't need to rest. I'm just fine. Well, maybe a little damp from the snow, but nothing that can't be fixed. Later. So, if you think you're going to plop me down and walk away after I've just asked you to kiss me, then you are strongly mistaken."

"Am I?"

"Yes. Strongly. I fell, yes, but I wasn't in the snow for long and—"

"Shh, Goldi. I can't kiss you when you're talking so much."

Oh. Well, then. "No more talking. I'll just…um… be quiet."

"Perfect." Still holding her, he sat down on the sofa. A second, then another, then another ten passed before he slowly helped her shift so she was sitting on his lap, facing him.

They were close. So freaking close. Eye to eye, nose to nose, almost lip to lip. And oh, how she yearned to stroke her fingers across the firm line of his jaw, up to his cheek, into his hair. But she didn't move, too afraid that he'd change his mind if she did anything other than wait. She couldn't bear it if he changed his mind. Now this kiss seemed of the highest priority. Over food and water and oxygen and sleep. It was all she wanted.

All she needed. Desired. Wished for. *Craved.*

"What are you doing to me, Goldi?"

"Probably the exact same thing you're doing to me."

"And that helps how?"

"Just kiss me, Liam. Please."

It must have been the please that did it, because the second the word slipped out, he groaned in a deep, almost guttural way, and in the space of half a heartbeat, his lips were on hers, pushing a soft moan from her throat.

His hands came to her waist and he brought her even closer as he deepened the kiss, his mouth firm, his hold secure. Curls of warmth trickled over her skin, suffused into her blood and seeped into her bones until nothing else existed. Except for them, his mouth on hers and friction and heat and want and need.

Just that quick. Just that effortlessly.

Made her want even more. She should've asked for an hour of kissing. Two hours. An entire night…the rest of her life. In this moment, that seemed reasonable. Necessary. Because she knew, really knew, that this kiss from this man would leave its mark. And she would never be the same. No matter how many miles she traveled or how many years passed.

Sliding his hands to the small of her back, he shifted them again, somehow bringing their bodies even closer together. Where did he start and she begin? She couldn't tell. Didn't know and didn't want to know. They were one.

His tongue pushed into her mouth, hungry and searching and demanding everything she could give, accepting nothing less. She opened her mouth and a moan, followed by another, whispered from the depths of her soul as she capitulated. Toe-curling? Yes.

Life changing? Yes, that too.

A frisson of fear swept in, momentarily overriding her desire. Not from the strength of her reaction, but from the knowledge that she would likely yearn for this man every day, in every way a woman could. The fallout of this action—a kiss—could be devastating. Somehow, more so than learning what she had about Rico. And that right there told her a hell of a lot.

She was already a goner. For Liam. A man she'd known for less than three days, yet her soul recognized from the moment she heard his voice. Her body recognized him, as well. Down to the bone, she knew this man. Oh, she didn't yet know the details that had built him, but she knew his heart. She knew his soul. She knew *him*. Had waited for him.

And here he was, kissing her, touching her, their bodies pressed together and nothing would ever be the same again.

Very purposely, she shoved the fear into a ball and pushed it as far down as possible. Whatever came next, whatever happened after this kiss? Well, she'd deal with it then. Later. When she had to. But she refused to allow her fears to weaken *this*.

Right now, he demanded her attention, her entire focus, and she wouldn't deny him the same pleasure he was giving her. So she returned his kiss with the same fervor, the same hunger, the same need and as she did, pushed her fingers into his hair and held on for dear life.

Maybe, just maybe, if she held on, he wouldn't stop. He would just keep kissing her…forever.

As if he could read her thoughts, he groaned and wrapped his arms around her body and pulled back just enough for their lips to separate. She missed him instantly.

No. Not yet. Please not yet.

"Dangerous," he said, his lips so close to hers, yet not touching. "But irresistible."

Before she realized exactly what was happening, he scooped her up in his arms again and was heading toward the stairs that led to his bedroom. "Guess I like the danger because I'm taking you to bed. If you're not okay with that, you better say something."

"Yes. Yes, I am okay with that," she said. "So long as you are staying there with me."

"That would be my intent, Goldi. Just—"

"I am sure, Liam. I know what I want. Trust me on that, okay?"

One swift nod and he carried her upstairs with the same ease he had through the snow. When they reached his bedroom, he gently set her down on his bed.

Doubt entered his gaze, concern perhaps that this wasn't a good idea. And maybe it wasn't, but she wanted him, wanted this, and she didn't want Liam to think otherwise, not even for a second.

She lifted her sweatshirt over her head and tossed it on the floor. Unclasped her bra and took that off, tossed it in the same direction as the sweatshirt. And Liam? Whatever doubt had existed a mere second ago seemed to be gone, replaced by the need she'd witnessed earlier.

The same need she had. For him. For *them*.

"Help me with my jeans?" she asked. "Please?"

He came to her then without pause and unbuttoned her jeans, dragged them down and off her legs. Her panties were next, and there she lay, naked in front of this man.

Gently grasping her arms, he started to lean toward her, his view unmistakably on her breasts…but no. Not yet. With a teasing grin, she pushed him back and yanked at his sweatshirt. "You're still dressed," she said. "That's a problem."

"Is it now?"

"Mmm-hmm. New rule. No more touching until we get your clothes off," she said, feeling powerful and beautiful and…sexy. "I need to see you, Liam. Feel you, too."

"I think I can manage that." He removed his sweatshirt with the same speed that she had hers, and his jeans came off quicker than she would've imagined possible. And there *he* was, naked save his boxers, and oh, was he a sight to behold.

Strong. Muscular. Long and lean and—in this minute—all hers. All hers.

"Boxers," she whispered. "Don't forget those."

"Patience, woman, geez." But then, he did as she asked, and there was nothing between them, nothing to get in their way. "Happy now?"

"Very much so." Breathless. A mass of trembles. Needy. But yes, happy.

"Trouble," he repeated. Kneeling over, he brushed his thumb over one nipple and then the other, rubbing in small, soft circles that dragged yet another moan from her lips. "You're beautiful, Meredith. And you're killing me with those moans."

"I can stop."

"Ah. Don't. Stop."

His mouth captured hers for another long, searing kiss, igniting this desperate, consuming need another degree.

Melting…she was melting. There really wasn't another way to state what was happening. From her bones to her skin, she became a puddle beneath Liam's touch. Beneath his hands and his mouth and his body. She became his, just as he became hers.

She lifted her hips, wrapped her legs around his torso and ran her hands down the warm length of his back.

All to show him that she was ready and that there wasn't any reason to wait.

But he had other ideas. "We're not there yet, sweetheart," he said, lifting his mouth from hers. "Not yet. We have all day. All night. Why would we rush this?"

Oh. Well, then. "Okay. No hurry."

Time disappeared into a vacuum. Five minutes, ten, three days, she no longer knew or cared. In this space of untraceable time, he skimmed his fingers down her stomach, to her thighs and then followed that very same path with his mouth. Tasting. Tickling. Teasing.

And as he did, her body came to life in an engulfing rush of shivering need, greater even than before, which hadn't seemed possible. She ached for him intensely. Viscerally. And regardless of what he'd said, she didn't believe she could hold out for much longer.

"Now, Liam. Please," she begged. "I can't wait. I need you inside of me."

"Oh, now, for a woman who fought against a snowstorm and survived? Pretty sure you can do anything you set your mind to," he said with a quirky, teasing smile. "Besides which, I don't think I'm quite done exploring your body yet."

She gave him another minute, maybe two, before reaching the decision that if he could torture her, she could certainly return the favor. She rolled out from beneath him and pushed him down, flat on his back with a lot less effort than it should've taken. Maybe he was melting too? A distinct possibility. "Now, it is my turn."

"Oh, is it?" he asked with a smile born of pure anticipation. Excitement was there, too, along with that desire and heat. "Well, if you're sure, I won't object."

"I insist." Lightly—ever so lightly—she trailed her fingers up his arms to his shoulders, leaned forward and brushed her hair across his chest, eliciting a delicious-sounding sigh. And that sound resonated just as strongly, just as deeply as what she experienced, with how he made her feel. Like he had done with her, she used her tongue to taste, to explore.

And everywhere she touched, his skin warmed, muscles tensed and released and then tensed and released again.

Yes.

Giving him pleasure was just as—if not more—satisfying than receiving pleasure. She kissed his chest, his stomach. He wove his fingers into her hair as she did, as she continued downward to his hips and his thighs, his hands tightening incrementally as she licked and tasted and pleasured and…loved.

Slowly, she crawled her way back up his body, one enticing inch at a time, to kiss him fully on the lips.

"You win," Liam said against her mouth as he gripped her waist. She did not object. She did not mind winning this particular battle in any way whatsoever. Together, they rolled, switching places. "No more waiting. No more teasing. You're going to kill me if this keeps up."

Oh. Here they were. *Now.* "If I remember correctly, you started the temptation game."

"You weren't supposed to turn the tables."

"Well, guess you have more to learn about me."

"Maybe I do."

The talking stopped again as he kissed her hard and then looked straight into her eyes as she opened her legs to him, for him.

He entered her in one long slide that, yes, stole whatever breath she had remaining clean from her lungs. And his eyes, hooded and dark and intense and beautiful, remained locked with hers. As if he couldn't bear to turn away.

Connected as one and so freaking intimate.

His hips moved against hers, over and over. She wrapped her legs tightly around him and pushed him in deeper. And then deeper still. Their bodies merged in perfect synchronicity, and Meredith gave herself to the sensations, lost in the power of the moment, in the pleasure swimming through her blood.

And all the while, Liam's gaze never left hers even for a millisecond. She kept her gaze on his, too, in the hopes she would remember every second of this encounter. Because forever and a day from now, she wanted to be able to pull it to her memory and see it exactly as she saw it now. Feel everything she felt now.

Impossible, of course, but she had to try. Had to.

Friction. Heat. Desire. All right here, all for the taking. The pleasure built and built and built and built some more, and then all at once, every sensation gathered into a tight ball, pulsated once…twice…three times before she gave up the fight.

She moaned and pushed herself against Liam, taking him as far as she could while the truest form of pleasure rippled and flowed through her body. This was…beautiful and sexy and somehow pure.

It was what was supposed to be. She believed this. She knew this.

Liam's body tensed, stilled and then he drove into her again as he found his release. His hands came to her arms, and he held on tight as he shuddered, as his eyelids drooped and one more long, satisfied groan rumbled from his throat.

Collapsing on top of her, he rested his head on her breasts, ran his fingers down her arms and together they lay there, still entwined.

Still one.

She wondered if he knew they belonged together. And if he didn't yet know this, if he would eventually come to the same conclusion. Because she was, without doubt, his. And he was, also without doubt, hers. Knowing what she did about this man, it might take him a while to figure this out, but she would wait. She would be patient. She would…

Do exactly as she had with Rico? Keep herself open and available in the hopes that he'd one day show up at her door, announce his love and carry her away?

Oh. Lord. No. She couldn't allow herself to fall into old patterns just as she was trying to find her own way in this world.

Meredith kissed Liam's shoulder, and while she didn't say anything, her soul mourned. Her heart broke. Because she wouldn't wait like she had with Rico. Not for years. She wouldn't do that to herself again, for anyone.

Even for the man she'd dreamed of. Even for the man she knew she belonged with. Even for the man who had just shown her more than she'd ever seen.

Her life was valuable. And she intended on living it, whether Liam was at her side or not.

So she would give him a little time, because she also knew he would need some. Demons of one sort or another raged a battle in his brain, his heart, and she couldn't do anything other than allow him some space to win that war. If he chose to fight it.

But if he didn't... If days melted into weeks, weeks into months, she'd force open her eyes, accept the truth and just live her life. If that happened, would she ever stop hoping?

Eventually, yes. Eventually. The question left unanswered was the precise length of "eventually." Maybe, if she were very lucky, she wouldn't have to find out.

Chapter 9

Liam waited for Meredith to fasten her seat belt before he closed the passenger's side door. It was midafternoon the next day, and while common sense dictated waiting until tomorrow to take her to her friend's house in Steamboat Springs proper, his heart needed her gone posthaste. Before he dragged her to bed and had his way with her again. It shouldn't have happened once. Or twice, later last night. Or...well, didn't matter how many times.

He couldn't let it happen again.

What had occurred between them would stay in his memory for a long while to come, because frankly, he'd never experienced anything like he had with his Goldilocks.

Not even with Christy. A realization that both stunned and shamed him. No one should be able to hold a candle next to the woman he married. Yet, somehow, this woman had. And that made him feel like a heel.

His thoughts hadn't turned that route until this morning, when he woke with Meredith curled against him, her hair in his nose and their bodies spooned. Initially, he'd felt joy and satisfaction and hope. Initially, he'd had the wild idea of asking her to stay.

But she'd slept for a while in his arms, and as she did, thoughts of his wife returned.

That was when the guilt set in, quickly followed by all those logical reasons why he was better off alone. Far better to trust in decisions that had already proven beneficial and solid than it was to blindly grab at a smoky, fog-covered dream that held zero substance.

By the time Meredith awakened, his resolve had become steel. An awkward type of intimacy had set in. There was no denying what they had experienced, and he hadn't yet figured out how to talk to her about any of it. She couldn't have expectations. He needed to be sure she realized this, yet…like always, he despised hurting this woman's feelings.

There was also a profound sense of emptiness that had set in.

Nothing new. He'd felt that way before, had combatted that emptiness with work and then later with Fiona and Cassie and eventually with Max and Maggie. He could certainly beat away that emptiness again. The doing shouldn't be nearly as difficult this time. There wasn't a comparison to saying goodbye to a woman he'd only just met and the woman he'd planned on spending the entirety of his life with.

Or there shouldn't be.

Max and Maggie pushed at his heels, waiting for him

to open the door to the back seat of his truck, knowing they were going for a ride. He did and they jumped in, tails wagging.

At the driver's door, he paused, breathed in the cool air and tried to let the serenity of the mountains, of his home, seep into his blood and calm the churning storm. Didn't work. Not yet, anyway.

But it would. Once he was on his own again.

He slid into his seat, forced a smile in Meredith's direction as he put the truck into Drive. He tried not to notice the tense set of her shoulders, the stubborn lift of her chin. Tried not to give in to this instinct to reach over, pull her into his arms and beg her to stay. Offer the world if she'd only stay with him and his dogs here on his mountain. Lord, that temptation was strong, but he resisted. Had to. For her, for him. For his sanity and well-being.

Hers, too, as far as that went.

"Bet you're happy to finally see your friend, huh?" He turned the truck around and headed down the slope of his driveway, taking care to go slow. "Sorry there isn't phone service yet, but I bet you'll have a signal on your iPhone soon enough. Can check in with her, then. Let her know you're safe and sound and on your way."

She held up her phone and nodded with an equally forced smile. "I'm ready."

"Hey," he said, turning onto the road, "do you remember where your car is? Might be able to get your luggage if you do. Would be nice to have your stuff back, right?"

"It wasn't far down this road, just after that first hill and curve, but… I don't know if I can remember the exact spot. I would like my clothes, if it isn't too hard to find the car. Just don't want you to go out of your way," she said quietly. "You've done more than your fair share."

"Well, let's see what we can do. Try to remember the best you can and tell me when to stop." What he didn't say, what he barely admitted to himself, is that he would do almost anything for this woman. Almost. "Maybe we'll luck out."

They did indeed luck out. Her car wasn't that far off the road, but getting to it would take a fair amount of effort.

He told her to wait for him in the truck—he didn't want to see her fall again—and he kept the dogs there, too. For company. And as he made his way through the snow, he couldn't help but think of her on that night, with the storm raging, all alone and lost and…terrified. He'd known since she'd told him the story that she could've died out here by herself, and he'd felt for her, had been damn glad Max and Maggie had come to the rescue.

But now a different type of terror took hold. He could've lost her before he'd ever even known she existed. And while there wasn't a lick of sense in his next thought, he couldn't rid himself of it, either: he hadn't been there to protect her when she needed protecting.

Ripped him to shreds thinking of that, again, with another woman he…well, cared about. Strongly.

When he arrived at the car and saw the open suitcase in the back seat, clothes strewn about, he could almost see her, panicking and dressing herself in the layers he found her in, scared and gathering her courage, her strength, to do what she needed.

It amazed him, really.

Hurriedly, he shoved the loose clothing back into her suitcase, latched it tight and went back the way he came, toward his truck, his dogs and Goldi. He'd ask her for the rental information, so he could call the company and tell them where the car was located. It wasn't a lot, but he wanted to take that weight off her shoulders since he couldn't reverse time and save her from the ordeal to begin with. But yeah, he would if he could.

He tossed the suitcase in the back seat with the dogs, smiled at Goldi who had pivoted to see him. "Got it," he said. "Not a problem, and now you're all set."

"Yes," she said, somewhat faintly. "All set. Thank you, Liam."

"Welcome."

A minute later, they were once again driving toward Steamboat Springs in silence. Painful silence.

But hell, he didn't know what to say. Didn't have a clue as to how to explain everything in his head and heart. Didn't know. But he wished he did. Wished he had the words to tell this woman that she had affected him deeply but that his life and future were set. And why. Yeah, he really wished he could tell her the whys. That, he knew, was out of the question.

He didn't speak of Christy or their child. Didn't utter a word of his loss. To anyone.

"Talk to me," he said, somewhat gruffly. "You're too quiet."

"Oh, my," she said with a hint of her old, spunky, adorable self. "I'm too quiet and you're asking me to talk? Did *you* fall and bonk your head out there?"

"No, I just…like hearing your voice." Oh, hell. Where had that come from? "And it will be slowgoing for a bit here, might as well have a conversation. Right?"

"Sure. What would you like to talk about?"

"How about your plans, once everything settles

again?" Like how long was she planning on sticking around Steamboat Springs? And did he want to know so he could avoid her or so he could find her? "You never mentioned how long this visit was meant to last."

"Anywhere from a few weeks to open-ended. I'm not really sure yet. Will depend on…well, several factors that remain unknown." Meredith shrugged and closed the heating vent nearest her. "As to my plans, those are rather loose, too. Rachel and I have a lot to catch up on, and I've never met her husband. We'll start with that, I guess, and see where we end up."

"Gotcha. Why…ah, did you quit your job?" He just wanted her to talk. Didn't much care about the topic. Just needed to keep hearing her voice. "Feel like sharing?"

"Oh. Well, that's a long story. Are you sure you're up for it?"

"Yup. I will listen to anything you want to share."

"Okay, then," she said. "I can't remember if I already told you, but I grew up in a wealthy family. We never lacked for anything. But my parents—and they're wonderful people, really, so please don't think they aren't—have a view of the world that they wanted me and my brothers to have. So, we were…what's a good word? Sheltered, yes, but also shown our paths from early on. The paths they decided we were meant to take. And that was that."

She continued to talk, weaving the story of her life for Liam's benefit. How her parents formed decisions for her, their expectations, her desperate want to make them proud even above her own happiness.

He hated that. Hated that she ever gave up even a second of what would make her happy for another person's benefit. It didn't surprise him, though. Not in the least. It was the way this woman was built.

Kind. Caring. Giving. To a fault.

"I met Rico in college, and with him, I suddenly no longer cared about what my parents wanted or thought. Love," she said with a sarcastic edge. "I thought we were in love."

The rest of her tale came out in a short, succinct manner. There wasn't a lick of emotion in Meredith's voice, but Liam recognized her hurt, her numbing shock, at learning how she'd gotten her job and what had really occurred with this man she'd believed loved her. And frankly, he wanted to punch both her father and this Rico square in the jaw.

For hurting this woman. She should never be hurt or betrayed. By anyone.

She wrapped up the story by saying, "So that is why I quit my job. What brought me here, to Steamboat Springs. I am determined to figure out my life without anyone else's interference. From here on out. My life, my choices and…well, I guess that's it."

"That was a lot, Goldi. And I'm proud of you." He was. Massively so.

"Thank you. I…it's time, I guess. Nothing more, nothing less."

"Right. I agree." Now what? "My parents died when I was a kid," he said, shocking himself. Where had that come from? And *why*? He didn't want to talk about that. Did he? "Doesn't matter, I guess. It was a long time ago. Not sure why I brought it up."

"Probably because some part of you wants to talk about it, and I am more than happy to listen." He felt more than saw that she angled herself toward him, and he could clearly imagine the look of compassion and sorrow decorating her features. "Maybe we're just finishing our conversation from yesterday, when you told me you were raised in Florida with your grandfather. I wondered then how that happened. I'm guessing this is why?"

"Yup. After our parents' deaths, Fiona went to live with my mother's sister. Neither our grandfather or our aunt had the room for both of us, but I know it was a tough decision for them. They hated separating us. They—" Liam cleared his throat "—made sure we spent holidays and summers together, though. Every year. So, that was good. Not the same, but good."

"No, not the same." A heavy sigh, as if she were imagining how that might have affected Liam and Fiona. As if the facts of his childhood somehow hurt *her*. "I'm so sorry. What happened? Your parents must have been pretty young still, right?"

He didn't want to answer. Yet, he did. Since he'd broached the topic, he figured he'd keep talking. Was only fair. More to the point, he couldn't ignore the sudden desire to let her in, to show her just a sliver of his foundation. Just a little, mind you. Not too much.

"Well, yeah, they were," he said, taking a careful right onto a cross street. The roads weren't in great shape. He should've waited until tomorrow for this drive for safety. "It was their anniversary. They went out for an early dinner, and with the sitter's help, Fiona and I baked a cake. It was rather ugly, actually, but we wanted to surprise them when they came home. Fiona drew a bunch of pictures, and we hung those around the living room."

"Sounds perfect. How old were you?"

He cleared his throat again. "I was ten. Fiona was seven."

"So young."

"Yeah. Anyway," Liam said, now wanting to get through the telling of this particular story as quickly as possible, "our plan was to hide when they came home, jump out just as they opened the door and show them the cake we'd made. They…ah, never made it home. It was raining that night, pretty hard. I remember the sound of it hitting the roof, the windows of our house. Found out later that Dad took a curve too fast, lost control of the Jeep." Here, he stopped. He hadn't thought about this for most of his adult life. "The car went down a ravine, rolled and crashed at the bottom. We…ah, didn't even know what happened until the next day."

Meredith's hand came to his thigh, and the weight and the warmth and the woman behind the touch offered comfort. Security. Understanding. "Oh, Liam," she said, her voice soft. Soothing. "I guess I'm not sure what to say, other than how sorry I am for you and your sister."

"Thank you. The ravine was steep," he continued, unsure why he felt the need to say more. But he did, so he did. "Even so, they probably would've survived if they'd worn their seat belts. Can't figure that one out, because they always did when we were all in the car together. As it was, Mom died pretty much instantly. Dad followed a few days later."

He waited for another "I'm sorry" and all the typical platitudes that people gave in moments such as these. Oh, he didn't doubt that Meredith would mean every last one, but they always came across—to Liam—as somewhat shallow. What a person said when they didn't know what else to say, how to react, how to really be there for someone else.

He supposed that was why they called them platitudes, and that was fine. No one had to be there for him. He had all he needed. All he ever would need.

A minute or two of silence passed. Then, "Did you still eat the cake?" she asked in a somber tone, surprising him clear through.

Why? He should've known better than to expect the typical from Goldi. Nothing about her fell into the ordinary range. "I think I would've smashed it on the floor, tossed it out the back door, threw it against a wall. I don't know. Something."

Those words, the vehemence behind them, struck deeply. She was right on the money. They *had* destroyed the cake, two days later, but in the sink. Water from the faucet running at full blast and two angry, distraught children wielding wooden spoons. They'd kept at it— Fiona crying and Liam stone silent—until the cake had become mush and most of it had gone down the drain. "Curious, Goldi. Why that question? Why do you think you'd behave in that way?"

She squeezed his thigh lightly. "Because the cake was made to be a happy surprise, a gift and a celebration to have with your parents. I would think that learning what had happened, that they were never coming home, would never see what you and sister had done for them out of love, would've made that cake... I don't know, an enemy, I guess? I would need to demolish the cake." She shook her head, sighed. "Not sure if that makes sense."

"More than you know." She'd nailed it. And why was he surprised? "And that is what we did, and for about an hour afterward, we felt a hell of a lot better."

Until, of course, they realized that cake or no cake didn't change their reality or their sadness or their loss. Their parents were gone. They couldn't escape that.

"Thank you for sharing," she said. "I know that wasn't easy for you." Were those tears he heard in her voice? Maybe. Probably. She was that way. "But I am honored you did."

"It was a long time ago." Emotion lodged in his throat. He pushed it down deep, just as he always did. "I wouldn't have shared if I didn't want to. So there's that."

"Right. There's that." A small laugh. "I can still be grateful and honored."

"I suppose you can."

A silent calm enveloped the interior of the truck, and Liam no longer felt the need for either of them to talk. The quiet soothed, connected. It was the same sensation that his solitary lifestyle in the mountains offered. He didn't question or analyze why—his stance on that and Meredith hadn't altered—but he allowed himself to accept the peace. Allowed himself to accept that, for whatever reason, this woman soothed the beast inside.

"Oh!" she said, breaking his concentration. "I have a signal! Let me call Rachel."

So she did, and he continued to drive. The squeal from the other side of the phone was easily heard from his position, as was Meredith's explanation of what had transpired after her plane had landed: getting lost, her accident, her unusual rescue and that she was on her way to Rachel's and should be there soon, but no, she didn't know exactly how long it would take.

To that, he said, "Within twenty to thirty minutes, I'm guessing. Roads are getting better the closer we get to town, and we're...almost there." Almost. There.

Why hadn't he waited another day?

"Thank you, Liam," Meredith said before repeating the information to her friend. The two talked for another five minutes or so before she disconnected the call. "People were looking for me. I guess Cole's brother, Reid, is a ski patroller, so he apparently knows the mountains even better than you! He and his friends have been on the search since yesterday."

"I'm not surprised. I'm just glad they didn't have anything to find, because that would've meant you weren't safe." Again, a kick of nausea hit his stomach. "You should know I despise that thought. Be more careful in the future, Meredith, okay? Stay safe."

"Oh, trust me, I don't plan on anything like that ever happening again."

"Of course, you don't. But come on, Goldi, you didn't plan on that, either," he said. "Which is what I'm talking about. If you're going into a new area, do your research. Know where you'll be, figure out more than one path to get you there and make damn sure you have a backup plan. I—that is, my dogs—won't be around. Gotta count on yourself."

"Why, Liam," she said. "You sound concerned. That's sweet."

Concerned? More like out of his mind with gut-wrenching worry that she'd get herself in another predicament and he wouldn't be there, couldn't be there, to help. "Just some solid, practical advice that you should take to heart. Danger doesn't typically announce itself."

"I realize that. And yes, of course, I will take more care in the future."

"Good." Then, trying to lighten the moment, he said, "Don't make me hire a team of bodyguards to follow you around. Take care of yourself, that's all I ask."

"And I already agreed."

Maggie took that moment to wedge her head over the

back of the seat and laid it on Meredith's shoulder. Max followed suit with her other shoulder, and in that strange canine unison the two had, they whined. Loudly. Voicing their unhappiness, their own concern, at the possibility of Meredith being in danger again? Wouldn't surprise him. More likely though, the dogs had somehow sensed they were about to lose their new friend.

Snuggling into the dog-head embrace, Meredith said, "It's okay, guys. I'll be fine! Maybe instead of body-guards, you two can just follow me around. I would… like that."

"They would, too," Liam admitted just as they officially entered Steamboat Springs. "Read me your friend's address again? From what I remember, her house isn't too far."

Meredith did, and yeah, another few minutes of her company was all he had left.

"Thank you, Liam."

"For?"

"Everything. Just…everything." She breathed in quickly, sharply. "This is odd, isn't it? I feel as if I've known you for far longer than a few days, and we're about to say…goodbye?"

"You're welcome, and yeah, I know what you mean." He didn't miss that she'd ended that sentence as a question, rather than a statement, and that meant she was curious if they'd see each other again.

Logical, with how they'd spent last night. He had to give her something. Not just an answer, but some type of understanding of what she'd come to mean to him, because it was the truth. And she deserved that. *They* deserved that. But words were not his strong suit, and he still hadn't figured out how to say all that should be said.

"I'll be around. And Meredith? Thank you, too. I've… enjoyed these days with you. Please don't doubt that."

"Okay. I… I won't. Thank you."

Not enough. Not nearly enough. But it was all he had. Probably was all he'd ever have.

Whether it be the mood or something undefined, Max and Maggie began whining again in long, serious notes of dismay. Hell. Knowing Liam's luck, they'd do the same all the way home in their distress over losing Meredith, likely increasing in volume with each mile driven.

And, hell, again. With how fiercely his heart ached now while the woman remained sitting next to him, he might just join them. Because yeah, this might be the right—the only—action to take, he despised the idea as much as his dogs seemed to. Unlike his shepherds, though, he knew what was best.

And this, regardless of how much the loss burned in his gut, was best.

Sitting up in bed, Meredith stretched her arms and yawned. Looked around the guest room she was staying in at Rachel's and yawned again. It would be a long day. Longer than yesterday, which had been longer than the day before.

Her third day with Rachel. Her third mostly sleepless night in a row. All due to Liam. She couldn't stop thinking about him. Wondering what he was doing. If he was missing her with the same strength she missed him.

Obviously not. He knew where to find her and he hadn't come looking.

When they'd arrived here together, he'd given her this long, searching look, a quick hug and then without a backward glance, had driven off. Literally into the sunset.

Fortunately, she hadn't had the time to think too hard on that until later that night, when she'd finally fallen into this bed. First, there had been hugs from Rachel and her husband, Cole. Next, she'd had the difficult phone calls to make to her family, which had been emotional and supportive.

Her father had wanted to fly out there immediately, when he'd learned she was missing in a snowstorm, but Rachel had convinced him to wait until the storm cleared. Until they had more information.

Surprising that he'd capitulated, but he had. She didn't think he'd have waited a lot longer, though. For a man who was used to getting what he wanted when he wanted, Arthur Jensen had shown incredible restraint. But he'd been scared. She heard it in his voice.

And when he apologized for cutting her communication from the family, she almost cried. Probaby would've if Rachel and Cole hadn't been nearby.

Not even once had he mentioned that she wouldn't have been in that predicament to begin with if she hadn't made the decision she had, to go out on her own. He even said he was proud of her, for sticking to her guns. They had a lot more to talk about, but she felt sure they would repair their relationship and that he finally understood her need to find independence. She hoped so anyway.

The remainder of the day had been spent with Rachel, drinking wine and catching up, learning about all the gaps in each other's lives. They'd stayed up so late, had giggled so hard, that Cole—who had tried to turn in hours earlier—finally gave up the fight and joined them.

A pleasant night. Except, of course, for missing Liam.

Yesterday had been much the same: more talking, more laughing and a quick tour around Steamboat Springs. They'd eaten lunch at Cole's family's restaurant, Foster's Pub and Grill, and she'd had the opportunity to meet both of his brothers, Reid and Dylan, and his sister, Haley.

What hadn't happened, what she thought was on the agenda for today, was the reason she came here in the first place: to think about her future, determine what that might look like, with Rachel as a sounding board. A difficult proposition from the beginning, but meeting Liam had made that even more difficult. A future. Her future. With or without Liam?

Standing, Meredith made the bed and grabbed a change of clothes, went to the log cabin's bathroom and took a shower. Mostly cold, to wake up her tired brain.

Even with missing Liam, she couldn't deny the pleasure of being here with Rachel, especially after so long. And oh, she seemed happy, living in this house with her handsome husband. Such a different life her friend had chosen from that in which she'd been raised.

While the log cabin was gorgeous, it wasn't a large home by any stretch of the imagination. Two bedrooms. One bathroom. Dollhouse-sized when compared to what Rachel had grown up with, to what *Meredith* had grown up with. But yes, she could see being happy in a place like this, with a love like her friend had so fortunately found. Deliriously so, even. Except in her head, it was Liam's face and his mountain cabin that she saw.

Damn that man anyway.

"'I'll be around,'" she mimicked as she towel-dried her legs. "'I've enjoyed these days with you. Please don't doubt that.'"

With any other man, she would have instantly taken those words as a brush-off. Would've instantly felt taken advantage of, even though she'd walked into their love-making knowing how it could, probably would, end.

But with Liam?

She didn't believe he'd just coldly brush her off, as if she wasn't anything more than a one-night stand. No, what she believed was that he was confused and didn't know how to handle the situation. That he had done the best he could. But that she meant something to him, something important, and that maybe he just hadn't reconciled himself with that yet.

The possibility also existed that she had finally reached the delusional stage and her brain refused to accept the truth. Or her heart. Or both.

She'd give him time. She'd wait it out for a little while before deciding on the delusional, blind and naive love-sick choice.

Dressing in a pair of jeans and a long, butter-yellow sweater, Meredith brushed her damp hair and rolled it into a clip on top of her head. The scent of coffee and cinnamon wafted through the closed door as she finished her morning routine. Rachel and Cole must be awake.

She found them both in the kitchen, sitting at the table over their coffee, chatting easily.

They were quite the attractive pair. Rachel with her long, straight blond hair and wide blue eyes and Cole with his black hair and dark brown eyes. And whenever they looked at each other, you'd have to be in a coma not to see the love they had each for other.

Beautiful. Something to aim for someday.

"Morning," she said with a smile. "That coffee smells amazing."

"Thank Cole," Rachel said. "I was out early this morning. But those cinnamon rolls you smell? All me, I'll have you know. And they're just about warmed up, so hope you're hungry."

"Morning to you, Meredith." Cole stood and poured her a cup of coffee, which he brought back to the table. "Don't believe a word my wife says. Those rolls came from a coffeehouse called the Beanery and were baked by the owner, our friend, Lola. You'll love them. I guarantee you've never tasted any as good."

"Hrmph. I said they were almost done warming, not that I baked them with my own two hands, and I bought them, didn't I?" Rachel wrinkled her nose in Cole's direction. "But he is right. They're delicious and I thought they'd be the perfect start to our day."

"You guys are already like an old married couple. It's cute." And even this friendly, warmhearted bickering brought about a yearning. Geez. She was a mess. "And I am hungry, so can't wait to try Lola's famous cinnamon rolls."

She did a few minutes later, over light conversation about the weather—which was, thankfully, back to normal for this time of year—and an upcoming baby shower for their sister-in-law, Chelsea, who was married to Cole's brother, Dylan. Mostly, Meredith just listened, enjoying the camaraderie between husband and wife. How effortless they were together, from their speech to their body language to those intimate smiles they so often exchanged.

Yes, Rachel had found her nirvana. And from their conversations the past few days, Meredith knew it hadn't come easily. She and Cole had to work for this, and okay, some of their choices fell into the questionable range, but they had done the best they could and their path brought them to this table, in this house, sharing coffee and cinnamon rolls and intimate smiles.

Could make a person believe that anything was possible.

"Okay, ladies, I'm due at work," Cole said, standing. In addition to the restaurant, his family also owned a sporting goods store, which he managed. He smiled at Meredith before kissing his wife. Then, "I should be home around seven, I think. I'll bring dinner."

Rachel's eyes followed him until he vanished down the hallway. When the sound of the front door closing reached their ears, she jumped from the table and grabbed a notebook and pen from the counter. Back in her seat, she flipped open to the first page and pushed it with the pen across the surface of the table to Meredith, saying, "Here. Let's see what we can figure out."

Picking up the pen, Meredith twisted it between her fingers. "Yes. It's time. The practical should come first. What type of job I want and then the job itself. A place to live."

"Well, maybe we should begin with location? Seems that should come first, right?" Tapping her pink-painted nails against the table, Rachel said, "Do you want a completely fresh start, or are you thinking of staying in San Francisco since you still have your apartment?"

"The lease expires in two months." Good question. "So that isn't a huge issue. I have enough in savings to deal with that and probably a couple of months of expenses." She should give that money back to her father, really. She only had it due to his interference and help with her salary, but...that suddenly seemed of such little consequence.

Her goal was a whole new life. If she needed some help from her old life to make that happen, why not take it? And without her savings, she had...zero money. So, okay.

"Want to stay on the West Coast? Or try something different?"

"I am going to stay here, in Steamboat Springs." Meredith said the words before she'd even thought them through, but once she had, she knew that was the only choice she could make.

Oh, she still didn't plan on waiting for Liam for years, like she had with Rico. But...she couldn't be far away from him just yet, either. Yes. This was the right decision. Besides which, "You live here, Rach. I'd rather start over with my best friend close by than in a strange city all by myself."

She didn't talk about Liam. Wasn't ready to share her feelings on him just yet.

"Yes! I was hoping you'd come to that conclusion. I've missed you!" Rachel's smile stretched from ear to ear. "And you know, you can stay here as long as you need. Don't feel as if you have to move out anytime soon. I like having you around."

"Aw, thank you. I like being around you, too, and I certainly won't be moving out in the next week. Depends on how long it takes me to find a job."

On the notebook, Meredith wrote the number *1*, which she circled, and next to it: *Live in Steamboat Springs*. Such a simple yet complex decision. Making it felt positive. Like the exactly right first step.

On a slippery, treacherous slope, perhaps. One that could cause her more harm than slamming into a tree and almost freezing to death. But oh, the possibilities—

the reality of her dream—were endless. Beautiful. *Her* nirvana. *Her* happy ending. With Liam.

"Actually, I have an idea on the job front," Rachel was saying as she refilled her coffee cup. "Didn't want to bring it up until I knew what you were thinking about location."

"Yeah? What sort of a job?"

"The same sort you were doing in San Francisco. This is a vacation town, you know. Plenty of homes need staging. With your experience, you shouldn't have too much trouble getting a door to open. Relatively quickly, I'd imagine, and without your dad's help."

Well. If that were the case, she had to believe that her heart, that fate, had led her in the exact right direction. Now, she just had to keep walking. Keep following this path she was on and see what existed beyond the next bend in the road.

Chapter 10

One week. Two weeks. Three weeks. Time just kept on ticking away, and it didn't friggin' matter if Liam was at home, working, outside, inside or asleep, that damn ache in his chest hadn't let loose for a millisecond since dropping Goldi off at her friend's place. That never-ending ache gave him pause, made him rethink what he shouldn't.

Hell. He'd even started listening to ABBA. "Mamma Mia," in particular.

And today he'd had enough. He *had* to see her, or try to, even if the doing was about the stupidest action he could take. First, though, he had to get through this meal with Fiona and Cassie.

His sister had phoned that morning, told him that enough was enough and to get his butt over there, or she'd barge into his sanctuary and wouldn't leave for a week.

She meant it, too. She'd done it before.

So here he was, with Fiona and Cassie, eating pot roast and vegetables on Sunday afternoon, trying to behave like a normal man instead of one hovering on the brink of insanity. He'd probably fooled his niece, but with the questioning looks his sister was directing his way? Nah, he hadn't fooled Fiona. She might not know what the problem was, but she'd honed in that there *was* a problem. Unlikely he'd get out of here without giving her a few answers.

"Will you be able to come see me in the Christmas play?" Cassie, who was cuter than any kid had the right to be, asked over a mouthful of mashed potatoes. "Please?"

It never failed to amaze Liam how much she looked like Fiona, with her light, strawberry-blond hair and vivid green eyes. Folks who didn't know better automatically assumed the two were mother and daughter and were astounded when they learned the truth, that Cassie was Fiona's foster daughter. Fiona was trying to change that, trying to untangle all the red tape to adopt Cassie, who had been in her care for the past three years.

Unfortunately, there was a lot of red tape.

"Wait a minute? It's barely November," Liam said. "There's already a Christmas play in the works? And of course, I will attend. Wouldn't miss it for the world, kiddo."

"She's a little ahead of herself," Fiona said, smiling at her daughter. "But there's always a Christmas play, and she's hoping to be one of the angels this year."

"Can't think of anyone better." Plate now empty, Liam pushed it back some and finished his milk. Always milk at Fiona's table if Cassie was present. It amused him, having such a rule. "You'll be a beautiful angel, so they'd be crazy not to make you one."

Joy lit up the girl's eyes. "I can't wait! Christmas is my favorite holiday."

"Better than Halloween? What about your birthday?" he teased. "Say it isn't so!"

"Christmas has carols and presents and cookies and a tree with sparkling lights and Santa Claus and Frosty the Snowman and…and…lots of other wonderful stuff," Cassie said in a matter-of-fact, what-are-you-crazy sort of way. "'Course it's better. Cookies, Uncle Liam!"

A rumble of a laugh burst from his lungs. He loved his family. Thank the good Lord that Fiona was on top of keeping them together; otherwise he and his loner self would miss these moments. "Can't argue with that. Cookies are right up there on the top of any list."

The dogs, who had been plopped on the floor in between his chair and Cassie's, recognized the word *cookies* and leaped to their feet, instantly on the lookout. For the past three weeks, they'd spent more time pacing the living room and sniffing the sofa that had been Goldi's bed than doing anything else. They were morose. Seemingly lost without her.

Here, in a place she had never been, they were doing better. Made him think he should leave them here for a while to give them some relief. But he'd miss them, and then he'd be completely alone in missing Goldi. The thought didn't sit well at all, so he nixed it.

Misery loved company and all of that.

The rest of dinner was a mix of quiet and Cassie chatter as they ate, with his niece talking about school, her new music teacher—who was, apparently, *amazing* and *funny* and *beautiful*—and, naturally, a good deal more about Christmas and the play and being an angel.

At the end of the meal, Fiona asked Cassie, "Did you finish your homework from Friday yet? If not, please do that before any television or phone calls or anything else. Deal?"

"Deal! And it's almost all done. Just have to practice my spelling words."

"Why don't you do that and I'll quiz you later?" Clearing the dishes, Fiona directed a look at Liam. "You can help me before you scurry back to your hidey-hole."

"Sure," he said. "I'm happy to be interrogated...help. I meant, I'm happy to help."

"What's *interrogated* mean?" Cassie was already halfway out of the dining room.

"To be relentlessly questioned," Liam answered as he, too, began clearing the dishes. "But I am just teasing. Go do your schoolwork. I'll say goodbye before I leave."

Hearing Cassie climb the stairs to her bedroom, Fiona turned her green-eyed, all-seeing gaze on Liam. "So, what is going on? And don't tell me nothing, because I'm smarter than that and have known you my entire life. You can't hide from me."

"You know," Liam said lightly, "one would almost think you're the older sibling, rather than the younger. Bossing me around like that! Why, I swear I remember this sweet, quiet little girl who used to trail after me and listen to every word I said as if it were gospel."

"Oh, I remember those days, too. And then we grew up." She went to the kitchen, where she started rinsing the dishes. "Are you okay? Tell me that much, at least."

"Honestly, Fi? I don't know." And then, for the second time in less than a month, he opened up to another person. Sure, this was his sister and not the woman who'd managed to carve herself into his heart, but still. He talked, she listened and he finished with, "So, yeah. This woman shows up at my house out of nowhere and... I don't know. I might miss her."

"You love her," Fiona said without missing a beat or mincing words. "Only other time I've seen you like this, heard you like this, was when you met Christy. And yes, you miss this woman. Doesn't really matter how long you've known a person if love is involved. And when you love someone and haven't seen them in close to a month, you tend to miss them."

"Love? I did not say—"

Fiona patted his arm. "That's because you haven't admitted it to yourself yet, and that's just fine. You don't have to admit anything until you're ready to. But I can see the truth on your face, hear it in your voice, when you talk about her. You," she said with a grin, "just have to admit when I'm right and you're wrong. Don't worry, you'll get there."

He arched a brow. "Sarcasm, too?"

"Some. But I don't think I'm wrong this time, either. Do you?"

"I don't know. That's my point." Running his hand over his eyes, he frowned. "Love. I haven't known this woman long enough to be in love. Have I?"

"Huh. How long did you know Christy before you—"

"Shh, you." Days. Mere days after meeting Christy and he knew. Then, he hadn't doubted that instinct, the surety or the strength of what he felt. "Doesn't matter. Meredith isn't Christy, and I'm a different man today than I was then. I don't really know her, Fi."

"Gee, let me think how you could fix that. Hmm.

Oh, I know! Perhaps, rather than standing around in my kitchen, you should be with her? Talking to her instead of me? Getting to know her?" His sister gave him a sugary sweet smile brimming with innocence.

He wasn't fooled. Oh, she was concerned, and she certainly could be one of the sweetest women on the planet, but she was also enjoying his torment. That sibling thing. More than that, though. She hated him being alone so often. Worried about him far too much. "What do you think?" she teased.

"I sort of reached that decision on my way here, actually."

"Guess you needed some reinforcement?"

"Guess so."

"Well, you have it." She gave him a tight hug. "Go on now, say goodbye to your niece and follow your heart. Try not to let your shields get in the way."

Yeah. That was always the problem, wasn't it? His damn shields.

He nodded, started to walk away when a thought occurred. What had Meredith asked him for their last day together, when they were going to build a snowman? Oh, right. Turning on his heel, he said, "You wouldn't happen to have any carrots, buttons and…ah, coal?"

"I have those," Fiona said after a moment's pause. "But I don't have a corncob pipe."

"Why would I need a corncob pipe?" Then, shaking his head, he said, "Doesn't matter. Don't need a pipe. Just the other stuff. And maybe an extra scarf if you have one."

She had that, too.

The doorbell rang just as Meredith disconnected the call to her former employer. She'd asked for a reference letter, as she had an interview later that week with one of the city's larger real estate firms. The position was only partially described as a stager, and she didn't yet know what the rest of the responsibilities were, but she felt confident that she'd be offered the job.

She just wished she'd thought of requesting the reference letter sooner. Easy to understand why it had slipped her mind, with it being so occupied by a missing mountain man.

The Get a New Life to-do list seemed a mile long, but retaining a job with dependable income had to come before locating an apartment or returning to San Francisco to pack her belongings. If she couldn't find a job, she couldn't stay. No matter how much she wanted to.

A knock on her bedroom door, followed by someone cracking it open, diverted her attention. It was Rachel. "Meredith?" she said. "Liam is here at the door, asking for you. He has those dogs with him, too! And oh, my, they are gorgeous animals."

Lightning fast, all thoughts of a job and a place to live evaporated, and Meredith's heart went into overdrive. "Yes. Yes, they are beautiful animals." Oh, Lord, was this it? Had he realized…did he miss her…did he want what she did? Pressing her hands down her jeans, she said, "How do I look? Should I change or…?"

"Um. You look gorgeous, just like always." Blue eyes narrowed and then widened in understanding. "Oh! It's that way, is it? You should've told me!"

"I was going to. Eventually. I…well, there might not be anything to tell." Shivers of apprehension whisked along Meredith's skin, bringing about a multitude of goose bumps. "But he's here. And he didn't call or text or…he's here. With the dogs. So, that seems good, doesn't it?"

"I don't know the story," Rachel said, laughing, "so I can't really comment. But when a handsome man shows up unexpectedly, well… I'd say the possibility of good is right up there."

Rachel was right. Liam's presence here had to mean something good, otherwise, why bother with any type of a visit? She hadn't left any of her belongings—mostly because she hadn't had hardly anything with her—at his place. They'd had that amazing conversation on the drive over and they'd said their goodbyes. There wasn't any reason for him to be here.

So, something good.

The thought—that freaking hope—settled her brewing emotions enough that she was able to force her legs to move. She left the bedroom and walked the short distance to the living room, to the front door, opened it and…there they were.

Her guardian angels and the man she hadn't been able to stop thinking about, on Rachel's front porch, looking to Meredith like a dream—her dream—come to life. A flurry of anticipation and hope swam in her stomach.

Both of which she immediately tempered and reminded herself to keep her head out of the clouds. This man might want nothing more than to check in, make sure she was okay.

"Well, hi there," she said, managing to keep her voice level and smooth, as she joined them on the porch. The second she did, the dogs were butting their bodies against her legs, pushing their heads against her hands. Dropping to one knee, she accepted their kisses and scratched behind their ears. "I missed you guys, too!"

Another few minutes of this went on while Liam, who looked as if he hadn't slept in days but somehow retained that rugged sexiness he so effortlessly carried around with him, stood by and watched with a stern expression. Almost as if he were…not angry, exactly, but upset in some form or fashion. So, maybe this wasn't good after all?

Only one way to find out and stop her brain's incessant spinning.

Standing, she leaned against one of the porch's rails for stability, firmed her shoulders and settled her gaze on Liam's. There it was, that sizzle of electricity, that punch of recognition that she'd felt from the very instant she'd first looked into his eyes.

Unfair, really. Glorious, though.

"Hey, Goldi," he said, his voice sounding almost as tired as he looked.

"Hey, back." They stood there quietly, their gazes locked for a few seconds that could've just as easily been a year. "What brings you this way?" she asked, trying to sound natural and not as if her knees were less than ten seconds from buckling. "Everything okay?"

"Yup. Everything is fine." Shoving his hands into the pockets of his coat, he leaned against the porch rail near the steps. "Had lunch with my sister and niece. They live fairly close by. Just figured I'd stop by and see how you were doing. Plus, I…ah…the dogs missed you."

"I missed…them." She was going to leave it at that, but to hell with it. "I missed you, too. And you look tired. Been working a lot?"

"Well, you know, there's all that wizarding that requires my attention."

"Yeah? Saving the world or causing chaos?"

The corners of his lips curled into a grin, wiping away that stern expression. Good. She adored seeing his smile. "Maybe a little of both. And yes, Goldi, I missed you, too."

"Did you now?"

"I just said that, didn't I?"

She laughed. She couldn't help it. "Don't be a grump. I'm glad to see you."

"Feel like seeing me for the rest of the afternoon?"

Happiness bounced through her like a kid's rubber ball, and it took all of her willpower not to jump up and down and clap her hands. "Depends," she said, modulating her voice to hide her extreme joy. "What do you have in mind? I mean, a girl's gotta be a little choosy in how she devotes an entire afternoon. You only get so many of them, you know."

Green eyes narrowed, and those lips of his? They widened into a bona fide smile. "Well now, I have something in mind, but I'd prefer it be a surprise. What do you think, Goldi? Can you put yourself in my care for a few hours without knowing the details?"

"Sure. I think I can trust you for a few hours at least." Or the rest of her life.

"Excellent." He looked her over from head to toe. "We'll be outside, so you need a coat and gloves. Actual gloves, Goldi, and not just a pair of socks slipped over your hands."

Tipping her chin, she shrugged. "Those socks worked well enough, didn't they?"

"That they did." Another long, searching look that sent her head spinning even more. She'd be lucky to get through the next several hours standing if he kept looking at her that way. Though, maybe that wouldn't be so bad. Considering what happened the last time she couldn't stay on her feet. And then, as if he knew exactly what she was thinking, he did that headshake thing and said, "You're dangerous. Entirely too much so."

"I think you're the dangerous one. Or maybe neither of us is dangerous," she said, once again deciding to just freaking speak her mind. "Maybe there's something else going on here."

He didn't speak; she didn't, either. Max went to Liam and braced his body against him, as if offering support. And Maggie did the same with Meredith. These dogs. Too smart for their own good.

The air between Liam and Meredith thickened somehow, as if all the unsaid words weighed it down.

Finally, Liam pushed himself off the rail, saying, "Get your coat and such, Goldi. We'll…ah…be waiting in the truck."

She might have nodded, but she couldn't swear to that fact. But she also didn't move from her position until Liam and the dogs had reached his truck, her eyes glued to him, his long-legged walk, the confident manner in which he carried himself.

She loved him. Without doubt, now that she'd seen him again, heard that voice again, looked into those eyes again. And she did not care how illogical or improbable or even impossible the realization. She *knew*. Love existed.

How far that love would take her, how much it would grow and deepen, remained unknown. But it was there for this man, and she saw no reason to deny that truth.

"Why are you still standing there?" Liam hollered, waking her from her trance. "I have plans for you, woman. Don't make me wait all day."

"Don't you call me woman!" she hollered back. "I have a name, you know."

"*Meredith*," he said, "will you please get moving, so we can commence with the afternoon I have planned? I would be ever so grateful."

She laughed. Loudly. And turned on her heel to get her coat and gloves. He had plans. For her. And didn't that sound so very pleasant? Not to mention…intriguing and hopeful and just breathtaking with all the possibilities? Lord. There were *so many* possibilities.

So many possible paths. Some included Liam, some didn't. And she did not know what he had in mind for the day, or if this was the start of a new path, one that would extend beyond a couple of hours on a Sunday afternoon.

But he was here. He wanted to see *her*. Had admitted to missing her! Right now, those three facts were glorious enough. Miraculous enough.

And the rest? Whatever loomed, she'd take it and run. One second, one minute, one afternoon at a time. Because that was life. *This* was life. She refused to waste any of it.

For the first time in a full friggin' month, Liam's heart didn't ache with emptiness. His head wasn't overflowing with annoying, complex questions he did not want to answer. Wasn't ready to answer. And damn it, the way this woman made him smile.

His cheeks hurt from the strain. Which was both annoying and wonderful. Astounding and irritating. Why did anyone need to smile so much their cheeks hurt?

He did not know, but all in all, he felt better than he had since that afternoon he'd dropped off Meredith. With her, he was…what? Restored? Ridiculous thought, but one he could no longer discount or ignore. Hell, even his bones felt sturdier.

Which seemed to state that Fiona's take on the matter might hold water.

He might be falling in love with Meredith—because he wasn't ready to fully admit he was already there—and if so, he was just going to have to decide what to do about it. Embrace and accept and move forward or tuck his tail between his legs and run away. Pretend and hide.

Sighing, he set the mess aside and decided to just sink himself into the day, into this time with Meredith and let the rest sort itself out as needed. Right now, he was restored. He'd admitted it. More than enough reality for a man like him to absorb at once.

He took her to a local park, showed her the bag of snowman accoutrements he'd gotten from Fiona and told her they were finally going to build that snowman, but that she would have to instruct him on the proper method. Since, yup, he did not have that experience.

Damn it, the smile that wreathed her face made his smile even larger. Made his cheeks hurt even more. The whole world brought into focus by a woman's smile. And he found he…liked that feeling. That realization. Almost as much as—

"No! Liam, you're making his head too big," Meredith said, interrupting his thoughts. Delusions? Maybe that, too. "Now you have to start over."

Cheeks pink from the cold, lips, too, and her hair a disarray of golden curls that all but glittered in the late afternoon sun. Beautiful. Spunky. A pain in the ass.

"I'll have you know that this ball is the perfect size for our snowman's head," he said, wanting to rile her up a bit more. For no other reason than it was fun. "Besides which, what's wrong with having a big head? You've seemed to get along just fine and—"

An icy cold splash of snow hit his face. "I'll have you know that my head is perfectly proportioned to the rest of my body," she said, as she lobbed another snowball his way. This time, he saw it coming and got out of the way. "Now, your head? That's a different story."

Another smile. Another laugh. Another half dozen snowballs before they got back to the question of the correct size for a snowman's head. He gave in. Because doing so made her laugh, tease and smile all that much harder. Good stuff, in Liam's opinion.

"There, look at that," Meredith said, moving to stand beside him when the snowman was featureless but built. She handed him the bag from Fiona's. "Go on. Give him his personality. His eyes and nose and mouth. Bring him to life, Liam. And then…give him a name. Because every snowman needs a name."

Bring him to life? Like she had done with him?

Asinine thought, so he put it out of his normal-sized head as fast as it had arrived. That thought was for later, when she wasn't in his immediate area messing with his logic.

"Sure. I can do that. Let's see, where to start." He fished through the bag and laid the carrot, buttons and chunks of coal on the snow in front of his creation. And he decided to rile her up a bit more.

Because…why not?

So, while she played with Max and Maggie—tossing them snowballs to leap after—he used the buttons for the eyes and nose, the coal in a nice, even row down the body and then he took that carrot and pressed it flat into the snowman's head for his mouth, instead of sticking out straight for the nose.

She hadn't noticed yet, as she was too busy with the

dogs, so he finished by wrapping the scarf around the arms—two tree branches they'd found—instead of circling what would be the snowman's neck.

"There. All done. I now have the experience of building a snowman," he said to Meredith. "And I name him Oliver. Because…well, he looks like an Oliver, don't you think?"

She stopped playing with the dogs to give Oliver the proper amount of attention, and yup, she laughed. Walked to the snowman and gave him another long look. "I have never seen a carrot smile before," she said. "But you know what? He's perfect. Because you made him."

Well, his plan to rile her up had failed. He didn't mind. Not with that smile.

"I like him, too," Liam said. "Thank you. I can now say my life is complete."

Large blue eyes blinked once. Twice. Three times. "Well, every person should build a snowman at least once in their life. So, you're welcome. Thank you for bringing me here, for letting me do this with you. I… I don't know, Liam. You have a way about you."

"So do you," he said, wanting nothing more than to grab her in his arms and kiss her. Long and hard. Soft, too. The want to taste her again wove in next, to claim her as his, to give himself to her and just let the dice fall wherever they landed. *Not yet.* Maybe not ever.

But he might be able to…

Before he could swallow the need that suddenly came over him, wiping out even the desperate want to kiss her, he held out his hand. "Come with me," he said. "I want to talk for a while. I want to share something with you, and I'll warn you. It isn't an easy story."

Curiosity along with a good dose of surprise flashed

over her expression, but she nodded. Held out her glove-covered hand to his, and he clasped it tightly. "Whatever you want to talk about, I'm happy to listen. Anything, Liam."

"Oh, I know how you like to talk," he teased. The moment didn't lighten as he'd hoped, but that was okay. It wasn't going to be a light conversation.

He led her to a park bench, where they sat side by side. And then, before he could change his mind or allow the million reasons—*valid* reasons, damn it—why he shouldn't let this woman in any more than he already had, he just pushed out the first sentence. "I am a widower, Meredith. Going on ten years now."

"Oh." Her grip tightened on his, and a bolt of courage, strength, existed there. Comfort. Desire. Acceptance. So much he felt from this woman. So much he felt *for* her. Too much, really. Too fast and too furious. "What was her name?"

"Christy." And then bit by bit, word by word, the story fell from his lips. As if it had just been sitting there, waiting for all this time for Meredith to hear.

He spoke of how they met—via a mutual friend—their courtship, their spur-of-the-moment decision to get married and how they didn't tell anyone until after the fact. Her pregnancy. His assignment. And the horrible tragedy that stole his wife and child while he was photographing birds in the Amazon Basin.

As he spoke the words he never really had before, she listened in silence. She never let go of his hand. She didn't interrupt with questions or her sorrow. She just let him talk.

And oh, he talked for a while. Longer than he'd expected to when he began. Longer than he thought he had it in him to talk about anything, let alone the greatest pain of his life. It was hard, but it wasn't. It was sad, but it was also…freeing in a way he hadn't imagined.

"Remember that picture of the birds? In my office?" he asked when he was done with the rest. "I took that the day before they died, and I remember… I remember thinking that those birds were like Christy and I with our baby on the way. That they represented our life. Happy and bright and colorful, full of song and…hope. So much hope. And I couldn't wait to get back to her, to be there with her, to start our journey as a family."

He heard a deep intake of breath, and her hand tightened another degree. She got it. He didn't have to say anything more. She understood.

But in a way that he couldn't understand, he also felt as if the burden of this pain, this loss, was now halved. As if Meredith had taken on some of the burden for him and was now helping him carry it.

Ludicrous thought, but it fit. It…yeah, it fit.

A hard, almost desperate shudder rolled through his body from head to toe, and she just kept holding on to his hand. Following the shudder, after years of existing without oxygen, of feeling as if the wind had been permanently knocked out of him, he took the first real and true breath he'd inhaled since the moment he'd learned of Christy and his unborn child's fate.

He breathed in as long and deeply as he could. Even then, Meredith didn't talk. But she leaned over to put her head on his shoulder.

The soft brush of her hair smelled like honey and almonds and…home. Lord help him, everything about her resonated as *home*. He supposed he'd have to layer in that realization with the rest, see where it brought him. Form some decisions.

But not now. Perhaps not for a while. He just didn't know. Time was called for.

They sat there for a while longer. The dogs, spent from their boisterous play, were resting on the ground in front of them. Again, there was serenity and peace and a sense of…rejuvenation? Maybe that.

"You're something special, Meredith," Liam finally said. "My dogs knew that about you instantly, and I wasn't too far behind. I…thank you for listening. For sitting with me in that memory and for allowing me to… well, just talk it out, I guess. I'm not used to doing that."

"I know you're not, and Liam? You're welcome." She kissed him softly and quickly on his cheek. "I'm always here for you. That is something you should know."

And that was it. All that needed to be said. For now anyway.

Chapter 11

The interview went well. So well, that Meredith expected to hear good news within the next day or so. Once she did, assuming she did, she could go about checking off the rest of the items on her to-do list. An apartment here in Steamboat Springs. Returning to San Francisco to pack up her belongings and officially move her life here. And she couldn't wait.

Today, though, she had more important matters on her mind. Her period was late. By one full week and that had never happened before.

Never.

So, while she tried to convince herself that she was likely worrying for nothing, that stress and the accident and everything else that had occurred could be more than enough to mess with her body...she *knew*.

And she was petrified.

The second she left the interview, in her second

rented car that matched her first, she drove to a local convenience store and bought two pregnancy tests. Two. So she could verify the results of the first, because yeah, she'd have to for her peace of mind.

And then she'd returned to Rachel's, relieved to find the house empty, and tore open both boxes. Read the instructions. Locked herself in the bathroom and...peed on the first stick.

She waited with her forehead pressed to her knees, forcing air in and out of her lungs. Trying to ignore the panic brewing in her blood. She couldn't be pregnant. She had zero symptoms: no morning sickness and her breasts weren't sore or swollen. Her body felt completely normal, just as it always had. She *couldn't* be pregnant.

She wasn't ready.

Not when everything in her life was finally starting to come together and feel right. Not when everything with Liam was starting to come together and feel real and possible more than blindly and illogically hopeful. Just not now. This wasn't the time. For her, for him, for them.

And oh, God, not after learning about his heartbreaking, tremendous loss.

A wife he'd loved. A baby on the way. Both gone in the blink of an eye, and a man who had already suffered great loss in his lifetime—his parents' deaths and all that missing time with his sister—had to prevail over another loss. It wasn't fair. It made her problems even less important, almost ridiculous, because she'd never had to sustain anything like Liam had.

Enough time had passed to look at the stick. To see if a plus sign or a negative sign had appeared.

But she didn't want to. In this second, she could remain clueless and hang on to her hope that she wasn't—

couldn't be—carrying Liam's baby. Her baby. Their baby. Because it wasn't time for either of them. What would she do? What would he do?

Think this through.

Right. Follow the possible paths. Determine the likeliest scenarios. Put some weight behind the what-if to bolster her courage and remind her that she could handle whatever came her way.

She'd survived getting lost in the mountains during a freak snowstorm, hadn't she? Yes. Okay, so that was nothing compared to the possibility of being pregnant, becoming a mother and raising a child. Even so, it showed she was tenacious. Strong. Capable.

So, she didn't lift her head from her knees. She forced the brewing panic to calm. If a plus sign existed when she looked, then what?

Well, the first thing would be to process the information. Second would be, naturally, telling Liam, because he deserved to know as soon as possible. A difficult, emotional conversation would likely follow. But how would he react? Shock would come first, no doubt. Anger? No. Liam wouldn't be angry, he'd be... scared? Probably even more frightened than she was at this moment, but he wouldn't admit that to himself, let alone to her.

Shocked. Scared. What else? Protective? Based on everything she knew about him, how he'd been with her, then yes...protective. Accountable, too. He wouldn't run from the financial responsibility or the hands-on day in and day out of being a father. She *knew* this. He might attempt to corral the situation into a neat little box so that he felt it was under control. Doable.

What would that mean? A shotgun wedding? Meredith sighed. Yeah, he very well could suggest they marry for the best interests of the baby. And as much as she yearned for…well, everything with this man, she wouldn't settle into a marriage of obligation. That was *not* the life she wanted.

For herself or for Liam.

Of course, if they were to arrive at that beautiful place from her dream where they truly loved each other, couldn't imagine a life without the other…that was an entirely different story. But they weren't there yet. Whether or not she was pregnant.

Breathing deeply, Meredith considered the least likely alternative: that she was wrong and that Liam would run from her, the baby and the responsibility.

No. That was not the man she knew, but…she had to follow through with the thought. For her sake. If the impossible were to happen, what would she do?

Well. Pretty much what she was already doing: creating a life of her own making. The same necessities existed: a job she enjoyed that paid what she needed. A safe home. Friends. Family. Laughter and love and more happiness than sadness.

Yes. The very same framework for a life she had already started to create. That life would simply include one extra person; her son or daughter.

Meredith's panic didn't fully disappear, but the smog in her head cleared. Her heart didn't beat quite so hard, and the nausea swirling in her stomach eased.

If she were indeed pregnant, she'd handle whatever came next. With Liam by her side, in the multiple ways that could occur, or without Liam anywhere to be seen. *She* could do this. On her own, if necessary.

Another deep inhale of oxygen and Meredith lifted

her head from her knees, closed her eyes and reached for the pregnancy test she'd left on the edge of the bathtub. Gripping her hand tightly around the test, she counted to three and opened her eyes.

A bold pink positive sign. She was having Liam's baby.

Whistling to the dogs, Liam tossed the last of his bags into the back of the truck. He'd been offered a last-minute, ten-day assignment in the Australian Outback due to another photographer cancelling because of a family emergency. Liam had almost declined but decided it would do him good on a lot of different levels to get away. So, he accepted.

He needed to think. He needed to separate his emotions from the almighty logic and find a balance. And he needed to do that somewhere else. Somewhere far enough away from Goldi that he couldn't be tempted to jump in up to his eyeballs before he was ready.

And he was *not* ready.

That being said, he couldn't leave the country without seeing her and letting her know where he'd be, how long he'd be gone. That felt necessary. And he wanted to do so in person, not via a text message or a phone call. Which meant he had to get moving as he was flying out of Denver early that evening. He had to drop off Max and Maggie at Fiona's, stop by Rachel's to talk with Meredith and then make the three-ish hour drive to Denver.

At the sound of Liam's whistle, the dogs emerged from the trees, bounding toward him at full speed in all their canine grace.

Ever since the snowman day, when Liam had split open his soul and began to breathe again, Max and Mag-

gie had been more themselves. They hadn't stopped staring and whining at the sofa each night, though, as if
hoping Goldi would appear in a flash of smoke.

There were too many nights he'd wished the same.

Just as the dogs swarmed around his feet, the sound
of a car driving into his long, twisty driveway pulled his
attention. Only took a second to see it was the woman
herself, Meredith.

Pride hit him first, that she'd found her way here without trouble. Happiness came next, because she was here
on her own accord. Curiosity as to *why* filtered into the
mix, followed quickly by the resurgence of his shields.

Oh, they weren't nearly as strong. But they were
there. Still. And he couldn't decide if that was good or
bad. Worthwhile or…useless. Protective or restrictive.

As she stepped from the car—another rental, he assumed—he was struck by her beauty all over again. She
had her long, curly hair swept back in a clip of some
sort, but the sides hung loose around her shoulders like
a shimmering cloud. A small, tentative smile curved
her mouth and she raised one hand in an equally hesi-
tant wave.

Something was wrong.

Apprehension tightened his gut, rippled through his
muscles. She walked toward him and he noticed the
slight tremble in her chin and the way she worried her
bottom lip with her teeth. Her skin, normally pale, appeared about as fragile as a sheet of tissue paper.

Yup, something was wrong. And that realization, the
many possibilities of what *could be wrong*, ignited that
natural need he had to protect this woman. Right alongside that need, however, existed fear.

Crippling, debilitating fear.

He didn't want to admit the fear. Didn't want to face it, either. So, he did the next best thing and set it aside, like a cup of forgotten coffee that had grown cold. It would be there later, to look at, analyze, consider. Decide how to better manage it or expunge it once and for all.

"Liam," Meredith said when she reached him. Max and Maggie, upon seeing her, had jumped back out of the car and were begging her for attention. Her smile widened at their boisterous, adoring affection. She petted their heads, scratched behind their ears, murmured her hellos. Then, lifting her eyes to Liam's, she let out a breath. "I…hope this isn't a bad time?"

"Never a bad time for you." Whoa. Where had those words, that sentiment, come from? They were true, he realized, despite his fear. He'd always welcome Meredith. *Always.* "I was actually going to stop by and see you, after I dropped off the dogs at Fiona's."

"You were? Drop off the dogs?"

"I was. I'm…heading out on assignment. Australia. I'll be back in a couple of weeks." He resisted the temptation to pull her into his arms and promise her that everything would be okay. He didn't know that anything was wrong, for one thing. For another, he didn't know if that was a promise he could keep. "So, I'm glad you caught me. We could've missed each other."

"Oh. I didn't know…but of course I wouldn't. Why would I?" Rubbing her hands together, she darted her gaze away from his. "Maybe this isn't the best time, then. We can always talk when you get back, and…yeah, that's probably what we should do."

She turned, ready to leave, and while he couldn't define how he knew, he was certain that letting her walk away would prove to be a horrible mistake. "Stop, Meredith." She faced him again. "You came here for a reason, and I have time for you, time for a conversation."

"You're sure?"

Yes. Something was wrong. "Wouldn't have said so if I wasn't."

"Well. I don't know. This conversation shouldn't be rushed. It's important. And…"

Her voice trailed away into nothingness. What was going on here? What thoughts, concerns, fears were swirling in *her* brain? He wished for the ability to take everything negative away from this woman and fill her with nothing but the positive. Let the sunshine wipe out the gloom. "We won't be rushed. I can always change my flight, if necessary. Let's go inside."

For about fifteen seconds, she didn't respond, just stood there with her back straight, looking over his shoulder into the distance. She nodded, pushed her hands into her coat pockets and said, "Yes. You're right. This… is important and it shouldn't wait."

They walked toward the house and Liam's brain went into overdrive. What could be wrong? What might they have to talk about? Was she leaving, going back home to San Francisco? He didn't like the idea of that at all. He wasn't ready to move forward, but he wasn't ready to say goodbye, either. Which meant…he couldn't do anything.

Even if she told him she'd decided to leave.

Less than an hour ago, he'd prepared the house for a two-week absence, and when he'd locked the front door, he certainly didn't know he'd be returning within fifteen minutes. And he couldn't have known that Meredith would be with him, following him inside. Whatever she needed to say, whatever the reason behind this visit, he had the sense that nothing would ever be the same again. That whatever she was about to tell him would change him. Forever.

For the good? For the bad? Yet another question he couldn't answer.

Once inside, Liam nodded toward the sofa, which would now and always be hers. If she was leaving… if he didn't have the necessary time to figure out what he wanted, how to move forward, if he *wanted* to move forward, he would have to replace this couch.

Or not. Hell.

She sat. He did, too, right next to her. Possibly a bad idea, but he had to be near her in case whatever she told him required his comfort. He needed to be close in order to hold her hand or put his arm around her or…well, offer his support. That was true, would always be true, regardless of the fear that seemed prepped and ready to consume him, from the inside out.

"Talk to me, Goldi," he said. "What brought you here today?"

Long lashes dipped in a blink, then another. She cleared her throat and fidgeted in place while a tremble visibly rolled through her slight frame. "I've tried to think of the best way to tell you this. All the way here, I rehearsed how to say what I need to say, but… I don't know if there is a right way. I don't know which words are best or which order to put them in. And… and I almost turned around at least a half dozen times. Because—"

She stopped speaking, shook her head and inhaled another deep, fortifying breath. Blue eyes glistened with the threat of tears, and Lord, all he wanted was to see her smile. Hear her laugh. Let her know that no matter what battles she faced, he'd stand next to her, sword

raised, ready to protect and defend and keep her…whole.
Safe. Again, words he couldn't say. Wouldn't say until
he *knew* he was ready for this, for her and that he could
give her all she deserved.

"Tell me, Goldi. Please?"

Yet another breath, deeper than the last. More fluttering of her eyelashes as she blinked. A firm nod. Shoulders straight, jaw set, she reached for his hand.

He held it tightly and with his other hand, tipped her
chin so they were eye-to-eye. "Don't you know that you
can tell me anything? I'll listen. Whatever it is, you have
nothing to be afraid of."

Those words? True. Heartfelt. Real.

Naturally, none of the truth there altered his own fear.
His own inabilities. His desperate desire to remain un-
scathed for the remainder of his life, to never again face
excruciating loss. He'd barely survived the first time—
with his parents, and hell, he still couldn't figure out if
he'd survived, as in *really survived*, losing Christy. All
these years, all this time, all his solitude and refusal to
become close to anyone and really…how many steps
had he traveled?

He couldn't answer that. Not now. Not when this
woman stared at him with shiny tear-filled blue eyes and
glimmering cloud-like hair. Not when her body shook
with shivers. And certainly not when he felt her confusion and fear as if it were his own.

"I'm pregnant, Liam."

That was it, all she said, three little words that held
the force of a tsunami. Three little words that sucked
every bit of oxygen from his body. Three words. Just
three. Yet they changed…everything.

"I'm sorry," he said, feeding the all-consuming need

to be absolutely sure he'd heard her correctly. "What did you say?"

More blinks. More breaths. More trembles. "I said that I'm pregnant. I… I found out earlier and…you needed to know right away. I wouldn't keep something like that from you. So, here I am and I know… I know what a shock this is and I—"

She broke off, waiting for him to offer…what? Reassurances, probably, to promise her that he was fine. That she had nothing to worry about. That she wasn't in this alone. And of course, she wasn't. Of course.

But he couldn't breathe. Couldn't think. Damn it, why couldn't he think? She was pregnant. A baby—*his* baby—was even now growing inside of her, and that baby would require the world. Deserved everything he could offer and more.

"You're pregnant?" He'd heard it twice. Why'd he have to hear it a third time?

"Yes. And yes, I am sure. And—" here, her voice strengthened, grew in confidence, and even in the storm of his emotions, he was proud of her "—yes, the baby is yours."

Well, he knew that. Didn't need that fact confirmed, but he understood why she'd put that out there.

No doubts. She didn't want him to worry or question, and he didn't. Wouldn't, with Goldi. But with that unnecessary confirmation, the smallest kernel of joy appeared in the center of the chaos. *Joy.* It was there. He felt it. And damn it all again, that joy increased his fear.

Joy was dangerous. It needed hope to exist, to flourish. And hope…well, he hadn't had a whole lot of luck with hope. Hope, he'd learned, was treacherous. Could make you believe the world was yours for the taking and then suck you down into the pits of hell. In less than a second, without warning. Did he have it in him to hope again? To let that joy flourish and take root?

He did not know.

"Liam? Say something," Meredith said, her voice a tangle of want. "Anything. I don't care what, but you have to say something. Don't let me sit here in this alone."

"You're not alone." The words flew from his throat, his heart and his soul effortlessly. And he meant them completely, but his voice sounded flat and without warmth. He heard it, so yeah, she had.

He tried harder with, "You are never alone, Goldi. I'm sorry for… I just need a minute to catch up, to let this news sink in. But I'm here with you, and this baby will have everything he or she needs. So will you, as far as that goes. Know that. No matter what else."

She swallowed hard and turned her body away from his. Dropped his hand. "I do know that, Liam. I do. And I'm not asking for anything from you that you don't…or won't…want to give. But you had to know. And…well, I guess now you do. So. Okay. You know."

"I *am* here. I swear to that."

"Okay."

Unsaid words weighted the air, and he fought to find…whatever it was she needed to hear. Fought to be a better man for her, for this child he'd just learned would one day be and, yes, for himself, too. A better man than who he had been. A man who'd lived in seclusion, choosing to separate himself from the world in order to create a structure he could exist in without the possibility of anything real ever happening again.

He wanted real. Yearned for real. But yeah, that

want, that hope was treacherous. So, he couldn't find the words, the emotion, the sentiment, the confidence and strength she surely needed from him in this space of time. He didn't know how to breach this gap that had appeared between them.

This woman had popped into his life out of nowhere, and he hadn't yet accepted and embraced that miracle, that *hope*. Moving from that to this so quickly was too much.

Time. He needed that time to process. To put everything into perspective and see if he could allow that kernel of joy to flourish into…well, a life. A full, real life that would include Goldi and a child and…a future he'd long given up on.

No, he didn't have the words or the strength or the courage. He didn't have any of those, and explaining all of that seemed impossible. Instead, he opened his arms and said, "Come here, Goldi. Let me hold you for a minute, because you need to know that I am here with you."

A slight hesitation, a quick breath and then there she was, her head pressed against his shoulder, her honey-and-almond-scented hair tickling his jaw. He brought her to him as tightly, as securely as he could. In those minutes, his world felt…right. Sturdy and secure.

No longer fragmented into pieces. So, whole, he guessed. Real.

"You can count on me," he said into her ear with the only promise he was able to offer in this minute. It wasn't enough. Not nearly enough. But he refused to give her hope he did not yet believe in, so really, all he could do was speak the truth. What he *knew* to be true. "You and the baby will never have to worry. You'll be taken care of. I promise."

"I appreciate that," she said, pulling herself free of his hold. "And I know you're a responsible man, Liam. I didn't expect…well, I didn't expect anything less."

Meaning she had expected more? Or just…hoped? Hell if he knew. But saying words he couldn't back up would only hurt them both, even if they would offer a momentary comfort.

"We'll figure this out," he said. "Soon. I just… I'm sorry. It isn't fair to you, but I need a little time, to think and plan. I'm not running away. I'm here. Please believe that."

Remembering his flight, that he had to take the dogs to his sister's, he looked at his watch. He had a few minutes before he absolutely had to leave, but he'd give her however much time she needed. He'd cancel the assignment. He'd stay if she asked.

But he wanted to go, wanted to have that time to sink into his work so he could process. Consider the past, the future. What he was capable of offering this woman.

Perhaps that made him awful and selfish, just having that want. Yet another mystery he couldn't solve. It was, he decided, what it was. But yes, if she asked him to stay, he would. Without hesitation.

As she had from the very beginning, she seemed to see straight into his brain and read his thoughts. That still disconcerted him, startled him.

"You probably have to leave soon, right?" she asked, pulling herself up to stand. "I won't keep you any longer, and of course take whatever time you need. I have to process, as well. I just found out a few hours ago, so I'm…thinking, too."

"I can cancel the job," he said. "Just say the word, and I'll do so. Or change my flight until tomorrow, if you want to…have more time to talk right now. Seriously. I will do that."

Bringing her fingers to her temple, she rubbed as if a headache brewed. "No. You have a job, and you should go. A couple of weeks, you said? That will give us both plenty of time to think about this, about what we want to do. So, no, don't cancel. Don't delay your flight."

Silence filled the space between them. Uncomfortable, tense silence.

He should cancel. That should be *his* decision. To show her that he meant what he said, that she wasn't alone. That he would be here, through everything and that he would see to her needs. To their child's needs.

But he couldn't quite find the will to say those words, to follow up on them, so he kept his mouth shut. The selfish side of him wanted to escape. Not forever, just for two weeks.

And the longer he didn't say those words, give that offer, make that decision for them, the more tense and hungry the quiet between them became. It was a monster, that silence, demanding what he *could* give but selfishly did not want to. She would have to ask for him to comply and that…well, that did not seem to be happening.

Both of them. More stubborn than anyone had a right to be.

Sighing, he gave into the selfishness. Knew he'd question that decision every hour for the next two weeks, but even that didn't stop him. He needed the time. Desperately. And he'd have to believe that she would understand and that she spoke the truth, that she needed it just as much. Otherwise, why tell him to go? Why offer those assurances if they weren't heartfelt?

Right. So, yeah, he gave in. "Okay, if you're sure. We'll...plan on talking when I return?"

"Of course." Her modulated tone didn't show whatever she felt, what she might be thinking. And as she spoke, she pivoted her entire body away from him, so she faced the door. She wanted to leave. Was waiting to get the hell out of here, so he could do the same. For him? For her? For both of them? "We'll talk when you return. That...sounds like a doable plan."

"It is the plan. Two weeks, Goldi, and we'll figure this out." He came to her then, started to reach for her but had second thoughts. Now wasn't the time. Even if he ached to hold her again, reassure her, give her the world. "Come on. I'll walk you out."

"Oh. I'm fine. I can find the car." And then, she angled toward him just enough that he could see her face. She smiled, but he could easily see it was forced. "It's right outside in your driveway, remember? No chance I'll get lost. I will even swear that I won't get lost going to Rachel's. So, no worries!"

Her attempt to lighten the moment as they went their separate ways on easier ground didn't go unnoticed. She was something, this woman. In such a moment, she wasn't crying or begging him for so much as a glass of water. She wasn't pushing him to do anything at all.

She was, he realized, trying to remind him that she was independent. That she would be okay on her own, without his help or presence. To give him...what? The freedom of choice?

Probably that. But all at once, his fear altered direction, became even fiercer, and he wondered if she was really saying goodbye. As in, a forever goodbye.

"Goldi?" he asked, hearing the fear that resonated

through him mirrored in his voice. "You'll be here, right? When I return? You're not going to disappear on me, are you?"

"Oh. I won't disappear." Another smile, this one less forced. "You'll always be able to find me, Liam. If and when you want. Don't worry about that, either. Okay?"

"Two weeks. I'll see you in two weeks." And then, because he needed to know the *precise* moment he'd see her again, he said, "Two weeks from tomorrow. Meet here around three? That will give me plenty of time to get the dogs and…how does that sound?"

She nodded and started toward the door. Paused. Breathed. And he thought, for barely a second, that she was going to say something else, but in the end, she didn't. Just pushed herself forward and walked away, leaving him alone.

Which was the precise state of being that he'd worked so hard for, had fervently believed he'd wanted and had drowned himself in for going on a decade. Truth was, he'd done just fine in that life, had survived without too much trouble.

But that was before Goldi.

Chapter 12

Closing her eyes, Meredith sat on the edge of her bed and waited for the bout of nausea to subside. Within days of learning she was pregnant, the morning sickness had begun with a vengeance, as if her body had patiently waited for her brain to be let in on the secret. She'd already started carrying saltine crackers and peppermints in her purse, because she'd also quickly discovered that "morning" sickness really meant "sick all the darn time, so get used to it."

A lot had happened in the last ten days since she'd told Liam they were having a baby. The job had come through, so she was once again gainfully employed. On her own merits. She had that initial flush of satisfaction, that she'd done what she'd set out to do, proven to herself that she didn't require her father's name or input to locate a good job.

And yes, that had felt empowering. Fulfilling.

In the end, though, she discovered that she'd always known that about herself. Always. Which was yet another powerful realization, though one she wished she'd come to earlier. It might have saved her a lot of angst over the years, that knowing. She knew now, and she supposed that was more than good enough. Better now than later, right?

She didn't start her new job for another ten days, but that worked out just fine. That gave her time to start scouting for an apartment, plan for her return to San Francisco to pack and empty her former apartment and see her family. Make those final amends with her dad.

Tell him and the rest of her family that she was pregnant.

Initially, there would be reservations on her parents' part, she knew. They would want her to move home, so they could take care of all that would need to be taken care of. But no. She'd keep her ground, she'd thank them for their support and she'd return here to her new home. Steamboat Springs, Colorado, where she would raise her child.

With Liam? Well, in one way, yes. He'd be here for their son or daughter, she had zero doubt. But that was it.

All that would exist between them was the shared, unconditional love for the baby they created. There wouldn't be anything more. His walls were too thick, too sturdily built, and the force between them—as strong as it was—wouldn't break through.

The look on his face when she'd told him she was pregnant would forever live in her memory. It was one of intense pain. Loss. And in that moment, she understood more about the man than she ever had before. Somewhere in that amazing heart of his, he might love her…or have the stirrings of love, the beginnings of what she already felt so strongly.

She just didn't think he was ready, would never be able to get himself there, to latch onto that seed and let it grow. Not with the loss he so obviously still fought, existed with, and she couldn't blame him or pretend she knew what that felt like. Walking around, day in and day out, after losing what he had? No. The strength, the courage he'd had to wrap around himself to just breathe was likely more than she'd ever had to gather.

Even more than she'd had to when she was lost and desperate in a storm.

Nothing could compare. And she hoped to God she'd never experience what Liam had, almost as much as she hoped he'd never face anything similar again for the rest of his life.

When she'd left his house that day, the only thought in her mind was to *run*. Far and fast, before the pain of his expression burned into her soul and never let go.

Her heart heavy, she'd driven to Rachel's and considered her options. She wanted to run. Wanted to return to San Francisco and give up on this idea of a life of her own making. Wanted to hide.

By the time she reached Rachel's, however, she knew she'd live up to what she'd told Liam: that she would be here, when he returned, so they could talk. He would always be able to find her, not only because of their child, but because…well, that was how it should be. What was supposed to be. She knew this, even if he didn't. Even if he never reached that conclusion.

As the days continued to pass, the tiny amount of hope that remained drained into nothingness. And oh, she mourned the loss. Not the loss of what could have been, but the loss of what never was…would never be.

The pain on Liam's face, in his eyes, was too deep, too severe for a man to come back from. Her dream was merely that: a dream. A glimpse, she supposed, of what life could be like with the right person, the right type of love, the right foundation.

It just wouldn't be a life she would have with Liam.

But at least she knew what to aim for someday down the road, when the hold Liam had on her heart let go and set her free. Might be years. The baby who grew inside her might very well be married and have a child of their own by the time that occurred. If it ever would.

If it ever could.

He'd be home in just a few days now. She would drive to his house in the mountains, and they would talk.

The conversation would surround the financial responsibilities, she was sure, along with more promises to take care of her, of their child. Maybe they'd discuss if he'd go to obstetrician appointments with her, if he could be there for the birth and if he was thinking far enough ahead, they might delve into how they would parent, visitation, the baby's last name.

Or they might simply sit and look at each other, with that heavy air choking them, so neither could breathe, let alone speak in complete sentences.

One of the two. Or both, in intermittent gaps.

The only rule she had was to tuck her emotions down deep, so they remained under wraps, to remain stoic and logical and keep her focus on the reason for their conversation: the life they were bringing into this world. How they would do that together without being together.

Meredith's hand went to her stomach. *A baby.* Joy

existed there, growing inside of her, alive and strong and beautiful.

This was her future. Joy and beauty, and her choice was to revel in that truth, what *would* be, instead of wish for what would never be.

Sweat beaded on the back of Liam's neck. He looked over at the clock, saw that the minutes were ticking away and he wasn't ready yet.

Everything had to be perfect for when Meredith arrived. *He* had to be perfect. So she could see that the time away had done what was needed: gave Liam clarity, allowed him to separate crippling fear from true, unadulterated hope and determine the stronger of the two.

In those first awful days, it seemed that fear would be the champion. Whenever he considered opening his heart more to Meredith, to that life he yearned for, he just couldn't see beyond his past to get to the hope. And hell, the last thing he would ever do was drag Meredith down a path that he couldn't believe in, couldn't be sure he'd be able to travel.

But on day eight, just as he'd reached the decision to remain in his comfortable solitary existence—save for being there for his child, of course—an epiphany had occurred. In the form of three colorful birds, rainbow lorikeets. They were gorgeous creatures, with bright red beaks and exotically hued plumage that included their green wings and tails, blue-to-purple heads and the vivid yellow-orange that circled their necks and dripped down to their breasts.

And just like before, with the paradise tanagers in the Amazon Basin when Christy was pregnant and awaiting his return, these three birds perched on a branch, huddled close together.

A family. Bright and happy and so beautiful to see that it took his breath away. His heart had ramped up to the speed of a runner about to win a marathon, and he waited for these birds to startle and fly off, just as the paradise tanagers had the second he'd snapped their photograph.

But the lorikeets didn't startle or fly off. They watched him boldly, without fear, and remained steadfast on their branch. In their life with each other. As if to state that nothing, not even a man that didn't belong in their world, could chase them off from where they wanted to be, had chosen to be. A grandiose thought, perhaps, but it resonated just the same.

The similarities between the past scene with the paradise tanagers and the present with the rainbow lorikeets were there and couldn't be denied.

Three colorful birds. A branch. That same feeling of belonging together, looking out for one another, as a family should. All that existed, yes, but they were different birds perched on a different branch in a different location.

More than anything else, though, the time was different.

And these birds? They hadn't disappeared in a flutter of wings, rushing off to find a new branch, a *safer* branch to perch on. They'd stayed. They weren't going anywhere.

Silly, probably, that it took three birds to wake Liam the hell up, but wake him up they did.

So very much came into perspective. So very much

clicked into place. Obvious conclusions. Most of which he'd known all along but hadn't allowed to gain a foothold.

Christy and Meredith were two different women. The love he felt for Christy was real and solid and would've lasted a lifetime. He was sure of that. They would've been happy. His love for Meredith—because, yes, he did love her, he knew this now without any doubt—was also real and solid and he believed to his soul that it could also last a lifetime.

But different women meant that love altered some, too. It meant the life he would have had with Christy if she hadn't died would also be different than the one he could have with Meredith. Had to be. He had changed. That loss had altered how he viewed pretty much everything. Before, he'd chosen seclusion to shield himself from facing that type of hurt again. Now, due to an epiphany brought on by three steadfast birds, he understood what he hadn't before.

What he most needed to understand.

Yes, losing Christy and his child had given him a front-row view of how precious life was. But rather than hide from more loss, he should be using that awareness to grab on and go for every bit of happiness—of joy— he could. He should be steadfast and sure, refuse to let go and cherish every damn second of good. And hell, Goldi was pure good.

She was light and love and hope. She'd swept in out of nowhere and stolen his heart.

And now she was having his baby. Some would call this a second chance, but Liam…well, again, two different women. Two different lifetimes. Any of the blessings that existed with Meredith weren't his "second chance," they were his *everything*. They were his present. He hoped his future.

Today, he was going to jump in up to his eyeballs and pour himself into that everything. His shields, his want for seclusion, were gone. She might reject him, might reject all he now saw and was ready to grab onto, and yup, that thought rightly scared him. But it was not going to send him running, nor would that possibility change his mind. He was in.

He just hoped she'd listen. Give him a chance. Give them a chance.

The rumble of her car in the driveway brought him to his senses and that sweat on the back of his neck doubled. No, tripled. But that was fine. He *should* be nervous.

This was life. He wanted to feel it all.

When he drove into Steamboat Springs this morning, he'd stopped by the jewelry store before picking up Max and Maggie. Had looked for and chosen a ring. Some would say he was moving too fast, but frankly, he felt as if he'd already waited, had gotten stuck in the mud of his fears, for too damn long. So, yeah, he was set on changing that dynamic.

No more waiting. No more getting stuck.

The ring box was in his pocket. The fire in the fireplace burned softly, gently. His dogs were snoozing by the fire after romping outside for close to an hour. It wasn't the most romantic of scenes, but it was what he had, and he figured Meredith—*Goldi*—would approve. This room was, after all, the very first place they'd ever laid eyes on one another. Seemed fitting.

Hopeful. Possibly joyous.

The knock on the front door came, rousing his dogs,

both of whom lifted their heads and looked at Liam in such a way that he would swear they were telling him not to screw this up. That Goldi was theirs, too, and it was about time he brought her home.

"Tell you what, guys," he said. "If I screw this up, you can go with her. I'll visit a lot, don't you worry, but I won't keep her from you. Deal?"

Now the look they gave him could only be described as pity. Max growled low in his throat, and Maggie whined. Well. They didn't like that idea any more than they enjoyed being with him without Goldi. Seemed they wanted it all, just as he did.

"I'll give it my best shot," he said, just as Goldi knocked for the second time. His stomach turned over and his legs held the consistency of a bowl of jelly. Pitiful. But glorious, too, that this woman could do this and so much more to him, for him. He went to the door and after sending a silent prayer upward, opened it. And there she was.

The woman he loved.

"Hey, there," he said, holding the door open wider and doing his level best to ignore the swarming of bees— couldn't be butterflies—in his gut. She wore her hair long and loose, her eyes were bright and that smile... he lived for that smile. "Come on in. I...how was the drive?"

"I didn't get lost, so there's that." She walked in and unzipped her coat, which she handed to him. Her voice, calm and cool and modulated, told him a lot. Told him she was hurting beneath her collected, easy-breezy facade, and he hated that he'd put her in such a place. "How was your trip?" she asked. "Did you get everything you needed?"

"I did. More than I expected." He hung her coat in the closet. "It was the best trip I've had, ever. I…got more than I hoped for. More than I thought possible." And because he did not want her to continue to think he was referring to his job, to the photographs he went to Australia to shoot, he said, "I thought about us. Constantly, Goldi. And…well, I'm so glad you're here."

She blinked. Nodded. "I thought a lot about us, too. Every day."

"Well then, I'd say we each have a lot to talk about."

"Yes. We do." A sigh teased from her lungs, and her shoulders shook just a little. "I'm glad I'm here, too, Liam. Happy to see you. It seems like I haven't in… forever."

"I know. Me, too." There was so much he needed to say that the words were all but fighting each other to come out. But not yet. Holding out his hand, he waited for her to take hold. When she did, he said, "Come with me. Let's sit down and have that conversation."

They moved into the living room, and he assumed she'd sit on the couch, but she didn't. She didn't sit anywhere, just stood in front of the fire, holding his hand for dear life.

Her chin trembled and she shifted her gaze away from his to stare at the floor. She was nervous. Scared, maybe, of what he would say. And while he'd wanted to ease her into the moment, into sharing all that he saw for them, he now believed that would be a mistake.

She looked like those paradise tanagers. A second away from startling. A second away from flying into the sky and leaving him alone, watching her departure. Wishing she'd return.

And his Goldi wasn't a paradise tanager. She was a

rainbow lorikeet, even if she didn't yet know that. So. Whether it was the right time or the wrong time, he let go of her hand to reach into his pocket. Felt for the ring box to assure himself it was still there and then…he threw caution and common sense and logic and every last one of his useless fears into the wind.

And he knelt in front of Goldi. Took her hand again and, ignoring the buzzing bees in his stomach that refused to settle, said, "I meant to do this differently. I meant to explain everything I've realized and why. I meant to turn on some music, so you could hear ABBA. I meant to be…ah…clear and eloquent, maybe a little romantic, but I can't wait."

Those blue eyes of hers narrowed and a shiver, long and loose, ran through her from head to toe. "If you're about to do what I think, then you should probably stop," she said, her words wobbly. "I don't want a marriage of convenience. I don't want you to think you have to marry me out of some form of responsibility, to ease your conscience. I… I…"

Her words disappeared into the air, but she didn't let go and she didn't look away.

That bolstered his hope, despite what she'd said. And of course, she would think that was what this was about. Of course she would. Well, Liam would have to change that mindset.

Pronto. "Close your eyes for me, Goldi, so you can really listen to my voice as I talk," he said, operating on pure instinct. "The first time you heard my voice, your eyes were closed and you had that dream. The one you still haven't told me about, but based on the little you said, I believe it was an incredible dream. About us. Am I correct in that belief?"

Moisture filled her eyes. "Yes. It was incredible and it was about us."

"Okay, then. Close your eyes, darlin', and let me talk. Listen. And see if you can hear the truth in my voice without any other distractions." He paused for a few seconds, mostly to try to find the words he *would* say, now that the moment was here. "Can you do that for me?"

She breathed in and nodded. "I can."

Max and Maggie, who hadn't yet greeted her, padded to her from the fireplace, standing sentry, one on each side. Even in this moment, one with so much riding on the outcome, he was amused by their stance. As much as they were Liam's dogs, Goldi belonged to them.

And they weren't going to let her fall.

Their presence seemed to offer her a sense of comfort. She closed her eyes, he tightened his hold on her hand and while he hadn't yet chosen the exact words to say, he decided to let his emotions lead his tongue. And he started with the most emotional of them all.

"I love you, Goldi. I do. And I have for what feels like forever, for far longer than the actual time we've known each other. So, I can't define when this love began or when it became so big that it could no longer be ignored. I just know, with every bone in my body, that I am in love with you. Completely."

Another breath, this one larger than the last, but she didn't speak. She didn't open her eyes. Just stood there, holding on to him, in…well, trust was there. Belief of some sort. And perhaps she had the same hope he did. He wouldn't know unless he kept talking.

"But see, even though I recognized this fact, that I love you, I wasn't ready to do anything with it, wasn't even ready to admit it to myself. I was edging in the right direction, but I think…no, I know, I would've proceeded slowly. With caution. But I was getting there."

"You started opening up to me, about your life," she said softly, eyes still closed. "So, I thought so. Wondered. But I didn't know for sure. I…just didn't."

"How could you?" His turn to breathe. The bees were still there, but not quite as many and not quite as strong. "When you came here to tell me about the baby, I… and it shames me to admit this, Goldi, but I got scared. Because you were already so important in my life, and you'd already chiseled into my shields. Add in a baby and the past seemed to be repeating itself."

"I get why you were scared. I have been scared, too."

That pained him incredibly, to hear her say this. "I'm sorry, sweetheart. So damn sorry I couldn't see the past from the present, couldn't stop them from merging together. I just didn't have the ability to do so in that moment, but I wish I had. I wish I could go back and—"

"You don't have to apologize," she said quickly, her words running together. "It was a shock for both of us, and you were still good to me, Liam. Still calm and patient. You just weren't ready to dive in deep, and I don't know if I was, either. Not really."

"I'm still sorry. Forgive me?"

"There is nothing to forgive," she said, as stubborn as always. God, he loved that about her, too, that she didn't back down. That she held her ground. "Can I open my eyes yet?"

"Not yet. Soon." Swallowing, he continued the path he'd taken, telling her about the paradise tanager photograph, how when he'd shot it, he'd been filled with happiness for the future he'd surely have with Christy and as a father. He told Meredith what those birds had represented and how they'd flown away almost instantly.

"It was later that day that I found out that Christy had died, and ever since, I've connected that photograph to my future crumbling into dust. To losing what I loved most. That beauty…well, that it doesn't last, I guess."

A sob escaped from between her lips. "I can see how you would make such a comparison. I think I would, too. And, Liam, I am so very sorry. You don't know how—"

"Shh. I'm okay, Goldi. I wasn't, for a long time, but I am now. Thanks to you." Then, before this woman he loved keeled over because he'd made her stand with her eyes closed for minutes on end, he then told her about the rainbow lorikeets, about what had transpired mere days ago. How in that moment, all he'd already known became crystal clear, solidified and sent his fear into the shadows. How hope and joy had done that.

How *she* had done that. For him.

Now came the most important, the most vital, of all he wanted—needed—to say. And Lord, he prayed he got it right. Or close enough to right that it wasn't wrong. He'd take that. He'd count that as a win.

Pulling the ring box from his pocket with his free hand, he said, "You can open your eyes now, but only if you promise not to say a word until I'm finished."

She nodded, said, "I promise," and opened her eyes. Looked down and saw the ring box, which he'd opened, so the diamond solitaire sat front and center. "Liam! I just said—"

"That you promised to let me finish, so let me do so." Another nod, but it came slower. "I love you, Meredith. I do. With my heart and my soul and my brain. I can no longer imagine waking up every day without you beside me or without 'Mamma Mia' playing too loud and you dancing in the kitchen. Or without you kicking my butt in Hedbanz. Or," he said, "though it is difficult to admit this, your incessant questions and love for talking. I can't live...my—"

Here, he broke off as emotion overwhelmed him, caught in his throat and stole the words he needed to say the most. Okay. He could do this. What was the worst that would happen?

She could say no. That was the worst, and he would respect her decision. But he wouldn't give up easily. Couldn't. Not for this woman.

Steadier again, he looked straight into her eyes, cleared his throat and said, "My life doesn't work without you, not how it should. Not the way it is meant to. So, I'm asking you to marry me. Because I can no longer see a life that doesn't include you beside me."

"Liam." She breathed his name more than she said it. "Are you sure?"

"Very sure. And we don't have to marry tomorrow or next week. Or hell," he said, feeling his confidence grow, "next year."

"Next year, huh?" she said, a glimmer of amusement in her voice, her expression. "I don't know about that. Seems a little too undefined for my liking, but Liam, you—"

"I'll marry you tomorrow," he said. "Now, if we could. But I want this to be your choice, when you feel confident that I have your heart and will keep it whole. Forever."

"I love you so much." Tears welled and spilled down her cheeks. "Have for a while now and, yes, I know this about you. You've shown it to me from day one."

"Is that a yes, Goldi?" He knew it was, but he had to hear her say the word. Had to know that she was his, that he was hers, before he could fully welcome the joy and revel in the promise of the life he would have with this woman. "Will you walk with me down this path of ours?"

"Yes, Liam," she said, her voice strong. Sure. Steadfast. "I will walk with you."

And with those words, Liam reached for her left hand and slipped the ring on her finger, sealing the deal.

She was his. He was hers. From this moment forward, he would cherish and treasure his Goldilocks, care for her, raise his sword in defense. And he knew without question that this woman would do the same for him. Each day. Every day.

For the rest of their lives.

Epilogue

Warm, brilliant sun shone down on Meredith's shoulders. Today marked her and Liam's daughter's first full month of life, and they were celebrating with a picnic outside their house. It was Liam's idea, his surprise, and since Teagan, which meant "beautiful," hadn't given them many hours of sleep last night, Meredith had agreed.

Her infant daughter always seemed calmer when they were outside in nature, which seemed to show she took after her father in that regard. In other ways, too. She had Liam's rich, dark hair and green-and-amber eyes. What she had of Meredith's, so far, at least, was a love for ABBA and a very vocal set of lungs. This amused Liam to no end.

He liked to tease Meredith—whom he still called Goldi most of the time—that she'd brought sound back into his life due to her love of talking. She didn't think he'd ever fully understand that her love of talking hadn't existed until she'd met him. It was with Liam that she had truly found her voice, and it was their conversations she loved.

Stretching her legs on the quilt Liam had laid on the ground, Meredith waited for her husband—they'd married when she was six months pregnant—to bring actual food to their picnic and looked over at her sleeping daughter who rested next to her, protected from the sun by the arch of the tree's branches above them.

This tiny baby was…everything. Happiness and love and sweetness all bundled together in one beautiful, if loud, package. And Meredith couldn't wait to see the person her daughter would grow into. What her interests would someday be, what her smile would look like and if she would laugh in Liam's booming or in her mother's softer, yet no less joyous, manner.

The storm that had brought her to this life, to the man she loved, no longer held any remnants of the terror she'd felt that night.

How could it? If not for that storm, she might never have found Liam, never dreamed about the life she now led, never become a mother to Teagan.

Of course, when she said such things to Liam, his logical brain forced him to point out that she wouldn't have known the difference. That she couldn't have missed what she didn't have, hadn't known about. But he was wrong. She would've known in her heart and her soul that her life lacked something. *Someone.* And she would've yearned.

Now, the most she yearned for was more than three hours of sleep at a time, but that, too, would come to her again. Until the next baby and then the next.

Three was the number that she and Liam had agreed upon, but she kind of thought they'd end up with four. In her dream, they'd only had two children, but…well, dreams could change.

Her husband appeared then with a picnic basket in his hands and Max and Maggie at his heels.

The shepherds came to her first, to show their love, before carefully taking up their guard-dog positions around Teagan, one at her feet and the other above her head. She was theirs, too. One of the pack. And they were never far from the baby for very long.

"Hope you're hungry," Liam said, dropping onto the blanket next to her. "And if so, you better eat up fast. Before the little one decides she's hungrier."

This man treated her so well. Cared for her. Protected her. Allowed her to do the same for him, so what they ended up with was a true give and take. A true partnership.

She was easily the luckiest woman in the world.

"I am hungry," she said. "But first, if you don't mind, I could use a hug. Maybe a kiss."

His arms came around her, his lips met hers and just like their very first kiss, the world disappeared and all that was left was just the two of them. The emotion that existed between them, their friendship and…yes, the heat that erupted into being.

Instantly.

She fell into the kiss, into the man, and could've stayed that way, locked in his embrace, with his mouth on hers, for all eternity. If not for Teagan deciding that now was the precise time to wake up and demand to be fed.

Her whimper turned to a wail, which led the dogs

to whining and then howling, which softened Teagan's tears, rather than ramping them up in volume.

Liam broke off the kiss, ran his hand down the side of her face. "I love you, Goldi."

"I love you, too." Meredith turned to reach for the baby. "More than you know, even."

"Oh, I have a good idea. Even so, I am pretty sure I love you more," he teased. "I mean, ABBA. In the morning, afternoon and when I'm trying to work. Just saying."

Shifting Teagan so that she could feed her, Meredith smiled at her husband. He did put up with a lot, especially for a man who had lived in these mountains for so long in almost complete solitude.

"A good point. I can start using my earbuds more often, to give you some peace."

"You could, but that wouldn't be you," he said, playing with Teagan's tiny fingers. "And you are the woman of my dreams. So, don't change. A thing. Okay?"

And that…well, that said it all.

* * * * *

SPECIAL EXCERPT FROM

♦ **HARLEQUIN**

™

SPECIAL EDITION

USA TODAY *bestselling author Judy Duarte's*
The Lawman's Convenient Family
*is the story of Julie Chapman, a music therapist who
needs a convenient husband in order to save two
orphans from foster care. Lawman Adam Santiago fits
the bill, but suddenly they both find themselves longing
to become a family—forever!*

*Read on for a sneak preview of the next great book
in the Rocking Chair Rodeo miniseries.*

"Lisa," the man dressed as Zorro said, "I'd heard you were going to be here."

He clearly thought Julie was someone else. She probably ought to say something, but up close, the gorgeous bandito seemed to have stolen both her thoughts and her words.

"It's nice to finally meet you." His deep voice set her senses reeling. "I've never really liked blind dates."

Talk about masquerades and mistaken identities. Before Julie could set him straight, he took her hand in a polished, gentlemanly manner and kissed it. His warm breath lingered on her skin, setting off a bevy of butterflies in her tummy.

"Dance with me," he said.

Her lips parted, but for the life of her, she still couldn't speak, couldn't explain. And she darn sure couldn't object.

Zorro led her away from the buffet tables and to the dance floor. When he opened his arms, she again had the opportunity to tell him who she really was. But instead, she stepped into his embrace, allowing him to take the lead.

His alluring aftershave, something manly, taunted her. As she savored his scent, as well as the warmth of his muscular arms, her pulse soared. She leaned her head on his shoulder as they swayed to a sensual beat, their movements in perfect accord, as though they'd danced together a hundred times before.

Now would be a good time to tell him she wasn't Lisa, but she seemed to have fallen under a spell that grew stronger with every beat of the music. The moment turned surreal, like she'd stepped into a fairy tale with a handsome rogue.

Once again, she pondered revealing his mistake and telling him her name, but there'd be time enough to do that after the song ended. Then she'd return to the kitchen, slipping off like Cinderella. But instead of a glass slipper, she'd leave behind her momentary enchantment.

But several beats later, a cowboy tapped Zorro on the shoulder. "I need you to come outside."

Zorro looked at him and frowned. "Can't you see I'm busy?"

The cowboy, whose outfit was so authentic he seemed to be the real deal, rolled his eyes.

Julie wished she could have worn her street clothes. Would now be a good time to admit that she wasn't an actual attendee but here to work at the gala?

"What's up?" Zorro asked.

The cowboy folded his arms across his chest and shifted his weight to one hip. "Someone just broke into my pickup."

Zorro's gaze returned to Julie. "I'm sorry, Lisa. I'm going to have to morph into cop mode."

Now it was Julie's turn to tense. He was actually a police officer in real life? A slight uneasiness settled over her, an old habit she apparently hadn't outgrown. Not that she had any real reason to fear anyone in law enforcement nowadays.

Don't miss
The Lawman's Convenient Family *by Judy Duarte,*
available January 2019 wherever
Harlequin® Special Edition books and ebooks are sold.

www.Harlequin.com

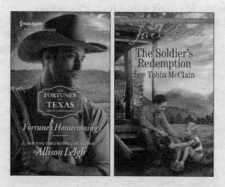

Reward the book lover in you!

Earn points on your purchase of new Harlequin books from participating retailers.

Turn your points into **FREE BOOKS** of your choice!

Join for FREE today at
www.HarlequinMyRewards.com.

Harlequin My Rewards is a free program (no fees) without any commitments or obligations.

MYR18